Also by Michael Gruber

The Good Son

The Forgery of Venus

The Book of Air and Shadows

Night of the Jaguar

Valley of Bones

Tropic of Night

The Witch's Boy

The
Return

The
Return

A NOVEL

Michael Gruber

HENRY HOLT AND COMPANY   NEW YORK

Henry Holt and Company, LLC
Publishers since 1866
175 Fifth Avenue
New York, New York 10010
www.henryholt.com

Henry Holt® and 📙® are registered trademarks of Henry Holt and Company, LLC.

Lines from "Return" by Octavio Paz, translated by Eliot Weinberger,
from *The Collected Poems 1957–1987*, copyright © by Octavio Paz and Eliot Weinberger.
Reprinted by permission of New Directions Publishing Corp.

Library of Congress Cataloging-in-Publication Data

Gruber, Michael, 1940–
    The return : a novel / Michael Gruber. — First edition.
        pages cm
    ISBN 978-0-8050-9129-8 (hardback)
    1. Book editors—Fiction.   2. Revenge—Fiction. [1. New York (N.Y.)—Fiction.]
I. Title.
    PS3607.R68R48 2013
    813'.6—dc23   2012045307

Henry Holt books are available for special promotions and premiums.
For details contact: Director, Special Markets.

First Edition 2013

Designed by Meryl Sussman Levavi

Printed in the United States of America

1   2   3   4   5   6   7   8   9   10

This is a work of fiction. All of the characters, organizations, and events portrayed in this novel
either are products of the author's imagination or are used fictitiously.

For E.W.N.

Sobre el pecho de México
      tablas escritas por el sol
escalera de los siglos
      terraza espiral del viento
baila la desenterrada
      jadeo sed rabia
pelea de ciegos bajo el mediodía
      rabia sed jadeo
se golpean con piedras
      los ciegos se golpean
se rompen los hombres
      las piedras se rompen
adentro hay un agua que bebemos
      agua que amarga
agua que alarga más le sed

      ¿Dónde está el agua otra?

      OCTAVIO PAZ
      from *Vuelta* (Return)

On the chest of Mexico
      tablets written by the sun
stairway of the centuries
      spiral terraces of wind
the disinterred dances
      anger panting thirst
the blind fighting beneath the sun of noon
      thirst panting anger
beating each other with stones
      the blind beat each other
the men are crushing
      the stones are crushing
within there is a water we drink
      bitter water
water that increases thirst

      Where is the other water?

The
Return

1

Mexico.

This was Marder's first thought when the doctor explained what the shadow on the screen meant, what the tests implied. Mexico meant unfinished business, put off for years, nearly forgotten, until this unexpected deadline: now or never. That was the decent part; the cowardly part was the terror of explanation, of seeing the faces of his friends and family wear that look, the one that said, You're dying and I'm not and as much as I care for you I can't treat you like a real person anymore. He could see this very look in the doctor's face now, presaging all the others to come. Gergen was a good guy, a fine GP; Marder had been seeing him for years, the annual checkup. Something of a joke this, for Marder was hale as a bear, arteries like the bore of a Mossberg 12-gauge, all the numbers in the right zones, remarkable for a man in his fifties. They had a good relationship; if not quite pals, they'd always joked through the exams, the same jokes. Marder always said, "Tell me you love me first," as the doctor slipped the greased, rubbered finger up toward the perfectly normal prostate.

And other humorous repartee before and during: current events, sports, but mainly books. Marder was a book editor of some reputation—he'd been editor in chief of a major house before turning freelance some years back. Gergen fancied himself a literary fellow, and Marder usually remembered to bring along the latest thing he'd worked on, a history, a biography; today it had been one explaining the origins of the financial crisis. That was his editorial specialty, doorstops dense as nougat that explained our terrifying new world.

Gergen was explaining Marder's own new world now. The thing was deep in the brain, immune from surgical intervention, immune even from the clever methods by which a tube could be passed up the arterial pathways to fix the deadly little bubble. When Gergen finished, Marder asked the usual question and got the usual answer: impossible to tell. It could stop growing, which occasionally happened, for reasons unknown; the most likely scenario was leakage, stroking out, the hideous decline, stretched out over months or years; or it could just pop, in which case, curtains, and the next world. Marder had believed in the next world all his life, more or less, and did not entirely dread the journey, but lingering—in paralysis, helplessness, idiocy—filled him with horror.

They shook hands solemnly when Marder was dressed and ready to leave. Gergen said he was sorry, and Marder could tell he meant it but also that he was glad to see him go. Doctors are irritated by those beyond help; Marder knew the feeling—he'd worked with any number of authors who couldn't write and wouldn't learn. Irritating: death, like lack of talent, an embarrassment to be avoided.

Marder left the doctor's office and walked toward Union Square, through the thronged streets, weaving in the practiced New Yorker's way through all the people who were going to outlive him, who would be in their lives after he was not. He found that this knowledge did not depress him. His step was light; he cast his eye almost benevolently at the passing faces, so many of them bearing the grim mask of the New Yorker, guarded, intent on the next deal or destination. The world seemed sharper than it had when he entered the office just a few hours ago, as if someone had wiped clean his smudged glasses. He had almost reached the park when it struck him that the last time he had felt this preternatural clarity was years ago, when he was a soldier in Vietnam, in the night forests along the Laotian border. This, too, was strange: Marder almost never recollected that war.

Ordinarily he would have taken the subway home, but now he walked. The day was fair, sunny, cool, a nice September afternoon in the city; nature did not mourn for him, no pathetic fallacy on offer for Marder. As he walked, his mind bubbled with plans; it was free with the liberty of the void. This is the first day of the rest of your life, as the happiness advice books always said, but since there was also a chance that it was the last day, the silly phrase took on a more interesting, more cosmic overtone, what the sages meant about living in the Now.

Marder was a deliberate man, a careful thinker, a detail guy, but now his mind seemed to be running with unusual speed, concentrated with the prospect of dying, at some date to be determined. So bemused, he nearly stepped into the path of a cab at Houston Street. Yes, that would solve it: the black bubble of suicide floated across his mind, quickly punctured. Quite aside from the religious objections, Marder knew he couldn't do that to his children, not *two* parents checking out that way, but now came the thought that placing himself in a situation where he was likely to be killed was not at all the same thing, especially if by so doing he could accomplish his purpose down in Mexico. His mind steadied, plans started to jell. He didn't know if he could do it, but it seemed right to die trying.

At Prince Street he passed a group of street musicians, South American Indians by the look of them, in woven ponchos and felt hats—a pair of flutes, a drummer, a woman with a rattling gourd who sang in a high and nasal voice. Marder spoke fluent, almost accentless Mexican Spanish, but her lyric was difficult to follow, something about a dove, something about the ruin of love. When the song ended, he dropped a twenty in her hat among the singles and coins, was rewarded by a brilliant flash of white teeth, in the shining obsidian eyes a look of amazed gratitude. She blessed him in the name of God, in Spanish; he returned the blessing in the same language and walked on.

Marder's generosity here was not connected to his recent news; he often gave ridiculous sums away, although always privately. Proust, he'd heard once, habitually tipped 100 percent, and Marder occasionally did the same. Although born into modest circumstances, Marder was rich, secretly rich, through a stroke of luck so absurd that Marder had never accepted it as his due, making him different from nearly every other rich person of his acquaintance: wealth without feelings of entitlement was something of a rarity, in his experience. That he still worked at all, and in a profession not noted for excess remuneration, was a bit of uncharacteristic deviousness, a cover story. Only his lawyer and his accountant knew how much he was worth. His children and a number of other beneficiaries would be *extremely* surprised at probate.

Continuing south on Broadway, he passed a massive industrial build-ing with an ornate cast-iron front. The ground floor of this structure boasted a strip of elegant eateries and boutiques; the rest of it contained luxury condos. During his boyhood, however, it had been a printing plant, where his father had worked for thirty years as a Linotype opera-tor. It always gave Marder a tiny pang when he happened to pass by. Maybe it was mere nostalgia, but he thought there was something wrong about a city that had become largely a dwelling of the very rich and the people who serviced their needs. He missed the city of his boyhood, then the greatest port, the largest manufacturing entrepôt on earth. He recalled it as exciting and comprehensible in a way that the current city was not—a place that now shipped only digits, that made nothing but money. He thought he wouldn't miss this aspect of the city in the time he had left.

The Tribeca loft he lived in was currently worth a bit over a million, but this was easily explained: he'd bought it back in the early eighties with an insurance payoff from his father's death. "Lucky stiff!" was the usual comment. Real estate bonanzas were hardly unusual in the city, and no one thought it remarkable. It was even true, but not nearly as remarkable as the larger story.

Having reached this loft, Marder went to the area he used as his office, sat at his desk, and began to disassemble his life. He had a book in process, and this he passed off on a subcontract basis to another free-lancer he knew, who had a pregnant wife and a pair of school-aged kids. Marder stifled the man's effusions of gratitude; that was the easy part. Then he called the author and broke his heart, pleading unspecified health issues as an excuse, assuring him that the work would be compe-tently done and that, to make up for dropping the project, he would reduce the contracted completion payment. He would have to make up this fee to the substitute editor (a wonderful man, several books on the List, you'll *love* him, and so forth), but that would not be a problem.

Third call: Bernie Nathan, the accountant, who asked, when he heard what Marder wanted, whether he was in some kind of trouble. No, he was not, and could Bernie have the cash on hand this afternoon? Fourth call: Hal Danielson, the lawyer. A few little changes to the will. A similar question, similarly answered: no, not in trouble at all.

Fifth call: H. G. Ornstein answered on the first ring. Ornstein's busi-ness, which was running a tiny left-wing journal, was clearly not pressing. After the pleasantries and the usual damning of the condition into which our once-great nation had fallen, Marder asked, "So, Ornstein, you still living with your mother?"

Yes, and it was driving him crazy; wonderful woman, but not so wonderful living in the same house. Ornstein's wife had, after many years of noble poverty, despaired of the inevitable victory of the people and filed for divorce. Ornstein, a decent man, had done the decent thing and moved out. Marder did not believe in the ultimate victory of the people either, but he admired grit and selflessness. He'd known the man since college, when Ornstein had also tried his hand at stand-up comedy in the angry lefty mode of Mort Sahl or George Carlin. The man was a dead-on mimic but lacked edge, and had failed at that too.

When Marder told him he needed a friend to look after his loft for an indefinite period, the phone line hissed silence for nearly thirty seconds, then another undesired gush, to which Marder replied, "No, don't thank me, you'll be doing *me* a favor. I'll drop the keys and paperwork in the mail today. Can you move in Friday? Great."

Now Marder's finger brought up the contact list on his cell phone but hesitated above the next necessary number. Time for some procrastination. He went to the closet in the loft's bedroom and pulled out a battered leather gladstone bag of Mexican manufacture. He had not used it in some time, for now he traveled with a black nylon roll-aboard like the rest of humanity, but he thought that this one was the right container for his truncated new life. Into it went lightweight shirts and trousers, the usual underwear and toilet articles, a linen jacket and a leather one, leather sandals, several softly worn bandannas, a real Panama straw hat, the kind you could roll up. He hung his best suit in a garment bag, providing for any formal event or to be buried in. He placed the packed bag at the foot of his bed and then opened a tall, narrow steel safe.

Marder was not exactly a gun nut. He disliked the policies of the National Rifle Association and thought the general availability of powerful semiautomatic weapons in his nation was insane, but, despite that, he liked guns. He admired their malign beauty as he admired tigers and cobras, and he was a wonderfully proficient shot. From his gun safe he brought out a rifle and two pistols, together with all the boxes of ammunition he had on hand. It was irrational, he knew, but he did not want his survivors to have to dispose of them. Besides, it was always convenient to be armed on road voyages through the regions of Mexico where he intended to travel. He asked himself why he cared, since the thing in his head was more or less in charge of his life. Mr. Thing, as he now decided to call it, had its own agenda. Mr. Thing could discharge him from his life without notice, but in the meantime he would remain Marder, although a Marder who would not be an occasion of pain to the people he cared about.

In furtherance of this goal, he now placed himself at his computer and shopped for a truck, for he did not want to fly commercial, which could be traced. It took him only half an hour to arrange for the purchase of a Ford F-250 fitted with a seven-foot hardwall Northstar camper, model name "Freedom," which Marder thought pretty amusing under the circumstances. The seller was in Long Island City, and Marder made an appointment to pick it up late that day. Another call to Bernie: courier a check over to the dealership. This time Bernie did not ask questions.

Marder spun on his chair and looked around the office, reflecting that he'd spent an extraordinary amount of time within these walls. Two of them, the ones in view of his desk, were painted eggshell. Set into one of these was the big industrial-scale window looking out on Worth Street. Behind him, the rear wall of the room and the remaining sidewall were painted bloodred. That had been Chole's section of the home office. He had his elegant steel-and-rosewood desk, his back-saving leather chair, infinitely adjustable with little wheels and levers. Her desk was the antique rolltop with pigeonholes he'd bought her for their fifth (or wooden) anniversary. She had used a wooden office chair she'd brought in from the sidewalk in the days of their poverty, its cushion upholstered in bright serape cloth. Above her desk, a broad section of the wall was covered in thick cork panels, on which she'd stuck family photos, posters, found objects, cartoons, newspaper and magazine clippings from the Mexican press. The report of the murder of her father and mother, for example. A photograph of Esteban de Haro d'Ariés, that father, when young and smiling and holding his daughter, aged four, for example.

She'd been doing this for a long while, and the corkboard had become a palimpsest of her life in exile, untouched in the three years since her death. Marder had long since stopped looking at it closely but had a good look at it now. On one side of the cork hung a torero's shining cape and on the other an enormous crucifix, its corpus gray-skinned, bloody, twisted, agonized, nailed to the rough wood of the cross with real iron nails. It looked as if it had been sculpted from life, and considering that it had come from Michoacán, it might have been. A lot of strange things happened down there, where she was from.

He removed the newspaper clipping about the murders. It had been torn roughly out of the pages of *Panorama del Puerto*, the newspaper in Lázaro Cárdenas; on it his wife had written lines from a poem by Octavio Paz on the occasion of the famous massacre of students in 1968. He translated it silently:

> Guilt is anger
> turned against itself:
> if an entire nation is ashamed
> it is a lion poised
> to leap.

Maddened by grief—an antique concept perhaps, but Marder had seen it played out in this very dwelling, this room. No one had been punished for the murders, just another pair out of the forty thousand or so that the *narcoviolencia* had claimed. Everyone knew who had done it, and by all reports he was still enjoying his life, buoyed by an ocean of dollars and his apparent impunity. Marder carefully folded the clipping and placed it in a slot of his wallet, as if it were a set of a directions for the operations of a complex mechanism. A trap of some kind—no, an ambush: a lion poised to leap.

Marder had no corkboard. Instead, he had a whiteboard, inscribed in dry marker. It listed book schedules, chapter outlines, things to do. He took a rag and wiped it clean; so much for his life. A transient weakness passed through his body, and he had to sit in his chair for a moment and catch his breath. Then he turned to the file cabinets. His and hers: twin four-drawer wooden models. Hers was empty—the kids had cleared it out after she died. The upper three drawers of his contained his professional life: editorial notes, contracts, and so on, most of them from years ago, before the world turned digital. A good proportion of the paperwork was in Spanish because, for the last ten years or so, Marder's fluency in the language had led him into the business of arranging Spanish translations of works in English. For many big Latin

American media firms, Marder was one of the go-to people in New York. No more, obviously.

He got a black forty-gallon trash bag from the kitchen and opened the top drawer. Out went the impedimenta of former labors, plus the financial stuff, old tax returns, business letters from before email arrived—rustling and thumping into the bag. The bottom drawer held more-personal papers. Here was an old-fashioned red cardboard file marked RICHARD on the index tab in his mother's parochial school cursive.

He flipped it open. It contained his birth and baptismal certificates, report cards, school awards, a collection of handmade Mother's Day and birthday cards of increasing competence, right up through his elementary school years, until he had money enough to buy from Hallmark. Then there were the letters he'd sent from his time in the military, scrawled in ballpoint on cheap PX stationery, several smeared with the red soil of Vietnam. He recalled the ones she'd sent him in return, one every few days: quotidian cheerfulness, a recounting of prayers she'd sent up from St. Jerome's for his safety, and, unconventionally, a series of commentaries about the Catholic antiwar movement, of which Katherine Devlin Marder had been an ornament. He didn't know where those letters were and felt a pang of regret.

A thin file was marked DAD in Marder's own neat capitals. This contained a sheaf of papers from Augie Marder's own military service in the Good War. Here was the honorable discharge in a tattered, yellowing envelope printed with the army seal. He'd been with the Sixth Army under MacArthur, in New Guinea and the Philippines, that grim, inglorious campaign of which no movie with major stars had yet been made, of which his father had hardly ever spoken. He'd been leg infantry all the war long, discharged as a corporal with two Purple Hearts and a Bronze Star. That had been one of the only two pieces of advice he'd offered when his son had gone off to the Less Good War: stay out of the goddamn infantry. Marder had followed it, had entered the air force to beat the draft, but, ignoring the other piece of advice (never, *never* volunteer!), had ended up in an outfit compared to which the leg infantry in New Guinea was a day at the beach.

There were also pension papers, union papers, canceled savings passbooks, a couple of yellowing photos with deckle edges: a stringy young man, bare-chested, smiling by a howitzer, jungle in the background; the same man, now unsmiling, with two others of the same age, in their liberty duds, on some dusty street, three of the legion of teenagers who had destroyed the empire of Japan. And an insurance policy, the word PAID punched through it in tiny holes.

His father had been no fool. He'd known what happened to men who spent their whole working lives punching out hot type, sitting next to pots of molten, fuming lead. All linotypers died nuts, he used to say; he even joked about it, until it stopped being funny, until the rages and paranoia ate up the decent workingman he'd been and he'd died at sixty, raving, in a state hospital. But he'd taken advantage of the insurance program run by his union and never missed a payment, and after his death came the astonishing letter and the check for $550,000, of which a hundred fifty grand was Marder's. The rest went to his mother, and it turned out to be just enough to pay for the best possible care during the following year, the final year of her life.

Another, much fatter file, marked APPLE STUFF on a machine-made label. It contained decades of broker's statements. They wanted to send them over the computer now, but Marder liked the paper in his hands. He looked at the latest one: the balance was a colossal, an unbelievable sum, forty times more than his father had earned in a lifetime of noisy, filthy, deadly toil. And all Marder had done to earn it was to walk into a Merrill Lynch office one day on his lunch hour, knowing nothing about stocks but having seen the famous *1984* commercial during a drunken Super Bowl party, and use his insurance money to buy thirty-five thousand shares of Apple, Inc., at $3.22 per share. And he'd held on to it, feeling stupid for decades as the stock stayed flat, dipped, rose, dipped again, but clinging to his faith, until the technology had blossomed in recent years, sending the stock into financial heaven and making him a multimillionaire. Dumb luck, yes, but Marder also thought of it as the Linotyper's Revenge.

The Apple file went into the trash, but he returned RICHARD and DAD to the drawer, for the kids to find. He thought of these as a part of their family history, no longer his to destroy. There were files marked with the children's names too, Carmel and Peter, although the Peter one was empty. His son had taken all his stuff out of the loft after his mother died, the circumstances of Chole's death having estranged father and son, and Marder no longer had any hope that they'd ever connect again.

For a moment he thought of calling his son and, presuming Peter would even take the call, telling him about the medical thing and . . . and what? I'm dying; you have to forgive me for what happened with your mother? No. He'd screwed up and he'd have to take the fall. Carmel was a different story. He could call *her*. Not to tell her the truth, of course.

Before he could chicken out again, he grasped his cell phone and touched her name. A couple of shaky rings sounded, and when the call went to voice mail he felt a shameful relief. He knew she'd call back as soon as she was free of whatever consuming thing she was into at the moment. She was like her mother in that regard. Peter however, was like Marder—cool, cerebral, a harborer of grudges. While he waited for her callback, he turned to his computer and went to a website for a firm called Su Hacienda. It was a property agency that sold villas and estates to wealthy Americans who wanted to vacation or retire in Mexico and bask in the sunshine and the plenitude of cheap servants. There were a number of such agencies, but for Marder's purpose only one would do. He took the phone number from the website and dialed a number he hadn't called in three years.

He felt sweat flow in his armpits, on his forehead, while he listened to the ring.

"Hello, Su Hacienda, Nina speaking." A wonderful throaty voice, slightly accented; this had been the first attraction.

"Nina, this is Rick."

A pause on the line, a crackling etheric hiss in his ear. He could imagine the small solo office with the framed pictures of properties, and he could imagine *her*, although he didn't want to, for she was the one pathetic infidelity of his long married life, an affair of six weeks.

During the last of which his wife had mixed up an unusually powerful version of her usual cocktail of prescription drugs and tequila, after which it had seemed good to her to climb to the roof of this very loft building, remove her clothes, and go dancing alone on the parapet, in a driving snowstorm. She'd landed in the air shaft and been covered by the drifts, had lain there for the better part of a week, a period during which he was with Nina Ibanez, in one of her properties south of Acapulco, screwing his brains out.

Amazement in her voice. "Rick *Marder*?"

"Yeah, it's me."

A chuckle. "Well. Someone I never thought I'd hear from again. It's been years."

"Yes. Look, Nina, I want to buy a property."

Another pause. "Ah, Rick . . . if you want to see me, you don't have to buy a property. A drink will do."

"No, it's not about that, us. I really want to buy a property, a house, a nice one, isolated, on the coast. You know, as a getaway."

"You're not thinking of *that* house, are you? Because it's been sold, and it's not on the market as far as I know."

"No, I don't want it in the Acapulco area. I want to buy a house with a good chunk of property in Playa Diamante."

"Playa . . . ? You mean Playa Diamante in *Michoacán*?"

"Yeah. Do you have anything? I need it sort of now."

Dead air on the line, for so long that Marder thought the system had dropped the call.

"Hello?"

When she spoke, her voice was chillier, more businesslike and precise.

"Sorry . . . It's just hearing your voice after all this time. I'm a little rattled. Getting dumped with the three-line email was a little harsh."

"Nina, maybe this was a mistake. Should I call someone else?"

"Oh, not at all. Frankly, I could use the commission. Second homes in Mexico—you know, a slightly shrunken market since the crash. And the violence. Not to mention the mortgage situation—"

"I don't need a mortgage. I'll pay cash."

"Oh, in that case, I tell you what—let me do some research, we'll have a drink somewhere, and I'm sure I'll have something nice for you to look at."

"I don't think that's such a good idea, Nina."

Another, shorter pause. "Well—all business, then. As a matter of fact, something just came to mind. Are you near a computer?"

"Yes, I'm in my office."

"Then I'm going to let you look at the Guzmán property. Did you know Manny Guzmán at all?"

"The name's sort of familiar but I can't quite place it. Who is he?"

"Was. He came up here from Michoacán in the eighties, made a fortune as a lawyer and property developer. He went back home a few years ago and built a big house on the coast in Playa Diamante. He had plans to build a resort, poured some concrete for rental units, but . . . he sort of disappeared. The house has been vacant since, but apparently it's been maintained. I'm sending the photos and specs now."

Marder waited in front of his computer, while Nina chattered on, trying and failing to generate a conversation. Marder liked Nina Ibanez well enough, a charming and sexy woman, but he never wanted to see her again. Images rose unbidden, her face and body, yes, but it hadn't been just about sex. It was the lack of all the tangles, the relief from what his life with Chole had become since some men had snatched his father-in-law from his car and chopped him into pieces and left them in a pile on the side of a road in Playa Diamante. And, being careful about witnesses, they'd shot her mother too.

Which was Marder's fault, ultimately, he having removed Chole from Mexico all those years ago. Marder had not been prepared for that, for his wife going crazy, and he'd cracked a little himself, the fling with Nina Ibanez being one result.

A shudder ran through him thinking of it, and then the email tone pinged. Marder opened the attachment and studied the set of pictures. One was an aerial view of what appeared to be a small island connected to the mainland by a short causeway; the property was listed as 112 hectares—277 acres. The other photographs were exterior and interior shots of what the accompanying copy described as a two-story six-bedroom concrete-block stucco house with a separate unit for the servants, a four-car garage, and a swimming pool. Some hundred yards distant from the house, built on a curve facing the sea and a broad shining beach, were what looked like bungalows in various stages of construction and behind these an excavation for another, much larger swimming pool. The listing claimed the house had seven bathrooms, a modern kitchen, air-conditioning throughout, a desalinization and sewage treatment facility in operating order, and a diesel generator in its own little building. The house was square, with a flat roof and a squat tower at each corner. It looked like a Spanish colonial fortress, which suited Marder very well. The asking price was a reasonable $1.2 million.

"This is available immediately?" he asked.

"They'll kiss your hands. The family, I mean. They've been paying maintenance through the nose ever since Manny disappeared. They're terrified it'll be looted and stripped. There are some people living in the servants' wing, watching the place, but you don't need to feel responsible for them. The taxes are practically nothing. If you let me talk to them, I'm sure they'll come down a little."

"No, I'll take it," said Marder. "I'll have my accountant send you a check for the asking price."

He heard a sigh over the line. "It must be nice to have money," said Nina Ibanez.

After that they discussed the details of the sale in a businesslike way and then Marder's phone buzzed with an incoming call. He said a quick goodbye and pressed the call-accept button.

"Hello, babe," he said to his daughter. "I'm not interrupting anything important, I hope."

"No, I was just in the fabrication lab, running some trials. Is anything wrong?"

She always asked that when he called, and he wondered why. Perhaps he should have called her more often. He knew other parents had more contact with their kids, but he'd always felt that after they were grown, excessive contact was an intrusion. Or maybe it was because his own father, in his madness, had called Marder oppressively often, full of paranoid complaint and mad schemes to reform the world. Chole had always been the caller, the main contact with the children.

And even though something *was* wrong now, and even though he'd always tried not to lie to his kids, he replied in a cheerful tone, "Not at all. I just called to find out how you were doing and to tell you that I'll be traveling for a while."

They'd had enough misery dealing with their mother's sickness and death, and he told himself he was actually doing them a favor.

"Where are you going?"

"Not determined yet. I thought I'd buy an open ticket and take some time off. There's a lot of the world I haven't seen, and I'm not getting any younger."

"But you hate to travel. You're always bitching about airports and the food."

"I changed my mind. Anyway, I'll be leaving in a day or so and I didn't want you to worry."

"You'll keep in touch, though, right?"

"I always do. How's work?"

"We're having tempering problems. Three-D printing in metal's easy if you're only doing art stuff or prototypes, but if you're trying to manufacture actual machine parts, it's a different story."

"I'm sure you'll solve the problem, dear," he said. "I'm sure you'll be in at the end of mass production as we know it," and she laughed. Marder was constantly amazed at how both of his children, the spawn of two literary types, had become engineers, and brilliant ones by all accounts. Carmel was in grad school at MIT; Peter taught at Caltech, as far as possible from New York and his father.

"Still keeping up with the swimming?" he asked.

"Every day. Still with the shooting?"

"Every week. How are your times?"

"Static. I'm devoted but not *that* devoted. Don't expect me at the Olympics. I hope that doesn't break your heart."

"As long as it doesn't break yours. Meanwhile—anything new on the social front?"

"The usual. Don't rent a hall."

"So you're saying no grandchildren anytime soon."

"When they have cloning maybe. I'd kind of like an instant ten-year-old with freckles and a gap-tooth grin."

He couldn't think of any response, couldn't think of any final paternal words of love or advice. "Well, I'll let you go now. You'll let Peter know, yes?"

"You could call him yourself," she said.

"I could. But if he doesn't take my call . . ."

He heard her sigh. "Okay. Have a great trip and keep in touch."

He said he would, said he'd loved her, said goodbye, pushed the button to end the call. For an instant he felt he'd switched himself off, as if he'd already died. Not staying in touch was the whole point.

As he often did when he was annoyed with himself and the world, Marder decided to go shooting. He packed his two pistols and their magazines and ammunition into their customized aluminum case and took a cab to the Westside Shooting Range on 20th Street. On the ride, he thought of a way to save himself a trip, so he called his accountant and told him to have the money he'd asked for ready at his office in an hour. The accountant asked him if he seriously intended to carry a hundred fifty thousand dollars in cash through the streets of Manhattan. Marder told him not to worry about it.

Marder had been coming to Westside for years and paid in advance by the month so he was always assured a lane. The firing line was crowded with nervously chattering newbies taking a firearms class, and he was glad he was wearing ear protectors.

He clipped a small paste-on circle target to the line and sent it a-flapping to the seven-yard marker, then loaded the first of the two pistols he was going to fire. This was a .45-caliber Kimber 1911, a high-tech, super-accurate version of the sidearm that American soldiers had carried throughout most of the twentieth century. He loaded it, took a stance, and fired a shot. A hole appeared in the center of the bull's-eye, rimmed by the fluorescent-yellow paint built into the target's paper. He fired again. No change was apparent, and he fired five more times, then placed the pistol on the little shelf and drew the target back. On examination, the hole had become slightly larger than the original puncture, which meant he had shot six bullets through the hole made by his first one. It was a feat he'd accomplished often. He loaded another magazine and shot at ten yards and again at twenty, each time blowing the center out of the target.

He now took from his case the elder brother of the Kimber, an actual military .45 his dad had brought back from the Pacific. It was still formally the property of the United States Army, but he thought they probably weren't looking for it too hard. He shot three magazines with this, not as accurately as before but still well enough: at seven yards, all the holes touched.

Marder then did something he hadn't done before. He slipped a fresh magazine into the old .45 and he stuck the pistol into his waistband, where it hung heavily, concealed by the raincoat he wore. Feeling a little foolish at this precaution, and in violation of the laws of New York, he cased the other pistol and left the range, for the last time, he supposed. He walked to Sixth Avenue, and in one of those miscellaneous-goods stores he purchased an aluminum suitcase and then took a cab to his accountant's office uptown. He gave the driver a fifty and told him to keep the meter going, then went in and and collected his cash. Packed in his new suitcase, it felt heavier than he'd expected.

From the cab he called the last person he needed to contact before leaving. Patrick Francis Skelly was not at home. An old-style answering machine picked up, and Skelly's voice said, "Skelly isn't here, obviously. Leave a message." Marder called back several times on the ride downtown but reached only the machine. From home he called several more times, then gave up for the moment. He hadn't eaten all day, had fasted before the doctor's visit and found that, though dying in a way, he still liked eating. He liked cooking too. He grilled a steak and made a Caesar salad with a soft-boiled egg and lots of anchovies and ate it while watching the news, rather enjoying the idea that he no longer had to pretend interest in what was going on in the world.

He tried Skelly a few more times, then called the car dealer and learned that the check had arrived and that he could pick the vehicle up anytime. He spread an old towel across the kitchen table and cleaned his pistols, an activity that always calmed him, although not tonight. Perhaps it was the money. He placed the cash in his gun safe, double-locked his door, left the loft, and hailed a cab.

The driver was not enthusiastic about going to Long Island City, but Marder waved some large bills and off they went. At a small lot on a dull commercial boulevard, he bought his camper and truck. Marder had never actually been in a truck camper before and was favorably impressed when he stepped inside. To the right as he entered was a clever shower–toilet combination and to the left a large wardrobe. Along one side were arranged a three-burner propane stove and a sink, with a refrigerator below. On the other side was a padded bench with a dining table that swiveled out of the way so that someone could sleep on the bench. There seemed to be plenty of storage in the overhead cabinets. Up a stepladder, extending out over the truck's cab, was a sleeping loft equipped with a full-sized bed. The thing was full of light and smelled faintly of plastics.

Marder had spent nearly all his life in the city and so was not much of a driver, and the bulk of his new vehicle was a little daunting. But after a bit of awkwardness and overcautious driving, he got used to the smooth power of the V-8 and the inability to see what was directly behind him. By the time he drove onto the Brooklyn–Queens Expressway, he had started to enjoy himself.

He soon became confident enough in his driving to use his cell phone but achieved the same irritating result. Skelly was the only adult of his acquaintance who refused to own a cell phone, and so it was always a pain in the ass getting in touch with him. Marder left the expressway at Brooklyn Heights and drove slowly through the prim green-shaded streets. He parked illegally in front of a modest brownstone, got out, and pushed the bell button next to a slot with no name in it. The door issued no welcoming buzz. He looked up at the top floor, where Skelly lived. It was dusk now, but no lights shone there.

When he returned to the truck, he realized he had forgotten that the previous day was September 19, and so of course Skelly would not be at home. He would be on his annual commemorative journey to oblivion on the anniversary of Moon River. Marder always forgot; Skelly always remembered.

Oblivion was in any case a regularly scheduled stop for Skelly. It was something they occasionally did together, but this anniversary trip was one that Skelly did alone. Skelly was Marder's longest-surviving continuous relationship. Forty years now they'd known each other, but they were not what most observers would have called best friends. Skelly spent a lot of time out of town. He called himself a security consultant but was closemouthed about what he actually did, and Marder had learned not to inquire. Skelly must have made decent money at it, for Brooklyn Heights apartments were not cheap, and he always paid for more than his share of drinks and meals and tickets. Skelly did not like going to movies and sporting events alone, and Marder was happy to accept his invitations. Marder did not have many friends in his profession, and these few were not the sort to go to hockey games at the Garden and then tour the saloons, usually ending the evening in some bucket of blood in Greenpoint or Red Hook, at which Skelly often got into fights. Young men or bigger men would take him on and find themselves pounded into the ground. Marder often had to pull Skelly off a surprised and bloody opponent and scatter cash around to assuage complaints.

Now Marder drove south on Fourth Avenue, then cut over to Second, passing under the Gowanus Expressway. At a stretch of waste ground near the rail yards, he spotted a group of homeless men standing around a fire barrel. Dressed in the usual thick layers of clothing, red-eyed, their faces demonic in the lights of the low flames, they were passing around a bottle, laughing and joking. The fights and assaults had not yet started. Skelly always brought good times to these gatherings, and Marder thought it was fortunate that the evening was young and the crack pipes were not in evidence as far as he could observe. Skelly on crack was not amusing.

He approached the group, waved a greeting, and sidled next to one of them, a small but powerfully built man with a shaved head partly covered by a filthy Red Sox baseball hat.

"Hello, Skelly," Marder said. "Are we having fun yet?"

Skelly looked at him with a belligerent stare; his eyes were unfocused and he stank of peach schnapps. "Marder. If you're here to join the party, have a drink. If not, fuck off!"

"Let's take a little walk, Skelly. I want to show you my new camper truck."

With the exaggerated diction of the very drunk, Skelly said, "Fuck you, Marder, and fuck the camper truck you rode in on. I'm having a little drink with some old army buddies. These are my good buddies here. Hinton, say hello to Marder. Marder isn't an old army buddy. Marder was in the air force. He was rear-area motherfucker."

The men laughed at this, Skelly loudest of all. If this anniversary celebration went the way of all the others, Marder would receive a call from a pay phone at three A.M. a couple of nights from now and he would call a hire car and drive to where Skelly would be waiting at some all-night place, sans wallet, cowboy boots, watch, coat, and other items, plus any number of bruises and abrasions. Once or twice he'd been standing there in his T-shirt and shorts. Marder no longer had time for that.

He tugged at Skelly's coat. "Come on, man. I need to talk to you."

Skelly pulled away so hard he staggered. "I'm busy," he said. "Get the fuck away from me!"

The other men were observing this with interest. Marder started to feel crowded. Hinton, the buddy, a large person with a wild Afro escaping from his knitted hat, and eyes like spoiled eggs, growled, "Yeah, leave him alone. Skelly's our friend. We having a good time here and we don't need no rear-area motherfuckers, you know?"

This remark was funny too. Marder addressed the big guy. "Yeah, I get that. Look, I need to talk to my friend here, and I'll give you each fifty bucks to help me get him over to that camper there. What do you say?"

Money changed hands. The men, ignoring Skelly's protests, picked him up and stuffed him in the passenger seat of the Ford.

"Nice camper," said Skelly. "Now can I go?"

"In a second. The thing is, I'm leaving, and I know you'd've had to call me later and I wouldn't be here. I wanted to let you know."

"So? I could've called somebody else. I mean, fuck it, Marder, you're not my *mom*."

"Somebody else? Like who? You mean I have a backup? I wish to Christ I would've known it sometime during the last—what is it?—forty *years* you've been pulling this shit. I would've told you, 'Get fucked, Skelly. It's three in the morning, call number two on the list.'"

Skelly was silent for a moment, and then asked, "So what's with the camper? You becoming a Good Sam?" In a familiar way, he seemed to have dumped his drunk by an act of will.

"Yes. It's always been my dream to tour America's national parks and meet wonderful people along the way."

"That's good, Marder, I like how you're easing into being an old fart. You need to get you some of those pants with no belt and wear more bright colors. And a plastic hat. Of course, it shouldn't be much of a change—you were sort of an old fart when you were young."

"I'm glad you approve. Should I drive you home or drop you off at the nearest saloon?"

"A saloon, thank you. If you cut right up there on Forty-Fourth Street, there's Mahoney's on Ninth Avenue."

Marder drove as directed. After a while, Skelly asked, "So how long do you figure this trip is going to take?"

"I don't know," said Marder. "It'll be a while. Ours is a big country."

He pulled the truck to the curb across from the dimly lit little tavern. He held out his hand and Skelly took it.

"Goodbye, Skelly."

Skelly gave him an odd look, a smile edged onto his mouth. "Yeah, well, I'll see you when I see you. Have a safe trip, and I know you'll obey all the relevant traffic laws."

Skelly left the truck and crossed the avenue. More than anything else, more than giving up his profession and his home, more than bidding his child farewell, this parting told Marder that the life he'd known was truly over. Or not. It would depend on Skelly.

2

In the morning Marder made himself a plate of eggs and bacon, toasted a bagel, and dripped a full pot of coffee. He had worked hard on making this kitchen as perfect and as well supplied as he could, and he had vowed not to miss it, but he knew he would. After eating his meal and drinking a couple of cups, he poured the rest of the pot into a thermos. Marder was traveling light, but it took several trips to load his truck. He put the rifle in the back of the wardrobe in the main cabin, together with his pistol cases, stuck his bag in an overhead, locked everything up, and went back for his laptop, the money, and the blue ceramic urn that held the earthly remains of Maria Soledad Beatriz de Haro d'Ariés y Casals, or Chole Marder, as she was known in New York. He placed this in a cabinet drawer, buffered by towels so it wouldn't roll. His bedroll he tossed up into the sleeping loft. The time was just past dawn; the garbage trucks rumbled, a siren wailed from afar, the sky above the canyons of Manhattan was taking on a tint of blue. It would be a good day for traveling.

As it turned out to be, the weather clear and mild, the traffic light until he got to Philadelphia and caught the morning rush on the interstate. Yes, something terrific about leaving a city at dawn on a long journey. He planned to drive a simple, swift route, down 95 to Jacksonville, where he'd pick up 10 west, and then across the bottom of the country to Tucson, hang a left, and cross the Mexican border at Nogales. He would leave the interstate when he became tired, would stay at no-name RV parks and pay for meals and parking space with cash. He was behaving like a fugitive, he knew, although he had committed no crime under the law. But he often felt like a fugitive, like someone who would be found out someday and brought to justice. He'd felt like that for a long time, since the war, in fact. Survivor's guilt? He had that, and plenty of the other types as well.

He stopped at a plaza north of Richmond, Virginia, dashed in for just a moment to pick up a bag of burgers and coffee to go, looking nervously out the window at his rig. When he got back to it, he found it untroubled by thieves and Skelly sitting in the passenger seat. Marder was not surprised; he had counted on it, in fact, but now he assumed a hard face, stepped into the driver's seat, and put his paper bag on the console between the seats.

Skelly said, "Hey, great! I was starving," and lifted out a foil-wrapped burger. "So where are we going, chief?" he said around the first mouthful.

"To the nearest airport and put you on a plane back to the city."

"Not a good plan, chief. You need someone to look out for you."

"*I* need someone? That's a laugh. Look, Skelly, no offense, but this is a one-man trip. For one thing, this camper has only one bed."

"Bullshit! It's rated to sleep three. There's a padded seat in the main cabin that'll do me fine."

"Oh, the camper expert! No, I'm sorry, it's impossible. This is not what you call a fun trip."

"Really. What kind of trip is it, then? By the way, I was interested in your gear. A ton of cash. You're packing enough artillery for a minor war, and I couldn't help noticing Chole's along for the ride. I peeked in there looking for something to eat. Unless that's someone I don't know."

Marder cranked up the truck and rolled it out onto the interstate. So far, so good. Keeping Skelly in the dark as long as possible was part of the plan. He did not bother asking how Skelly had entered a securely locked camper and inspected a locked suitcase, because he knew Skelly would say, Hey, I'm a security consultant.

Skelly leaned back in the seat, adjusting its angle to a more comfortable slant. He pulled out and lit a cigarette. Marder rolled his window down.

"And you're going to stink up my new truck too."

"Am I going to get a lecture on secondhand smoke? Don't pretend to be more of a pussy than you are, Marder. It's unseemly. Face it—you're going to Mexico and I'm coming with you."

Marder snapped a startled look at the other man. "How did you know I'm going to Mexico?"

"I checked the email on your laptop. I see you're still dealing with the lovely Nina. Are we still getting any in that quarter? No? A pity; it looks like a nice place. So you're traveling to Michoacán with a lot of guns and a shitload of cash and won't say why. That's not characteristic of my pal Marder. So I'm thinking you're in trouble and you need a friend to watch your six."

"I'm not in trouble and I don't need my six watched. My *six*? Now we're talking army talk. Jesus, the war's been over for forty years and we lost. Get over it."

"You never get over it, and if you think *you're* over it you're more of an asshole than you usually are. How about passing this semi here, unless you want to breathe diesel fart for the next hundred miles."

"There's an airport in Richmond."

"I'm sure, but we're not going there. Look, chief, I saved your life. We're mutually entwined. Why do you think I let you hang out with me all these years and do all the shit I do for you? Believe me, it's not your charm. I'm responsible for you, end of story." Skelly yawned, stretched, and said, "And now I believe it's rack time. Actually, I fell into conversation with a young lady in Mahoney's last night, and with one thing and another I didn't get much sleep. Wake me when we arrive at a point of historical or scenic interest."

With that, Skelly lay his cheek against the window glass and was asleep in thirty seconds. It was a talent he had, one that Marder envied. Skelly could sleep in a helicopter under fire. Marder had seen him do it many times; he'd seen him sleep through a rocket attack. He could sleep in mud, on concrete, and of course he'd be perfectly comfortable on the padded bench of the camper. His sleep seemed deep and genuine, but if anything occurred that needed his attention he would be instantly awake, focused, ready to receive information, act, or give orders.

Marder drove past the Richmond exits. Of course, he was not going to take Skelly to any airport; he was going to take him to the house in Mexico. Mutual entwining, yes.

The last time Marder had spent any extended time on the interstates was after the breakup of his first marriage a long time ago, when he'd driven a motorcycle from New York to Mexico, a fateful journey, and one that he was repeating now. The difference in mass between the camper and the Harley Shovelhead he'd ridden then, with his every earthly possession in the saddlebags, was indicative of the draggy accretions of maturity. He always looked back on that lightness as particularly sweet, and he wished to taste it again, if but a little. He could have bought a bike, but the thought of old guys on motorcycles violated his sense of seemliness, like an octogenarian wearing a miniskirt.

He found that when alone at the wheel his mind spun free. The journeying being mere limbo, the mind of the highway traveler casts forward into plans or backward into memory. Marder's plans were still too immature to bear much thought, quite aside from the death-at-any-moment thing, but his past was rich, solid, there for the viewing. Marder glanced over at his sleeping companion, and his thoughts rolled back through the years to the first time he'd met Patrick Francis Skelly and started whatever this connection was, farce or tragedy, he couldn't be sure.

Marder had joined the air force right out of high school. By 1968, in the working-class neighborhoods of New York, boys Marder had known, who had been in and out of his mother's kitchen, had returned in coffins or shattered, and he knew she could not bear the thought of her only child slogging through jungles. Marder would actually have liked slogging, despite his father's experience in New Guinea, for jungle slogging was clearly what a real man did; besides which Marder was a reader, and much of his reading had been tales of manly adventure—Kipling, Hemingway, and their lesser epigones. Not to mention the war movies. The antiwar movement then roiling the media of the nation seemed an affectation of the higher classes, like golf or yachting.

From the start he'd done well in the military. It took him only a few days to understand that the service was a game, like baseball, and separate from real life. You had to take it seriously but not personally, and therefore it was as absurd to fight the system as it would have been to bitch and moan that there were only three strikes in baseball. He also understood that the USAF labored under the rep of being the most pussy service, so that its NCOs were at pains to be extra tough, although it was easy to see that this was a faux toughness and easily distinguishable from that of, say, the marines. After basic training and after blowing the top off the air force qualification tests, and after a certain amount of communications and radar training of a most select kind, he found himself at Nakhon Phanom, Thailand, at the huge air base that everyone called Naked Fanny. He was attached to a unit of the Infiltration Surveillance Center, an outfit known as Task Force Alpha.

This was the heart of an immense project code-named Igloo White. Its purpose was to stop the flow of supplies along the so-called Ho Chi Minh Trail, a vast braided network of roads and tracks issuing from communist North Vietnam and threading through Laos and Cambodia to Vietcong supply points in the south. The theory was that if you interdicted the supplies, the communist resistance would collapse.

When Marder first arrived in Naked Fanny, he was amazed by the scale of the operation. The building in which the center lived was the largest structure in southeast Asia; there were hundreds of airmen involved and scores of aircraft flying and billions of dollars being spent. During the briefings that accompanied his arrival, he learned that Igloo White depended on large numbers of electronic sensors capable of picking up the sounds or vibrations of trucks or sniffing out human effluvia. The sensors sent their messages to circling aircraft, which in turn sent data to the analysts at Task Force Alpha, of whom Marder was one.

He spent his shifts in a darkened room with dozens of other airmen, staring at video screens hooked up to the IBM 360 computers that stored the data flowing from the circling aircraft. These men, known as pinball wizards, looked for activity in a particular string of sensors, seeking the patterns of sensor response that signaled the passage of trucks or personnel. Most of the time there was nothing, but when something did light up, Marder would seize on it and pass the information up the line. High above his own pay grade, intel officers would collate the information, make a decision, inform the airborne battlefield command-and-control center, and before too long the forward air controller would lead a strike to just that spot, more or less, and the jungle would erupt in flame. Marder was good at this work, careful and alert, although bored out of his skull.

With a start, Marder snapped himself back to the present. He realized he had been driving for an uncertain period of time with his mind in long-ago Thailand, watching green digits on a screen and not the lights on the darkened interstate. Marder shook himself, felt chill sweat on his palms and forehead. This was strange. He never thought about the war; he could not really recall more than a few incidents of his time in-country. He never dreamed about it, although sometimes it seemed as if it all had *been* a dream; sometimes a face in the street or a sound or a certain situation would pluck a chord, give him a funny feeling—*this* was something that happened back *then*—but he could never quite pin down the source memory. Skelly, in contrast, was a walking encyclopedia of Indochinese events; *his* problem was that he recalled everything.

Marder had been driving for over five hours since his last stop. It now occurred to him that being hungry and tired was what was forcing up this buried stuff, that or the hypnotic effect of the moving lights on the highway, the glow from the instrument panel, the man sleeping in the seat next to him, all setting up a psychological predicate for a trip down memory lane. He didn't like it. Marder preferred always to focus on the present, on the instant: why he'd been excellent as a pinball wizard at Task Force Alpha, why he was a good shot.

An exit sign glowed greenly in the near distance, a town he'd never heard of, and Marder took it, braking on the ramp, throwing off the near-hypnosis of the open highway, recalibrating his sense of speed. Going thirty felt like being parked. The ramp debouched on a state two-lane with the usual gas plaza and fast-food mills, the road stretching past these into piney rural darkness.

Skelly was up and alert in his usual spooky way the instant the wheels hit the exit ramp.

"Where are we?"

"Somewhere south of South Carolina. I need a piss and the truck needs gas. I could eat too."

Marder pulled into a gas station, used the can, and came out to find Skelly filling the tank.

"There's a Hardee's over there," said Marder, pointing.

"Yes, but the last I heard, Hardee's didn't provide a full bar. I'd like a drink before dining, as they do in civilized lands. Give me the keys."

Marder experienced a moment of unaccountable panic. Things were getting away from him, his careful plans.

"Come on, Marder. I'll find us a place, we'll have a meal and a couple of scoops, and then we'll get back on the road."

"I thought we could find an RV park and start in the morning."

"What's the point of that? Yes, you look whipped, but I'm fresh as a fucking daisy. You're forgetting we have *two* drivers and a *camper*. One of us can rack out in the back while the other drives. We can be in Mexico the day after tomorrow."

Marder didn't have the energy to argue. Skelly got in the driver's seat and roared off down the road, away from the highway and the lights. This was *like* something, thought Marder as he slumped exhausted in his seat: being driven down a black road toward an unknown destination.

It was Thailand again. He was in a three-quarter-ton truck with two other guys from his unit. He could not recall either their names or their faces; they were just a trio of young fellow pinball wizards on a pass, tired from staring at the screens, looking for action.

By agreement they'd driven away from the neighborhood of soldier bars and whorehouses clustered like crab lice upon the sweaty carcass of Naked Fanny, driven south into the tropical night. They were looking for the real Thailand, though even the fake Thailand had been thrilling enough for young Marder. Having been raised in a Catholic parish in Brooklyn in the late fifties and early sixties, his sexual experience had amounted to teenaged fumblings with the bad girls of the block, these fumblings dulled by the terror of pregnancy and the anaphrodisiac strictures of the old Church. And here he was translated overnight to a society in which sexual prudence was a risible and scarcely believed rumor. The quasi-Americanized precincts of the great air base had been electrifying enough—the thin brown girls and their elastic, willing bodies! What could the deeper and presumably more genuine country have in store? They drove, the tropical night fell all at once, they drove on, getting lost, driving through streams on increasingly poor roads, youthful bravado pushing them on into the warm, velvety dark, and then they'd seen lights ahead.

There were lights ahead. Skelly was slowing down to take a look. A roadhouse, a mean concrete block, pillbox windows lit by two beer signs, hairy guys and their blunt-faced smoking women hanging out in the dirt yard in front, and a row of chopped Harleys too, their chrome reflecting the colors of the beer signs. Skelly passed it, braked; Marder said, "Maybe not here, Skelly."

But of course he backed neatly into the lot, as far from the motorcycles as he could. Marder didn't even bother to start an argument. Instead, he went into the camper and came out wearing a flannel shirt with the tails out.

Skelly said, "You know, I don't think there's a dress code here."

Marder said, "I was chilly," and then Skelly took off, striding through the parking lot with his cocky small-guy walk, waving, calling out, "Good evening, fine evening, gentlemen," to the bemused bikers standing around, and the same inside, a low-ceilinged joint, thick with the stink of cigarette smoke and stale beer. In the rear a pool table, a jukebox pumping out a Merle Haggard song; behind the bar a manly tattooed woman with dyed blond hair, and behind her a large Confederate flag.

Walking into a strange bar in a strange country, feeling ill at ease. Again, unbidden, a memory bloomed, the recollection of when he'd first met Skelly. It was in a bar they'd found in a town forty klicks distant from the air-base fence, a large open shack raised on poles above the earth, with a rusting tin roof and a split bamboo floor, the sweet stink of rice wine in the air, and the culinary odor you smelled throughout that part of Asia: charcoal, rice water, grilled meat, oily spices. The darkness of the place was barely relieved by colored lanterns; everyone looked up when the three of them walked in, and not in a friendly way. The furnishings comprised a bar made of teak planks stretched across oil drums, two round tables made from wooden wire spools, and a scatter of miscellaneous rattan stools. Four men were sitting around one table, three of them small and thin and brown with close-cropped hair. They were wearing tattered plaid shirts and shorts cut down from jungle fatigues.

Montagnards, thought Marder. He'd never seen one before, but he'd heard of them, the highland tribesmen who fought for the CIA and the Special Forces. They wore the telltale brass bracelets on their wrists. You could buy crude copies of them in the Saigon markets, and a lot of American soldiers wore them, but he could see that these were the real thing, thin and intricately incised. The fourth man was an American, a smallish pug-faced guy with major muscles, his hair worn longer than was usual for the military but obviously a soldier. He was wearing some kind of light-green uniform shirt of a type that Marder hadn't seen before, with the sleeves cut down and unraveling. He had a bracelet like the others.

This man stared briefly at the three young airmen and into the silence spoke a phrase in some nasal twittering language, and the place broke up in laughter. The two bar girls laughed, the toothless woman behind the bar laughed out of the dark hole of her mouth, the montagnards and the other men in the bar all thought it was hilarious. Marder wanted to know what the joke was but was too embarrassed to inquire. One of the men with him caught the vibe, pulled at his arm. Maybe we shouldn't . . .

But Marder walked in boldly, went to the bar, held up three fingers, said "Bir khap," and the woman, covering her mouth against the giggles, brought forth three bottles of Singha. As Marder drank his beer, his gaze kept turning back to the American. Without being loud or boisterous, the man was the center of the room's attention. The bar girls vied for a word; the three montagnards clearly regarded him as the sun around which they orbited. Marder had never seen anyone like that close up before, but he'd read about such men, born leaders, natural warriors, not at all like his own officers, who were more like petty bureaucrats. He'd been fascinated by Lawrence of Arabia in the movie: here was another in real life.

After a period of sneaking looks, Marder found the American looking back. Blue eyes, but with the flat, uninformative gaze of the tribesmen who were his companions; uninterested, hostile, but only mildly, as if to say Marder was not significant enough for serious hostility. Marder felt his face flush, and he turned back to the quiet nervous chatter of his companions and his beer. Finishing it quickly, he had little trouble convincing the other airmen to seek out a more welcoming venue.

In the biker bar, the only food seemed to be packaged bacon rinds, bar nuts, and the contents of large glass vats filled with murky liquid, in which floated pickled eggs and pigs' feet. Skelly, meanwhile, was taking in all his calories via Jax beers and shots of Jim Beam. Marder sucked at the lip of a longneck and waited for the inevitable. Half a dozen of the bikers were in the back, playing pool, and ten or so were at the bar or at tables. They were ignoring the newcomers but also watching them, looking for an opportunity. On the neighboring stool, a big man in a studded denim vest kept jostling Marder every couple of minutes. He imagined a similar thing was going on on the other side of Skelly, delivered by a bushy-haired big-belly who had an SS skull tattooed on the back of his neck. It was not going to be hard to initiate proceedings.

"Madam, what is that flag there? What does it signify?"

This was Skelly, pointing at the Confederate banner, speaking loud and in the cultured tones of an eastern preppy, which, remarkably, he had actually once been.

"It's a rebel flag," said the woman after a scrutinizing pause. The place quieted down, waiting. The click of pool balls stopped; people started to drift in from the back, so there was a substantial audience for Skelly's peroration.

Marder took a hundred-dollar bill from his pocket and stuck it, folded, under his beer bottle and eased himself away from the bar.

Skelly evinced curiosity as to why a respectable saloon would display the symbol of an atrocious treason, a symbol, moreover, of the right of rich guys to fuck helpless slave women, many of whom were whiter than the people in this bar, and to sell the daughters thus produced to whorehouses, but perhaps only after first encouraging their sons to fuck their half sisters. Yes, long may it wave, the glorious symbol of the right of sister-fucking by rich men and the fact that poor assholes could be deluded into fighting for that right, and in his opinion Bobbie Lee and every fucking treasonous rebel officer over the rank of major should've been hanged from the highest—

Mr. SS Skull swung the first punch. Marder had seen Skelly in operation many times and was always amazed at how fast the man still was, still a perfect machine of harm. Skelly time ran just a little faster than the time of everyone else and, up to a certain point, alcohol didn't seem to slow him at all.

The punch landed on air, because Skelly had crouched down under the blow and had buried his fist up to the wristbone in the fellow's crotch. The man screamed and fell on his side, retching heroically. Mr. Studded Vest attempted to throw a choke around Skelly's neck but instead, mysteriously, found himself flying through the air into a table and chairs. At that point the bartender pulled a cut-down ball bat from under the bar and swung it at Skelly's head. He deflected it with his left hand, which turned into a grip, pulling the woman forward. Her face smashed down on the bar with an awful crunching thump, a splash of blood, little droplets falling on Marder's hundred, and now Skelly had the bat.

He was just wading into the crowd with it, clearly to his doom, since there were at least a dozen people armed with cues, chairs, bottles, one with a thick bike chain, when Marder pulled his fancy pistol out from the small of his back and fired a shot into the ceiling.

Everyone paused, and for an instant the place was as quiet as an art museum. Skelly turned and looked at Marder inquiringly, frowning a little, like a child called from the sandbox. Marder jumped toward him, embraced him in a bear hug with his free arm, shouted out, "You'll have to excuse my friend, he's still crazy from Nam, crazy from *Nam*! There's money on the bar, drinks are on us. Sorry for the inconvenience."

He dragged Skelly toward the door and out into the lot. The people outside backed off when they saw the pistol, but Marder knew one of them was bound to have a gun and it was only a matter of minutes before they started using it.

The first shot sounded and Marder heard the snap of the bullet. He shot out the two beer signs. People scattered. He let go of Skelly and they both reached the camper, putting its bulk between them and the crowd of bikers.

"Give me the keys," said Marder.

"Oh, please!" replied Skelly, scooting into the truck from the passenger side, slipping into the driver's seat, and cranking the engine. Marder got in. More shots and the sound of bullets striking the sides and back of the camper as they roared away.

Then Skelly slammed on the brakes and jerked the wheel violently, sending the truck slewing across the road. It teetered for a hideous second, all four wheels crashed to the pavement, and they were pointed back toward the roadhouse, accelerating. A bullet holed the windshield as Skelly drove the big truck's brush guard into the line of Harleys, which went over like dominoes, some skidding away, others crushed under the heavy tires. More shots: Marder could hear them thudding into his new camper.

Skelly did yet another 180, swinging across the two-lane and sending a road sign flying. Marder slid off the seat into the foot well and wrapped his arms over his head. A horrible metallic grinding from below, the sound of gunfire from above, Marder literally praying and then laughing inwardly at the absurdity of it.

Now they were heading at high speed back toward the interstate. In the side mirror Marder could see the glow of flame—perhaps the gas from the smashed motorcycles had caught fire. Amazingly, no one had shot out the tires, no one had sent a lethal bullet into either of them or punctured the fuel or propane tanks. Marder got up on his seat. Skelly said, "Christ, you know what? I'm starving. I could go for some Hardee's. What do you say?"

"Hardee's would be good," said Marder. "To go, I think."

He awoke with bright sunlight in his eyes. A shaft of it, thin and bright as a laser, was coming from a bullet hole in the over-cab compartment. It took Marder a moment to recall where he was and how he'd come to be there. The truck was not moving. The only sound was wind and, faint and distant, the twang of a country song. He left the bed and slipped down into the camper's main cabin. Well, so much for his fourteen-thousand-dollar investment. Most of the windows were shattered, and the cabinetwork was marred by bullet holes. The floor was covered in broken glass and splinters and bits of pink insulation. Besides the cosmetic damage, it seemed that the camper had not suffered functional impairment: the lights worked, the refrigerator was cold, the toilet swallowed his pee, and the shower gushed. He stripped and jumped under it.

Dressed in a fresh T-shirt, jeans, and worn leather huaraches, Marder left the camper. He found that it was parked in a small lot facing what appeared to be a public beach. He presumed that the oily green swells he observed rushing shoreward and pounding a slight surf against the sand were part of the Gulf of Mexico. He could see a large gray naval vessel moving slowly against the horizon. Skelly was nowhere around.

Marder used his iPhone to find out where he was. He ignored the many messages indicated and consulted the map app, which told him he was off Highway 90, in a park near Pascagoula, Mississippi. Skelly had driven well over seven hundred miles during the night and early morning. He must be exhausted now; Marder wondered where he was.

As he was not about to leave an unlockable camper with a lot of money and weapons in it, Marder busied himself with light housekeeping. He charged his iPhone. He used the little broom and dustpan that came with the camper to clear away the glass and debris from the floor and surfaces, made himself a cup of instant coffee on the stove, and ate a packet of cold, greasy fries left over from the previous night. Thus restored, he sat in the passenger's seat, switched on the radio, and waited.

Marder was good at waiting. He had learned the skill from Skelly, in fact, long ago. Skelly said that survival in combat was largely a matter of knowing when to move and when not to, and not moving—becoming so still that you essentially disappeared—was a discipline hard to acquire, especially for the large, anxious, jittery Americans. But Skelly had acquired it and so had Marder, under Skelly's strenuous direction.

Waiting in a truck, with the heat just starting to build, it had been early, just after first light. Marder had been ordered to report to his commanding officer, a bottlecap colonel named Honus "Honey" Folger. Folger was out on the pistol range at Nakhon Phanom. One of his policies was that every person in his command be a proficient shot and that every person carry a sidearm when on duty, although the possibility of any of his airmen ever having to defend the base against enemy attack was remote—more than remote, absurd. Still, he was the CO of all the pinball wizards and they all had to qualify, including their leader. There he was in the approved stance, blasting away with his .45 while his aides stood in a worshipful little group behind the firing line.

After he was done and had cleared his weapon and stuck it back in the romantic leather shoulder holster he wore, an aide motioned peremptorily to Marder, who jumped out of his seat and moved smartly over to the line, where he saluted and reported as ordered.

Colonel Folger looked him up and down and indicated the holstered army .45 on Marder's hip.

"Can you shoot that thing, son?"

"Yes, sir," said Marder.

"Then do so."

The pit crew set up a new man-shaped target at the ten-meter line, and Marder produced a single ragged hole in the silhouette's head with his seven bullets.

Honey's fleshy red face lit with a grin. "See? That's what a little training can do," he crowed to his assembled aides, and then in a lower voice said to Marder, "You didn't learn to shoot like that in the goddamn air force, did you?"

"No, sir. I shot pistols as a boy. A lot."

"Country boy, were you?"

"No, sir. I'm from Brooklyn."

A surprised grunt from the colonel. He said, "Come on over here, I want to talk to you."

They walked over to where a table and chairs had been set up under a distinctly un-military striped umbrella and sat down.

"Marder, I've had my eye on you for some time," the colonel said. "You're smart, and I think you're tough. I have an instinct about these things. You're not meant to spend the war staring at screens. Am I right?"

"Yes, sir."

"So tell me what you think, son. I mean about Igloo White and Alpha. The air force thinks it's a great program, a war-changing program. Charlie needs three hundred tons of supplies every day to function in the south, and if we can strangle him on the trail, the VC will dry up and blow away. And we can, we can! I want to know every time a mouse farts along the whole length of the trail, and if that mouse is a commie mouse, I want to drop a bomb on him—not just near him, mind, but right on top of him. So tell me, son, why can't I do that yet? Why in hell are those supplies still getting through?"

"I couldn't say, sir. I'm pretty low down on the intel food chain."

"That's why I'm asking you, Airman. I want the view from the trenches."

"Well, sir," replied Marder after a moment's thought, "the first problem is the whole idea that it's a trail. It's not a trail; it's a whole road network constantly being expanded and improved by an army of workers. I mean, you can just look at the maps, sir. Plus, the sensors are scattered by aircraft, sort of approximately where we know they have road networks. Some of them supposedly go into the ground like lawn darts, and others supposedly hang from camouflaged parachutes in the treetops. But we don't know that. It's a crapshoot. And the other thing is, the VC are no fools. They have to know about the sensors; they've probably taken them apart and know how they work. For all I know, they've found a lot of them and moved them to where they can't do us any good. And also, well, the whole thing you said about strangling them. Basically we've got million-dollar computers and millions of dollars' worth of aircraft, costing God knows how much to operate, just so we can drop a bomb and blow up a World War Two Russian truck and a thousand bucks' worth of rice. I mean, won't we run out of dollars before they run out of rice?"

The colonel frowned. "Don't you think that's a little above your pay grade, Airman Marder?"

"Yes, sir. Like I said before, but you asked me—"

"Yes, yes, but the other things you said are quite true. Very perceptive, Marder. I see I wasn't wrong about you. Now let me ask you this: What's the solution? How can we know the location of every vehicle on your vast road network? What would we need?"

"I don't know, sir. The logistics and routing schedule of the Central Office for South Vietnam in your pocket, updated daily?"

Folger laughed. "Yeah, that would do it. But failing that—and, son, I'm going to tell you something that maybe ten people in this theater know about—we've got something just as good. We've got a new kind of sensor a little bigger than a regulation softball. It gets buried by the trail, and when trucks or personel pass by, it sends out data on speed and vector. I'm talking exact location now. What do you think of that, Marder?"

"It sounds pretty cool, sir. Who gets to bury these softballs on the Ho Chi Minh Trail?"

"Ah, SOG has been tasked with that by MACV—you know, the so-called Green Berets and their little jungle helpers. I'd argued that the air force has the capability to get in there and do the job and place its own sensors, but unfortunately I was overruled. Basically, it's the army's war, and they get to do it their way. However, we did prevail in one respect. MACV has authorized USAF liaison teams to work with the Special Forces, to calibrate the equipment when emplaced and do maintenance on the repeaters."

"The repeaters, sir?"

"Yes, like network amplifiers. The little balls don't have much range, and for technical reasons I won't go into, their signals have to be picked up by a man-portable stationary unit and relayed up to the EC-121s. These repeaters will have to be buried at precise locations along the road network, and that task naturally will fall to us. To, uh, volunteer technicians who will infiltrate with the Special Forces and their montagnard allies and do the job. You understand what this means, right? For the first time we'll have a true electronic fence, with defined sensor locations, across the whole trail complex. Nothing will move south that we don't know about. It'll be an order of magnitude increase in accuracy from what we've got now. We'll bomb the living shit out of the bastards. And one other thing: such a technician would have to, uh, ascertain that the VEDUUs were properly deployed."

"Voodoos, sir?"

"Vehicle detection uplink units. The softballs. We don't want the little friends to just toss them anywhere, do we?"

"No, sir. So let me see if I've got this straight. These volunteer technicians are supposed to go unsupported into the most hostile area on earth in the company of the most dangerous men we've got, to deploy an untried technology, which, if it works, will focus the attention of the entire People's Army of Vietnam on these volunteer technicians, and, in addition, these volunteer technicians are supposed to spy on the most dangerous men we've got, who are the only people protecting them from the PAVN. Do I have it right, sir?"

The colonel stared at him; Marder returned the stare. "Well, you're certainly a direct bastard, Marder."

"Yes, sir. I try to be. It saves time, and I figure if you want ass-kissing you've got all those guys over there to do it." He gestured broadly to the waiting staffers.

"And dangerously close to insolent in the bargain."

"Yes, sir, but I try to stay on the good side of that line. I figured you for an officer that can handle a little straight talk. You know and I know that you're talking about something very close to a suicide mission. On the upside, obviously, any volunteers would get a full step up in grade and hazardous-duty pay."

"Obviously. But I want you to know that should any of these volunteers get into trouble, the entire resources of the Seventh Air Force would be devoted to extracting them."

"That's good to know, sir. In that case, I would be happy to volunteer for the mission. Does it have a name, by the way, sir?"

"Yes, we're calling it Iron Tuna," said Honey Folger. He stood; Marder stood. "You'll report to squadron immediately for your new orders," said Folger, now looking intently off at the horizon, as if he could with enough effort see the trail. "And, Marder? Not a fucking word about any of this to anyone."

Marder reconstructed this dialogue in his head, found it interesting and satisfying that he could still do it. Whether it was literally true or not he couldn't have said. He did recall the feel in his hand of the little devices, which they immediately rechristened "voodoos," and of the grinding, Sisyphean weight of the man-portable repeaters on his back. His view of Honey Folger was conflated with other images: the man left the USAF in '71, still a light colonel, went into defense contracting with Raytheon, made a bundle, ran for Congress in Arizona, won a seat, and then wrecked himself like so many others in the savings-and-loan scandal. Marder could recall the man's face, fleshier than it had been, with the deer/headlights look they all had coming out of the courtroom after the indictment. He remembered that shot more clearly than he did the interview that had changed his life, that morning under the striped umbrella at the Naked Fanny pistol range.

There was one other vehicle in the lot, a large RV, the source of the faint music Marder had heard earlier. As the morning wore on, other cars and campers arrived. Marder was trying to think of the names of the other two volunteers in his volunteer group, one a tall pale boy from Tennessee and the other an Italian from Providence they called Sandhog. Sandhog and . . . ?

While he was thus engaged, the rear door of the RV opened and Skelly emerged, and after him followed a middle-aged woman with teased blond hair and a tanned, ferrety face. She embraced Skelly warmly and her laugh rang across the parking lot, louder than the sound of the gulls. Then another woman stepped down, the same teased straw hair, the face less ferrety, pretty even, somewhat younger than the other. Marder figured them as sisters.

Skelly waved goodbye; the sisters blew kisses and waved back. In the driver's seat of the truck, he inserted the key and said, "How about some breakfast, chief? I'm hungry as a mule."

"So breakfast wasn't part of the package over there?"

The truck roared to life and started rolling. "No, we were otherwise engaged," said Skelly. "Those were the Cromer sisters of Amarillo, by the way. Sunny and Bunny. Touring this great land even as you and I are."

"A little more mature than your usual taste, no?"

"Has nothing to do with taste, chief. That was what you all call an act of corporal mercy. I don't believe those ladies have had a serious gentleman caller in some time. Good Christian women too. How often did they call upon the deity during our exertions! You know, I should've invited you in there. The gratitude of those girls would've melted your cold, cold heart. Whoa, there's a Pancake House."

"They must've been really hard up to settle for an old guy," said Marder as they pulled in to the restaurant lot.

"You know, that kind of cruelty doesn't suit you, Marder. As a matter of fact, they had all the necessary supplemental devices and chemicals, some of them that would probably shock your right-wing Catholic killjoy sensibilities, so I won't mention them at this time."

They got out of the truck, and Marder made sure to head for a seat with a good view of the parking lot. When they were seated, he remarked, "You know, speaking of Sunny and Bunny, I was just thinking about old Honey Folger. Do you remember him?"

Skelly wrinkled his nose. "Yeah, that douche bag. What made you think about him? You never think about the war."

"I don't know. Maybe hanging with you has unstopped the waters of memory. But it's got all kinds of holes in it. For example, those two guys who trained with me. One of them was called Sandhog—"

"Sweathog Lascaglia. Edward G. The other one was Hayden, Ford T. They called him Patches, or Pinto, because of that white thing he had in his hair."

"I didn't have a nickname, did I? You were Skull, as I recall."

"No, I don't believe you did. We just called you Marder. You were too bland for a nickname, everything hidden away under your poncho, if memory serves, a cryptic person. As you still are."

"Unlike yourself, as open as the southern skies."

"Just so," said Skelly, and to the waitress, through a blazing smile, "Yes, black coffee, miss, and a stack of pancakes as high as pretty you."

3

Carmel Marder cruised through the water of the Zesiger Pool at MIT, her long arms consuming the meters, a niggling worry afflicting her thoughts. She understood that this constituted lack of focus, that real champions thought of nothing but the perfection of their movements while they worked out, but she was not that sort of champion. She was training for a meet in the eight-hundred-meter freestyle, her best event, which meant that every single day she had to come to this excellent Olympic-style pool and swim that distance at least ten times. Responsible to a fault, she rarely missed a day, but she also knew she lacked the killer instinct of the true champion; you simply could not think about anything else except (as a true champion had once said, and truly) eating, sleeping, and swimming.

She, in contrast, thought about many other things; she was thinking about them now as she completed lap fourteen, probably adding fractional seconds to her time, tiny bits of psychic drag on the wetted surface of her body. Her work also had to be stuffed in there somehow, between swimming and eating. She was part of a group designing the future of manufacturing, in the form of a 3-D printer-plus-robot that could actually make copies of itself. Theoretically, you could put one of these babies in an open field, supply it with power and raw materials, and after a time you could have a complex that could make anything makeable out of metal or plastic, at virtually any scale, since your original machines could also be programmed to make parts of larger copies of themselves. Of course, they'd had 3-D printers for years, but these were largely toys for producing prototypes or art objects. Her team was interested in making real things, starting with the machine itself. They called it the Escher Project, from the famous drawing by that artist of the hand that draws itself drawing a hand.

The work ran on its own track; a constant, it danced in her dreams, it invaded her infrequent romances. (What are you thinking about, he would say, smiling, and she would say, Nothing. But it was the work: everything.) Now, however, this extra non-work thought, this niggling worry: Where was Dad? And what was he doing?

Sixteen laps. She slid up onto the edge of the pool in one motion, like an otter mounting a rock, and checked the time of the final lap on her watch: 8:29.12. Better than virtually every female on planet earth, except the hundred or so women who competed at the international level, almost all of whom could swim the eight hundred meters in less than 8:20. Sighing, she let herself hurt, let the muscles dump their lactic acid, allowed her breathing to recover its normal tempo.

Then she rose, snapped a tiny crescent of buttock back where it belonged, and pulled her cap and goggles off, revealing pale-green eyes and dark-red wavy hair, parted in the middle and cut into short wings. As she picked up her towel and logbook and headed for the locker room, those who knew high-end swimming could observe that she possessed the ideal female swimmer's body—the small head, the broad shoulders, the exiguous breasts and hips, hands like shovels, feet like flippers. There was also that face.

"Yo, Statch," said a young man, another pool rat, as he walked by on the corridor leading to the lockers. She waved back, not pausing to chat. When strangers asked her the origin of the odd nickname, she would shrug off the question—a family thing, she would say, and partially true, since her older brother had been the first to bestow it. Later, if she liked the person, and in private, she would strike the pose: foam-rubber spiky green crown on her head, right arm upraised and holding a flashlight, large volume under the left arm, and her remarkable features set in a stern expression.

"Holy shit" would be the usual response, or startled laughter, for Carmel Beatriz Maria Marder y d'Ariés, her brow broad, her nose bold, wide-bridged, and straight as a die, her eyes deep set and heavy lidded, her mouth a set of generous petals, looked (except that her complexion was rosy gold and not verdigris) exactly like the Statue of Liberty. Her appearance both fascinated and terrified the typical male denizens of

MIT engineering labs, which was fine with her: she tended to treat her male colleagues asexually, as if they were somewhat rude but endearing little brothers. Nor was she interested in professors or the occasional touring genius. She had no trouble getting dates when she so desired but selected the lucky men from nerd-free venues far beyond the university districts of Cambridge.

She changed from her tank suit into jeans, Converse high-tops, and a khaki safari shirt with lots of pockets, all of which bulged with various bits of gear she felt naked without: knife, tools, Rotring pen, notebooks, cell phone, electronic scraps. She walked across Mass Avenue to Building 3, where she shared a tiny office with a Chinese-Vietnamese grad student named Karen Liu and where the Escher Project was located. Liu was there, as she almost always was, earbuds socketed, staring at a CAD/CAM screen's representation of an effector arm. Statch sat at her own machine and continued with what she had been working on before she broke for swimming, which was the design of a three-fingered hand that was supposed to take a part out of the sinter bath, expose it to an air blast that would blow the steel dust off it, move it into the oven, take it out when it was finished, and send it down to the assembler. As with all parts of Escher, the problem was constrained by the requirement that everything in the machine would also have to be made by the machine, using the same 3-D manufacturing process. It had to be simple and it had to work. Either of these goals was easy to achieve; doing them both at the same time was Engineering. A Schue Saying, as it was called in the lab.

She lit up her screen and brought up tables of various materials, strength vs. weight vs. cost, plus whether or not they could be used in 3-D, and made notes, then brought up her CAD/CAM and tried them in her designs. But none of them worked, which meant she would have to redesign from scratch, which meant she would not have a prototype ready by next Monday. Dr. Schuemacher would give her a sad, disappointed look and not say anything, which was worse in a way than if he'd been a ranter, and then go on to the next member of the team—Liu, maybe, whose design would be perfect.

Liu let out a yell, jerked off her headset, and said something in Chinese, which by its tone was something her mother would not have liked to hear.

"What does that mean?" asked Statch.

Liu colored and rolled her eyes. "It means someone has mixed pubic hairs in the bean sprouts. You know, when something doesn't work because of one detail? What do Americans say?"

"A fly in the ointment? What's the problem?"

"The problem is that the space allotted for this arm is too short. I could use a compound lever, but then the part would be too complex, a bull to assemble, yes?"

"A *bear* to assemble," Statch corrected automatically. She leaned over Liu's shoulder and studied the vast screen. After less than a minute she saw the solution.

"You could use two smaller arms, above and below. That would fit."

"Two arms? Can I do that?"

"Sure. It's 3-D manufacturing—material is a minor constraint. They'd have to be mirror reversed, but that's a piece of cake."

"A piece of cake," Liu repeated. "Yes, I see. Thank you, Statch!" She replaced her headset and applied her supernatural intelligence once again to the screen. Not too good outside the box was Liu, but matchless within its walls.

"No problem," said Statch, returning her attention to her own screen. She could solve other people's problems with ease but not her own, story of her life—or, no, stupid, let's not descend into despair, self-pity's a mug's game, pull up your socks and drive on. One of her father's sayings, that. And another one: if you're stuck, don't pound on yourself; take a break, do something you like, and let your unconscious work out the solution. She'd tried that with her swimming, although swimming was yet *another* demand, not quite the same thing as a trashy novel or a walk in the woods.

She pressed a key. A chime sounded and a new window appeared. "Call Dad," she commanded. A pause, some warbling rings, and a machine voice told her that the cell-phone customer was not available. She waited for the voice-mail beep and asked her father to call her. She was about to add that she was getting worried but did not. In fact, she *was* worried. She'd been trying to reach him for three days, with no response. Of course, she knew how to track the location of a cell phone and had done so, but the last time Richard Marder's phone had been turned on it was located in Pascagoula, Mississippi, and it was either still there or had been turned off since. She could not imagine what her father was doing down in that Gulf Coast city or why he had stayed dark since.

She now decided it was time to use a program her father did not know about, which was not exactly a legal program either, but, like most technically adept people of her generation, she had a fairly shriveled idea of what privacy and legality meant. The program was an exploit of a defect in the credit-card-charge recording system of a major bank. She patched herself into her personal computer, brought up the program, ran it, and discovered that her father had not used his credit card this week. Moreover, there were no travel-related expenses—neither air tickets nor hotel reservations nor ground transport. She knew that Richard Marder never carried significant amounts of cash, so this meant either that he had another credit card she didn't know about, had modified long-standing habits, or (impossibly) was out traveling without spending any money at all. It was easy and barely illegal to check for other credit cards in his name; she did so and found nothing.

This was seriously disturbing. Statch had been spying on her father in this modest and caring way for some years and increasingly in the three years since her mother's death. She'd heard of people going batty after the death of a spouse, spending money on weird stuff, getting involved with malignant people, and she wanted to keep tabs on what he was up to, especially since he was involved with at least one malignant person already. She had, of course, also tried to keep tabs on Patrick Francis Skelly, to no avail. According to the all-knowing Internet, such a person did not exist: no credit cards, no bank account, not even an email address.

The possibility that her father had gone off with Skelly popped into mind. Her father had never gone off with Skelly before. Why should he start now? Skelly had been a presence throughout her childhood, an attender of parties, a giver of large, generally inappropriate presents. The family, her mother especially, had treated Skelly like an unruly but beloved dog; a dish was always full for him, but he was not to be taken seriously. The Marder kids had used him as a Dutch uncle, of the sort always good for forbidden pleasures—the R movie, the first sip of bourbon, the straight skinny on sex, on bad stuff kids were not supposed to know about, secret lesson in driving a car, age ten. The Marder kids had no uncles—Marder was an only child, and their mother was deeply estranged from her Mexican family—so Skelly was it in that necessary role. They knew he'd saved their father's life in Vietnam and was thus responsible for their own existence, which conveyed a certain primal fascination, but they'd also picked up some of their father's attitude toward the man—a slight diffidence, a vague boredom. Statch did not think her father would willingly spend more than a long evening with Patrick Skelly. So where was he?

With a mumbling curse, she closed down the snooper program and scrubbed all traces that she had used it off the university system. She sent the latest version of her design to her laptop as a sort of promissory note. Perhaps she would work on it later after she . . . after she what? Got rid of this antsy feeling, this unease in her mind and limbs, after she determined where her father was and what he was doing.

In the next moment it occurred to her that a single phone call might resolve both the dad problem and the tension, which she now identified as at least partly sexual in nature. Like many women of her generation and cast of mind, Statch had an engineering relationship to her own body and its requirements. She knew what she liked, she knew how to get it, and the only problem was getting it without entanglements—that is, with a minimum expenditure of emotional energy. Someday she would reset the program so as to enable marriage and children, but not just yet. It puzzled her when she heard women say there were no good men left, because she'd found plenty. She thought that what women of the educated classes meant when they said this was that there were no good upper-middle-class men making six figures who were not metrosexual wimps or work-obsessed assholes or gay persons. Possibly true, but Statch did not require her lovers to hold a degree from a good college, or even one from high school, or to work at high-status, big-bucks jobs. She demanded only a sense of humor, a nice body, a certain edge, a competence in the physical world, and that they liked her. Recent guys had included a chef, a stock-car racer, the stock-car racer's chief mechanic, a Boston police detective, and a boatbuilder.

She told her machine, "Call Mick." This was the cop.

* * *

Marder decided to stop in Baton Rouge, believing that the Louisiana city might host craftsmen skilled at repairing bullet holes in vehicles, and so it proved. At Bob's Body, out on Airline Highway, he waved thick wads of cash in the greasy little office, until the eponymous Bob got the idea: no insurance, no records, no taxes, double pay for a one-day job starting this minute.

When that was settled, he dodged across the highway to a McDonald's. The day was warm and would get warmer, the dense, white-skied sticky heat of the gulf south, a climate Marder particularly disliked. He didn't mind heat as long as it was dry; he liked to bake, but boiling annoyed him. He felt he'd boiled enough in his life, in both Vietnam and New York summers.

He paused outside the restaurant and looked through the glass. Skelly always sat strategically in public places, and here had chosen a booth in a corner, with a good view of the street, back to the wall, close to the rear exit. Marder hung for a moment, slightly outside Skelly's angle of view, and watched—silly, really, but being with Skelly tended to make one conspiratorial.

Skelly was drinking iced tea and writing with a cheap ballpoint in a small notebook. Despite the heat, he was wearing a tan cotton jacket over his T-shirt, and he had his old Red Sox cap pulled down over his eyes, which were obscured by Vuarnet sunglasses. Holding the notebook with one hand, Skelly reached into an inside jacket pocket and, to Marder's surprise, pulled out a telephone, a thick black thing with a pencil antenna. Marder walked in. Until he started this trip, he had not been in a fast-food joint since his kids were grown, and now, in the chill of the A/C, smelling the familiar slightly sickening odor of cheap food, he resolved not to do so again. He slid into the seat before Skelly could slip the phone back into his pocket.

"I thought you didn't own a cell phone, Skelly."

"I don't."

"Then what was that thing you just stuck in your pocket, a bagel? Your personal vibrator?"

"That's a sat phone."

"Really. Who were you talking to on it?"

"A guy. What's with Bubba across the way? He going to fix your truck? Not that I thought it needed fixing. I thought the bullet holes took some of the respectable old-fart asshole shine off the thing, added a little street cred."

"We don't need street cred where we're going. We want to be invisible."

"Yeah, I sort of got that part. You mind telling me why?"

"Asks the most invisible man in America. It's simple. I don't want to be bothered. I want time for peaceful contemplation in my Mexican hideaway. Why is that hard for you to understand?"

"Because it's complete bullshit. You're armed to the teeth, you're paying cash, you got your cell switched off. This tells me you're on the run from something. If I knew what it was, maybe I could help."

"I appreciate that, Patrick, and let me assure you, in all sincerity, that there is nothing I am fleeing from or hiding from. Like you, I'm an aging man entitled to a few eccentricities, of which this trip is one. I didn't invite you along, but now that you're here I'd like you to respect my wish for a certain anonymity. Tell me one thing—are you packing heat this fine morning?"

"What, you mean guns? Hell, no!" Slight pause. "Just the Sig is all."

"Oh, wonderful. I'm really looking forward to spending my . . . my vacation in some southern jail." Marder had almost said "last days" but checked himself in time.

"Right, so this is why you haven't said twelve fucking words to me since those guys jumped us in that roadhouse in Buttfuck, Georgia? Because you're scared I'll disturb your contemplation?"

"Jumped us? *Jumped* us? You walked into a biker bar and provoked a violent confrontation, from which I had to rescue you with a firearm, after which you destroyed maybe a quarter-million bucks' worth of—"

"First of all, who're you talking to? Your grandmother? 'Rescue' was not the operative word, my friend. Interference I'll give you; escalation, yes. If you'd kept that cannon in your jeans, in three minutes every one of those Confederate assholes would've been shit out of action. You've seen me do it."

"I have. When you were twenty-three, when you were thirty—"

"What're you saying? I'm past it? I'm fucked?"

Skelly's voice had risen to the combat decibel range, suitable for good communications over small-arms fire, and the usual mix of Mickey D patrons was staring at them, some with avid interest, some with fear. A chubby youth in a white shirt with a plastic name tag on it had eased his cell phone out.

Marder stood up abruptly. "Yes, you're a superannuated bag of gas. To prove it, we're going to call a cab, find a pool hall, and I'll whip your ass in nine ball while we wait for Bob to fix my proletarian vehicle."

"In your dreams," said Skelly.

* * *

Marder was actually a somewhat better pool player than Skelly was, but Skelly had won the majority of the games they'd played over the years, simply because he wanted to win more than Marder did. They played a match of eleven games, win by two, and Marder dragged the thing out to twenty-three games, enjoying Skelly's increasing discomfort, before easing off and throwing the last game, enjoying also the boyish triumph on his friend's face. Not a competitive guy, Marder, although he wondered sometimes whether his remaining life might present him with some combat worth giving his all for. It'd be interesting if that happened.

There was a seafood joint a little ways down the highway, so they walked over and had a meal, Cajun-style seafoods, rich and spicy. When they'd finished, Marder said, "Why don't you call Bob and see if the truck's done. He said five-thirty."

Skelly obligingly took out his costly brick and made the call, then called a cab. Bob turned out to be an artist with Bondo and paint. The holes were all neatly patched and the glass had been either plugged or replaced. Bob didn't ask questions about whatever had caused the bullet holes, nor did he comment when he observed Skelly attaching Louisiana license plates to the Ford.

Marder did, however.

"May I ask what the fuck?"

"Yeah, well, a little insurance. As you pointed out, we may have damaged some fascist motor vehicles back there and started a fire and so forth. I thought maybe the word might've filtered through to the police."

"Where did you get the plates?"

"Some guy I know."

"Some guy? What guy?"

"A guy who sells phony plates. It's a need-to-know thing, Marder. Leave it lie. The papers're all in the glove, your name and everything. So, are we rolling or what?"

After that, interminable Texas. Marder drove through the night, sometimes straying off the interstate to find a place to eat that wasn't a chain and finding some good little places: once a Chinese restaurant that, incredibly, made delicious egg rolls from scratch, another with biscuits from heaven. The food gradually became more Mexican-ish as they headed west from San Antonio but never became really Mexican. Marder found that he had a hunger for the food that his wife used to make, the food of her native soil, the place where he was going.

The country had changed since the last time he'd been through this way. Many of the little country towns, which had seemed prosperous, even smug, back in the seventies when he'd last made this drive, had been hollowed out, their storefronts empty, their economies wasted by out-migration, the collapse of small farming, the big box stores; their civic life was composed largely of the high school football team, the big signs painted on the water tank, the brick walls of the low, sunburned buildings: GO COUGARS! GO HAWKS! GO REBELS! On the dusty streets of towns named for nineteenth-century cattlemen, pioneers, heroes of the Civil War, they now saw few descendants of such people, only little clots of dark-skinned men and signs in Spanish. The Indians were slowly reconquering the land, for the white people had everything but enough children, and the children they did have wanted the life they saw on television, not the life of the small American towns.

Marder thought of himself as a patriot, but, like many men his age, he was a patriot of a nation that seemed no longer to exist. Modernity had failed, obviously, and now he was going into a country that modernity had failed even more spectacularly; all the bright ideas of the imported religion, of the imported economics, of the imported revolution, of industrialization, of education, of freedom even, had all failed or had been attempted in such a warped fashion that they could not work, could not change the immemorial nature of that land and its people. What remained was the strange country, inexplicable, that he did not understand but that he loved, as he had not understood but had loved his wife.

The land rose. Marder had left the interstate and was now climbing into the Davis Mountains on a state road. He had forgotten that Texas had mountains, but here they were, damp, cool, verdant, with trickling rocky streams, smelling of pine and sage. They passed through a state park and Marder pulled off the road at an overlook.

"Nice country," said Skelly, who was sitting in the passenger seat, unusually, for he typically spent the daylight hours back in the camper, sleeping and doing various bits of business that required the use of his special laptop and his special phone. He also claimed it embarrassed him to watch Marder drive.

"Wasted on Texas, of course," he added. He lit another cigarette and held it out the window between drags, which was the acme of consideration for him. The cigarettes came out of a Marlboro pack, but they were unfiltered, hand-rolled, and laced with hash oil.

"You don't like Texas?"

"No. But I don't like any of the states. To be honest, I've never been in North Dakota, so it could be an exception and not full of stupid, fat, arrogant, ignorant, money-grubbing, whining, hypocritical American assholes."

"Come on, Skelly, we're not that bad."

"Yes, we are: fat, doped up, and dangerous. Did you see that parody poster? Picture of some nice country like this here and the caption goes, 'America! It's more than bombs and fat people.' Actually, not."

"We've had this conversation before."

"Yes, we have, and you always lose. I'm going for a run. You want to come along, fat boy?"

"I am height and weight proportional for my age."

"You're soft as cream cheese. And don't think you're going to ditch me, 'cause I got the keys."

Marder watched the man trot down the road with his usual effortless lope.

He recalled now the first time he'd seen it and how much he had hated Skelly then. The three of them—Marder, Hayden, and Lascaglia—set off just after dawn one morning in 1969, in the dry season, in a helicopter with the gear and hopes of Iron Tuna aboard, one of a dozen such little teams of volunteer air force technicans. They'd trained on the equipment for three weeks, and now they were off to the Special Forces base camp for jungle training. Not one of them had ever been in a helicopter before or in a jungle. They were headed toward a Special Forces base called Bronco One.

They were set down in a clearing, Marder recalled, and humped the heavy containers that held the repeaters and the voodoo devices, plus their personal gear and weapons; then the chopper lifted off, leaving them alone somewhere in Vietnam or maybe the Kingdom of Laos. Marder didn't recall the details, only the feeling of absolute vulnerability and the waving saw grass and the threatening dark tree line. Again, he could not bring to his mental screen the faces of the other two men. Lascaglia was jumpy, a nervous dark kid from Providence or Boston, and Hayden was an Appalachian person with more than the usual reserve such people had, a silent, almost passive presence.

A group of small dark men in mixed uniforms, some wearing brimmed jungle hats, others with cloth headbands, emerged from the tree line. Lascaglia grabbed his M16 and started to curse, but Marder said, "Relax, man, those are montagnards. They're the good guys."

Or something to that effect. At any rate, the Yards helped them carry their gear, each man lifting a heavy olive-drab case up on his tiny shoulders as if it were a feather pillow. They walked down a jungle trail for what seemed like miles but was probably only a klick or two. Marder had got hold of a Hmong phrase book in Nakhon and said "Nyob zoo" to anyone who passed him, but he was ignored. But he'd read enough to know that Hmong was impossible to learn from a book, since a syllable could mean wildly different things depending on which of the seven tones you spoke it in, so he wasn't worried. He had a good ear—the nuns had told him that in Spanish and Latin class— so he figured he'd learn it with the daily exposure. The boyish adventure novels he'd grown up on all stressed that imperial troopers in foreign lands did well to learn the native tongues. He recalled being happy walking down that trail, not afraid at all; it was Kipling brought to life.

Stupid, of course, looking back on it, but he'd never seen a man killed in action and he was nineteen, and he knew in the depths of his soul, as sure as he was that he was breathing air, that nothing bad would happen to him, that he would come home to his mother. He knew it, she knew it, God knew it: it was a settled thing.

Bronco One was located next to a village called Hli Dlej, which sounded something like shleek-leh, with the first syllable hissed through the sides of the mouth and the second with a high falling tone. It meant Moon River, which the air force guys thought was pretty funny, because of that song. They found that none of the Americans ever called it anything else. This and other information was conveyed to them by their liaison NCO after they had put their gear away in a Hmong longhouse that had been reserved for the Americans. There were a dozen or so Special Forces troopers at the base, a lieutenant and the rest sergeants, who, as they soon learned, formed part of what the army coyly called the Studies and Observation Group. SOG ran operations for which the ordinary Special Forces were deemed too conventional: Iron Tuna was one of these. There was also a platoon of LLDB, who were South Vietnamese Special Forces, posted there for liaison and translation services and to pay the montagnards, which they often failed to do. Their unit initials stood for Luc Luong Dac Biet, but the Americans called them Lousy Little Dirty Bastards, and the montagnards felt the same, only with more reason. Marder picked this up during the first afternoon at the base and thought it was not a good sign.

Another unpleasantness occurred when they met their liaison NCO, Sergeant First Class P. F. Skelly. Marder immediately recognized him as the American from the lantern-lit bar, but Skelly didn't recognize Marder, or pretended not to, and even later Marder never mentioned this earlier encounter. Maybe it hadn't happened at all. Marder realized that he had any number of false memories rambling around in his head. He knew Skelly did too. It was one of the things about war, that war scrambled time and place, the intensity of it made the brain unhinge, and soldiers signified this unconsciously when they said of some colossal event they'd experienced in their very flesh: "It was just like the movies!" But it wasn't.

During that first interview, or lecture, SFC Skelly made a number of salient points:

That since they were mere air force pukes, suited only for eating BX burgers and getting more lard on their desk-bound asses, they should not dare to think of themselves as actual soldiers;

That in their present form they constituted a danger not only to themselves, which he could not care less about, but to himself and to his Yards, the least pubic hair of the least of whom was worth more than the three of them put together;

That the foregoing pissed him off, and he intended to take it out on them, preferably by killing them during training or at the very least making them wish sincerely for death;

That they were undoubtedly going to die on this mission, being far too soft and stupid to live, and that they should put any and all thoughts of returning to the world and their loved ones aside;

That if they abused any montagnard, or messed with a montagnard woman, he would personally stake them out on an anthill, having reserved several cans of C-rat strawberry jam for purposes of smearing on naked sniveling air force pukes so staked out;

That training would commence at 0500 tomorrow.

He asked for questions. There were none. The three air force pukes retired to their hooch, ate their C-rats, and waited fearfully for the dawn.

SFC Skelly's training consisted at first primarily of running. They ran over hills and through streams, through saw grass and vicious thornbushes, carrying the load they would carry on their missions, not only weapons, food, ammo, water, and bedding but also the pack frames holding the repeaters and the voodoos and the diagnostic equipment necessary to set up the data nets. Marder thought their loads could not have been less than eighty pounds each. Lascaglia and Hayden both collapsed several times in sobbing heaps, were screamed at by Skelly, prodded into motion by the short bamboo stake he always carried. Marder didn't cry but fainted on two occasions. Skelly, who was smaller than any of them, carried the same load, plus more ammo, and ran literal circles around them, seeming to float above the trails, while they suffered the terrible pull of gravity, which wrenched their limbs and pressed their webbing cruelly into their flesh.

Those were the mornings. In the afternoon and into the evening, they had target practice. Of the three, only Hayden had ever fired a rifle before, so this was another imposed misery. They were using cut-down CAR-16s, carbines as they were called, or AK-47s captured from the enemy. The targets were playing cards that Skelly would affix to trees and bushes along a set course. (Skelly seemed to have an infinite supply of new playing cards, and they figured he had boosted them from some rear-area PX. Even this early they had understood that SOG supplied its needs largely by scamming the army or by naked theft.) During these exercises, they would walk along the trail, still burdened by their gear, sweat and gnats in their eyes, holding the unfamiliar weapons, and when they walked past a card without shooting it, Skelly, walking on their heels, would jab his stake into their short ribs and scream, "You're dead, asshole!" in their ears.

After target practice they would play hide-and-seek. The air force men would walk off into the boonies and, after an interval, Sergeant Skelly would find them. When he found them, he would poke them with his stick and comment on their brain power and ancestry in vile language.

On one of these sessions, however, Marder snapped and said something to the effect that if the sergeant ever poked him with that stick again, he, Marder, would shoot him through both knees and laugh about it every day of his sojourn in Leavenworth.

A little staring after that, and then Skelly grinned and said, "Brooklyn, huh?"

Marder said, "Fuckin' A, Sergeant!"

"And you think you're a fucking wise guy. But understand this, Airman: I am a trained soldier and am superior to you in every military art, and besides that I am superior to you in every conceivable human activity, mental and physical. So don't you even think about threatening me again, because if you do I will take that weapon from your shaking hand and ram it up your asshole."

"I would beg to differ with you there, Sergeant," Marder replied. "I can outshoot you with a pistol on any target over any range."

After which, as Marder had expected, Sergeant Skelly had to demonstrate his superiority in this matter, and they organized the Moon River Invitational Shoot-Out, which later became legendary among the Special Forces and marked the time and place when his long friendship with Skelly had begun.

As soon as Skelly vanished, Marder went into the camper and poked around. He found Skelly's sat phone and looked at it. He turned it on and the little yellow screen asked him for a password, so he turned it off. In the overhead storage, he found a thin magnesium/titanium suitcase and a plastic gun case. The gun case had a foam cutout that approximated the shape of a Sig P226 9-mm pistol. This was vacant, but the case also contained a box of hollow-point rounds, three magazines, a box of .410 #3 shotgun shells, and the matte-black cylinder of a Gemtech Tundra suppressor. He put the case back, and as he did so, he noticed another case, shoved deep within the compartment. It was long and extremely heavy. Marder dragged it out, found it was locked, and lifted it back into place. He figured it must contain a shotgun, or shotguns.

He did open the titanium suitcase, however. In this he found a Getac B300 ruggedized laptop and a Thrane satellite modem connected to the folded panels of its antenna, all neatly nested into the case's foamed interior. He pulled out the laptop and turned it on. It, too, wanted a password. He typed in "Hli Dlej," which was rejected. He thought for a moment and typed in "Joong Mang."

The screen went dark for an instant and then a photograph appeared. It had the dark, grainy look of an enlarged cell-phone photograph, and its setting looked to be a cheap hotel room. There was the corner of a bed showing, and a washstand, and a bright triangle that meant a window. To one side a table supported what looked like a Getac B300, perhaps this very machine. In the center of the frame was a dark-skinned man in a white shirt, lying on the floor near an overturned chair. He was apparently dead from a bullet wound to his head, and his features were completely obscured by blood.

The picture had a caption: "This is the last guy who tried what you're trying." As Marder stared at it, blue letters started to dance across the screen, like a news crawl: "Marder, you asshole! Stay clear of my shit!"

Marder turned off the laptop and put everything back in the case. Apparently, whatever business Skelly was engaged in, he was continuing to run it via some cryptic subunit of the Internet, and unless the picture was a scam, it was the kind of business that got people killed. No surprise there, thought Marder. He took a beer from the refrigerator and sat in the truck, waiting for his friend to return.

4

"You're looking good," said the cop, Mick Kavanagh, when Statch got into his car, which was a 1974 powder-blue El Dorado convertible—not the best car for Boston, with gas running close to four bucks a gallon, but this politically incorrect impracticality was one of the things she liked about the man. She *did* look good too, having taken some pains with her appearance: leather biker jacket (with many pockets) over a red translucent shirt with tiny seed buttons, a clingy black calf-length skirt, and silver-toed elaborately tooled cowboy boots. She wore a jade-and-silver necklace, heavy and very old, that she'd inherited from her mother; also a silver-mounted belt, ditto. And round, heavy-framed spectacles, in red plastic. Her hair was gelled into a kind of friendly Medusa effect. As far as she knew, the nerd-punk-vaquero look was original with her. It tended to frighten off the men she didn't care for and attract those she liked, thus achieving the only true engineering function of fashion. She didn't much care what women thought.

Kavanagh put his car into gear and said, "So what would you like to do? There's a pretty good card at the Fleet—you could cheer for the Mexican fighters and I could cheer for the Irish, if any. That'd be fun. Or we could catch a movie. The city lies before us."

"No, let's just go to Monahan's and get tanked with your cop buddies and then go to your place and fool around."

He ignored the traffic to give her a fast look. He could never tell when this one was being serious. But she was.

"Okay, you're not going to get much of an argument on that one. Tell me, do all you college girls require this little wooing?"

"I wouldn't know. I kind of always go for the optimal solution: maximized output with minimized inputs, frictionless as possible."

"Meaning?"

"Oh, you know, get to the yield, the finished product, which in our case is mutually pleasurable sexual intercourse, with lots of orgasms."

"And you don't find that a bit, uh, cold?"

"You mean unromantic. No, I don't. My parents were the most romantic people you can imagine. They had this wild affair down in Michoacán, had to escape from Mexico with gangsters on their heels, and they were always mooning at each other, exchanging love poetry and secret glances. They were literary types." She hesitated, looking out the window. "And it didn't end well. Or maybe it was just a reaction. Both my brother and I were lousy in English, great in math, and became engineers. I guess it's inevitable; everyone's embarrassed by their parents: your parents are hippies, you become a banker, and vice versa."

"Not inevitable," said Kavanagh. "My dad was a cop. I thought he was the greatest man in the world."

"Whatever. Why are we talking about parents?" She looked out the window again. One of the problems with Kavanagh: everything became an interrogation, an unearthing of the past. She liked new stuff, not old stuff. They were crossing the Mass Avenue Bridge into Boston, sludgy with rush-hour traffic.

"Can't you turn on your siren, flash some lights? It'll be an hour before we can get a drink."

"Not unless you know of a crime in progress. No? Then we'll have to converse. How's work?"

"Awful. I'm totally blocked, no ideas at all. How's work?"

"Crime's down. We sit around all day eating donuts and making sexist jokes and bad-mouthing liberals and the darker races."

At this point Statch almost came out with what was on her mind, what had made her irritable and not entirely her usual sunny self, but she forbore. She thought he might be more amenable to a sort of nonkosher favor later on, after a few drinks and some of those orgasms. Although she understood that most people got the favors promised *before* the sex, she thought this dishonorable and corrupt.

Kavanagh had been around the block a few times with women, but this one was a bit outside his range. He was not exactly complaining, for she was unconstrained, almost violent, noisy, and enthusiastic in the throes of sex, insanely wonderful, a cornucopia of delight; besides which there was the erotic multiplier of being fucked by a national shrine. But afterward he always felt as if he'd been ridden, like a horse, urged on to do this, to do that, squeeze here, rub there, faster, slower, up a little, yeah, that's it, but harder, harder! He always had blue bruises on him after an evening with La Marder. Kavanagh didn't exactly mind being a horse, but he was somewhat more romantic than she was, or than he let on. Besides, he was a cop and used to figuring out people; he was drawing a blank here, and it made him uncomfortable.

Now they were entwined on his king-sized bed in the upstairs bedroom of the small house he owned in Dorchester Heights. The window was opened a crack, and evening air was cooling their lately steaming flesh.

"Kavanagh, could I ask you something? A cop question?"

"Ask away," replied Kavanagh lightly, but inwardly he quailed. He did not think it would be a question about police procedure; no, it would be a someone's-in-trouble question.

So it proved. "It's my dad," she said. "He, well, he seems to be missing. God, that sounds more dramatic than I meant. It's just he's been a little weird since my mom died."

Kavanagh understood, having watched what became of his own father after the death of his wife of forty-two years. "Yeah, it's always rough, that kind of thing. Weird how?"

"Oh, nothing you could put your finger on. Bascially, he blames himself for her death. Not to get into details, but he did a bad thing and she, well, not exactly killed herself but like that. Not a good scene at all. So he called me up the other day and said he was taking a trip, no destination mentioned, and since then I haven't been able to get hold of him. Everything goes to voice mail; he doesn't answer texts. The last time his phone got turned on it was in Mississippi, and let me add that that's not a location my dad would be likely to settle down in. So I thought it would be good if I knew who he'd called in the days before he left, maybe get some information on his plans."

"How would you do that?" asked Kavanagh, well knowing.

"You could pull his phone logs."

"Uh-huh, I could, if your father were a master criminal and I had a court order."

"What if he was in danger? Like kidnapped."

"Do you have any evidence of that? Does your father normally consort with criminal types? Is he fabulously wealthy?"

"No, none of the above. But I just *know* something's wrong. He's always been *extremely* careful about keeping in touch. And he never goes off like this. He's a planner, even fussy about arrangements. And he does know at least one criminal type, or shady character, I should say."

"Really? Who would that be?"

"A guy named Patrick Francis Skelly. He was in the Special Forces in Vietnam, and my dad served with him there. Since the war he's been doing weird stuff—'security,' like in quotation marks? He's a little nuts, and it wouldn't knock me flat if I found out he was a drug lord or an arms dealer or whatever. I'm thinking he might've got my dad involved in something. That's the only thing I can think of. And *he's* not home either and doesn't return calls."

"Well, they're both adults. They can take off without telling anyone."

"Yeah, I *know* that, Kavanagh! I feel like a jerk for worrying, plus, according to my father, Skelly is exactly the kind of person you want with you if anything dangerous is going on. But I am worried. Isn't there anything you can do that's not illegal?"

"Call him now."

"I told you, I've been calling him every couple of hours for days."

"Humor me. Just call him again."

Statch slid away from him and walked over to the chair upon which she'd dropped her bag, pulled out her iPhone, and pressed the buttons. Kavanagh did not really expect the results of the call to be different from the dozens of earlier ones, but this way he got to see his girlfriend walk across the room naked, which he thought was something special.

"Hello?" said Statch, and then began a short conversation that Kavanagh didn't understand because it was in Spanish, but he understood what was implied by her yelling into what was obviously a dead line at its end.

When she turned to look at him, her face was bleak. "It was a kid," she said. "He said he found the phone in a trash can in Ojinaga. He didn't see who put it there."

"Where the hell's Ojinaga?"

"I'm looking it up now," she said, punching away at the tiny device. "It's on the border, in Chihuahua. Oh, Christ, he's going to Mexico!"

"Come here," Kavanagh said. After a little coaxing, she was lying against him once more, with his arm protectively around her.

"What's the story with Mexico?"

"I'm not entirely sure. That's the romance part. My mother was a dish, educated and much sought after; the son of a big political boss wanted her, and her father had to go ahead and agree to the marriage, or else. It was apparently that way in the part of Mexico they were in, and still is, I guess. Anyway, along came my father and stole my mom from this big shot, and they eloped. My grandfather was real bitter about it and never answered any of my mom's letters, and my grandmother had to sneak out of the house to get phone calls. We never went to Mexico, my mother never saw her family again, and I got the feeling that if my dad ever went back there, he could get in serious trouble. Why would he go there? I don't get it!"

Kavanagh studied the ceiling for a while and stroked the area of warm girl flesh that was at hand. Then he said, "Okay, look, there's a guy I know, owes me some favors. He works for a telecom that will remain nameless, and sometimes he looks over the logs for me. I could ask him to check out your dad and this Skelly character. But, really, Statch—not a word to anyone, ever. And if anyone ever asks me, I'll deny it; I'll say it was a lie I told you to get laid."

"But you're not lying."

"I would never do that."

"No, and I'm not just trading sex for help, am I?"

"I don't believe you are, no."

She shifted on the bed, threw a thigh across him, and sat up in the saddle. "In that case," she said, "would you please fuck me into oblivion? I don't want to think about this shit for as long a time as we can manage."

Skelly came back from his run, barely sweaty but powdered with dust. Marder asked him if he always ran armed. Skelly pulled his T-shirt over his head and grinned.

"You've been poking through my shit, Marder. I assume you poked far enough to know you can't poke anymore."

He took off the nylon fanny pack he'd been wearing and placed it on the counter, where it made a pistol-ish clunk.

"Or what?" asked Marder. "You'd have to kill me?"

"No, but others might. The security business is highly competitive. In some parts of it, when they say they want to eliminate the competition, it's not just a business metaphor. I don't want to have to keep rescuing you."

"No, I wouldn't want you to go through the trouble," said Marder after a moment, but Skelly had already stripped and entered the camper's tiny shower. Marder didn't want to bring up the subject of rescues, since he and Skelly had difficulties in coordinating their memories on that subject, and Marder found it best to avoid it, even when Skelly was sober.

When Skelly got out of the shower, Marder said, "Speaking of pistols, I was just thinking about the Moon River Invitational Shoot-Out."

"Really? Why was that?"

"Like I said, traveling with you is loosening the mystic chords of memory."

"Also because it's the one pathetic time you beat me at anything. I would have caught up with you by the fourth deck, if Handlebar hadn't stopped it."

Marder thought this was probably not true but said nothing.

He did recall the actual event fairly well. Handlebar was the lieutenant commanding the detachment of Special Forces and their montagnard allies and was so called because of his remarkable mustache, grown, Marder assumed, so that he would not be carded in bars. Not a bad officer, for an officer, was the scuttlebutt, and a man always up for morale-boosting activities. When the contest was explained to him, he arranged to have two sets of bamboo posts erected in the cleared ground that surrounded the village, between which some lines were nailed, and upon these were hung with wire hooks two complete decks of playing cards. At a range of ten meters, Marder and Skelly were to shoot all the pips out of the cards with their .45s and finish by shooting out the heads of the face cards. This made 244 targets per deck. The rules were that a shooter couldn't go on to the next card until he'd shot out all the pips (or heads) of the previous card, and the man who finished first won, except that Skelly insisted that the winner had to be at least four cards ahead to win. Marder stayed two or three cards ahead through four whole packs of cards.

Everyone in the village—soldiers and tribespeople—was out watching this, the soldiers drinking "33" beer and the Hmong drinking their horrible *rnoom* rice brew through straws. It got dark, in the usual lights-out fashion of the tropics, and Lieutenant Handlebar called the match, declaring Marder the winner, with Skelly insisting they shoot by the light of flares and the lieutenant explaining in an intoxicated way that this was a good way to silhouette the entire population for the VC, who would in any case have been drawn to the area in droves by the shooting. Some of the other sergeants, laughing like maniacs, had to physically pick Skelly up and haul him away. The VC were in fact drawn, the base got rocketed for a brief time, and there was a nice little firefight, but that was a normal evening in Moon River.

Marder had thought that he was in deep shit, that Skelly would come down hard on him, but such was not the case. Skelly became if anything almost friendly, no more yelling or nasty remarks, or fewer than before. In any event, training, such as it had been, was over. The air force team had to earn their hazard pay now, by mounting helicopters, flying to various predetermined parts of Laos and Vietnam, and burying the repeaters so as to cover the whole broad delta of supply routes that made up the trail. The long repeater aerials, disguised as vines with fabric sheaths the men called "sweaters," had to be hung just so from the nearest trees. Then they planted a few voodoos on the trail proper, to see if the system worked.

After that, back at the village, the airmen made sure the machines were alive and transmitting and that they could pick up the voodoo signals. Which they could: the voodoos talked to the repeaters; the repeaters talked to the planes overhead. All they had left to do was to actually bury the little spheres in a dense belt across the entirety of the Ho Chi Minh Trail, or at least that portion that fell within their area of operations. This was the hard part, which no one on the team had really thought about during this preparation period but now had to. During this phase, Marder had been impressed by the skills of Skelly and his SOG team, by the helicopter crews from the 21st Special Operations Squadron that ferried them to and fro, and by the enormous effort being made to ensure the success of their operation. The air force staged diversionary raids; the Spectre gunships hovered overhead; each mission was accompanied by flame and explosions and the racket of miniguns establishing a zone of death around their working areas.

Several times they had experienced ground fire, or so Marder recollected. He had a mental image of glowing green balls rising from dark woods and floating by and the sound of metal banging against the aluminum of the helicopters. He did not recall being afraid, but perhaps that was the salve of forgetting.

What he did recall, with startling clarity, was a conversation he'd had with Skelly the evening before they left for their first run to plant voodoos. The sergeant had come by the Hmong longhouse where the airmen lived. Marder couldn't remember where Hayden and Lascaglia were that evening, but he had the sense that the sergeant and he were alone. Skelly dropped a duffel bag on the floor.

"Your uniform of the day," he said. "I figured you're a large."

Marder dumped the bag out on his cot: a light-green shirt and pants in nylon, a soft, brimmed hat of the same color, a pair of tire-rubber sandals, plus a set of web gear of unfamiliar design.

"What is this?" asked Marder, holding up the shirt.

"It's a garbage man's uniform from South Korea."

"Are we allowed to wear this?"

"Well, the rules say we can't wear civilian clothes and we can't wear enemy uniforms, and this is neither. It's cool to wear and it blends in pretty good, especially with a little mud on it. The footwear is Vietnamese, as worn by Charlie, in case anyone is inclined to follow tracks. We've had guys walk right by NVA patrols in that gear, and even if they think it's fishy, it gives us a couple of seconds, which is all you need sometimes."

Marder waited for Skelly to leave, but Skelly did not.

Instead, he plopped himself down on Lascaglia's cot and lit a cigarette. A strange sight: since arriving at Moon River, Marder had never, as far as he could recall, seen Skelly other than upright, usually moving to some purpose.

"So, Marder, where did you learn to shoot a pistol like that? Not in the fucking air force."

"No. I've been shooting pistols since I was seven or eight. My dad had a Colt Woodsman .22, and he brought a .45 back from the Pacific. We used to shoot the .22 at a range in the basement of the VFW hall near our house. It was probably illegal as hell, but nobody minded in those days. Also, my dad knew a guy down in Coney Island who had a kind of rinky-dink arena for fights and bike races, and he had a real range set up behind his place; we'd go down there, take the subway a couple of times a week, and blast away with the .45. The guy had, like, a ton of condemned army ball ammo and he'd let us shoot it off, and in return my dad would print up posters and shit for him—I mean for his arena. He died about five years ago, so we stopped going."

"Your dad died?"

"Oh, no, the guy. With the arena. O'Farrell was his name. So after that I just shot with the Woodsman." There was a pause. Skelly watched his cigarette smoke in silence.

"Where did you learn to shoot?" Marder asked, to keep the conversation going. "Did you shoot with your dad?"

"No, the only thing my father ever taught me was how to lie. He must have envisioned this war. And if I had access to a gun in his presence, I would've probably shot him."

"Didn't get along, huh?"

"You could say that. What does your dad do for a living?"

Marder told him, speaking easily and happily about his father, and then, by easy stages, prompted by what seemed like genuine interest from Skelly, he talked about his mother and his family and his neighborhood. Only later did he understand that Skelly's interest was not merely polite. It was very nearly anthropological. The kind of normal urban American family life Marder had enjoyed was as alien to Skelly as the customs of the Hmong in whose midst they lived—or even more so, since Skelly, it turned out, knew a great deal about the Hmong.

After a period of this exposition, Marder began to feel a little uneasy, as if he were in the classic small room with a skilled interrogator and the humble data of his life a matter of substantial import. So he asked Skelly about his own background, and Skelly answered with the question: "Did you ever read a book called *The Catcher in the Rye*?"

"Yeah, I did, as a matter of fact. I got it on Fourth Avenue. It was something my mom and I used to do. There're all these used bookstores on lower Fourth, and we used to take the subway up from Brooklyn. Starting when I was about six and up 'til, I don't know, 'til I was too old to go out shopping with my mother, I guess. I picked it up, the paperback, because of the red cover and the title."

"What did you think of it?"

"I don't know. I couldn't figure out what the guy's problem was. I mean, he went to prep school, so he must've been loaded, or his folks were, so what did he have to complain about? But the whole book is one long bitch about how phony everything is, how everything isn't just right for wonderful what's-his-name, Canfield—"

"Caulfield. Holden Caulfield."

"Right. Why did you ask?"

"Because I'm what Holden Caulfield turned into." He laughed then and shook his head. "You know, Marder, we're probably the only two people in northern Laos capable of discussing *The Catcher in the Rye*. I might have to keep you alive after all."

"Thank you, Sergeant. So you got kicked out of prep school?"

"Yep. I thought they were all phonies. You never thought your parents were fucked up?"

"No, I thought they were decent, honest people. I told you, my father's a union guy, a printer. He's proud of what he does; he thinks he's preserving the printed word, the backbone of civilization, and then he always said the printers were the aristocrats of the labor movement, the vanguard. And my mom—I'd come home from school and there'd be this stranger, some old bum off the street, and she'd be feeding him soup. Ladies would come up to me at the grocery store, or wherever, and say, 'Oh, your mother's a saint.' I didn't think anything of it. And she was a reader too; she read to me for as long as I can remember, and she made sure the nuns didn't mess with me. In our neighborhood, I'd walk down the street with the two of them, I'd be smiling, I was so glad they were my folks. So, no. The army is fucked up, the world may be fucked up, but not the Marders. Why did they kick you out?"

"I got liquored up and took a big crap on the school seal. They had it inlaid in marble in Byron Hall, the main building there at Vaughan Preparatory Academy. Then my father sent me to the Christian Brothers, where he'd gone to school, to see if they could, as he put it, beat some sense into me." Skelly lit another cigarette and gazed upward at the smoke rising through the thatch, weaving like a serpent around the thin shafts of light that descended from above.

"And did they?"

"Well, they sure beat me, I'll give them that. I didn't think *they* were phony. They were extremely sincere about whipping boys. I thought they were nuts, all that God bullshit, and I wouldn't do it—I mean pray or pretend to believe in it—and I got beat, and I still wouldn't, and basically I lasted about a month and I just took off. I broke into the school office and stole all the cash that the students had on deposit for pocket money and like that, a couple of hundred bucks, I guess, and then I hitched south. I got to Florida, got a job in a restaurant in Orlando, slept in a crash pad with a bunch of other runaways. It was a nice time, really, and then I got picked up and the cops sent me back to Dad."

"He must've been pissed."

"Not really. He'd sort of written me off. He delegated his executive secretary to deal with me, Mrs. Tatum. Actually, she was the only person I can recall who took me seriously when I was a kid, I mean as someone who had a mind of his own."

"What about your mom?"

"Oh, the lovely Clarissa? After I ruined her figure, the lovely Clarissa took off and married an Argentinian polo player. I get a check and a card from her on Christmas and birthdays. Anyway, Mrs. Tatum handled it perfectly— asked me where I wanted to go to school, if anywhere, and I said I wanted to go to a regular public high school, and she sent me to Hancock High and I loved it. Girls, for example: I'd never had daily access to girls before, and to guys who were just regular assholes and not rich assholes, which is a completely different level of assholery and much harder for me to take, my father being the classic rich asshole. And it was the whole fucked-up urban high school thing you see in the movies. No one's interested in anything but who's cool and who's not, and it's all about getting sex and having laughs and getting high, with the actual studying as something you did as little of as possible. And nobody beat me or told me I was a disgrace to the school, because in a school like that, if you weren't arrested for murder you were considered an honor student.

"In my senior year, Mrs. Tatum asked me if I wanted to go to college and I realized that I didn't, that sitting at a desk or going to the library or writing bullshit was not what I wanted to do, and one day I was downtown with a bunch of my pals and I passed a recruiting office and I walked in, just curious, and there was this master sergeant there, a big black guy with rows of ribbons, and, what can I say? He saw me, he knew who I was, what I was supposed to do. I realize that he was only doing his job, that he wanted me to fill a quota, but the wanting part was real. And no one had wanted me before, I was a pain in the ass to everyone, and even if the army just wanted me to get killed, that was cool with me. I was only seventeen, so I had to get my father to sign off on the form, and Mrs. T. didn't even bother him with it. She ran it through the autopen and there I was, in a place where I could either die or kill somebody, which were the only two options that interested me at the time."

Marder recalled that last line very well, although the rest of it might not have all come through that first evening. There were a lot of such evenings. Looking back, sitting in this camper with the sun rising over the peaks, warming the day, Marder thought about how astonishingly young they'd been, himself scarcely more than eighteen, Skelly two or three years older. Skelly was the first contemporary Marder had found with whom he could discuss the ideas found in books, who thought as he did that the things in books could form your life. It had been intense, frightening almost, almost as memorable as the slender, skillful girls of Thailand.

They entered Mexico at Presidio, a little-used border crossing in the Chinati Mountains. Marder was driving at the time, and when he handed the passports to the Mexican border agent, he could not help noticing that Skelly's was in someone else's name. They drove south on the two-lane, through Ojinaga, a typical Mexican borderland town, bustling, American-looking, but clearly a different country. They filled the gas and water tank here and had a meal in a *taquería* near the gas station.

Skelly said, "Well, we're in Mexico."

"What was your first clue?"

"You know, guys in serapes, señoritas with flashing eyes. My point was, now we're here, did you have any particular place in mind?"

"Yes, I'm going to stay in my house. It's in Playa Diamante on the Pacific coast in Michoacán."

"Where Chole was from."

"Right. I'm going to bury her ashes in her family crypt."

"And . . . ?"

"And I hate these commercial flour tortillas. I'm really looking forward to getting some handmade corn tortillas."

"You're being mysterious again, Marder. It doesn't suit you. I'm the mysterious guy. You're the solid family guy, with the straight job and the loving friends and family. Have you called Statch recently?"

"Recently enough."

"I doubt that. Your phone's been off since Pascagoula. I haven't heard a beep from it, no text, no mail, no calls."

"I don't see why the state of my cell phone concerns you."

Skelly shrugged. "Suit yourself, chief. But if you're not going to use it, I'd advise you to get rid of it. They can trace them when they're turned on, and since you're behaving like a man who doesn't want to be traced, that would be a good move. I speak as a man who knows a little about hiding traces."

Skelly finished his beer and walked out of the *taquería*. Marder took out his iPhone, looked at it for a while, and felt a pang of regret. The silly thing had grown on him, had become almost a part of his brain, another organ. Yes, his brain: it would continue to maintain a record of his family and friends, his musings, his tastes, his curiosities, long after he was gone, and when he thought this he all at once could not bear the sight of the once-dear glassy slab. When he followed Skelly out the door, he shrouded it in a paper napkin and slipped it into the trash.

They drove southwest on Highway 16 through the sere countryside of Chihuahua state, past the scarce straggling towns, over the lizard-backed violet hills, over the few grass-green watercourses. They didn't speak much or, rather, spoke only in spates and then were silent for a while, in the manner of men who know each other very well but have very different lives. Skelly smoked, occasionally smoked marijuana, and Marder remarked that he must be the only man in history to import marijuana into the Mexican republic, and Skelly answered that a man couldn't have too many distinctions.

Marder found that Mexico had not changed all that much since the last time he'd been down this very route, thirty-odd years before. The cities they passed through were somewhat more Americanized, more cars traveled the streets, the public spaces appeared in somewhat better repair, but this surface modernization seemed to him like a scrim over a deeper Mexico, which had not changed, which nothing could change, or ever had.

"Did you ever read *The Plumed Serpent*?" he asked Skelly as they drove west out of Durango.

"D. H. Lawrence? No, not that I recall. Does it have dirty parts?"

"No, but it's about Mexico, about Michoacán—not the coast, where we're going, but up north, around the lakes."

"Any good?"

"Oh, it's a little dated, with a lot of that racist horseshit they went in for back then. He thought men in western civilization had all lost their balls because of Christianity, and he thought Mexicans were in contact with the dark, fertile forces and that made up for them being dirty, lazy, and corrupt. Chole hated it. The book, I mean. All that stuff about yearning for Quetzalcoatl and the return of the dark and powerful gods. It's about an Englishwoman who despises the men of her own culture and falls under the spell of Mexican machismo. Lots of purple language about true manhood and true womanhood and how materialism and reform have poisoned Mexico and how Christianity is the worst poison of all. Chole used to say it was typical gringo colonialism: it's okay for the darker people to be brutalized and poor and stupid, because they still have something the white man has lost, animal power, plugged into the natural world, full of the true juice of life, open to the old gods of Mexico."

"And it's not true?"

"What do you think?"

"Makes sense to me and will make a lot more sense when I finish this fat joint. So, besides the ashes, is that why you're going down there, to get in contact with the old gods and the juice of life?"

"No, and to talk about why that stuff is bullshit, I'd have to mention my religion, and then we'd have to have fight number three thousand four hundred and twenty-seven on the subject. But I recall you making similar comments back then, about the Hmong."

"The Hmong are gone," said Skelly. "All that's over."

He took a deep drag on his dope and closed his eyes. It was one of the many subjects Skelly did not care to discuss.

Outside, the sky was darkening and blushing toward the horizon, preparing for yet another gorgeous desert sunset. The pale tan of the land was going mauve in response, and the isolated yucca were entering their nightly transformation into the shadows of mythological creatures. Marder didn't buy the whole Lawrence agenda, but he knew that something was indeed sick in his culture and he knew that Mexico, while itself sick almost unto death, had within its own sickness the possibility of a cure.

Or such was his hope, now near the unpredictable hour of his death. He realized that he had started to think of Mr. Thing as a Mexican, with a stony face and indifferent, merciless black eyes, a D. H. Lawrence figure perhaps, careless of death but possessed of a heedless, violent, passionate life. Mr. Thing had a wide Villista sombrero and crossed bandoliers and a big revolver stuck in his pants; he was drinking and brooding in his cantina, but soon he would rise and do what he was meant to do. Marder smiled inwardly at Mr. Thing, or Sr. Thing or Don Thingado, and he thought that Mr. Thing smiled back. They understood each other now.

He switched on the radio and fiddled with the search button until he found the kind of music he liked, the Mexican equivalent of an oldies station, playing straight *ranchera*, not the pestilent *cumbia*, the Mexican version of rock, or, worse, pathetic rap derivations.

He glanced at Skelly, who was stone-frozen, the dead joint poised in his hand, a silly smile on his face. Marder actually preferred Skelly when he was a little wasted on dope, when the sad, ruined boy emerged from the depths of the man and occupied his face, softening the grim lines cut by war and worse things than war.

They listened for a while; the sun sank down in flamingo hues; the road rose quickly and grew serpentine as they climbed into the foothills of the Sierra Madre Occidental.

"What's he singing?" Skelly asked.

"I thought you knew Spanish—you can't get the lyrics?"

"I can barely get the lyrics to songs in English. My Spanish is entirely concerned with making money, eating, and fucking."

"Okay, this is a famous song by Cuco Sánchez. It's called 'The Bed of Stone.' It goes, 'Let my bed and headboard be made of stone. The woman who loves me must love me truly. I went to the courtroom and asked the judge if it's a crime to love you. He sentenced me to death. The day they kill me, may it be with five bullets, and I will be very close to you, so as to die in your arms. Give me a serape for a casket, give me my crossed ammunition belts for a crucifix, shoot a thousand bullets into my tombstone for my final farewell.' And the chorus—"

"Yeah," said Skelly, "I got that part: 'Ay yay yay, my love, why don't you love me?' Nice song. He sounds like my kind of guy."

The *rancheras* played on; they drove upward into the dark, into the sierra. Marder felt a lightening of his spirit. He saw, as from high above, as on a cosmic GPS map, the dot of his being climbing into the mountains of Mexico, and he had the thought, for the first time in many years: I am in the right place; it's okay if I die this very minute. He waited in this state for what seemed like a long time, but life went on.

5

"Where are you going?" asked Kavanagh out of the torpor that followed this latest bout of sexual congress. He could see her white shape moving from place to place in the room, vanishing once and then returning.

"Nowhere," she answered after a moment. "I just needed my notebook."

"How did I do? Do you have, like, a star rating system?"

"If I did, you'd have three stars, Kavanagh. No, I had an idea I wanted to sketch out before it disappeared."

"What kind of idea? And who gets four stars?" He watched as she fell into an armchair and arranged her long, flexible legs over its arm, forming an intriguing sort of desk.

"What kind of idea?" he asked again, and she said, "For work," in a tone that did not encourage further inquiry.

Carmel often received ideas from her unconscious in the spacey moments after particularly rewarding sex, and she had removed from her life those men who objected to women who leaped out of bed to tap upon their laptops immediately subsequent to the ultimate moist spasm and tender cry. Or a paper notebook in this case. Kavanagh was thus not an objector to such shenanigans. He rolled over and drifted off. When he awoke in the morning, she was gone, leaving a note instructing him to send you-know-what via encrypted email, if possible during the current day, because she planned to leave that evening for New York, to try to trace her father's movements. "Thanks, love," she wrote, and signed the note with a smeary pink lipstick kiss.

Kavanagh decided on a couple of things after he read this. The first was that he would call his telecom pal and get the logs he'd promised. The other thing was that he was going to stop seeing Statch Marder. He was starting to fall in love, which he thought was like starting to main-line heroin after a period of enjoying an occasional snort. He wanted to be in love, but he thought that falling in love with this particular woman would lead to a life fraught with sorrow, possibly including violations of the penal code. He did like them a little crazy, true, but this one was over the line. And the thing with her father too. He sighed, regretting his loss, and made the promised call.

Carmel got to the lab a little after six a.m., made a pot of coffee, drank a pint, and set to work on her computer. Liu came in at eleven-thirty, caught the vibes, sniffed the odor of her roomie, and decided to spend the morning at the library. The lab director, Erwin Schuemacher, dropped by around noon, as he usually did, to kibbitz with his students and to receive the sort of informal progress reports upon which the reputations of graduate students (and the progress of science) largely depend. He had heard rumors all morning that Ms. Marder was onto something and he wanted to see what it was.

He knocked, heard a half-snarled rejection of human contact, opened the door, and studied the girl and her screen.

"What's up, Statch?" he asked after a few moments of staring.

She looked over her shoulder and blinked at him, as if in her concentration fugue she didn't immediately recognize the trim, tanned fellow with the gray ringlets as her boss and mentor.

"Oh, sorry," she said. "I was really into it."

"So I hear. What is that thing?"

"It's a . . . I don't know. A new kind of actuator system. I'm not sure yet, but I think it'll work."

"What's it for?"

"Well, I think it's a solution to the internal transport problem. We've all been screwing around with designing custom arms and spoons and pincers to move parts inside the machine and each one is a bear and each one practically has to be unique and they don't fit in the available corridors and—well, the whole general problem is a pain in the ass. So I thought why not just carpet all the internal transport corridors with a zillion of these things. Look, I did an animation of how they would work."

She pressed keys. A wire drawing appeared of an arbitrary brick resting on a bed of what looked like tapered nails. In the animation that followed, the nails elongated in complex waves; the brick moved back and forth, was rotated by the tiny fingers, was stood on end, was deposited into a hatch.

"Each unit is real simple—it's basically just a fancy solenoid; they'd be cheap as shit to mass produce—but the beauty part is we can adapt the same programs we use in animation, I mean to populate a screen by flashing pixels. Each of them is like a pixel or a voxel, a sort of moving voxel—"

"A moxel," said Schuemacher, naming the thing henceforth and forever, as was his right. He was nodding, his eyes alight. "Well, well—that's actually extremely interesting. The problem, obviously, is will it work on the manufacturing end? Let's get a meeting together, like today. I want Sepp and Chandra and the other team leaders to see this stuff and get their ideas, and we'll talk about it at the regular lab meeting this afternoon, and then tomorrow we can try to set up some initial manufacturing runs. We need to find out if this is real, because if it works, it changes practically every subproject."

"Right, well, I don't see why it shouldn't work. It's just a basic principle—like the assembly line. But I can't come tomorrow—I have to go to New York. And I'm not sure when I'll be back."

Schuemacher had kindly bright blue eyes that could become unkindly under certain conditions, as now. "Uh-uh, kid, you *have* to be here. This is your play. I'm not going to tell fifteen engineers to rethink all their designs because you had a passing thought that's not even worth attending a couple of meetings for. What's so important in New York that you have to go there?"

"It's a family thing," she said, knowing that it was not an acceptable answer, that science at this level and her junior status precluded family things. She felt her face flush; it was like saying you didn't do your homework because your grandmother died.

He gave her an unkind glare, twiched his mouth, shrugged, said, "Well, at least you'll finish the concept presentation. Maybe you can get Liu to work on it while you're out."

On the train to New York that evening, Statch turned this conversation over in her mind, as well as the day's other interactions with her colleagues.

It had been a horrendous day, a ruin built on what was certainly the most important breakthrough in her career and probably, if it proved out, the most important idea she would ever have. Moxels. Everyone was calling them that now; the news had flowed like AC throughout the Escher Project. People she barely knew were stuffed into her little office, asking to watch her animation, asking her questions she couldn't answer, essentially stealing her idea, going back to their machines to run with it, to do the development she should be doing. And, of course, Schue was encouraging this process, spreading the word, maybe even starting to squeeze her out of the development work. No, he wouldn't do that, but he had two divorces to show the world that the work came first, that when an idea was fresh was the time to go balls to the wall on it, because if one doctoral drone had come up with it, it meant that somewhere in China, or Germany or Japan, a similar drone would be thinking along the same lines.

And she was not there, not in the center of the most exciting part of engineering, turning the sketch into working substance, otherwise known as Changing the World. Instead, she was on this fucking train to New York, because her father had somehow, after a lifetime of being sane as toast, gone batty and disappeared.

At Springfield, she actually jumped off the train and stood on the platform for a dreadful minute, then jumped back on as the door slammed shut, transported by guilt as much as by the contraction of her bountiful fast-twitch muscle fibers. She'd been in Cambridge when her mother died. She'd been busy, she had let the messages pile up in her voice mail, because parents were supposed to be grown-ups, they were supposed to handle their own shit; she hadn't realized what the woman was going through, hadn't seen the signs of derangement, of increasing desperation. She was the daughter, she was *supposed* to have this cosmic relationship with the mother, but what she had now was ineradicable shame, and so fuck the career right now, and fuck the sort of nice relationship with Kavanagh too, because it was obvious from their last conversation, when he'd told her the phone logs were on their way, that this one little illegal favor was the kiss-off; he wouldn't be around for the next one.

And she hadn't had her swim; stupid thought, but there it was. She felt her muscles turning into useless flab as she sat in the tickly plush seat, watching America's industrial wasteland roll by, borne at a pathetic sixty miles an hour on century-old technology. Maybe people like her could turn it around, maybe the country could leap a generation in manufacturing, maybe she'd be one of the saviors, but not now, not this week.

Marder and Skelly stood on a peak in the Sierra Durango, looking out at the clouds below, not exactly with a wild surmise but with deep appreciation, for they were both people who liked the mountains, and these were nice ones.

Skelly said, "This is pretty cool. I didn't think Mexico had anything like this. It looks like Oregon or western Kashmir, the Hindu Kush foothills."

"Most Americans only know the northern border from the movies, little burnt desert towns with banditos." Marder looked at Skelly, who was smoking his first reefer of the day, and had an intense and disturbing déjà vu of the type that had become increasingly frequent: standing with Skelly on a mountain ridge, looking out at a cloud-strewn forest, in the morning, as he could now, feeling damp, too, on his face, and the scent of the vegetation. The weird feeling passed over him like a vagrant breeze and was gone.

The smell was different. He felt Skelly looking at him. "Anything wrong, buddy?" he asked.

"No," said Marder, "just remembering the last time we were up in the mountains. We've had a pretty urban relationship over the years, haven't we?"

"Yeah, I guess we lost our taste for camping out. I'm going to go run. Don't get into trouble."

Skelly took off down the foggy road and was lost to sight before the sound of his footsteps had quite faded.

It was on their first RON mission to plant voodoos; they were going to Remain Over Night, as the army peculiarly called camping out. It was Marder and Skelly and another SOG guy, named—he couldn't recall the man's name, only what they called him—Popeye, and two of the Vietnamese LLDBs, and a dozen or so Yards. Marder and the SOGs were wearing the garbagemen's uniforms, and the Viets were in civilian black pajama outfits, and the Hmong were wearing their traditional garments. Each of the Hmong would be hauling a woven straw pannier of rice on his back; the idea was that they would walk down the trail as if they were a gang of Hmong impressed as porters, and the LLDBs were the guards, and the three Americans were, what—making a movie? Tourists?

At the mission briefing, they'd learned that the SOG people did this all the time, that there were Russian experts, engineers, and so on working on the trail, and besides it was dim and jungly and they would walk on by like they owned the place and in general no one ever stopped them. The lieutenant's opinion was that no NVA would believe they had the balls to just stroll along the sacred Ho Chi Minh Trail like that, especially not that far north. Marder hoped he was right. He personally thought it was nuts, but at the same time he was excited, he was glad to be there with Skelly instead of calling down fire on the place from the safety of Naked Fanny. The plan was to try to sensorize the whole road complex where it was narrowed down by having to go through the Mu Gia Pass. It was near impossible to place sensors accurately by air drop in this area, because of the terrain and the concentration of antiaircraft fire, which was of course the whole reason behind Iron Tuna.

They'd been flown in by a couple of CH-2s the previous evening and been led upland from the drop zone by Skelly, whose theory was that the Viets were lowland people and that soldiers in general would avoid climbing while on patrol, so the safest place to RON was up high on a ridge. In fact, they passed a peaceful night. At dawn Skelly had taken Marder up even higher, to an actual outcrop of rock, where they stood and looked out over the unbroken green rug of the Laotian forests. Skelly said they were looking directly at the Ho Chi Minh Trail, invisible under its canopy. "Why we had this little problem," he added.

The two ARVN Special Forces had been picked by Skelly as being the best of the lot. One was a dour whippet named Dong—called Ding Dong, naturally, by his American friends—and the other was a man who smiled unusually often and was unusually large for a Vietnamese, who was known as Charlie. The running joke (an example of the kind of constant, irritating military joshing that passed for relationships in the war) was that he was so good at impersonating a Vietcong that he probably really was VC. Skelly would joke that "Charlie is going to stab us all in our sleep" and Charlie would grin and say, "No, no, I not VC, I hate VC, VC number ten!"

The LLDBs carried Kalashnikovs, and the SOG guys carried small Swedish K submachine guns. Marder had his sidearm and, stuck in his rucksack, a cut-down M79 grenade launcher. Besides that, he carried no other warlike devices but only several dozen of the incredibly heavy voodoos and an entrenching tool.

Marder went back into the camper and poured another cup of coffee. What was that guy's name, Popeye? He couldn't bring up his face either. And maybe it wasn't Popeye at all.

He had an image of walking along a road, in dappled shade, and watching the motion of the man's huge rucksack and the weapon he had slung over one shoulder, not a Swedish K at all but a cut-down Russian RPD light machine gun, a captured weapon that looked like a giant tommy gun. He could recall the gun perfectly but not the man's name or face. What did that say about him?

He did remember the trail, though. They'd come down on it from the heights above, and he remembered being surprised to see it was not what Americans thought of when they heard "trail" at all but a finished road, well shaped and gravelled and almost twenty feet wide. They walked south along it, and every couple of hundred yards, Marder would slip into the bush and bury a voodoo. They had short aerials that stuck up above the earth and they were flexible like pipe cleaners; you were supposed to bend them artistically so they'd resemble roots or creepers.

After an hour or so they heard traffic, and a convoy of trucks passed them without incident, dozens of trucks, the men inside them looking incuriously out at the line of montagnards and their supposed keepers. Later they'd come on a scene of devastation, the jungle blackened and trees blasted and the carcasses of trucks with big holes in them from the cannon on some gunship. There were NVA troops here and workers salvaging truck parts. As they walked on by this busy scene, an NVA officer called out and Ding Dong answered him without stopping. Marder felt as if he were in a dream, something like reading a report to your third-grade class in your underwear; he was strolling down the Ho Chi Minh Trail! He felt Skelly come up next to him and say something in a loud voice, in a language he didn't know, perhaps Russian? Marder replied, "Arise you prisoners of starvation, arise you wretched of the earth," the only Russian he knew. It appeared to work. The NVA officer went back to supervising and Skelly said, after they were out of earshot, "Where the hell did you learn that Russian?"

Marder said, "My mom had a record of the Red Army Chorus. She was always playing it in the house and I picked up some of the words. It's the Internationale."

Skelly laughed out loud. "Yeah,I got that. That's what this war needs, Marder, a little more irony. Amazing!" And again he said, "I might just have to keep you alive."

They were not bothered for the remainder of the day, passing without challenge through the bustle of what seemed to be a stretch of busy highway in a small town—but studded with antiaircraft cannon—and finishing their assigned portion of burying sensors. After that they turned sharply into the bush and climbed and did another RON, then descended the next declivity, at the bottom of which was an even better road, one scarcely inferior to the Mexican federal route he was looking at now.

That wasn't the time they got into the firefight. That came later.

The clouds thickened and turned to drizzle, so Marder went back into the truck cab, drinking his coffee and wishing he still smoked cigarettes. He could start again now; that was a gift from Mr. Thing he hadn't considered. The traffic here was light, a lot lighter than it was on the Ho Chi Minh Trail. A white SUV with government markings and a light rack on the roof zoomed by and then a few minutes later returned and passed, more slowly this time, and then returned again and stopped on the other side of the road. Its doors opened and four uniformed men got out, holding assault rifles. One of them approached Marder's truck and asked to see his papers.

Marder handed over his license and passport and registration. The man studied these for a while and passed them back, saying, "I must inspect your vehicle."

"Be my guest, señor," said Marder.

The policeman climbed into the camper body and studied the interior, while Marder studied him. He had sergeant's stripes and a smooth fleshy face, well shaved except for a brush mustache. An arrogant face, used to having orders obeyed, but his eyes were nervous, darting here and there.

He flipped open an overhead compartment and peered in.

"What is your business in Mexico?" he demanded.

"I've bought a house in Playa Diamante and some land. I was thinking about opening a small business. I intend to emigrate here."

"You've been to Mexico often?"

"No, just once, a long time ago. My wife was Mexican, though, and I learned my Spanish from her."

The sergeant opened another compartment. "What is in that case?"

"Money," said Marder. "Around a hundred and fifty thousand dollars in cash."

The man stared at him. "Open it!"

"Open it yourself. It's not locked."

The sergeant looked at the hundreds, all crisp and green in their paper bindings.

Marder added, "We have weapons as well. A rifle and several pistols, and there may be others I don't know about. I have a companion who likes to travel armed."

"Where is he?"

"Oh, out and about. He's probably armed at this minute. Let me check."

Marder opened the other overhead locker and pulled down Skelly's gun case.

"Yes, he's a carrying his Sig P226, which as I'm sure you know is a very expensive and accurate weapon. And I see he's carried his suppressor today. He likes to practice shooting without attracting attention."

The sergeant said, "I think you will have to come with me. To be questioned at the police station in Durango."

"And why is that, sir? I've done nothing wrong."

"You have cash and weapons. I have reason to believe you're another gringo narcotics trafficker coming here to buy drugs." In a practiced motion, he unslung his carbine and pointed it at Marder. "Down on your knees and put your hands behind your head!"

Marder didn't move. "You know, that makes no sense. This is not Tijuana or Juárez. As I said, I'm an American businessman with deep family ties to Mexico. You're thinking of all that money and how much of it you can take for yourself and how much you may have to share with your men and with your superiors. And you may also be thinking that if I should meet with a fatal accident, you could simply keep all of it. But you've forgotten my companion out there."

The policeman raised his weapon so it was pointing at Marder's chest.

"There is no companion," he said. "I told you to get on your knees. Do it now!"

Marder sat down on the long cushion that ran along one side of the camper body.

"You know, Sergeant, this is either the luckiest day of your life or the last. My companion is certainly real, and I have to inform you that he is one of the deadliest men in the world, an experienced soldier who has been trained to kill efficiently and silently. He is very fond of me for some reason, and if you shoot me, he will certainly dispatch your men with his silenced pistol and then he will come after you, and I'm afraid he will not make your death pleasant. You have as much chance against him as a high school football player would have against Ronaldo. On the other hand—tell me, do you have a daughter? I do. A daughter and a son. Have you been so blessed?"

The gun barrel wavered a trifle. "Yes, I have a daughter. And two sons."

"I congratulate you, sir," said Marder brightly. "And as you are a young man, I doubt that your daughter has yet had her *quinceañera*. Mine has, and let me assure you that they don't come cheaply, not if a man wants to do honor to his daughter and to his family, as I'm sure you do. As a token of our good relationship, therefore, I would like to contribute to your charming daughter's *quinceañera*—let us say, oh, five hundred dollars. Feel free to take that amount from the case. And I'm sure you won't abuse my generosity."

Marder smiled genuinely at the policeman and he saw that the policeman saw it, that the man at gunpoint was not in the least afraid, and it confused him, as it was entirely outside his ordinary experience— for he had held guns on many men—and more like a dream. This more than anything would convince him that the gringo was telling the truth and that five hundred dollars was a very fine *mordida* and without the complications that would ensue if he brought the man and his treasure into Durango. And if he did steal it all, how could he hide a hundred and fifty thousand dollars? He took a pack of hundreds from the case, stripped five bills out, and left, without looking at Marder or saying another word.

Twenty minutes later, Skelly climbed into the camper.

"What did the cops want?"

"The usual. They thought we were narco traffickers."

"Taking the scenic route. What did you give them?"

"I gave the sergeant five."

"That's high, chief. Now he's sure you're a dope lord."

"Well, he had a daughter," said Marder, and he observed that Skelly picked up what he meant. This was one of the charming things about Skelly: after so many years, there were things that didn't need to be tediously explained.

When they were driving again, Marder asked, "What was the name of that guy in your outfit—they called him Popeye. Big guy with a shaved head; he always carried that Russian RPD."

From the driver's seat, Skelly gave him a long look, then turned his face back to the road. "It wasn't Popeye; it was Pogo. His name was Rydell, Walter E., master sergeant. Why are you asking about all that Vietnam shit now?"

"I told you. I've been thinking about our time there and I realized I can't remember stuff. I can recall some things, but I can't get the faces and I can't bring up the names."

"That's because you weren't really there, Marder. You were a fucking tourist the whole time."

After that, one of the dismal silences that often followed when Marder brought up the war—one reason he hadn't done it often during the ensuing years. He knew Skelly talked about it with ex–Special Forces; he'd been in bars with Skelly and had heard the stories. He had even heard stories he knew were fabrications. But for some reason Skelly never wanted to talk about it with him. A less charming facet of his relationship with Skelly but one he could live with, for there was no one else who could confirm the memories of that time as they floated to the surface of his mind.

Now they were descending the winding, precipitous road from the peaks of the sierra, Skelly taking the curves somewhat faster than was safe, but there was little traffic and, despite several close calls, they survived to reach Mazatlán on the Pacific coast. The last time Marder had come this way, he'd been carrying everything he owned strapped to the back of his motorcycle, and the country had seemed as poor as he was himself and free with the freedom of poverty. The roads were rough but the people were gentle, or so he recalled, but that journey was colored by the wonder that had revealed itself at the end of it, when he had found Chole.

Now there was an American-style turnpike with toll booths and service plazas that took you from Mazatlán to Guadalajara, saving time over the old road that led through the fantastic volcano country around the great dead cone of Ceboruco. Marder did not want to save time, however; he felt that saving time was not what one came for in Mexico, the land of *mañana*. And so he left the Carretera Federal de Cuota at Tepic and went south on Route 200 to the sea and in easy stages past the tourist beaches and high-rise hotels of Puerto Vallarta and Manzanillo, through the smaller beach towns and resorts of Michoacán, with the glistening sea on the right, below the green loom of the Sierra de Coalcomán.

"So what do you think?" asked Marder. They were sitting at a tin table outside the cantina El Cangrejo Rojo, facing the palm-lined central plaza of Playa Diamante. Hector was the proprietor and already a pal. Hector could get the señores anything they desired in the way of dope and girls and, Marder suspected, would be happy to split the bribes with the cops in the event of their arrest. But a nice guy, a fat, pleasant, crooked man, eager to please.

In the center of the plaza was the typical kiosk, and this faced a tiny park from whose entrance Lázaro Cárdenas, Friend of the People, gestured toward the future in bird-spattered bronze. A mild breeze whickered in the palms and in the fringes of the umbrella overhead, smelling of the sea and, more faintly, of some of its deceased inhabitants. A gray monster of a cat sunned itself in the cantina window under the neon depiction of a red crab.

Skelly held to the light the shot glass from which he had just drunk a slug of tequila and seemed to be examining the oily residue.

"What do I think? It's a beach town. It could be in Thailand or Malaysia or East Africa. It could be America if there were more fatties walking around. It's got the usual favela stuck on the hillside for the servants to live in."

"Yeah, they call it El Cielo. Ironic."

"Indeed. Besides that it seems unusually clean and well policed, although probably not by the police. You're intending to settle here? This is your dream of paradise?"

"It is."

"Because it's Chole's hometown?"

"Partially. As a matter of fact, we passed where she used to live. That yellow adobe two-story place with the white awnings? When I first came here, they ran it like a traditional Mexican inn, meals with the family and so on. It was named after their hacienda, from the old days, Las Palmas Floridas."

"You could've stayed there. You have to admit, it's a little strange buying a house sight unseen in a place you haven't been for over thirty years."

"Unlike you, Skelly, I sometimes commit irrational acts. I was tired of the way I was living and I have enough put away, so why not spend my golden years in the sun?"

Skelly put on the kind of false smile that appears when one has not believed what was said but does not think it worth calling the lie. "Well, good for you. A couple of things, though. You picked a place that's about as much under military occupation as Kandahar, and also whoever's being occupied doesn't like it."

"You think?"

"Yes. One clue was that a number of the walls have those little holes in them, lots and lots of little holes. Another thing is, we passed the police station on our tour just now, and it's got scorching fanning out from the window frames, and it's probably not because a guy forgot to stub out his butt. I'm thinking gasoline bombs. Maybe Sarasota or Scottsdale would've been a better choice."

"Maybe so, but you can't get handmade corn tortillas like we just had in Sarasota." Marder drained the last of his Dos Equis and stood up. "Come on, let's go look at the place I bought."

They were about to cross the plaza to the truck when they heard the sound of powerful engines approaching. The life of the plaza, the children dashing about, the women shopping, the men lounging and playing dominoes in the shade, all seemed suddenly to stop. Women grabbed at their children, people ran indoors, as around a corner appeared three dark sport-utility vehicles in convoy. Marder and Skelly had to jump back to keep from being run down as the cars circled the plaza once and then came to a stop.

Marder looked around. Somehow, almost magically, everyone in the plaza had disappeared. Then, with another roar of engines, the cars departed to the east. Something that had not been there before was leaning against the base of the statue. They walked over to see what it was and found it to be a male human torso, facedown. On its back someone had written, "He deserved this!" in green marker.

"The justification is a nice touch," said Skelly. "It speaks to a certain formality of style, which I find endearing. Who do you think did it?"

"*Los otros*," said Marder. "La Familia or one of its factions, or someone wanting to send a message to all or any of them."

"A mobbed-up beach town? What's the angle?"

"It's not so much here, but Lázaro Cárdenas, up the road, is the only serious container port on the Mexican Pacific coast. All the precursors for making meth come through there, not to mention coke and heroin. It's a contested area for the narcos. And Playa Diamante has a nice little harbor itself, as you saw, if someone wanted to run stuff in and out."

"And you chose this town?"

"What can I say? I like the beach. Here come the newsies. They must have better intel than the cop."

"Well, it stands to reason—the cops are probably being paid off more than the newsies."

A white van had run up to the curb nearest the park, and a cameraman, a sound man with a mike boom, and a young woman got out. They did the usual getting-ready-for-taping routine, working efficiently as a team, and in something of a rush, it seemed. Marder watched the woman. She was wearing a tan suit, very chic, and had her light-brown hair cut close around her face, which was appropriately pale but bore stronger features than one typically saw on female reporters north of the border. She spoke, and Marder heard with a pang the Mexican accent called *fresa*, clipped and precise, that marked a member of the country's upper classes. His wife had spoken like that. The cameraman recorded the reporter's contribution and then moved to get tape on the torso. Sirens wailed, followed by the sound of heavy vehicles approaching.

Marder said, "Here comes the army. Let's get out of here."

They left just as several truckloads of soldiers entered the square. Marder drove out of town to the west, following Avenida Jaramillo until it crossed a bridge over a sluggish estuarine stream, the Río Viridiana, after which they turned left toward the sea. Before them was a low bluff with a cut through it, which led the red dirt road past a broad white beach to a causeway built on pilings and rough boulders. This in turn led to a humped green-clad island, on the top of which, through the thick vegetation, they could see the white terrace and the red tile roof of a large house.

Marder had seen the photographs, but these did not do justice to the magnificence of the setting and the palatial dimensions of the house. There was a high whitewashed stone wall around it with an open steel gate, the gatepost bearing a ceramic sign that read CASA FELIZ. Past the gate was a garden with fruit trees and flowering bushes, hibiscus and oleander, and then a gravelled courtyard before the house itself. It was two stories tall, capped by a little square tower at each of the four corners of what appeared from below to be a roof terrace. They could see the tips of folded umbrellas above the terrace wall, or parapet. On the left of the house, separated by a low adobe wall, was a less imposing structure of concrete-block stucco, and beyond that was a line of what appeared to be smaller houses in various stages of completion, as well as various piles of construction supplies and equipment. A thin plume of white smoke arose from a distant structure, and Marder wondered what it was.

They entered the main house through the front door. There was a small entrance hall, with a door to the left and one to the right and in the center a rounded archway. They went through this and found themselves in an enormous room, with a staircase in one corner leading to a gallery that ran around three sides of the room. Through the rails of this they could see the doors that must lead to the bedrooms on the upper floor. Great windows opened on a view of the sea, flickering palms, and the sky. Overhead was a black wrought-iron wheel chandelier of the type that Zorro liked to swing from.

"We'll be cramped, but I guess it'll do," said Skelly.

"Yes, it's a little hard to judge size from photographs. I thought they were using the kind of lenses that hotels use to make a closet look like a big room, but I guess not." He called out but received only a slight echo in answer.

They went through the kitchen and out a back door, toward the small house they'd seen from the drive, without doubt where the servants lived—and there must be servants here, and good ones too, for the place was spotless and still had its appliances.

He knocked. The door opened and there stood a thin woman of about forty, in a plain dress and apron, with a small girl and a smaller boy flanking her on each side. All three stared at him with a look that he had not seen addressed to him since Vietnam, a look of hopeless terror.

He said, in the mildest voice he had, "Señora, my name is Richard Marder. I'm the new owner of this property. May I ask your name?"

The woman moved her mouth silently for a moment, and then croaked, "I am Amparo Montez. I'm the housekeeper."

Marder extended his hand, and after staring at it for a dumb moment, the woman shook it. He felt her hand tremble like a bird.

"I didn't hear—I mean, no one told me the house had been sold."

"Well, it has. I can show you the paperwork if you like. And allow me to introduce my friend, Patrick Skelly . . ." Marder looked behind him, where Skelly had stood, but Skelly was not there.

"Well, perhaps later. And now, if you would be so kind, I'd like you to show me around the house and grounds."

The woman gaped, and then her face collapsed, and she began to weep and the children began to weep.

Marder watched this for a few moments, feeling increasingly confused and helpless, then said, "Señora Montez, I don't know why you're distressed, but let me give you a minute to compose yourself. I'll unpack, and when you're ready you'll come into the house, we'll make some coffee, and we'll have a talk."

Marder knew his Spanish was fluent, but the woman looked at him as if he were speaking Hmong. He left her staring and snuffling and retreated to the camper, where he began to unpack his things.

He had his own stuff nearly cleared out when Skelly appeared.

"Where did you get off to?" Marder asked.

"What happened with the woman?"

"She's the housekeeper, she says. She had a nervous breakdown for some reason."

"I can guess why," said Skelly, climbing into the camper. Unpacking sounds emerged.

"Why?"

"The place is full of squatters. There must be near a hundred people living back there, men, women, lots of kids. They're growing corn and peppers and beans and living in the unfinished houses, and they've got what looks like a commercial fish pond going. They used a big hole the previous owner dug for a foundation or a swimming pool."

"Oh, shit! That's why she was scared. She probably thinks I'm going to evict them and fire her."

"Are you?"

"I don't know," snapped Marder irritably. "Oh, hell, no, probably not, although becoming a *hacendado* was not part of my original plan."

"And what *was* that original plan, chief?"

"Obtaining peace and quiet in a pretty little village on the Mexican coast and returning my wife's ashes to her homeland."

"Uh-huh," said Skelly, emerging from the camper with a case in each hand, one of which held the sat phone and the other—a long heavy one—what Marder believed were shotguns. "I think I can pretend to believe that for a little while. Meanwhile, you should take a look at this."

He led Marder into the four-car garage, which held only a battered yellow Ford pickup truck of seventies' vintage.

Marder looked at where Skelly was pointing. In one corner of the garage, the concrete wall was pocked with what could only be bullet holes, lots of them, and the smooth white surface of the wall there and the floor below was spattered with dark reddish-brown stains.

"Someone was killed here," said Skelly. "Any idea who?"

"The previous owner is among the missing," said Marder.

"Then it's a good thing we brought all these guns," said Skelly, and grinned alarmingly at his pal.

6

"I'm really sorry, Statch, but that's all I can tell you," said Ornstein. "He called me up, he said he'd be gone indefinitely, and he offered me the use of his loft."

Ornstein was a little embarrassed as he said this and apprehensive too. Carmel Marder had shown up demanding to know what he was doing living in her father's loft and where her father had gone off to, and why, and while Ornstein could answer the first of these questions, he was perfectly ignorant as to the others. Perhaps he ought to have asked, as a friend, why Marder should have made such an arrangement, obviously, as was now clear, without telling his family anything about it. Besides that, Ornstein was frightened of Statch Marder. He was a small, retiring man, and while utterly prepared to battle global capitalism to the last drop of his blood, facing down a tall, angry young woman a few feet away from him was outside his normal range. And, he wanted (and, oh, how difficult it was to preserve the selflessness that any good red should exhibit!), he very much wanted to remain in this wonderful loft.

Statch glared, threw up her hands, said, "Okay, I got it—do you mind if I look around?"

"Oh, be my guest!" he replied, "or, really, since I'm *your* guest . . ."

Statch left the living room and the undrunk tea that Ornstein had made for them. She went immediately to the room her parents had used as their study, the Aladdin's cave of her childhood, and began to explore her father's desk and filing cabinets. As she did so, her apprehension increased. There was nothing besides the usual office supplies and some meaningless papers, receipts, odd notes, catalogs, family papers of no revelatory value.

She switched on his computer and cursed when she saw that it was password-protected. That had been Peter's suggestion, she recalled; he'd lectured his father on how vulnerable his machine was, had scrubbed it of accumulated malware and installed the password. And, being Peter, he hadn't used a word or memorable phrase but a ten-digit random string. Which meant that Marder had probably written it down somewhere, on a Post-it, or in his antique Rolodex. She looked; she found plenty of other passwords but not the master key.

She took out her phone and called her brother in Pasadena.

"It's me," she said.

"What's wrong?" he said.

"Why should anything be wrong?"

"It's six-fifteen here, a little early to call just to say hi. Gosh, I was deep in dreamland. Maybe this is still part of the dream."

"It's not. Look, Pete, I'm in Dad's loft and . . . have you heard anything from him in the last few days?"

A pause on the line, then, coldly, "Why would I hear anything from Dad? We don't talk much. As you know."

"Yeah, right, but the fact is, whether you like it or not, he's still your father, and he's gone missing."

"What do you mean, missing?"

"As in, he left the loft and gave it to Ornstein, no return date specified. I tracked his cell phone and the last time he used it was in Mississippi, and the last time I got through to it a Mexican kid answered, suggesting theft or abandonment, neither of which makes me happy. I'm really worried about him. Look, do you happen to have his master password? I want to check his computer."

"No. I don't keep other people's passwords. Unlike some members of this family, I'm not a snoop."

"Thank you. But do you know if he wrote it down? He probably didn't memorize a ten-digit random string."

"Yes, he wrote it on the back of his driver's license," he said, and heard his sister's short, vivid curse.

"And you can't think of any reason why he would disappear like this? I mean, Peter, it's freaky—he's totally cleaned everything out of his files."

Another pause. "Did he take his gun?"

"Oh, God! Wait a minute, I'll check."

She hurried to the gun safe and punched in the combination, a number she had known since the age of eleven, this quite outside the knowledge of her father, who had not discovered it until she was old enough to be taught how to use a pistol, at which point it didn't matter.

"The Steyr and both pistols are missing. The only thing he left was the Woodsman."

"Well, then, we know he didn't go off to commit suicide. He'd need only one gun for that."

"Jesus, Peter! That's a horrible thing to say. You really think Dad is suicidal?"

"I don't know. I don't know who he is. I thought I did, but obviously I was wrong."

"You're never, ever going to let that go of that thing with Mom, are you?"

"No, I'm not."

"Well, that just sucks. He's our father, for God's sake. He's your father, who made a mistake. I'm sorry he didn't live up to your standards of perfection, but we're still a family."

"Well. We'll have to agree to disagree on the subject. I still love you, if that's any help. And I get it that you're worried about him. Have you tried calling Hal Danielson? Or the accountant, what's his name—Benny?"

"Bernie. No, I haven't yet. That's a good idea." She said goodbye and closed the connection.

But Statch never called either the accountant or the lawyer, whose names and numbers appeared on the log from Kavanagh's friend, nor did she even notice the name of Dr. Gergen or Patrick Skelly on the list. Only one of the names interested her, and she called its number immediately.

"*Buenos días!*" said a recorded voice. "This is Nina Ibanez at Su Hacienda. I can't come to the phone right now, but leave a message at the tone and I'll get back to you as soon as I can."

She did not leave a message. Instead, she unlimbered her laptop, brought up Su Hacienda's website, and found Nina Ibanez's email address. Then she called a Cambridge number. She got voice mail and at the tone said, "Boro, this is Statch Marder. I need to talk to you right away. It's sort of an emergency."

While she waited, she went into her old bedroom, a place she used during trips to the city, which was therefore amply supplied with clothes and other necessities. She filled a nylon backpack with clothes suitable for a short stay someplace warm.

Her phone sounded. She checked the number and answered it.

"Boro, thanks for calling."

"What's the emergency, darling?" said a voice with a Russian accent. *Dolling*.

Statch was a competent computer jock, but she was by no means a hacker. Boris Borosovski, on the other hand, was an ornament of the computer sciences department and one of the best hackers at MIT, a very tough league.

"I need to break into an email account."

"Is illegal to do, darling Statch. I am hanging up right now."

"No, really. I wouldn't ask you if it weren't a matter of life and death."

"So. What is story?"

"It's complicated."

"Good. I love complicated."

"It's my dad. I think he's gone crazy and run off with a woman."

"Good for him."

"No, this is a very bad woman. She . . . she's been after my dad for years, trying to get her hands on his money, on his loft and everything. She's a manipulative bitch and I have to stop her. I mean, my dad's sort of going soft in the head and he's, like, nearly helpless. He's left town without telling anyone and I'm pretty sure he's with her. And I need to get into her email to find out where they've gone."

"Is like Shakespeare. Or *As the World Turns*."

"No, really, Boro—I *need* this."

"In this case, I can get you password. You will supply sexual favors at some future date, yes? Disgusting practices?"

She laughed despite herself. "I'll unleash all my exotic skills on your hairy little body."

"I will anticipate with great excitement, I assure you. What is email?"

She read it out to him, and he promised to text her with the information within half an hour. Which he did.

It required but a few minutes after that to log into the Ibanez account and find the correspondence beween Su Hacienda and her father. She'd made up the story about Nina chasing after her father's money, but maybe it was true after all. He'd actually purchased a house for the two of them in Playa Diamante!

She felt her jaw grinding and made herself stop it. How could he? He had sworn to her that the affair was over, that it had been a transient aberration, and now he'd bought a house—the words "love nest" appeared in her mind—in her mother's hometown so that he could . . . what? Start another half-Mexican family? After her mother had killed herself in despair over his betrayal with Nina? No, that was crazy thinking, that was how Peter thought, that could not be the answer.

But in fact her father had purchased a large property from his former, or maybe not so former, girlfriend, said property located in her mother's hometown. The whole transaction stank of weirdness, of crazy male menopausal hijinks, the kind of life-destroying error that dutiful daughters were supposed to save their batty dads from. And where did he get that money? Ponzi schemes and embezzlements—these went with the evidence of a secret life with Señora Ibanez. Her stomach lurched as she contemplated the notion that the beloved dad was not what he seemed, perhaps was a hidden monster like you read about in exposé biographies.

To distract herself from these disturbing thoughts, Statch called Karen Liu at the lab.

"Where are you?"

"I'm still in New York. Anything going on at the lab?"

"It's been insane. Schue got us all together today and said we're going to reboot the whole project, or at least the transport part of it, and convert to moxel surfaces. He was foaming in his teeth, Statch. I never saw him like that before."

"At the mouth. He was foaming at the mouth. What's everyone else doing?"

"Oh, tearing their hairs. We have an initial design for the moxel unit sketched out and we are waiting for the first prototype. You really should be here. Schue is unhappy with you, I think."

"Well, yes, but I have this family crisis that I can't get out of."

"Yes, family is the most important. I would leave in one minute if it was my family having bad times."

"Yeah. Look, keep me informed, okay? Email me the designs, and if you have any problems you want me to work on, let me know."

Crazy, she thought after she'd ended the call; I have to get back there right now. But in the event, it turned out that the Marder apple had not fallen far from the tree after all, for when she reached Kennedy that evening, instead of taking the Boston shuttle she had the driver take her to Mexicana, and she bought a seat on the first available flight to Mexico City. She had only the one small bag, but she had to check it because of the gun.

Marder told Señora Montez that he would be happy to have her and her children stay on and that whoever else was living on the property could stay where they were for the time being. She smiled at that, immediately shedding years from her face and showing herself to be a remarkably handsome woman. The señor inquired whether some food could be prepared. The woman looked embarrassed, smiled, nodded, and Marder felt stupid. Of course there would be no food in the house suitable for such grandees. Marder pulled a thick wad of thousand-peso notes from his pocket and pressed it on her, telling her to stock the house with food and keep the rest. She stared at him, at the money, started to say something, then left.

Marder and Skelly spent the rest of the morning jacking the camper off the Ford, unpacking all their gear, and stowing it in their rooms. After that, Marder sat down to his first meal at his own table, a meal cooked by Amparo Montez and served by her and her two children. These were Epifania, a thin, dignified-looking girl of twelve, and Ariel, a boy of ten. It was a good meal, built around *posole*, a corn and meat soup that requires a pig's head and pig's trotters and a laborious processing of each kernel of corn to remove the germ so that it will blossom like a kind of popcorn and give the soup its characteristic texture. The labor, Marder understood, was a compliment and a promise. He praised it enthusiastically. "This is a very ancient dish, Skelly," said Marder. "The Aztecs used it to consume the victims of human sacrifices. The Spaniards made them substitute pork. Apparently they said it tasted pretty much the same."

"It does," replied Skelly darkly, "and this is pretty good, but I thought food down here would be hotter. I can never get food hot enough in New York. Thai places, Mexican places, they see I'm a white guy, they hide the good stuff."

Marder said, "There are different kinds of heat, right, Amparo? This has *guajillo* and *ancho* chilies in it, I think. But I'm sure you have something hotter in the kitchen, if the señor desires."

Amparo smiled and sent Epifania off to the kitchen. She returned with a small unlabeled bottle containing an oily golden liquid and set it before Skelly. He took a soup spoon, filled it from the bottle, and supped it down. The three Mexicans goggled at him, Amparo with her hand over her mouth in shock.

"That's getting there," said Skelly, his face now brick red and glistening with sweat, and they all laughed with amazement and admiration. In a lower voice, and in English, he added, "Speaking of hot."

This was in reference to Lourdes, Amparo's niece, a teenager so stunningly beautiful that, when she walked into the dining room wearing cutoffs and a purple tube top, neither of which entirely confined her remarkable young body, both Marder and Skelly had paused with spoons in air and nearly gaped. She'd come in with a bowl and clunked it unceremoniously down in front of Marder and then exited with a rolling strut, as if she owned the place.

Skelly added, "That's trouble."

"She's a kid, Skelly," said Marder, who had begun to study the serving bowl as the girl had leaned over to place it on the table, so as not to have to study the flesh on display six inches from his nose. "This is interesting pottery, don't you think?"

"Fascinating. And I believe the traditions of Old Mexico almost require you to take a piece of that before you marry her off to a fine young lad."

"This is really good food, don't you think?" said Marder heavily, to change the subject, and then discoursed briefly on the remarkable sophistication of Mexican cuisine, which had as little to do with Mexican restaurants in the States as chop suey joints did with what they used to eat in the Forbidden City. It was nearly the only survival of the deep pre-Columbian culture of meso-America, conveyed by example and advice by women to their daughters across thirty generations since the fall of Tenochtitlán. In Amparo's kitchen there would be dozens of different clay pots, each designed to perfectly cook a single kind of food, and the number of ingredients—many of which existed nowhere else—was enormous.

And so it was a fine meal: *crema fría de aguacate*, followed by *tamales de harina* and a real *atole negro* with real toasted cacao peel and an unfamiliar steamed fish covered with crushed macadamia nuts. The younger children served him silently, with the occasional shy smile when they looked at him. Marder had eaten food like this all his married life, and eating it again struck at his heart as much as it satisfied his belly, but it was different being served it this way, like a *hacendado* by his servants. He felt like a fool and an impostor, but also, parodoxically, as if he was where he belonged.

Skelly was not big on food in general, but he said he could get used to this, and they talked in an easy way about meals they had enjoyed, or not enjoyed, around the world. Their conversation paused only when Lourdes drifted through the room, as people will stop talking when there is an explosion or a rain of frogs.

"I notice the dad is nowhere around," observed Skelly, after one of these passages. "In fact, this whole place seems unusually devoid of the male sex. I wonder why that is."

"A lot of them probably went to *El Norte*. Another chunk is likely engaged in the narco wars or has been killed in them. But most of them probably are hiding."

"From . . . ?"

"Us. No one told Amparo that the place had been sold to a gringo. When I showed up, she thought I was *los otros*, the gangsters. Which means *los otros* pay regular visits. I think we should stroll around the grounds and make smiley faces at the locals."

They set out north from the main entrance of the big house and passed the servants' quarters, a long, low one-story concrete-block structure connected to the big house by a breezeway. The former owner had intended to build a small holiday resort on his land and had started ten good-sized concrete, tile-roofed bungalows in an uneven line along the high ground at the center of his island, these separated by thick ornamental plantings. The first few were completed shells, the next few were roofless walls and the last ones were mere foundations, like a museum demonstration of how to construct cheap vacation homes. The squatters had used the typical inguenity of the barrio to improve these, using the piles of construction materials that lay in drifts all around the property. Some had built actual walls with mortar and block. Others had used plywood and studs, or even what looked like driftwood, to complete their homes. The roofs were a miscellany of tile, corrugated tin, tar paper, mud brick, and plastic tarpaulin weighted with rocks.

"They call this bricolage," said Marder as they strolled through what had been devised as an ornamental path but had become by default the street of a small hamlet. "The use of materials for purposes other than the intended one. That tennis court, for example."

The four-court tennis court, whose markings could still be faintly seen, had been turned into a barnyard. Shelters had been thrown together for goats, pigs, and chickens.

"All in all," he continued, "I think it's an improvement over tennis. Or don't you agree?"

Skelly wasn't listening. He was staring at the surroundings with a dark look on his face. He doesn't like this, Marder realized. He fears this kind of village. It was a village like this that broke his heart.

They greeted a large woman in the dirt yard in front of her house; she stood over a plywood table on which sat a blue plastic bowl of *masa*. She looked at them calmly, as if making tortillas was more important than they were. They introduced themselves and she did the same.

"I am Rosita Morales. Are you going to take my house away from me?"

"I am not. You can stay here as long as you please."

"So I have heard, but I didn't believe it. The former person wanted to make vacation houses for rich people here and get a lot of money. Why don't you do the same, Señor?"

"Perhaps money no longer interests me."

"Then you must be insane or a saint," said the woman, and laughed at the thought of someone uninterested in money, showing large crooked teeth.

Marder laughed too and said, "I'll let you decide as time goes by. Good day to you, Señora."

Skelly had walked through the village and emerged at the far end of the built-up area. Beyond lay the rest of the island, a stretch of undulating Mexican tropical dryland scrub: thorny low bushes, chaparral and various kinds of cactus, with some larger trees rising up above the tangled green mass. The edge of this growth was scarred by an aborted attempt at a road, at the end of which a small yellow Komatsu bulldozer sat crookedly, as if taking a break.

"He was going to put a golf course in here," Marder remarked.

"A good thing someone shot him, then," said Skelly. "How big is this place anyway?"

"A little shy of three hundred acres, including the beach. They used to call it Isla de los Pájaros, Bird Island. Guzmán was going to call his operation Isla Paradiso, but I think we'll retain the original name. That's a boojum tree over there. They call it *cotati* around here, or *cirio*. It has honey-scented flowers in the summer."

"You're full of information today. Hitting the Google key, are you?"

"No. When I was in this area the first time, Chole took me around and taught me the names of all the plants and animals. Let's take a walk through the woods."

They walked along the path toward the bulldozer, Marder pointing out the various trees: the gumbo-limbo, the manzanita, the *jicaro,* or calabash, the *acalote* pine. The land rose slowly, and soon the vegetation became mere scrub and they were looking down a cliff at a perfect oval of sand that capped the island's northern point.

"Let's go," said Skelly, and began to pick his way down the crumbly rocks. Marder followed him reluctantly, but there was a reasonably accessible path. They climbed over rocks and waded briefly and soon they had reached the island's main beach. They stared at the glittering Pacific for a while and listened to the thump of its surf. "A nice beach," said Skelly. "A nice break too. I should have brought my board."

"Yeah, it's a terrific beach—the whitest sand for miles." Marder stooped and let some of his property sieve through his fingers. "It's practically pure quartzite—that's why they call it Diamond Beach. If we walk south for a little while, we should be able to see the harbor breakwater and the mouth of the river."

He set off, walking on the damp sand. Marder had always liked the sea. He liked it in all seasons and had always taken his family on seaside holidays, renting houses on Long Island or the Jersey Shore in summer and taking occasional winter trips to the DR and Antigua. He and his wife used to laugh about this, the whole personals-ad cliché about loving long walks on the beach, but they did; they took long walks on the beach, she often stooping to pick up things mottled or faded by the sea and keeping them on a particular shelf in their office. The first of them must have come from this very beach—not this particular island but farther south, on Playa Diamante proper. Without warning, Marder was seized with a blast of emotional pain so strong that it clouded his sight and he stumbled. He would have fallen had not Skelly grasped him by the arm.

"You okay, buddy?"

"Yeah. I had a stitch in time. A flashback, if you want to call it that. I was walking on the beach with Chole, but it was now—I mean, I was with her but I knew the future, that I was . . . that she was going to die. Shit!" He shuddered like a horse. "You ever get flashbacks, Skelly?"

"Only nightmares," said the other, but did not expand. Instead, he pointed ahead to where they could see the tip of the long breakwater, with the red-lit channel marker, and beyond it the greeny-brown stain made by the outflow of the Rio Viridiana.

"There's your boat basin," said Skelly, pointing. "Like you said, it's a nice location for running drugs. Quiet little port, a boat channel, good communications inland. It tends to explain the torso in the plaza and raises once again the question of why you chose to spend your golden years in the middle of what looks like a narco war. Would you care to illuminate?"

"Not really," said Marder. "There should be a set of stairs just ahead." They continued walking, found the stairs, and climbed them to find themselves on the lower of the two terraces that lay beneath the house. This was lined with young mango trees, bearing green fruit, and there was a hammock slung between two of them. From the south side of the terrace they could see where someone (perhaps the late Guzmán) had built a pair of docks and dredged out a tiny bay to make a miniature marina. There were no boats in it.

"We should get a boat," said Skelly. "There's supposed to be terrific game fishing off this coast. And also . . ."

"What also?"

"To be frank, we're basically on an island with only one way off. I like to be in places with two ways out, or more."

"Okay, find us a boat. I like boats too."

"Not a sailboat, Marder. Something with legs."

"Hey, get a guided-missile frigate. Whatever will reduce your paranoia."

They strolled back across the terrace. Upon the adobe walls that rimmed this on the ocean side, posts had been implanted and heavy wire strung between them to act as a support for bougainvillea and trumpet vines, although these had not flourished. The wiring on one side was completely bare.

Skelly twanged a wire. "We could hang cards on this and shoot. Since there's no golf course."

"Yeah, we could have a rematch of the Moon River Invitational."

"I've got cards. When I win, will you tell me what the fuck we're doing here?"

"When you win," said Marder.

Skelly went off and came back with a deck of cards and a basket of clothespins. "The señora had all the necessities," he said, and attached a row of cards to the wire strand that faced the sea.

"Too bad if anyone's on the beach when we shoot," said Marder.

"Fuck 'em. It's a private beach. And it's Mexico. Want a round now?"

"I think it's siesta time," said Marder. "You've waited forty years for this; it'll keep."

He turned and climbed the broad stone steps that led to the upper terrace. There a pool shone with the aquamarine of advanced chemistry.

"Now that you've circumnavigated your kingdom," said Skelly, "you look pleased."

"I am pleased. It wasn't what I expected to find, but it's kind of neat. I don't have to wait for my next life to be a feudal lord."

"Yeah, but if you don't have them move the latrines from where they are now, you're going to have medieval levels of cholera. The subsurface flow has to be from the river, and the shitters are upstream from the well. In fact, you should put in a septic field if you want all those people to stay."

"You know about this, do you?"

"Yeah, the army cross-trained me in field engineering. It's part of the wonder of Special Forces."

"Well, we'll consider it *mañana,* as they like to say around here. First our nap."

Skelly laughed and said that some rack time sounded good. After he'd gone, Marder contemplated his pool and thought about his daughter and wondered how she was getting on. This line being too painful, he had changed his wonderment toward the question of who was maintaining a pool in an empty house so well when he heard young voices and saw the two Montez children trotting across the far side of the terrace.

"Hey, kids," Marder called out. "Who takes care of the pool? Do you have a service?"

The children stopped and stared at him. The girl, Epifania, said, "No, sir. We do it ourselves. We take the leaves out and put in chemicals, and Bonifacio makes the machine work when it breaks. But it only broke twice."

"We don't swim in it," said the boy.

"Not even when no one is looking?"

"No," said the boy fiercely. "We swim in the sea only."

They disappeared, whispering to each other.

As he walked back to the house, Marder heard a less innocent noise, a rattling in the bushes below the wall overlooking the lower terrace, and a gasping male voice. He peeked through an oleander and saw Lourdes in a clinch with a guy who had to be twenty-five. He was trying to get his hand into her pants and was kissing her neck, and she was laughing and fighting him off but not all that seriously. Marder walked down the steps, making noise. More shaking foliage, panicked whispers, and the sound of retreating people, fading around the side of the house. He'd have to deal with that situation but not just yet.

Marder went through the cool and echoing house to the room he had chosen. It was white-walled and full of light, with windows looking out at the sea. The bed was similarly huge, a brass item that looked antique, and the rest of the furnishings were Mexican provincial: light-colored, carved, painted, and distressed with dents and wormholes. It was the bedroom of a great *patrón*, or someone who wanted to be one. Marder felt that strange ambivalence once again: I shouldn't be here, but here I am, the lord of a mansion and a village. He felt something working behind the scenes in his life, as if he were on a ship captained by a hidden stranger.

He unpacked his scant clothing and put his weapons in a wardrobe that locked with an antique brass key the size of a can opener. As he finished this task, he heard the sound of a car on the gravel road, coming closer. He left the room, walked around the gallery until he came to a window that looked down on the drive. A white SUV was pulling up in front of the house. He watched three men get out, walked back to his room, grabbed the Kimber pistol, stuck it uncomfortably in the small of his back, pulled on his linen jacket, and went downstairs.

He waited in the living room, leaning casually against the back of a couch. He wondered where Skelly was and wished that he were here for the coming interview with whoever had just arrived in the SUV. Some-one pounded on the door, then flung it open. Through the open arch-way, Marder could see the three men, all as neat as Mormon missionaries: dark suits over open-necked shirts, short haircuts, shined shoes. They came toward him, one man in front, the others a little to the rear. They were looking around the room as if they wanted to buy the place, or had already bought it.

The leading man stopped in front of Marder, a little too close. He was dark skinned, shorter than Marder by almost a foot, but bulky. His face was pitted with old scars, and he had two blue teardrops tattooed at the corner of one eye. He folded his arms and glared at Marder.

Marder said, "Welcome to my house. What can I do for you gentlemen?"

The man said, "You can tell me who the fuck you are and what you're doing here."

"My name is Marder and I own this house. I intend to live here. And who are you?"

The man was shaking his head. "No, you don't want to live here, man. This is not a healthy place for you to live. Acapulco, Puerto Val-larta, that's where you should live, with the other gringos."

"I'm a gringo, true, but I'm also a citizen of Mexico. My wife was a Mexican and my whole family has joint citizenship. So thank you for the health warning, but I believe I'll stay."

The man smiled and shook his head again. "No, *pendejo*, you don't understand. There is too much lead in the environment here. If you stay you will definitely die." With that he reached into his belt and pulled out a Glock pistol. He waved it under Marder's nose. "You understand now, *coño*?"

"Yes," said Marder. "You make yourself perfectly clear. You want me to leave."

The man ran the muzzle of the pistol across Marder's cheek and tapped it a couple of times. "Good," he said. "You're a sensible man." He returned the pistol to his waistband. "I don't want to see you around here again. If I do—"

But Marder did not find out what he would do, because from up above came the unmistakable and ever-interesting sound of a shell being jacked into the chamber of a shotgun.

They all looked up. Skelly was standing on the gallery, pointing a Browning BPS 12-gauge shotgun at the three visitors. He said in Spanish, "Sit down on the floor, gentlemen, and fold your hands on your heads."

After a moment's hesitation they did so, and Marder disarmed them of three identical Glock pistols. He felt as if he had been propelled out of his ordinary existence for sure now and forced down what would have become an hysterical giggle. Somehow he had been translated into Skelly's life, and it was as unreal as Skelly would have felt had he been translated into a quiet room and given galleys to edit. And—this was the strangest part—Marder found it wonderful! He was cool, unfrightened. A thousand thrillers on the page and on the screen had taught him exactly how to act, what to say; the garment had been tailored by squadrons of hacks, and he slipped into it easily.

He stuck the three pistols in various pockets and said, "Gentlemen, we seem to have started out on the wrong foot. I didn't realize you were so interested in pistol shooting. As a matter of fact, my colleague and I were just talking about having a little target practice. If you please, follow me."

With that, he pointed toward the terrace doorway of the great room, Skelly came down from the balcony with his shotgun steady on the trio of gun thugs, and all of them marched out into the sunlight, past the pool, and down to the lower terrace. Marder dumped the Glocks on one of the metal umbrella tables, pulled their magazines, and cleared the chambers of each. He turned to the three men.

"I've given you my name," he said. "Permit me to know yours."

Pock-face was Santiago Crusellas. His associates were Tomas Gasco, a light heavyweight, sand-colored, with the brutal face of a Toltec idol, and Angel d'Ariés, a thin, boyish-looking man of about forty, with a sad, defeated look. Marder studied the face of this one for a good minute: high cheekbones, large tilted hazel eyes, a paler complexion than the other two. The man shifted uncomfortably under his gaze. Marder asked, "Are you related to Don Esteban de Haro d'Ariés?"

A pause. "My father."

"A man known for his probity and generosity, I believe."

"Did you know him?" said d'Ariés, a small light appearing in the dull eyes.

"A long time ago and not as well as I should have," said Marder, and then clapped his hands. "Well, let us begin!" he said, and pulled the

Kimber out. Skelly had arranged the four sevens from his deck on the wire. Marder took up a stance at a convenient crack in the pavement, twenty feet or so from the target, and with seven spaced shots blew the pips out of the seven of hearts. He put his pistol down on the table and handed Crusellas a Glock and a magazine. Behind them, Skelly raised his Browning.

Crusellas loaded his pistol and blasted away, missing entirely several times, but, having fifteen bullets to play with, he managed to shred the bottom of the seven of clubs, leaving the upper two pips unharmed. Marder went to the wire and removed the two targets. He looked at the seven of clubs and shook his head, then pulled out a pen and scribbled on the seven of hearts. He dropped both cards into Crusellas's breast pocket.

"You need to practice more, my friend, unless you confine your shooting to assassination at very short range," Marder said. "Tell me, who is the chief of the plaza these days?"

"Servando Gomez," answered Crusellas.

"Well, you can tell Señor Gomez that we've had a meeting. Tell him, if you would, that you didn't find another stupid gringo you could frighten away or perhaps dispose of as you disposed of the unfortunate Guzmán. Tell him I'm a dangerous fellow. And tell him I mean him no harm—I'm not a rival of any sort but perhaps an ally. Tell him also that I have dangerous friends, like, for example, the gentleman with the shotgun. Also tell him that I would be happy to visit him at any time, to discuss matters of mutual interest. My number is on my card, so to speak. And I believe I'll take that pistol back from you now. I'm sure you have others."

Crusellas handed over his empty Glock, a look of dull hatred on his face. Marder took his Kimber and tapped the man lightly on the cheek with it, then made a shooing motion, and after a moment the three men turned and walked away. They heard the front door slam and a car start up and drive off.

"That was very impressive, Marder," said Skelly. "A dangerous man. And here all the time I thought you were a candy-ass book editor. You know, those guys'll be back."

"I'm sure. That's why it's good that I have dangerous friends." He smiled at Skelly and then they both laughed.

7

Returning to the house, Marder heard a sound that he had not heard in a long while, a delicate clapping, like the applause of a single child: a woman making tortillas in the traditional way. Instantly, twenty years slipped away and he was back in his office at home, listening to the *pat-pat-pat* from the kitchen. A ridiculous activity in New York, where there were abundant Mexican groceries and very good tortillas available in plastic packages, but sometimes Chole had to slip back into what she called "deep Mexico" and make tortillas from corn *masa* she mixed herself, to be eaten with a *mole* of thirty ingredients, also made from scratch. Not always a pleasant time for Marder, these sojourns into *México profundo*. Sometimes it would be fiesta, sometimes a breakdown, tears and recriminations directed at him, the author of her long exile. Tears dropping into the *masa*.

And now as he listened, the same noise: sobs, barely stifled. Marder went into the kitchen, half-fearing that there would be no one there, that his brain was starting to go and he was hearing things.

He was delighted to see it was only Amparo, standing at the long wooden table, making tortillas, and sobbing. A small television was affixed to the wall, showing a telenovela with the sound off.

"What's wrong, Señora? Why are you crying?"

She stared at him, openmouthed, then wiped her streaming eyes with her apron.

"I heard the shooting. I thought they had killed you like—" She stopped, wild-eyed.

"Like they killed Guzmán?"

She nodded.

"These were the same men?"

Another nod. "It was Crusellas. Señor wouldn't pay them, so they killed him."

"In the garage."

"Yes. They said they would kill everyone if we told."

"Well, I think they will find it harder to kill people around here from now on. Tell me something, Amparo. How come this house is so orderly? Nothing has been stolen and you keep the place beautifully, as if someone is still living here. I was surprised."

"They use it. Or they used to use it. It is a great prize and no one knows who will have it. I mean *los otros, los malosos*. They say El Jabalí was going to give it to his son, but El Gordo objected and that is the reason they are fighting now. Or so they say."

El Jabalí—the Boar. And the Fat Man. Marder didn't know who these were, but he expected he would find out. He said, "So La Familia is having a war with itself?"

She shrugged. "I don't know anything about such things, Señor. I'm only a housekeeper. Some say if only they would all kill themselves off, things would be better, but others say the important thing is to have peace and no bullets flying around, and for that to happen one must win, because there will always be *ni-nis* to deal in the drugs for *El Norte*."

"*Ni-nis?*"

"What we call them, like those who came here. The boys: *ni trabajo, ni estudiar*. They're like weeds, and if they don't have a *jefe* who makes them behave, then life is hell for everyone. At least La Familia made them behave. Now, who knows?"

"Well, we'll see what we can do to make them behave," said Marder. "I intend to stay here, and I wanted to talk to you about arrangements. I want to put you in charge of the whole house. Hire staff, a cook, someone to clean, people to care for the grounds, and so on. I'll pay you a flat amount each month and then you can take a salary for yourself out of that, pay the staff and the bills, buy food, and so on. Can you use a computer?"

The woman stared at him. "Yes . . . no, not very well, but the children can. They have one at the school."

"Good. Epifania can be the accountant, and Ariel can be her assistant.

I'll get them a computer and show them how to work an accounting program. I'll set up a bank account for you too—" He stopped in the face of her obvious distress. She looked as if she might start crying again.

"What's wrong?"

"Oh, Señor! Why would you trust me with tens of thousands of pesos each month? How do you know I won't cheat you? You don't even know me."

"I know you enough. You have books on the shelf in the kitchen, which shows you have had some education, but you make corn tortillas by hand instead of buying them wrapped in plastic, which shows good character and suggests to me that you are not fool enough to risk everything for some scam. Am I correct? Good. Now, here's what I want you to do."

They spoke of business matters for half an hour, the woman contributing in a manner that only confirmed Marder's judgment that there were no flies on Amparo Montez. When this concluded, he said, "Two more things—no, three. First, that little community we have squatting here—do they have a leader? I mean someone who everyone respects and comes to for advice and help."

She thought for a moment and came up with some names, which Marder wrote down in his notebook. One of them was Rosita Morales, the woman he'd spoken with earlier. "Next," he said, "do we have any *ni-nis* on the property? Young men who might join La Familia or some other narco group?"

"A few. I'm sure Rosita would know who they are."

"Okay, I'll ask her. Could you send word that I'd like to see the people on this list after the evening meal, say eight o'clock? And you'll need to get yourself a notebook and a cell phone. I'll be throwing a lot of stuff at you soon, and you won't want to forget things."

"Yes, sir," she said, and then paused attentively. "And what is the third thing?"

"Right. I think we should talk about Lourdes."

"Oh, my Jesus! Has she done something again?"

"No, but I perceive a problem that I would like to forestall. The child has a certain form and face, which she can't help, of course, but she also seems unhappy. Sulky, even. That's not an atmosphere I wish to cultivate in my house. Besides that, there will soon be men shooting one another over her, and given the unfortunate situation in Playa Diamante, that is not merely a figure of speech. I caught her with a man ten years older than her just this morning. No, not that—she was merely playing with him, but such play tends to get out of control very quickly. What is her story, if I may ask?"

"She's my niece, my youngest sister's only daughter. Her father is dead, a *narcoviolencia* thing, now many years ago. My sister went to *El Norte* when Lourdes was five. At first she wrote, she sent money, but now, for five or six years we haven't heard from her. That usually means something bad. But after you shed your tears, there is still a child to raise." She sighed, shrugged. *"No importa madre,"* she said, using the general Mexican expression for things that can't ever be fixed, of which that nation had, oh, so many. "I have thought of sending her to my brother in Guerrero, to the *rancho*, you know? But she swears she will run away if I do, and she will. The girl is a mule. She won't work, she is failing school, and she is starting to sneak out, as you saw. All she thinks about is money and things and how to get things, all the things she sees on the television and reads about in the magazines. She thinks she will be a model or a movie star and have cars and jewels and fine clothes. But I think some *guapo* will take her and give her drugs and that will be the end of her, poor little thing!"

"Perhaps not," said Marder. He was looking up at the television, which had attracted his attention when the program changed to the spangled opening of a news show. Marder saw that they were leading with the incident in the square, with the torso. He saw again the pretty woman with the tan suit. He reached up and turned the volume on. He watched and listened, enjoying the *fresa* accent in the throaty voice, until the segment ended.

He turned back to the housekeeper. "Let me talk to her. Sometimes a young girl will listen to an older man."

He was watching Amparo's face when he said this and observed a variable display there: fear perhaps, doubt, then resignation. The animation that had appeared in her eyes while they were talking of the business of the house faded, and the servant's polite mask reappeared.

"Yes, Señor. I will tell her. May I get on with my work now?"

Marder nodded and went up the stairs to have his siesta. As he closed the blinds and lay down on the cool sheets, he thought, She thinks I want to have the girl myself and thinks it might be the best thing for her, a rich old American instead of a thuggy kid who'll get her pregnant. She read me wrong, he thought; I already had that life.

He stared at the ceiling, a flawless pale-cream field, and entered, as he often did when exhausted, a hypnagogic state, in which the past seemed more available. Was he more prone to this since the diagnosis? Perhaps he was running back through his life, as people are supposed to do at the moment of death, but more slowly, consideringly, as befitted an editor of encyclopedic works. In any case, now in his half-sleeping mind, he was on a different bed, narrower, harder, and the ceiling above was mustard yellow and cracked in a peculiar circular pattern, like the outline of a cat's head. He was in his room at the Las Palmas Floridas Hotel, after a motorcycle journey of several thousand miles. He had not planned to come to Playa Diamante, had never heard of the place, it was just where a series of spontaneous decisions had led him, not toward anything but away from a life he thought he had screwed up beyond repair. He was twenty-four.

He had left his wife, a perfectly nice woman he did not love. Like so many of his brothers-in-arms, he had married her on the rebound from Vietnam, seeking life, seeking warm human shelter from what had happened to him over there. Janice Serebic: he could hardly recall her face at a remove of over thirty years. Yet even back then, lying on that other, narrower bed, guilt had washed her features, her voice, from his memory. She'd been the cashier in the place where he'd worked as a cook, both before and after the service, a student place up on Amsterdam Avenue near the university. He was sad beyond words; she was funny and plump and made him laugh and steered him like a salvaged vessel into marriage's dry dock. He'd lost his caring machinery up there in the rainy mountains, and subsequently whatever happened, whatever someone else wanted, was okay with him, because he'd found out what making decisions and volunteering and wanting stuff came to: nothing good.

His parents liked her; that was big plus. His dad was starting to go weird and she was okay with that. She was a nice person he didn't love, and when it hit him finally that he was going to spend his whole life faking affection, he went a little nuts. One Friday, after drawing his paycheck, he cashed it and got on his Harley and, without really thinking too much about it, drove past 20th Street, where he lived with her in a second-floor walk-up, straight down Broadway and right at Canal and through the Holland Tunnel and through many a winding way and strange adventure, slowly building his courage up again, the numbness fading, until he was brave enough to call his mother and tell her what had happened to him and call Janice and bear the sobs, the screamed imprecations coming over the line, standing with a fist full of quarters under the snapping bug lights of a Gulf station somewhere in central Texas.

He'd heard Guadalajara was cheap and so it proved to be, but it was full of Americans, and he'd lost his taste for watching his countrymen boss around short brown people. Besides that, he was too broke after a month on the road even for Guada, but in that city he'd heard that the Mexican Pacific was even cheaper, and so he'd followed Route 200 down the coast and made a random right turn and followed a rutted road until it dead-ended at Playa Diamante.

He remembered the first time he'd seen her. Wasn't that the way when it's real love? You recall every detail of face and body and dress, even the smell, the feeling of keys sliding into a lock you never knew existed. She was waiting tables in the small restaurant the hotel kept to serve breakfast to its guests. He came down that first morning and filled his plate at the buffet; he loaded it, because he had a young man's appetite and no money and the breakfast was included with the room: eggs fried with salsa and scrambled with sausage, beans, enchiladas, warm *bolillos*— what they have in Michoacán instead of croissants—and a vast tray of fruits. Except for oranges and grapefruit, they were all unfamiliar to him. He loaded another plate with samples of each and sat down at a table, and then she walked out of the kitchen holding a pot of coffee. He stopped eating to watch her pour coffee for the other guests.

She approached his table, she smiled, and he was a gone goose. Her eyes were palest hazel, her cheekbones high and staring through skin like a creamy Bourbon rose, and, topping all, that mass of thick glossy red-black hair. She asked him if he would like coffee. He could barely answer yes. She poured, turned away, and he cried, "Wait!"

"What are these fruits?" he asked when she turned politely.

He made her explain the tejocotes, the cherimoya, the guanabana, the nanchi, and the puzzling guamúchil. In his halting high-school Spanish, he asked how one ate it. She showed him how to open the brown pods, exposing the shiny beans covered with pale fibers that tasted like cotton candy. She demonstrated how to suck clean the little bean and smiled again. It was like the Garden of Eden.

He lost interest in all else, planning his campaign; he was back in the jungle, collecting intel. He pumped the hotel staff without shame, tipping more than he could afford, cornering the bartender, the chambermaids, the gardeners. Her name was Maria Soledad Beatriz de Haro d'Ariés y Casals, known as Chole. She was a daughter of the place, a student at the National University in Mexico City, home for the summer to help out. Her mother was Carmela Asunción Casals, whose family had founded the hotel, and her father was Don Esteban de Haro d'Ariés. They were *criollos* of the highest water, reduced by the revolutionary depredations that took their estates in the thirties to the indignity of running a ten-room hotel in Playa Diamante. The girl had literary pretensions, always a notebook or a book of poetry to hand. She wished to be modern, to write, to have a career, but the father was set on a grand marriage, preferably to one of the local *caciques* of the PRI, the permanently ruling Institutional Revolutionary Party. One such had been found, with acceptably light skin tones, and an engagement was imminent. By this act would the family fortunes be restored: Don Esteban would expropriate the expropriators.

The daughter was currently mobilizing the traditional Spanish colonial response to absurd orders from the crown: I obey but do not comply. The suitor had been put off, tangled up in rivalry, manipulated, told to be patient. She was only seventeen, after all: perhaps next year.

Marder's heart lifted when he learned this. He knew some poetry. His mother had doted on Yeats, had dropped stanzas into his little ear throughout his tender years; he had earned cookies at the price of memorization: swaths of Yeats, of Poe, of Tennyson resided in his love-addled brain. And when she approached him with the morning coffee, and having learned that she understood English well enough, he gave forth a few lines appropriate to a fine morning, to a dull morning, to a particularly succulent dish, to her smile, her eyes, her form. She would blush and nod and smile, showing her small white teeth and that charming tiny gap between the two front ones. So, gradually, over the weeks (and Marder thanked God that it was the off-season and dirt cheap to stay in his tiny room), they formed a connection, consisting of brief conversation at breakfast and occasionally in the evenings, when they happened accidentally, purposefully, to pass in the dim walkways of the patio.

There was a bookcase in the hotel sitting room, a glass-fronted mahogany item, perhaps a relic of the old *estancia,* with a number of moldering leather-backed volumes in it, and here he located a thin volume of the poetry of Ramón López Velarde. Marder had never heard of this person, but he was clearly a Mexican poet of some standing, and so, as a way of generating a subject for mutual discussion with Chole, he undertook to read and understand some of the poems. But what began as a half-witted and desperate ploy became something else when he fell under the spell of the poetry and discovered that Velarde, whoever he was, had gone through *precisely* the emotional scarification with his honey that young Marder now endured with respect to Señorita d'Ariés. "She is so reticent yet welcoming," wrote Velarde, "when she comes out to face my panegyrics, the way she says my name, mocking and mimicking, makes gentle fun, yet she's aware that my unspoken drama is really of the heart."

He breathed these lines to her one evening in the garden of the hotel patio, just a wing shot as she passed by with a load of towels. He saw her pause—did she tremble a little as she asked, "Do you know Velarde?"

Did he ever! He recited, "May you be blessed, modest, magnificent, you have possessed the highest summit of my heart."

"Meet me on the beach in one hour," she said. The air smelled of orange blossom, or maybe that was her skin, or his brain.

Marder drifted off and awoke, almost expecting to see the cat-head crack in the ceiling, but it was only blank, dead cream. There was a knock on the door, and he told whoever it was to come in.

It was Lourdes, her perfect face marred with inexpertly troweled-on makeup, wearing a sleeveless black blouse with the top buttons open enough to show the gold crucifix and the tops of the breasts it nestled between and a white skirt big enough to drape a large doll. White plastic wedge sandals completed the outfit.

She regarded him with her usual expression of sulky indifference.

"My aunt said you wanted to talk to me."

"I do. Pull up a chair."

Instead, she sat at the foot of the bed and relaxed against a throw pillow propped on the brass pipes of the bed frame, cocking her leg up in a manner that afforded him a view, had he desired it, of her crotch.

"So, Lourdes," he said, "what are your plans?"

She stared suspiciously. "What do you mean?"

"I mean how do you want your life to work out? The reason I ask is that I'm observing the way you're going and it's possible that you're following a plan, which is to fuck a bunch of guys and get pregnant, then get pregnant again, until your beauty's a little faded, and then again, and then you're thirty with three or four kids, working as a servant. Or a whore. If this is what you want, it's fine with me. You're well on your way. But not in my house, please."

"I'm not a whore!"

"Then stop acting like one. Or, if that's your choice, I would be happy to introduce you to someone who'll teach you how to be a high-class whore. Diamonds, champagne, trips on jets and yachts, a little retirement fund when you get too old. How does that sound?"

"I'm not a whore," she repeated.

"I'm glad to hear it. Then what are you? I'm interested to know what you want. In your deepest desire, how would you be if everything worked out perfectly for you?"

Another suspicious look. "You'll laugh at me."

"I won't."

"I want to be in telenovelas. Like Thalia. Or Natalia. Or Pepa Espinoza, but she doesn't do them anymore. Or, I love Belinda—"

"Okay, a good plan. So how do you start?"

"What do you mean, start?"

"I mean you don't get to be a telenovela actress by watching telenovelas and reading fan magazines and fooling around in the bushes with guys ten years older than you. You have to work. Natalia was studying drama when she was eight. By the time she was your age, she'd been in a couple of dozen TV commercials. It's work, Lourdes; it's not all about going to parties and being famous. If you're serious about this, I can help you out. I know lots of people in Spanish-language media. I can get you lessons, auditions, whatever you need. I can fly you up to Defe, take you shopping at Mundo E, buy the clothes you have to have to make an impression, introduce you to people. . . ."

"Why would you do that? You don't even know me."

"I do it in honor of my late wife. She was only a few years older than you when I met her. I stole her away from the life she should have had, so perhaps by giving you the life you want, I can balance the books in heaven. That's one reason. Another reason is that I can't stand to be in the same house as a sulky, disobedient teenager. It makes my blood boil. So you have to stop acting like a slut, you have to be nice to your aunt, you have to stop being a *ni-ni*. Because it's my house and I won't have it."

"When will we go to Defe?" She had a stunned look now; she'd expected another lecture, but not this.

"When I see some changes. When you're back in school and doing well. When you learn how to act around men old enough to be your grandfather. You can begin by sitting properly—I've seen one of those before."

The girl moved as if shocked by a cattle prod, dropped her feet to the floor, and closed her thighs.

"And when I see you're showing proper respect to the people who care about you, we can talk about getting your career started. Are we clear?"

"Yes, clear." A long pause. "Thank you, Señor Marder."

"It's nothing. Now, scram."

Lourdes left but not before giving Marder a large kiss on the cheek.

He was in the bathroom, smiling at the scarlet lipstick blotch on his cheek, when the door to his bedroom crashed open and his daughter barged in. He turned around and gaped at her.

"What are you *doing*?" she yelled at him. "Have you gone *insane*? Disappearing without a word to your family and . . . and . . . having sex with *teenagers*!"

"I am not having sex with teenagers."

"Oh, thank you, Bill Clinton! I just saw your *chica* sashaying out of your bedroom, and she left half her mouth all over your face."

Marder sighed, and said with studied mildness, "And hello, Carmel. What a nice surprise! I thought you were in Cambridge."

"I *was* in Cambridge. And then you disappeared off the face of the earth. I called your cell and some Mexican kid answered. What was I supposed to do, sit in a lab and design machines? Oh, my father's vanished but, hey, he'll turn up, it's sort of like when the remote falls down behind the couch. You have no *idea* how you screwed up my life with this trick."

"Darling, pipe down and stop treating me like an Alzheimer's patient who wandered away from Shady Acres. I needed a change, I came down here. Do you inform me every time you go off someplace with one of your numerous boyfriends?"

"Oh, you *are* down here with a girlfriend, then."

"For God's sake, Carmel, have some sense! What the devil does it matter to you if I decide to change my life? I'm lucky if you call once a month."

"Oh, now it's my fault? I'm a neglectful daughter, so you had to come down to Mexico for the teenaged prostitutes?"

"What teenaged prostitutes?" said Skelly, appearing in the doorway. "Am I missing something? Hey, Statch! I thought I heard your voice. Come here and give your uncle Pat a big hug."

"Oh, you're involved in this too?" she said, making no move to hug him at all. "Maybe you can tell me what's going on with him."

Skelly stepped into the room and threw his arm around Marder's shoulders. "We're gay, and we're finally out of the closet," he said. "Richard bought me a lovely trousseau. And a ring."

A moment of stunned silence here, as Statch looked from one man to the other, until Marder shook off the other man's arm with a curse.

Skelly roared with laughter. "I had you for a second, didn't I? Not that there'd be anything *wrong* with it, of course."

"Oh, shut up, Skelly! Something's going on here, and I'd like to find out what it is so I can go back to my life. All you have to say is two old farts are having a midlife crisis and I'm out of here."

Marder slipped into his sandals, picked up his wallet, and said, "Two old farts are having a midlife crisis. I hope you'll stay for dinner. We could catch up. Meanwhile, I think I'll go out and get drunk."

"I'll come," said Skelly.

"Alone, if you don't mind. You can stay and explain to my daughter what sexual hijinks I've been up to without her permission."

"But take a gun," said Skelly, changing his tone down to grim.

Marder ignored him, leaving to the sound of Statch's voice: "Wait, why does he need a gun? *Why the fuck won't anyone tell me what's going on?*"

Marder took his truck out of the garage and drove off down the narrow causeway. As he turned toward the town, he saw a ragged boy squatting by the side of the road with a handful of browning bananas and a few papayas. He hadn't been there yesterday, and Marder briefly wondered if this was a gangster lookout reporting on his movements.

He didn't care. He was thinking about his daughter and how to ease her away from him without making her suspicious or, indeed, hurting her in any way, for though he loved Carmel more than anyone in his life, he did not ever want her to be in charge of him. That was the whole purpose of the trip. He felt a wave of self-contempt. A man tries to quietly slip away from his complex, fraught life and finds himself in a life even more complex and fraught than the previous one. Although there was still the real, the hidden purpose; he shouldn't forget that. Fraught was okay for whatever time remained to him, if he were able to bring it off.

The rough road caused something heavy to clunk in the driver's door caddy. He reached in and found his father's .45, which had rested forgotten there since the start of his now futile efforts to escape his life.

He drove aimlessly around the little town for a while, back and forth, on a few of the six *avenidas,* up and down a few of the thirty or so *calles,* past the two-story *palacio municipal* with its cop cars, its tiny jail, around the park, with its statue of Cárdenas shining gold against the foliage, past the hotels and dive and surf shops, the tourist traps, the six decent hotels and the fourteen lesser ones, and then down toward the beach. He would have a drink at the town's only real luxury hotel, the Hotel Diamante. Or three. He had to think, and he had to be away from his beautiful refuge to get some peace. What a joke!

As he approached the hotel, he noticed a dark-green SUV with smoked windows parked opposite the entrance. Two men were leaning against it. They had neat haircuts and wore dark suits, open-necked white shirts, and large gold crucifixes hanging from neck chains. Despite these signs, their faces did not indicate that they were on an evangelical mission. Both of them were big men, but one was big and snaky, with a long neck and a small head, and the other was big and fleshy, like a football lineman. This one looked at Marder as he slowed down, raising his sunglasses to do so. He had a pronounced squint, the eyes almost hidden but not hidden enough to conceal the malevolence of the look. Marder tapped the gas and swung into the hotel driveway. When he got out, he gave the valet kid a hundred-peso bill and told him to leave the car on the drive, with the key in it.

There was a bar off the lobby with a shady terrace out front. Marder took a seat with a view of the street below. One of the thugs with the SUV answered a cell-phone call. The other stared at the hotel entrance, as if he were waiting for a hot date to show. Marder ordered a tequila and a beer. When it came, he downed the shot, ordered another, and sipped the cold beer. The waiter brought chips and salsa and he ate some of that, although it was typical expensive-hotel crap, bland and watery. He looked around the bar. A trio of sunburned tourists speaking noisy German, a couple of Mexican business types, and, in a corner, behind a potted palm, a laptop on a table and someone—a woman, by her hands— tapping upon its keys.

A cell phone rang, sounding the first bar of a *ranchera* song he knew, "El Caballero," by José Alfredo Jiménez. The woman with the laptop answered it, spoke for a minute or so, then packed up her laptop and strode out of the bar, carrying her laptop case and a pale leather over-nighter. She was wearing a rose-colored suit now, but Marder could see it was the TV reporter, the one from the torso incident.

He watched her walk out of the bar, as did the two Mexican opera-tors, who froze and looked up from their important papers. Marder wondered idly how sick you had to get before you stopped watching the sway of a woman's ass. Then it clicked: the woman, the reporter, was who those guys were waiting for outside. He stuck a wad of pesos on the table and rushed out. She was down at the foot of the drive, looking both ways, as if expecting a car to pick her up. Marder went to his truck, reached in, and secured the .45, jacking a round in as he walked toward the street.

The two thugs were crossing the street now, heading for the reporter. She looked at them but didn't move, didn't scream or run, until they reached out to grab her, by which time it was too late. One of the thugs yoked the woman and clapped a hand over her mouth; the other knelt and swept her feet up. Together they carried her toward the SUV. The driver jumped out and opened the rear door, like a nasty parody of a chauffeur.

Marder was by now a few yards behind the men. A younger Marder was in control of the aging body, a Marder walking the trail, weapon ready, expecting action.

He fired two shots into the street-side tires of the SUV, puncturing the sidewalls. This got the attention of the men carrying the reporter, who stopped and looked over their shoulders, their faces showing the stunned look of jacklighted stags. The driver reached inside his jacket, and Marder shot him. He slumped down the side of his car, leaving a shiny trail of blood on the dark metal.

"Let go of the woman!" said Marder.

After a brief hesitation, they did so. The woman staggered, having lost one of her shoes. Marder said to the men, "On the ground. Face-down. Hands behind your head. Move!"

The snaky guy said, "What the fuck're you doing, asshole? Do you know who we—"

Marder shot him in the foot and he sat down, writhing; the other one did too, never taking his squinty eyes off Marder as he stripped them of their pistols and cell phones.

Marder turned toward the woman, touching her on the arm. She started violently, coming out of shocked paralysis. He said, "There's a red Ford truck up on the drive. Get into it and wait!"

"But someone is coming . . . I had an appointment."

"It's canceled, unless you want whoever's picking you up to get shot when they send another team after you. Just go!"

She took off her remaining shoe, picked up her case and bag from where she'd dropped them, and hobbled up the drive. Marder went over to the man he'd shot, who he was glad to see was still breathing, and took his pistol and cell phone too. He knelt down and said to the men on the ground, "I'm going to drive out of here, and if I see that you've moved when I come by, I will kill all three of you." Then he ran up the drive, got in his truck, tipped the valet, and backed down the driveway with the transmission screaming. The men were still lying where he'd left them.

"Where are you taking me?" the woman asked, when they were a few streets from the hotel.

"Bird Island. I have a house there. Just a second—I have to make a call." He made a brief call to Skelly on one of the cell phones he'd lifted from the thugs.

"I think you'll be safe there for a little while," said Marder in Spanish when he finished this call. "I'm Richard Marder, and, I'm sorry, I didn't catch your name, but I've seen you on television. The torso story . . . ?"

"I'm Josefina Mercedes Espinoza. Thank you for rescuing me, but if it's all the same to you, I'd like to contact my crew and have them pick me up. They'll be frantic when they show up at the Diamante and I'm not there."

"Okay by me, Señora Espinoza, but in my opinion it's better for them to be frantic than for you to be a torso on television, especially if someone else is covering your story. Which of course they would, if it was your torso. My place is fairly safe at this point, and you can call your guys on a landline and set up a secure retrieval."

They were crossing the bridge over the Río Viridiana. Marder kept checking the mirrors, conscious that the reporter was staring at him. A trio of SUVs had just appeared on the road behind them, driving in excess of the speed limit. Marder pressed more heavily on the gas.

"Who *are* you?" she demanded. "The police? No, Cuello owns the police. The army?"

"Not the army."

"No, because you have a slight accent. But you also sound like you're from Michoacán. You're an *American*?"

"Busted."

"Let me out of the car!"

"Don't be stupid, we're almost there." He turned off the road onto the causeway. The kid with the fruit was still there, and Marder gave him a wave. He slowed down on the narrow road, and as he rolled along he saw that someone had splashed the riprap on one side with small dabs of white paint at regular intervals.

"Who do you work for? The DEA?"

"No, I don't work for anyone. I'm a retired book editor."

"Really? I didn't realize book editors were in the habit of taking on three La Familia *sicarios* and rescuing reporters."

"As an editor, freedom of the press is very important to me. Why were they kidnapping you?"

"Or the CIA, maybe, hmm? What are you doing in Mexico?"

"Seeking tranquillity by the sea. That's my house up ahead."

Marder observed that the gate was closed, but when they approached, a young man whom Marder had never seen before opened it and stood aside, then closed it when they passed. Marder spotted a Glock pistol stuck in the waistband of his faded jeans. Skelly must have been busy.

"I heard about this place," said the reporter as they entered the front hall. "The previous owner disappeared."

"Yes, he was disappeared by a man named Servando Gomez. Do you know the name?"

"That's El Gordo. He's *jefe* of the plaza here. Why are you here, if you're not with a U.S. agency?"

Marder ignored her and shouted out for Skelly. Lourdes came out of the kitchen. She was dressed in a blue skirt, a short-sleeved white shirt, and new-looking sneakers. Her makeup was now restrained to a level more suitable for a schoolgirl, in Marder's view. That was fast, he thought, and then: she's really still a child inside that sexual flesh, and she could change back again tomorrow. Why am I responsible for this person? This was not part of the plan.

Lourdes said, "They're up on the roof terrace—" and then she saw Marder's companion and cried, "Oh, my God! Are you Pepa Espinoza?"

"This is Lourdes," said Marder. "She's a big fan. Look, why don't you two get acquainted—I need to see my friend."

Marder dumped the pistols and cell phones he had collected on a nearby table, jogged to the stairway, mounted to the second floor and then up a side stair to the roof terrace. He found Skelly by the front balustrade, kneeling by his long gun case. Statch was some yards away, looking out at the coast road with a pair of binoculars. She ignored her father.

"What in hell is *that*?" asked Marder. Skelly was screwing a tube onto one end of what appeared to be a gigantic weapon from a sci-fi movie. It was painted pale tan and looked to be more than seven feet long. It was supported at its center by a bipod and had mounted on it a long telescopic sight.

"It's a twenty-millimeter Anzio Ironworks rifle," said Skelly, as he arranged the thing so it was pointing out through the balustrade at the causeway below. "I figured we might need it if the guys you rescued your reporter from decided to come out here and get her."

"You always travel with a cannon?"

"Not when I fly—it doesn't fit in the overhead bins. You know, you should talk to your daughter. She's very upset with you."

"Why is that? Because I bought a house in Mexico without asking her permission?"

"That, and I think she's jealous of your paramour. You know, her mother dies, you jump into bed with your mistress, and, not only that, you buy her a house in her mom's hometown, where you refused to travel when her mom was alive."

"What!" cried Marder. "I didn't—I haven't—"

But these expostulation were now interrupted by a cry from Statch. "Someone's coming down the coast road. Three vehicles. They're turning onto the causeway."

Skelly dropped down to the deck and put the butt of his rifle to his shoulder. He said, "I think you'll want to get your Steyr up here. And plenty of ammo."

Marder thought of asking him what the plan was and then thought about ordering Statch off the roof but instead turned sharply and raced to his room, where he unpacked his rifle, stuck two spare magazines of 7.62-mm ball in his jacket pocket, and headed back to the roof. On the way he passed the reporter, trailed by Lourdes, who was admiring her at a respectful distance. The woman looked at Marder and his weapon and asked, "What's going on?"

"Just a small war. Why don't you stay indoors for a little while. I'll be back as soon as I can." He took off, followed closely by the woman, who was apparently not someone who stayed away from a war, small or large.

Marder dropped prone to the left of his daughter, who was to the left of Skelly and the Weapon from Outer Space. She was looking through the binoculars.

"Could you please go downstairs?" said Marder. "I don't want you up here."

She disregarded this and continued to study the approaching vehicles.

Marder looked through his own scope. Three green Lincoln Navigators were rolling toward the house. Now he understood what the paint marks on the roadside rocks had been for. Skelly had placed them there as range markers.

He heard a whirring sound behind him. Looking over his shoulder, he saw that Pepa Espinoza was crouched down and wielding a tiny video camera. Of course she'd be doing that. Tape at eleven. Statch noticed her too. "Is that her? The girlfriend?"

"No, of course not. I just met the damn woman!"

"I don't believe a word you say anymore."

At that moment came a bulky muffled sound, like a car door slamming. The cannon had fired.

Through his scope, Marder saw a large hole appear in the hood of the lead car. The SUV slowed, stopped, with black smoke gushing from under its hood. The middle car braked and slewed sideways on the loose gravel, clipping the rear bumper of the stricken car. The third car braked ten feet behind the middle car. A man got out of the middle car and began to walk forward. Through the scope, Marder could see that he was one of the two kidnappers, the one with the squint. He wants to find out why his guy stopped, Marder thought. He didn't hear the shot—he's thinking mechanical breakdown.

Skelly fired again, with a similar result. Smoke arose from the second car. Marder had seen the man on the road jump when the round struck. The man looked at the smoke and the huge hole in the car's hood; the penny dropped, and he ran to the third car.

Skelly said to Statch, "Darling, would you pass me that magazine of high-explosive incendiary rounds? That's right, yellow tops. Thank you." He took the heavy box Statch handed him, changed magazines, and chambered a round. Marder looked through his scope. The 20 mm fired again, and the last car, now reversing back down the road, lit up like a Chinese lantern and burst into flame. Men leaped out of it, some of them on fire, and plunged down the rocks into the water. The doors of the other two cars sprang open and men jumped out, more men than should have been able to fit in them. Marder thought it was almost funny, like the clown car in the circus. The not-funny part was that some of them had automatic rifles, and these began to fire in the general direction of the house.

"Lourdes!" Marder shouted. "Run down and tell your aunt and the kids to lie on the floor." The girl hesitated, unwilling to leave Pepa Espinoza for even a second, but then turned and vanished. The occasional bullet cracked overhead. Marder saw there was a porcine, stocky man down there with field glasses, apparently giving orders. Marder sighted on him, but he dropped down off the road before Marder could squeeze off a shot. He shot down two men firing automatic rifles, after which the other men took shelter behind the two forward cars. The trailing car was by this time burning hard, sending a column of black smoke up into the cloudless sky. Skelly fired an incendiary round into each of the other two cars, and these went orange as well, and the men behind them leaped off the road.

"They're in defilade down among those rocks," observed Skelly conversationally. "They could work their way toward us along the causeway and slip into the foliage down there and creep through the garden to the house. We should have mined the approaches and preregistered mortars all along the apron where the causeway meets the island. But you can't have everything. I tell you what, Marder, next time you want to start a war, let me know a little in advance. I'll lay a base coat down for you."

"I didn't plan to start a war," said Marder.

"Oh, yes, you did," said Skelly, but under his breath.

"Excuse me?"

Skelly sat up and leaned against a balustrade column. "I said, I was hoping you would introduce me to our new friend."

Marder did so.

"Aren't you afraid that they're moving forward, as you said?" asked Espinoza. She had shaken Skelly's hand politely, but now she raised the camera and turned the introduction into an interview.

Skelly looked lazily back at the wreckage he'd caused. "I don't think so. These are thugs, not assault troops. They're brave, but they're not paid for this shit."

And, indeed, the men were collecting their wounded and creeping back to the coast road, picking their way carefully along the riprap.

"Ah, victory is sweet," said Skelly, and stood up and swept Statch into his arms, bent her over backward and gave her a sloppy mock-kiss like in the famous photo of the sailor and the nurse on V-J Day.

"You people are crazy," said Pepa Espinoza. "La Familia has hundreds of soldiers. They have tanks, helicopters; they own the police. How will you fight that?"

They all looked at Marder, who placed his index finger next to his forehead and said, "I have a plan."

"What? What is your plan?" Pepa demanded.

"I am going to go downstairs and make a really big pitcher of margaritas," said Marder, and, placing his rifle on his shoulder, he walked stiffly from the terrace like a good tin soldier.

8

Marder was drunk. He was not often drunk—he didn't much like the woozies, and he suffered from post-drunk insomnia and hangover—but he thought that today was a special occasion, being the first time since the year 1969 that he'd shot and killed a human being. He'd been perfectly calm when he shot the gun thug at the attempted kidnap and calm when he squeezed off rounds from the Steyr (that hideous moment when the crosshairs of the scope rest on the target's vitals, and the shooter knows he has a kill, and he imagines, or Marder imagined, the final thoughts of the target, unaware that his life was about to end) and saw the men fall over in that cut-string marionette way they had. But after he'd walked away from the terrace, he shook like a set of castanets, tossed the rifle on the bed, and knelt at the toilet and tossed his lunch; he couldn't catch his breath. And he had another intense recollection of the last time he'd been in combat, sharp and vivid, as if the real life he'd had since then had been a dream.

They had argued, there in the command hooch at Moon River, about the scam with the fake Russians and the porters. Yes, they'd played it in different areas, but the NVA weren't stupid; they communicated. They'd be saying, "Who're those white guys driving those stupid Hmong? Who's the liaison with our command?" and they wouldn't find a liaison, they'd know it was a scam, and the next time they went out it'd be a massacre. Meanwhile, Colonel Honey was on the horn every day: When are you people going to finish my system? What is wrong with you, Marder, don't you realize this is the key to the whole war? And Lieutenant Handlebar was getting the same from his people up his chain of command. So, a lot of tension, with Skelly arguing that they had to be blown, that they should go out on the last mission at night and do the usual sneak play and emplace the last fifty or so voodoos that way. And he had prevailed.

Skelly volunteered to lead it, and Marder couldn't back out; not that he wanted to back out. The whole unit was psyched up by the prospect of finishing the mission and seeing how the new system worked. To Marder's surprise, Pinto Hayden also volunteered. Hayden said that he'd like to go because if they had another technician working they could get through it that much faster. There was a little silence and then Sweathog also said, "Yeah, what the fuck," and the lieutenant said, "Shit, we'll all go, we'll get another bird in."

The birds came, three Jolly Green Giants, and they almost scratched the mission because of the low ceiling, but it lifted later the next morning and they flew out to an old half-overgrown LZ on the east side of a mountain near A Yen, on the other side of which was a place where two main branches of the trail converged and it was therefore vital to sensorize. They flew in without incident, ascended the mountain, and Remained Over Night on the steep slopes, digging niches in the mud to park their exhausted bodies.

A chill mist covered the mountain as they descended the next morning. They were in three teams, each with eight montagnard soldiers, a Special Forces sergeant in command, a lone airman, and one LLDB along in case they needed to interrogate someone or confuse the enemy. Marder was in Skelly's team, walking just within visual range of Baang, Skelly's radioman, watching the sway of the big basket that contained their PRC-25 radio with the antennae rolled up and concealed. When they started out, they could barely see more than five meters and they kept bunching up for fear of becoming separated, and Skelly was trotting up and down the line calling out in a harsh stage whisper to keep their distance. Every so often the leading team, with Hayden and Pogo, would stop and they'd wait in silence, listening to the drip of water from foliage and the gurgle of the rushing stream whose gorge they were following. It was dangerous to walk down stream valleys— always a good place to get ambushed; it was safer to chop your way through thorn and bamboo—but for this mission they were taking the risk; they needed silence and speed.

As the morning wore on, the mist lifted a little, and Marder could see the line of men, maybe four or five in either direction, and he could see also that they had entered a zone of disturbed forest. Trees had been knocked over by blast and the area had been defoliated, which was how they knew they were close to the trail. The sergeants posted security teams and the airmen got to work, opening the little globes of the voodoos, turning them on, pinging the relays to ensure that they could communicate with the net, burying each in a shallow pit, and artfully stringing the antennae, rootlike, vinelike, around any conveniently upright vegetation.

That wasn't the memory. He really didn't recall the meeting in the command hooch, or Hayden or the others, or the flight in, or the overnight stay on the steepest slopes, or burying the sensors at the edges of the trail. He had reconstructed all of this tale out of supposition and from what Skelly had said over the years, usually when he was drunk; in other words, he had created a plausible fiction he could relate to himself and others, a literal war story.

What he actually remembered was:

The explosion. The disorienting sound, the soft whump of the shock wave a fraction of a second later.

Green tracer blossoming out of the gloom, the snap of rounds passing overhead. Screams, people running, shouting, and somehow more distantly the percussive pop of weapons firing.

Skelly grabbing at his rucksack, screaming in his ear to move, move, return fire. The cut-down grenade launcher being placed in his hand.

The acrid smell of propellant. A man maddened with pain, screaming God's name and obscene curses . . .

The sense of everything slowing down, of his body recovering from the paralysis of fear and perfoming simple operations—pointing the launcher, pulling the trigger, breaking open the smoking breech, inserting another fat sausage-like round; and again.

Taking cover behind an immense fallen tree, firing shotgun rounds at groups of men in green uniforms and pith helmets running by, seeing them fall, knowing he'd killed them, seeing one PAVN soldier raise his rifle and fire directly at him, and knowing, absolutely, irrationally, that he was invulnerable, that no bullet could kill him, the man shooting and the bullets flying overhead, and him struggling to get another round in the M79 and firing almost point-blank into the man, seeing his middle dissolve into a red jam. The man's rifle flying upward.

And the feeling. They talk about adrenaline, but Marder knew it was much more than adrenaline; it was a mystical cocktail that comes only from this one act, from killing men at the risk of yourself dying, a Pleistocene inheritance, disgusting and marvelous at the same time. Sports, even violent sports, were just a pale shadow of this. Why they'd never abolish war.

* * *

"Hey, buddy."

Marder felt a hand on his arm, shaking gently. Skelly's face was there, but strangely it was not covered in sweat and red dust. It did not have the unique expression melding terror, rage, and control that was Skelly's face in combat.

"You back with us?"

Marder shook his head violently and shuddered. "Jesus! I was somewhere else."

"Yeah, you were muttering and waving your arms around. You were scaring the girls."

Marder looked around. Amparo, Lourdes, and Pepa were standing frozen on the terrace, staring at him, looking like the decorative extras in an Antonioni movie tableau. He wondered vaguely where his daughter was.

"You ought to put away the pistol too, chief."

Marder stared at the gun in his hand—his father's .45—and dropped it on the table.

"How're you feeling, chief?" Skelly asked. "The margos going down pretty good?"

"I was back in the war," Marder said. "It was shooting those guys today. It was that firefight we got into in the blasted forest. When Hayden and Lascaglia got it. And we hauled Pogo out. I remember—I mean *really* remember it, but in flashes. I mean, I know what happened, but just now I . . . it was like I was there."

"What happened?" This was Pepa, coming over, offering to sit, getting the nod, sitting down, and pouring herself a drink from the seriously depleted pitcher of margaritas. "Marder here was having a flashback," said Skelly. "We were in Vietnam together."

"Really," she said. "A particularly stupid war, even among American wars."

"Yeah, but the part we were in wasn't stupid at all. We were protecting an indigenous people from a nasty regime that wanted to exterminate them, but somehow that cut no ice with the fine liberal sensibilities of the people who wanted us to leave. In the particular instance Marder is referring to, what happened, since you asked, is that a small party of Special Forces and montagnards ran into a reinforced company of PAVNs—North Vietnamese regular soldiers—who just happened to be in the area looking for just such operations as the one we were on. One of our people touched off a trip-wire mine, and we had a running fire-fight up a mountain."

"It was foggy," said Marder, "so we couldn't call for air support and we were out of artillery range. I thought we were dead."

"War stories bore me," said Pepa, "especially ones from lost wars."

Skelly ignored her. "Yeah, we were dead. A lot of us were actually dead by then. And then the wind picked up, the fog blew away, and a Spectre gunship that had been loitering in the area came zooming in and blew them up. There was no foliage and—"

Skelly stopped and looked off into the distance, as if had just remembered an appointment.

"—and I have to agree with the señora here. War stories *are* boring. I was going to take Statch around the island to look at some of the things we got going, she being a real live professional engineer. You want to come?"

"I would if I could walk," said Marder.

"Then I'll see you later," said Skelly. He nodded to the reporter. "Señora. I'll try to think up something more entertaining for next time."

"What a strange little man," said Espinoza, after a drink. "This is a good margarita. I'm surprised. What does he do, your friend?"

"He runs a security firm."

"That could mean anything. It's like import–export."

"True. But Skelly is unusually close about his business dealings. He spends a good deal of time in Asia."

"And you—you've retired from book editing, you said, and you're here to enjoy the sun and fun, taking the precaution of bringing an armory with you. Obviously you're under no obligation to tell me what you're really here for, but I would appreciate not being treated as a fool."

"I had no intention, Señora Espinoza—"

"In fact, if you're going to survive much longer in this lovely resort, you will require some information about the various players. Perhaps we could arrange a trade."

"Fine, but I'm sure my information is not nearly as rich and valuable as your information. It would hardly be a fair trade."

"We'll see. And call me Pepa, like everyone else does. Señora Espinoza is my mother."

"I see. And how *is* your mother, Pepa?"

"She's fine. She has a job in the Ministry of Culture and gives her old clothes to her maid. A model of socially responsible bourgeois womanhood."

"And your father. Is he also a model?"

"Yes. He's Cesar Teodor Espinoza."

"The architect?"

"That one. He travels a good deal and is generous to his wife and his several mistresses. No one could ask for a better father."

"I sense a tone of disaffected sarcasm."

"You sense correctly. I was raised in surroundings insulating me from the reality of my country. When I grew up, I decided to change that, to actually live in Mexico and not in the international icing that frosts its upper layers, and, if I could, as a journalist, to rub the faces of my class in the realities of their unfortunate nation."

"And how is the rubbing going?"

"Indifferently. It was scandalous when I became a telenovela actress, and, if possible, the scandal was doubled when I became a reporter on the narco beat. My mother's friends don't mention me to her anymore, as if I were a whore in the Red Zone. My father thinks it's amusing that I am playing at journalism and is always asking me when I'm going to forget all this nonsense and get married."

She finished her margarita, lifted the pitcher as if to pour another, then set it down with a metallic clang on the tin table, leaving her glass empty.

"I believe that is sufficient information about me. Oh, one other thing: I despise America. I despise your policies on drugs and immigration, the unconscionable hypocrisy, and I find that most Americans are exactly what one would expect from citizens of such a disgusting and destructive nation. Now, tell me why you are here in Playa Diamante. And no quotes from *Casablanca,* if you please."

"Well, that's a shame. I was going to open a saloon and call it Rick's. But you can call me that, since we seem to be on an informal basis now. Why am I here? The short answer is, my late wife was from here. I brought her ashes back here to be interred in the family crypt in La Huacana. Aside from that, I felt I needed a break. And, unlike you, I love my neighbor. I love Mexico, the top parts and the bottom parts. I love it as only an exile can love his country, even though it's not my country. I stole my wife from here, an act of selfishness I've always regretted, and so when I decided to retire, I chose to come here."

"You chose to come equipped like a small army, with an apparently deadly henchman in the 'security' business? And a cannon? I think you'll have to do better than that."

Marder laughed. "What can I say? Skelly attached himself to me without my invitation. You should ask *him* what he's doing here and why he brought his cannon along."

"Perhaps I will. Why did you buy this particular house?"

"It was on offer, and the price was right. A bargain, in fact."

She looked at him closely. "Interesting. You're lying about why you came but not about your reasons for buying this property. Let me ask you something: Have you been threatened at all since you came here? I mean aside from the events of today, which I suppose were directed at me."

"Yes. Early this afternoon some men came and told us to get out."

"Did you get their names?"

"Yes. Gasco and Crusellas. They said they worked for Servando Gomez."

"Well, in that case, you're in trouble with the Templos as well as La Familia. I wouldn't like to be your life-insurance company."

"And the Templos are . . . ?"

"An offshoot of La Familia. You know who *they* are, don't you?"

"The drug gang."

"More than a drug gang. A drug gang with religious pretensions, which is just what Mexico needs, another murderous cult justifying their crimes as ordered by God."

"Are they actually religious?"

"No one in Mexico is religious. Oh, there are some elderly ladies, I suppose, but besides that the Church has always been a racket to keep the people distracted while they're raped every day by their rulers. It's the same here."

"I'm religious," said Marder mildly.

She didn't seem to register this statement. "As far as La Familia is concerned, one of the early *jefes* got hold of some American evangelical's book of nonsense about how to be a heroic Christian man, and now they all read it and quote from it while they do their murders, which naturally are all defined as God's justice."

"These are the ones with the big crucifixes and the rosary bracelets?"

"Yes. The fine distinctions among the Christian sects elude them. In any case, one has to ask, why the current violence in a dinky little tourist town like Playa Diamante?"

"A rhetorical question, I hope."

Pepa sniffed and rolled her eyes. "About six months ago, the police killed Nazario Moreno, the *jefe* of La Familia, and there was a falling out among the subordinate leaders. Street signs went up all over the state, declaring that La Familia was no more and that the altruistic responsibilities of La Familia had been assumed by a group calling itself the Knights of the Temple—*Los Templos*—after the medieval order. Some of the plaza bosses went over to the new organization, and others stayed loyal to the original La Familia structure. Obviously, most of the action is up in Morelia and the north, but down here the big prize is the port at Cárdenas. That's where they import the chemicals they use to make methamphetamine, along with other dope from South America. The *jefe* of Cárdenas, Melchor Cuello, stayed loyal to the remains of La Familia. The *jefe* of Playa Diamante went over to the Templos."

"This is Servando Gomez?"

"Yeah. El Gordo, as he's known to his many friends. The rivalry between Cuello and Gomez is the root of all the recent killings around here. Of the two, Cuello is the most violent. They call him El Jabalí, the Boar. His trademark is the dumped torso with the crimes of the victim scrawled on the back in green marker."

"That's useful to know," said Marder. "What's the trademark of El Gordo?"

"The Templos display the head among a geometric arrangement of severed limbs, the legs on either side and the arms in a cross in front of the head. The eyes in the head are always propped open with toothpicks, and they stick a scroll in the mouth with the reasons for the execution. Another example of our quaint Mexican folk art."

"No torso?"

"In the sea, or so it is believed. In any case, all this theatrical posturing and violence is not the interesting part. The interesting part is the sociology and the economics. Sociology, because it is the ambition of every Mexican bandit to become respectable. This has always been the case. Every man in Mexico, in his secret heart, wishes to become a *chingón* and to render every other man the *chingada*. In order for this to become manifest to the whole world, however, he must have the young blond wife, the big house in Chapultepec, the yachts, the foreign vacations. But they cannot have these very easily or securely as long as they are *narcoviolentes*. So they must find a way to get out from under the burden of being gangsters, or at least to ensure that their sons do. These men are very indulgent of their sons. Having a son who is a handsome playboy is almost as good as having the blond wife."

"Do Gomez and Cuello have playboy sons?"

"Gomez has two, who go to an expensive high school in San Diego, where they drive hundred-thousand-dollar sports cars and date cheerleaders. Cuello's son, Gabriel, is right here. He has little interest in being a playboy. He likes being a gangster, and I'm sure it's a grave disappointment to the old man. He's known as El Cochinillo, the Piglet. But El Jabalí has several daughters being finished in Europe as we speak. He will have to be content with respectable grandchildren. Or perhaps not; perhaps he wants to make the transition in his present incarnation, like a bandito bodhisattva."

Marder grinned and thought he saw a little softening in the woman's severe expression. He wished to see her smile. "That's very good. You should try journalism. How is he going about this transition?"

"He's been investing. He's become a so-called partner in a number of legitimate businesses. He has interests in hotels, in agriculture, in shipping, in transport. He owns the cab company here and a bunch of bars and restaurants. He contributes to political campaigns and uses his people to rough up or kill reporters who write against his interests. And still the dope money comes rolling in, because the demand for dope in *El Norte* is insatiable—the only thing greater being the hypocrisy of your government—and therefore the cash position of his organization is increasingly perilous. It is hard, even in Mexico, to spend ten, twenty million a month without a declared source of income. So they must find a laundry for this money, one that does not involve traceable bank records. And what is the best kind of laundry? Do you know that, Rick?"

"Well, with the American mob it was distilleries first and then casinos. Vegas and so on."

"Casinos, exactly! Now, did you know that Playa Diamante was a marine turtle sanctuary?"

"No, I didn't. But I'm happy to hear it."

"Yes, every year in the summer and early autumn, the olive ridley turtles come up on this beach to nest, and therefore the beach frontage is closed to development. Obviously, Mexican zoning officials are eminently bribable, but environmentalists are watchful, and there would be an international scandal should new development be permitted. There is one exception, however, a large tract that was grandfathered in as a developable area when the refuge was established. It was an offshore island, and for some reason the turtles don't nest there."

Now she gave him the smile, which Marder thought was a good one, a charming one, although she meant it as malicious.

"You mean here? Isla de los Pájaros?"

"Exactly. And when two heavily armed American strangers arrive and immediately defend it against both the Templos and Cuello's people—"

"I didn't defend it against Cuello's people. I was protecting you. I had no idea that gangsters wanted to build a casino on my property."

She seemed about to say something, caught herself, and said something else: "And now that you know?"

"Now that I know, I will finish getting drunk. Then I will be hungover. Then I will decide what to do."

"What about me? How am I going to get back to my crew?"

"That's for you to decide, Pepa. We have plenty of bedrooms here, and you're welcome to stay as long as you like. Or you can go. This isn't a prison. Say, Amparo!"

He held the pitcher up to hail the housekeeper, who came over and took it.

"Could you fill that up for me again, dear," said Marder.

"Certainly, Señor," she said, taking it from him.

"Where is my daughter, do you know?"

"She is out in the *colonia* with Señor Skelly," she reminded him. "I think they are moving the well, as you ordered." She paused, regarding Pepa Espinoza, and asked, "At what time would you like to have your supper, Señor? How many will there be, and what would you like to have?"

"Roasted pig," said Marder. "And everybody will eat."

"Everybody?"

"Yes. Invite everyone on the property. There are plenty of pigs. I can smell them from here. And take the truck into town and buy beer. And mescal. And make a pot of *mole verde* the size of one of those clay planters. In fact, you can use the planter if you haven't got a big enough cauldron. Dig pits, gather mesquite wood, buy bags of cornmeal, give it out to anyone who can slap a tortilla. And let there be music!"

Marder didn't know how much all this would cost, but he didn't much care. The expression on Pepa Espinoza's face was worth every peso.

Statch stood spellbound in front of the forge where the blacksmith, Bartolomeo Ortiz, was putting the finishing touches on a massive drill bit he had manufactured out of an old crankshaft and sections of automobile leaf springs. She was reflecting on something remarkable—that in one week's time she had observed both the beginning and the end of the history of human beings making things out of metal. She gaped at the glowing steel on the anvil. As far as she could judge, it was a perfect artifact, a functional drill bit made entirely out of scrap and skill.

The drill itself was based on a motorcycle engine of some antiquity, dangerous as sin but perfectly suited to the task. Its cooling system was a kid with a water bucket and a ladle. Statch had appointed herself driller's mate, had made some trivial improvements in the rig, and now, with the new bit in place, she threw her weight onto the A-frame to keep it from shifting as Arsenio, the driller, put the thing in gear. It roared, it threw mud and lubricant, it drilled. She was as happy as a pig in shit, and no cleaner. In twenty minutes water gushed: cheers, she hugged Arsenio, then she helped him cap the gusher with a spigot.

She walked down to the far end of the village, where Skelly was supervising a gang using the Komatsu to excavate what was going to be the drainage field for the septic system.

"We have water?"

"We do," she said. "How's this going?"

"Great. It's amazing how some decent pay will turn these people into fucking Germans. No more *mañana* around here, no, sir! They'll bring the piping in tomorrow, courtesy of your dad. And now could you tell me why he decided to start his own Peace Corps in . . . you know, I'm not even sure what they call this place."

"Colonia Feliz, after the name of the house. I don't know anything about what my father does. He's always been a little secretive. Not as secretive as you—"

"I'm not secretive. Ask me anything. I'm an open book."

She laughed. "Yeah, right. As far as this place goes, I'm calling it midlife crisis, a bit late, but there it is. He hasn't been exactly stable since Mom died. You talk to him and he's somewhere else. But it's her home-town. Maybe he wanted to recapture the golden years or whatever."

"I get that," said Skelly, "but why this house in particular? On this site."

"What do you mean?"

"Check it out. It's a fortress. One causeway, the house commands all the eastern approaches; the beach side is overwatched by cliffs. We have our own water and a diesel. With enough food, and if we train up the guys we have on hand, we could hold off a small army. That can't be an accident."

"Is that why you brought your cannon? You were expecting a little war?"

Skelly became interested in the operation of the bulldozer and shouted some advice to its driver. "Mere coincidence," he said blandly, and she laughed again.

Now they became aware of heightened action in the *colonia*: kids running around, a man driving a small herd of pigs out of their pen, a pair of women carrying a large iron cauldron toward the big house.

Statch called out, "Yo, Ariel, what's going on?"

The boy stopped in mid-run. "The *patrón* is having a fiesta. I'm the messenger. We're going to kill pigs!" He ran off.

"Well, a fiesta," said Skelly. "A good way to start a war. Your father is a classy guy, when he lets himself be."

He walked over to the bulldozer and climbed up onto its seat.

"What are you doing now?" she asked.

"I'm going to go down to the causeway and push those wrecked cars off it."

"I'll come with you." She was filthy and tired but she didn't want this thing to end yet, this satisfying thing that she hadn't realized she desired, so different from the satisfactions of MIT and her life in Cambridge.

"There's only one seat," he said.

"I'll sit on your lap."

He grinned at her and made a welcoming gesture.

When she settled down and he shoved the joystick forward, he said, "A patriotic wet dream this is, a vibrating Statue of Liberty on my groin."

"Shut up, Skelly," she said without heat, and studied his motions as he guided the machine through the *colonia*, across the broad graveled drive, and down the causeway.

"This is like when you taught me to drive a stick. What was I, eight?"

"Yeah, your mother threw a pot at my head when we got back."

"Yes, and Peter was so jealous he didn't talk to me for a week. But she really liked you. I mean my mom."

"In a way," he said after a considering pause. "She liked me the way you like the pet that someone you love brings into the marriage. Basically, they were kind of wrapped up in each other."

"I guess," Statch said, a little surprised that Skelly had picked this up. He came on like the essence of brute insensitivity, but he didn't miss much. And what he'd said about her parents was a truth written into her life. They *had* been wrapped up in each other, and their children, although surrounded by love and every good thing, had understood from an early age that they were understudies in the Great Romance. Which was fine, really. They had developed early a kind of wild independence of spirit and had looked outside the family for the special flavors of love that their parents husbanded for each other: for example, the kind of gentle flirting that a father does with a daughter throughout girlhood so she knows she's attractive, potent, desired; all the small comments, the fond looks that become the foundation of a woman's deep confidence. Marder had tried, she understood that, but he didn't have the energy: Chole was a full-time job for him. So Statch had got most of that over the years from the man she was sitting on right now.

"Hop off now, kid," he said, bringing the Komatsu to a stop in front of the first of the wrecks. She did so and watched as he efficiently shoved the SUVs off the causeway and into the sea. It was no surprise that he could operate a bulldozer. Skelly could do a very large number of practical things, many of which (besides driving a stick shift) he had taught her over the years: how to be silent in the woods; how to hide; how to shoot, skin, and butcher a deer; how to clean a fish, a rabbit; how to ride a motorcycle; how to jump out of an airplane; and what guys, at least guys like him, looked for in a woman. It was probably no accident that the men she favored were more Skelly than Marder. Marder had taught her how to sail a small boat and how to shoot a pistol and about the uses of imagination. He was the one who told her stories. Skelly didn't tell stories. She had asked, many times, but she still had not heard his version of what he and her father had experienced in Vietnam. After the cars were gone, she made him let her drive the bulldozer back up the hill.

Marder could only assume that his fiesta had proceeded accordingly to plan, for he remembered little of it, or about as much as he recalled of that firefight on the Ho Chi Minh Trail. Small vignettes had been somehow recorded through the blear of alcohol.

Two men carrying a sheet of plywood upon which the meat of two dismembered piglets sat smoking; Skelly, stripped to the waist, feeding mesquite fires at the pits, grinning at him from a smoke-blackened face, like a devil; Amparo standing in the cool center of chaos, giving orders with magisterial calm, as if she was used to serving a hundred people at a moment's notice; the music of the mariachi band, with the costumes and sombreros, guitars and trumpets, and dancing to its music with his daughter, and with Pepa Espinoza, who noted that it was a cliché, who wanted to know what he thought he was doing, who disapproved of him, but who still danced with him, whirling in the colored lights; the colored lights shaped like little peppers—Amparo, again, had conjured them out of somewhere. Had he kissed Pepa Espinoza, or was that part of the dream?

He recalled giving a speech. Bartolomeo Ortiz, the blacksmith, a man he now understood was the mayor of the *colonia*, had called on the musicians to play a fanfare and in the ensuing silence had spoken simply and directly, thanking Señor Marder for this wonderful fiesta. Then Marder had to speak in response, and he had spoken, saying that he was gratified to have the privilege of hosting such wonderful people and that unless he was killed he would guarantee that the Colonia Feliz would exist and thrive forever. As he spoke, Marder sought out the faces of the three people he was most interested in. His daughter looked worried; Pepa Espinoza wore a sardonic grin, her head gently shaking in disbelief; Skelly had a grim and determined expression.

How it ended, or how he had returned to his bed, he did not know. Someone had undressed him to his shorts and covered him. In any case, there he now was, with sunlight slatting in through the closed shutters. He raised his head from the pillow, yelped, and dropped it down again. It was impossible to move with that head, yet he had to have water or die. And, indeed, some kind soul had left a bottle of water and a bottle of aspirin on the wicker table at his bedside. He washed down two aspirin and finished most of the liter.

He was engaged in the newly complex task of pulling on a pair of chinos when there came a light knock on the door.

"Yes?"

The door opened to reveal young Epifania in her blue school uniform. "Señor, my mother says to tell you there is coffee ready, if you care to come down, and she has made fresh *bolillos*. Also, Señor Skelly says to tell you that the army has arrived. And they have a tank."

9

"That's not actually a tank," said Skelly. Marder, dressed and with a cup of Amparo's excellent coffee in his hands, was standing with his friend on the roof terrace of his house, while Skelly studied the approaching column of vehicles through field glasses. "It's a Panhard Lynx, a budget-friendly armored vehicle suitable for midsized armies whose major opponent is likely to be its own population."

"It looks like a tank, though," said Marder, "and that's a pretty big gun."

"Yes, it's a ninety millimeter. I suggest we surrender."

"I agree. Where are you off to?"

Skelly paused at the head of the stairs that led down into the house. "I think I'll head down to the *colonia* and see about the septic field. I'm sure you can handle an armored assault all by yourself."

There were four trucks and a Humvee following the Lynx like obedient ducklings. As Marder watched, they drove in through the open gate, parked on the gravel, and spewed soldiers in battle dress, armed with assault rifles, while the Panhard moved to one side, knocking over some planters, and sat there. Marder could hear the sound of its turret and elevator motors as the long tube of the gun swiveled around to point at the front door of the house.

He turned away and moved rapidly downstairs to the kitchen. Amparo was sitting there with her two children by her, on her face the familiar expression the war photographers love to catch.

"Amparo, take the children to your house and wait there. I will talk to these soldiers and then I'll drive the children to school. Go now!"

Marder went to the front door and opened it, then went to the kitchen and poured another cup of coffee.

The soldiers entered in combat formation, weapons high. They shouted at him to get down on the floor, which he did, and then they bound his hands with plastic flex. He waited for some time, smelling dust and floor wax, listening to the sound of soldiers rummaging ungently through his house.

Then two soldiers picked him up by the arms and took him into the dining room. They placed him in one of the chairs. There was a plate of *bolillos* on the table, still giving off their delightful odor.

An officer came in and took a seat across the table from Marder. He was wearing a camo uniform with the brass star of a major and the pale-gray band that indicated he was a member of military intelligence. He seemed young for a major, mid-thirties perhaps, and Marder was glad to see that the eyes set deeply into his thin, angular face had a bright and curious expression.

The two men stared at each other for a long minute. When the major spoke, his voice was low and cultivated. He said, "Señor Marder, I've looked into your background, and what I find there surprises me. I'm curious as to why someone like yourself should have come here to Playa Diamante and immediately become involved in the operations of not one but two dangerous narcotics-trafficking gangs. Perhaps you could enlighten me."

"With pleasure, Major," replied Marder. "I purchased this house and the surrounding land both as a retirement home and as an investment property. This is a common event in Mexico, I believe, and is not discouraged by your government. I had no sooner taken possession than some men arrived and ordered me to leave. They showed weapons. I was able, however, to disarm them and I sent them on their way. Later, I was in town, at the hotel, when I observed a kidnapping in progress. Happily, I was able to thwart it and escaped here with the victim. A little after that, three vehicles full of armed men arrived and fired automatic weapons at my house. Again, I was able to discourage them and they left."

"I see," said the major, with a smile of the type conferred on small children when they claim that their dollies come to life at night. "And how, exactly, did you accomplish this discouragement?"

"A colleague and I returned fire. It is the right of every citizen to defend his home, I believe."

"Yes, it is. You know, I command a unit that is part of the effort of our president to eliminate the domination of drug gangs in this region of Mexico. In many parts of Michoacán, as you may be aware, civil government has entirely collapsed. The municipal authorities and the local police are either bribed or murdered, and the gangs rule. This cannot be allowed to happen, and so the army has been sent in to restore law and order. I have seen many odd things in my time here, but I was not prepared for the report that three vehicles belonging to La Familia had been destroyed by a cannon. This struck me as a dangerous escalation of violence, and so I decided to investigate. Have you any comment?"

"Yes. There was no cannon involved, only an exceptionally powerful rifle. I am what we in America call a 'gun nut.' I collect weapons of various calibers, which I daresay your men have already located, and one of these was involved in discouraging the invaders."

The major opened his mouth to speak but was forestalled by a shriek from the upper parts of the house.

"Get your hands off me, you pigs! Bastards! Homosexuals!"

"My daughter," said Marder. "I trust your men are not accustomed to abusing women, Major."

The major stood, shouted an order to one of the soldiers—a sergeant—standing by. The man snapped a quick "Yes, Major, right away!" and ran out.

"Who else is in the house, Señor Marder?"

"My daughter, as I said, and my friend Patrick Skelly, and the victim of the attempted kidnap, Josefina Espinoza."

The major's thick eyebrows rose at the mention of this name. "Not *the* Pepa Espinoza, surely."

"The very same. I believe La Familia objected to some of her coverage of their war. Major, my wrists are uncomfortable. Could you . . . ?"

The major snapped his fingers and pointed, and a soldier came over with a knife and cut Marder free.

"Thank you, Major. I hope you're now satisfied that—"

"What the hell's going on, Dad?"

The two men turned and observed the entrance of Statch Marder, dressed in shorts, a stained T-shirt, and a bad attitude, accompanied by the sergeant and two embarrassed-looking young soldiers.

Marder rose and put an arm around his daughter. "The major here was just trying to determine if this household was a danger to the peace and security in the state of Michoacán. I believe he's almost ready to decide in the negative."

The major looked back and forth between father and daughter, with somewhat more attention on the daughter, whose T-shirt was thin and revealing of what it covered and who was exhibiting an extraordinary length of leg below her very short shorts.

The major smiled. "There is the matter of the cannon."

"The rifle, actually. Major, let us not fence. I understand your position. This land is mine. I intend to stay here. The gangs want me to leave. They want to build a casino resort on this island and dispossess me and the people who have come to live here. This I will not allow, and I have the means to resist them, I hope. I also hope that the army will see me as an ally and not as a menace."

At this moment, Pepa Espinoza walked in. She was dressed in a terry-cloth robe that had obviously come with the house, her hair was wet, and her eyes were flashing mad.

"Well, Major Naca, we meet again," she said to the officer, who stood and lost his smile on seeing her.

"Señora Espinoza. Always an enchantment."

"Your men practically dragged me naked out of the shower."

"I regret the inconvenience, of course."

"Oh, please don't! It will fill the second paragraph of my story. The headline will be—let me see—ARMY ABUSES DAUGHTER OF WEALTHY AMERICAN INVESTOR. The subhead—'Beachside Residence in Playa Diamante Assaulted by Tank.'"

Major Naca's face darkened. "There was no assault and no abuse, Señora. As you well know."

Marder moved to stand between the reporter and the soldier. "That's right. It was a simple mistake, of the type that often occurs when soldiers are charged with civil operations for which they are not trained or equipped. I was once part of such an operation some years ago, in Indochina, and so I can appreciate the major's difficulties. Innocents are roughed up, property is damaged, and so on. But I believe there was not much harm done in this case, and I believe that the major is perfectly satisfied as to the nature of this household and will soon be on his way."

Their eyes locked briefly, then a little smile played on the major's lips.

He nodded, turned, snapped orders to his men, demonstrated his good manners by taking formal leave of the household (but without apology), and in ten minutes the soldiers were gone. The Lynx in leaving collided with a large jacaranda tree by the gate, shaking down a blizzard of violet blossoms that briefly covered the road like an imperial carpet, until the following vehicles ground it into pulp.

"That was nicely handled, Marder," said Pepa Espinoza when the door closed behind the last trooper. "I admire your skills at negotiation. It was not what I had expected from a book editor."

"That shows how little you know of the New York literary scene. I would much rather face a Mexican intelligence major than a literary agent pushing for an unreasonable advance. And, in any case, you were the critical factor. Even the army quails before the power of the press. I'm sure he would have torn the house down and hauled us all off to prison had it not been for your presence. Now, for almost the first time, I'm glad I saved your life."

She pasted an unpleasant aggrieved expression onto her face, which Marder thought was a relic of Mom, and then, to his relief, she laughed. He hadn't heard her laugh much, so it was like seeing a rainbow, joyful.

"Are they all gone?" This from Skelly, who strolled in from the kitchen holding a cup of coffee.

"Yes, you missed our writhing under the military boot. Where were you?"

"At Chiquita Ferrar's. I was stashing my cannon in her pigpen."

"I've never heard that particular euphemism before," said Statch. "Did you just make it up?"

"That was a *literal* description, dear. She's a lady of the *colonia*, married, four children. Her husband is in our employ, and we ate some of her pigs last night." He asked Marder, "How did you ditch the army?"

Marder told him, and Skelly gave Pepa an appraising look. "You're going to be a useful guest," he said.

"I'm not going to be a guest at all. I have to be back in Defe for a taping day after tomorrow. I'm going up now to get dressed and call a cab."

"I wouldn't advise that," said Marder. "As you told me yourself, Cuello owns the cab company. I don't think his drivers are going to take you to the airport."

It was clear to him that she had never thought of this possibility, and he wondered how the woman had stayed alive this long. A look of panic started to gel on her face, so he said cheerily, "I have a much better idea. I promised Lourdes I would take her to Defe if she stopped being a pain in the ass, and she has—so far—so we'll *all* go to Mexico City. We'll charter a plane, preferably not one owned by La Familia. You, me, Lourdes, Skelly—Statch, you're welcome too. We'll take Lourdes for her shopping trip and to launch her career as a big star."

"Sounds great, but who's going to provide security?" said Skelly. "There's a single two-lane from the foot of the causeway into town, and they have people watching it. You can see them from the roof. I mean, we could take your truck and maybe blast our way through, but that's a little risky. Or we could buy that boat we were talking about and take it to the Cárdenas marina, but then we'd have the problem of getting from there to the airport. Cuello probably has the port sewed up and, as you just said, cabs are out."

"So what do we do, security man?" Marder asked. "I defer to your wisdom."

"My wisdom says we had some guys here yesterday offering us protection and we turned them down. Maybe we should reconsider."

"You mean the Templos?"

"Why not?" said Skelly happily. "That's their business, after all, and they're already at war with La Familia. I think you should get in touch with Servando Gomez."

Marder smiled at the reporter. "And I bet Pepa here can tell us just how to do that."

"I can. But how are you going to get to where he is? Cuello will have hawks out watching the road."

"He'll have to make a house call," said Marder.

A white SUV arrived at the *casa* by arrangement the following afternoon, and two men got out of it.

One was very large, over six feet tall, with a belly that must have made it hard for him to see his feet. His head was shaved bald, and he wore a rectangularly trimmed mustache so deep and wide that the thing resembled the working surface of a small shoe brush. He was in his mid-forties, Marder estimated, with eyes as black and unfeeling as a shark's. Although he was fat, he did not look soft; rather, he seemed to be constructed of a dense solid homogenous substance, like beeswax, and, like old beeswax, he had a tawny smooth surface. He had two chins and jowls, but they didn't jiggle like jowls.

This must be El Gordo, Marder thought, and he could not suppress a thrill of fear. The man had committed, or ordered committed, countless murders and acts of torture, and Marder was entirely at his mercy just now. Then he recalled that his best friend had probably killed more people than El Gordo had and also (and this thought was never entirely absent from his mind) that he might die anyway at any moment when Mr. Thing popped, so what was he worrying about? He felt an idiotic little smile appear on his mouth.

The other man was smaller, a lot smaller than El Gordo, so that it was nearly comical to see them together, as in an old-time vaudeville act. He had a flat brown *indio* face with a scar under one of his dark eyes, and his hair was neatly trimmed into a military-style crew-cut, with faded sides. Marder thought at first that he had deep crow's-foot lines extending out from his eye sockets, but then he saw that it was tattooing, a line of tiny teardrops that reached almost to his ears on either side. Both men were wearing dark suits and white shirts, and both wore heavy golden crucifixes on thick gold chains.

Marder met them at the door. "Don Servando, it's good of you to see me. I believe I owe you an apology."

Both men stared at him.

"Yes, when your representatives came to my house, I sent them on their way with a card, carrying the meaning that I was not a man to be trifled with or easily discouraged. I hope there won't be any hard feelings because of this misunderstanding. I believe that we can in fact do some profitable business together, and I have two proposals in mind. Please come into my house."

He led them through the living room to the terrace and seated them at a table under an umbrella. There was a big bucket full of ice and long-necks on the table. Marder offered, but they both refused.

"Coffee, then?"

"What do you want, Señor Marder?" said El Gordo.

Marder said, "You may have heard about the attack on my house the other day by elements associated with La Familia."

El Gordo nodded. "Yes. I heard you used a cannon. I would have liked to see that."

The voice was surprising, a soft, cultivated voice. Marder remembered something that Pepa had said, that Gomez had been a schoolteacher before being sucked into the general *narcoviolencia* of his region.

"It was an interesting event. And it has some bearing on the second of my proposals. But first things first. You already know that I'm not what I appear to be. If you were to check, you would find that I was a book editor in New York, mildly prosperous, a model citizen. But I am not entirely that person. During the Vietnam War I was involved in highly secretive activities in Laos and subsequently maintained certain contacts that I made there. Tell me, are you familiar with the name Van Mang?"

One of El Gordo's bushy eyebrows rose a fraction of an inch. "I've heard the name."

"Yes, I thought you might have. So you probably know that General Van controls the production of heroin in the northern Laos area of the Golden Triangle. He gets his opium paste from Myanmar through Khun Sa's old network and ships the refined product out through Bangkok and south China to be couriered by air to America and Europe. The general, however, now desires to avoid the many middleman fees and official payoffs required by this routing. He would like, for example, to transship his product overland to Shenzhen, say, load it into a container, and deliver it to some organization in America. He has been shopping around for a distribution organization since the Chinese gangs were broken up over the last few years. So that would be the first opportunity—would you like to distribute General Van's high-quality heroin?"

"How would it come in?" asked El Gordo. "It can't come through Cárdenas port. Cuello has that tied up."

"Yes, I know. But he doesn't have Playa Diamante yet, and that brings me to the second part of this proposal. General Van also has a supply of weapons excess to his needs. I mean heavy weapons—ex-Soviet, ex-Chinese—and plenty of ammunition. This is the kind of machinery you can't get through straw purchases in Arizona gun shops. I'm talking 12.7 machine guns, rocket launchers, assault rifles, grenades, even mortars if you want them. As I understand it, La Familia outnumbers the Templos three to one, not to mention the other cartels just waiting until you kill each other off so they can move in. If you had such weapons, no one would be able to touch you. The *army* would barely be able to touch you. So, does any of this interest you?"

Gomez nodded. The other man stared silently at Marder as if trying to look into his head.

"The weapons interest me more than the heroin, to be frank," said Gomez. "And what interests me more than either of them is your property here on Isla de los Párajos."

"Yes, you want to build a casino here. But the fact is, I don't care to vacate the property at this time. I intend to develop it."

"As a casino?"

"As a craft cooperative, shipping ceramics, metalwork, textiles, and paintings to the U.S. market. You might be interested in participating in such a venture. I'm sure it'll be highly successful. Michoacán crafts have not been well-represented abroad, I'm afraid. I'm sure they'd sell like tortillas in a famine."

"I don't think so. I would prefer to have the casino. In fact, I think I will have to insist on it."

"Don Servando, with all due respect, I believe a certain flexibility is called for here. There are any number of half-legal casinos along this coast, in Acapulco, in Puerto Vallarta. Buy one of those if you need a casino. What I am offering you is, first of all, the assurance that Cuello will not have Isla de los Párajos and, second, the opportunity to make a good deal of money in heroin and, third and most important, the means to dispose of your rivals and defend yourself against all comers, now and in the future. It's the chance of a lifetime. I need not mention the fact that, should you turn me down, my principal will likely order me to make representations to La Familia, or to the Sinaloa cartel, or to the Zetas."

"If you live." This came from the thin *indio*.

Marder slammed his hand down on the table. "Oh, shit! *If I live?* You still seem to believe you're dealing with one of your little local businessmen or some small-town mayor. All right, go ahead—shoot me, or chop off my head, or whatever you like, but within a week after you do, a rocket-propelled grenade is going to come through your door, and a heavy machine gun is going to spray the wreckage. Have some flexibility of mind, Don Servando!"

A little staring contest here. Then El Gordo said, "What was your general thinking for the product?"

"Forty a kilo. This is the quality that's going for two hundred in New York and L.A."

"Still, forty thousand's too high. I'd have to pay ten a kilo to the

Arellano Felix organization to move it across at San Ysidro, and beyond that they usually lose at least ten to twenty percent to the narcs."

"You wouldn't have to use Arellano Felix or any other transporter."

A small smile appeared on the waxy face of El Gordo. "I'm not sure you understand the complexity of moving product in bulk. The Arellano and the other transport contractors have networks they've built up over many years: mules, drivers, vehicles, payoffs. That's why they're used, and that's how they earn their ten thousand a kilo."

"Yes, but you would have our craft cooperative. Every week, trucks would depart carrying pots and boxes of fabrics and statues, metalwork, whatever. Brightly painted trucks, with *indio* drivers. At odd times, the crafts would be packed in bags of your product. You wouldn't need mules swallowing condoms, and you wouldn't need Arellano Felix. Or the casino."

"How do you mean?"

"I mean, let us say that Juan the potter ships forty pots a month and gets paid for forty pots, but we invoice four hundred very expensive pots to fictitious merchants who send the organizers of the cooperative nice clean checks from American banks. And what is more innocent than helping poor Mexican craftsmen sell their work on the world market? Whereas, everyone knows that a casino in Playa Diamante would be a money laundry. You would have the *fiscals* in your hair from the first day."

"An interesting proposal. I will consider it."

"Good. And I'll send you a list of the weapons we can supply, although I believe General Van would prefer to do business exclusively with the buyers of his China White. Be that as it may, I have another item of business that would be a personal deal between the two of us."

"Oh?"

"Yes. Right now you provide protection for various parties in the region, and in the normal way of your business you are protecting them from yourself. I understand that, but what I would like to propose is that you provide actual protection to me and my associates. None of these good things that we're discussing will come about if I'm assassinated or if I cannot move freely about the area. Obviously, I would pay any reasonable amount for this service."

The other man spoke up. "Five thousand a week. Dollars, not pesos."

Marder looked at the man. "And you are, Señor?"

El Gordo said, "I should have introduced you. This is Mateo Reyes. Señor Reyes handles security matters for our organization. I presume you have an associate with similar duties?"

"Yes," said Marder, hiding his elation now. "His name is Patrick Skelly."

"Well, then, we should arrange for Señores Reyes and Skelly to meet."

"What happened then?" asked Skelly. They were sitting by the pool after Gomez and Reyes had departed. Chickens clucked in the streets of the *colonia.* Green parrots were making a racket above and dropping fruits from sapodilla trees onto the tiles of the terrace.

"I said I would arrange it, and then we all had a drink. Reyes said something about security services being payable in advance, and I pulled out my roll and peeled off five large. Then Gomez stood up— Christ, the guy is a truck! He must be six-three, three twenty at least. And he shook my hand and said he'd be in touch, and I asked him if he had my number, and he nodded and said, 'You've already sent your card, Señor Marder.' And then walked out."

"Good, then it's all set up. I get the impression he was more interested in the guns than in the dope."

"Probably he has enough product of his own."

"Yeah, but nobody doesn't like China White; it's like Sara Lee. He'll go for it."

"He'll *go* for it? Patrick, I agreed to this scheme because you said it was the only way the Templos would provide security and let us move around freely. I asked you at the time about how we were going to handle the fact that we have neither weapons nor China White. Now we've promised a gangster we're going to get him guns and high-end heroin. And our next move is . . . ?"

Skelly gave him a strange look. "Our next move is to obtain the dope and guns, what do you think?"

"I mean seriously."

"I'm *being* serious," replied Skelly. "And don't look at me like you're a girl who just saw her first dick. How did you expect to survive in this place and do whatever it is that you came down here to do? Which, by the way, we haven't had a discussion about yet. You wanted me to arrange security. In my professional opinion, this is the best way to do it."

"Right, but I thought we could just pay for it."

"You mean like the pool service? It don't work like that, chief. Why the hell did you think I gave you all that stuff about General Van and the weapons and dope?"

"I don't know," said Marder, "to generate an air of authenticity, to come on as a tough guy?"

"And it never occurred to you that this gang of mass killers would be, let's say, *annoyed* with us if we didn't deliver?"

"So you're suggesting that you can actually deliver this stuff?"

"Oh, yeah. I can deliver the dope. You wanted to set up this crafts deal anyway. As far as the weapons go, we'll see."

"Oh, Gomez won't like that. His beady eyes were shining when I talked about the weapons."

"Marder, think this through. If I have the kind of stuff I'm talking about in hand and the time to train enough of our *colonia* guys to use them, I couldn't give a shit about what Señor Gomez likes."

"You're starting a war."

"We're *in* a war, boss. I'm only escalating it so we can scare off the big dogs, make it more trouble than it's worth to get rid of us. Or we can just pack and go back to New York—your choice."

"I'm staying."

"Wonderful." Skelly finished his beer and rose. "Meanwhile, I got to get busy on the sat phone and set up contacts for the Mexico City trip. And find a plane. And buy a boat."

10

By that afternoon, there were two Templo trucks at the foot of the causeway, and when Marder drove his pickup out, they fell into formation, one in front and one behind. The Las Palmas Floridas Hotel was smaller and dingier than Marder remembered, but whether that was time, or neglect, or the absence of the bright varnish of youthful romance, he could not say. The flame tree at the entrance still stood, but now without its pool of bloodred petals. The fountain that had played and sparkled in the front courtyard was now dry and littered with food wrappers and plastic cups.

The lobby was dark and cool, as he remembered it, but there was a musty, greasy smell that his wife's parents would not have tolerated when they ran the place. A fat youth sat behind the desk with his feet up on a crate, reading a *fútbol* magazine. He looked up without interest when Marder walked in, then returned to sport. The tables in the little restaurant were the same, even in the same positions on the floor, but what he recalled as a softly glowing polished hardwood floor had been covered with cheap tiles in an annoying chemical blue. The brass wall sconces were still in place but bulbless, smeared with greasy cobwebs, their light replaced by a long fluorescent fixture screwed into the plaster ceiling. The dining terrace was deserted except for some small yellow birds picking crumbs off the unswept tiles.

Marder went in and sat at what had been his usual table. The plastic tablecloth had not been wiped in a while. He looked to the doorway where he had first caught sight of Soledad d'Ariés. Suppose it were possible, he thought, to return to this very spot on the earth's surface, to insert into the consciousness of his former self the history of the years that followed that first blast of infatuation. Would the youth he'd been divert his course? Probably not. He hadn't been able to greatly affect the lives of his own children, or so it seemed to him. No, if Marder now had appeared like the Ancient Mariner to Marder then and prophesied disaster, if he had appeared to the two of them in their passion and said in the thick voice of experience, Don't do it, kids!, they would have laughed.

Or, no, *he* would have laughed; she would have looked at the old specter with that wonderfully limpid look she had, deep seriousness in her eyes with that clear spirit shining out, and she would have said, Yes, I believe you, it will be a disaster. I believe my father will never speak to me again if I run off with this penniless gringo; I believe I will never see my mother again if I do, but still I do it. If it is my fate to die for love, prepare the grave! She could, in fact, say things like that, things that sounded right in Spanish but that no one would have believed if spoken in the English of America, that sensible, dispassionate, calculating tongue; and she did say such things, in her native language, throughout her marriage to him, and he had learned that language too.

So he never understood that he had torn her out by the roots. She kept that knowledge from him, and she made him believe that when she went mad in New York—which was not that often but violent when it came—it was because he had failed in perfect love, and he strove always to do better. He thought that to be flogged into passion was better than not having passion at all, better than being slightly dead, which was what he'd felt like when he came back from Vietnam and married in haste to poor Janice, then drove off south on the Harley.

And it had not been an illusion; it had not been a frosting of romance on ordinary life. No, the romance had gone down to the core; their life had been an opera—a comic opera, perhaps, full of transcendent emotion, ridiculous from the outside, but not from within. He'd developed the grand gesture; he brought her flowers and jewels he couldn't afford, vacations at the beach—ditto—and trips to Europe and Asia, to every place but Mexico. The point was the extravagance, the absurdity of a guy on a salary buying his beloved such things, a dozen gardenias in the dead of a New York winter because she'd mentioned that she missed the odor of gardenia that used to float through the window of her room when she was a girl.

Which was why, when the Apple fortune came in, he'd kept it from her, so that those gestures would retain their extravagance. It was his only secret from her, except for the one sad little affair.

Her secrets from him were more serious than that, as he knew now. He hadn't known about the drugs, that she'd been treated for depression for years. She'd never told him, she'd taken that secret with her off the snowy roof, and he'd had to piece it together later. There was a hidden journal, used infrequently, mere jagged impressions set down at odd moments amid the translated poetry. The hideous shame, for example— he hadn't known about that; the ache of exile, the insults borne. Because in New York, when you see a Latina woman with a couple of obviously American kids, she's a nanny and treated as such in our great democracy. He hadn't understood the hope that her father would relent, that as he aged he'd mellow, that he would call for his daughter to be at his side and they could return to Playa Diamante, that she could one day care for her parents as a daughter should. He'd had no fucking idea about any of this.

And it might have worked out, had Esteban de Haro d'Ariés not been a proud man, a descendant of *peninsulares*, Spaniards of the purest blood, or had he not lived in Michoacán during that particular historic juncture, when the mafia peace was broken and the drug wars blossomed in the streets, or had he not refused to sell his hotel to a certain *jefe* of La Familia. But such in fact was his fate. Therefore, one Sunday morning, he and his wife had entered their modest sedan—modest, for Esteban d'Ariés had refused the silver of La Familia—and had driven off to church.

On the way, a car had forced them to the curb, and Don Esteban had been dragged out at gunpoint. His wife had bravely attacked the kidnapper and been shot down for her pains. Silver or lead, as they say in Michoacán, and he had chosen lead, which had been duly delivered. Some of that lead, metaphysically speaking, had flown north of the border, an invisible illegal immigrant, and entered the heart of Maria Soledad Beatriz de Haro d'Ariés Marder, killing her too, also metaphysically speaking.

This Marder believed, for when she returned to New York from the funeral (and she'd insisted on going by herself, for how could she bring him, the gringo demon lover, the *cause*, when you came to think about it, of this disaster), she was a changed woman. At first he thought it was the shock of losing both her parents to the violence, but months passed, then years, and he discovered that he was married to a different person. It was just the two of them by then, the kids off at college, and the evenings of silence were exceedingly long. She stopped working, she watched television—American television, no less—she stopped cooking, or dressing. He urged therapy; she refused. But then she did go, secretly, for the drugs. She took them; she became calm. But as far as he could see, she was no longer Chole, the love of his life.

Marder caught a movement in the corner of his eye and there she was, dressed in the pale-blue dress with the white apron she always wore when she served. He thought: Mr. Thing has popped; blood is flowing into my brain and I'm having hallucinations, and now she'll come over and kiss me and take me to heaven, where it will be explained what happened, why she left me with a living corpse like she did, and how much of it was my fault. Or maybe not to heaven, considering the events surrounding her death. For a second or two a smile spread on his face, and then reality focused its malicious lens. The waitress was a thin slattern with a sour expression, and her apron was not perfectly white, crisply ironed, but limp, stained. She asked him what he wanted, and he ordered a coffee and an empanada to get rid of her.

She came back with muddy, thin coffee and an industrial pastry still glowing from the microwave. After a bite and a sip, he shoved a hundred-peso note under his plate and left. It was clear one did not come to Las Palmas Floridas any longer for the cuisine or the service, and he wondered how it managed to stay in business. As he approached the front desk, he found out. A gentleman, clearly drunk, clearly a foreigner (red-haired, chubby, middle-aged), was checking in with a young woman teetering on four-inch platforms; she wore a halter top made from a silk scarf and a skirt that barely hid her round, high buttocks. Marder watched them depart, swaying, clutched together, with giggles in two languages.

He asked the clerk where he could find Angel d'Ariés. The man shrugged and picked up his *fútbol* magazine. Marder snatched the magazine from his hand and asked the question again and was embarrassed by the brief look of terror that crossed the poor man's face. He stuck a hundred-peso note in the magazine and gave it back, and the man made a movement with his head toward a door marked OFICINA.

Marder was no stranger to this room. In his day it had contained an old-fashioned rolltop desk with pigeonholes, a glass-fronted bookcase, two wooden filing cabinets, a swivel chair, two bentwood chairs seconded from the bar, and a horsehair couch, upon which the young Marder once delightedly, clandestinely, rolled with the girl of his dreams.

This couch was now occupied by Angel and the two chairs by a pair of young louts, *ni-nis* without question. They were watching three people fucking on a large wall-mounted screen, which hung in the place Marder remembered had once been occupied by a glassed and framed representation of the Virgin of Guadalupe. The room stank of marijuana smoke and stale tequila.

All three looked up when Marder entered.

"Hello, Angel," said Marder.

"What do you want?"

"I want to talk with you. Could you turn that thing off and ask your friends to give us a few moments?"

Angel did nothing, only stared at the screen. His face was colored by the reflected writhings, a sickly pink like a skin ailment. Marder moved to block the screen and addressed the louts. "Gentlemen, if you would?" he said, and made a courtly wave of his arm that swept back his jacket and showed them the butt of his pistol. They looked to Angel for direction, and he made a gesture and said a few words that enabled the two to rise and strut out without loss of their pathetic honor.

When the *oficina* door closed on them, Marder pointed his finger at the porn and Angel lifted a remote and made it stop. Marder said, "Angel, do you know who I am?"

"Yeah, you live in the big house on Bird Island. I heard you were connected and we're going to do business with you."

"I don't mean that. I mean I was married to your sister."

A puzzled look appeared on his face. "To Juanita?"

"No. To Soledad. She left a long time ago, with me. You were a little kid, maybe five or six. You're looking confused—you never heard anything about Soledad? I mean from your parents, or neighbors, or relatives?"

A shrug here. "No, not really. Oh, I get it—that's why you asked about my father when we were at the Guzmán house. I wondered about that. Yeah, Soledad—I sort of remember her, but she was a lot older, and there weren't any pictures, and my father got pissed whenever anyone in the family mentioned her name. I guess I thought she was dead a long time ago."

"She is dead, but recently," said Marder. He wanted to get out of here, away from this obscene parody of a place that had lived in his mind for nearly forty years as a kind of gateway to paradise, like the place where Dante first caught sight of Beatrice.

Angel shrugged again. Marder asked him, "How did you come to work for the Templos?"

"It's in their zone, you know? Before that I was in La Familia."

"Even though they killed your parents?"

"My mother was an accident. The guy that did it was taken care of."

"And your father?"

"He made his choice."

"And you're comfortable with this? Running a hot-sheet hotel for gangsters? This is your life?"

"What the fuck do you care? You're a gangster yourself, from what I hear."

"I care because you're my *cuñado*. Family is supposed to be important. And also, when I look at your face, I see part of her. You may not remember her, but she remembered you. She sent money and packages for your birthday and Epiphany. She never got anything back."

Angel's face grew more tender when he heard this, as if a lost person was trying to come out from behind the thick shellac of the thug. "Truly? Shit, I never knew that," he said. "You know, come to think about it, I found some pictures after my folks died. I got them here someplace."

He got up, rummaged in one of the file drawers, and drew out a flat black cardboard box. "Here's the only one with her in it."

Marder took it from him. It was a large-format studio photograph of the whole family, in the formal pose favored years ago by Mexican families of a certain status. There was Don Esteban seated in a large chair, with Carmela, his wife, standing at his right side, their children Juanita and Angel stood on either side of their mother, and on the other side of the father's throne was the eldest daughter, Maria Soledad, glorious in her innocence.

Nasty animals clawed at Marder's gut and raked his throat. He said, or croaked, "Angel, can I borrow this?"

A final shrug. "Fuck, you can have it, man. The Templos are my family now."

* * *

"So, old home week didn't work out, I see," said Skelly when Marder returned.

"Is it that obvious? I remember him as a bright, pretty little boy and now he's a skanky thug running a whorehouse. He gave me this."

Skelly looked at the photo. "Ah, *la familia d'Ariés*. That is one pretty miss, my friend. Although, in fairness, I'd have to say she was not a patch on our Lourdes."

He started the truck and they began the drive back to the house.

Marder studied the photo some more. Yes, her nose was too large for perfection, her face had not the perfect oval, the eyes were smaller than they should have been. And yet even in this photograph you could see the living poety there, the perfect integrity of a wonderful soul. Which Lourdes, he thought, did not have, and which was what had wrenched his heart when he'd first seen it; he thought it still would have, whatever the size of her nose.

"Speaking of Lourdes, what's the story with this trip? You're going to buy her clothes and get her in the telenovelas?"

"That's the plan."

"Huh. Well, that's funny, because I didn't figure you for short eyes."

"Oh, you think I'm buying a sixteen-year-old a bunch of stuff and helping her out because I want to fuck her."

"You don't? God, *I* sure do. And she wants it too. Some little pistolero is getting all of it these days, or that's what it looks like."

"What do you mean?"

"She's taking off that chaste school uniform and slipping into the tube top and hot pants and sneaking out at night with some dude. Looks to be late twenties. Giggling in the chapparal, and a blanket down on the beach under the cliff. Little cries of delight. Pretty horny-making, as a matter of fact. I almost had to cover my ears."

"Well, it's her life," said Marder after a pause. "She's not my daughter."

"He says wistfully. Your rescue complex is kicking in again. You need to watch that, chief. Many don't want to be rescued, and a lot of the ones who want to can't be."

"Yes, and you speak as a fellow sufferer, I know. In any case, fuck it. It's Mexico."

Marder's actual daughter was at this moment standing disconsolately outside the smithy of Bartolomeo Ortiz. She'd been there since this morning, trying to make herself useful in the hand manufacture of ornate door hinges and wrought-iron chandeliers, but the blacksmith had indicated by increasingly gruff responses that she was not welcome to help at the forge.

She wandered away down the main street of the *colonia,* through what looked ever more like a permanent construction site and miniature industrial area. She could hear the distant sounds of the bulldozer flattening brush and clearing land, and, closer, the whine of power saws, the rumble of the diesel generator, the whir of potters' wheels, the clack of looms, and throughout the expanding settlement the peculiar clink of concrete blocks knocking together. New residents were arriving hourly, it seemed, for these people all had cheap cell phones and they had been quick to inform their friends and relatives that a crazy gringo was giving away homesites and money and funding start-ups for anyone who had crafts to sell or labor to contribute.

She entered the pottery workshop of Rosita Morales, an open shed roofed with rusty corrugated steel and even hotter than the hot street outside. Statch could see the heat coming off the kiln in wavy ribbons; its bright yellow eye gleamed in the shadows. Rosita was at her kick wheel, throwing a pot, and Statch watched as what looked like a cow plop morphed in the brown, slick hands into a pot: delicately walled, round, tapering, elegant.

As always, Statch was fascinated by the fact of making, of the human ability to turn nothing into something beautiful and useful. This whole experience is important, she told herself, this is going to make a difference in what I do with my life. But at the moment she could not tell how.

"Where did you learn to do that?" she asked the woman.

"My mother," Rosita said, as she took the finished bowl and placed it on a rough plywood shelf with the other unfired pots. "And my grandmother taught her. We've always been potters in my family, from way back, way back before the Spanish, when we lived up by the lakes."

Statch was looking at a line of glazed ware, pots of different sizes, each designed for a traditional purpose, for some particular domestic task, and each glazed with an original design of iridescent black figures against matte white—a woman grinding corn, a raven, a squash blossom. We don't really do this anymore, she thought, decorate our tools like that—we would think it kitschy to stick a picture of a flower on a Cuisinart—but this is just a kind of delight in making common objects beautiful. We still have it, but we call it design, and it's not the same thing at all.

"My mother used to sell pots like this in the market at Guadalajara for fifty pesos. *El patrón* says I can get a hundred dollars for one like this if I sell to the *comuna*. Do you think he was serious?"

"I'm sure he was. These are works of art. I've seen pots not as good as these for sale in New York for two, three, four hundred dollars in fancy shops."

Rosita shrugged. "It seems crazy to me. They're just pots. You can help me now if you like. I'm going to load my other kiln, and the girl who usually helps me went to Cárdenas today with her cousins."

"I'd be glad to," said Statch.

"Yes, you can do this work, because, you know, it's proper for women. But stay away from the forge. They say if women are around, it weakens the metal."

Statch's jaw gaped for a moment and then she laughed inwardly. She thought, Girl, you are a long fucking way from MIT.

Three hours later, hot, dusty, and besmirched with clay, Statch went back to Casa Feliz. As she passed the front of the house just beyond the gate, she saw a line of people waiting patiently in the scant shade of the ornamental trees. Amparo and a young man she hadn't seen before were talking to the first man in the line, an *indio* in worn jeans and a clean but ragged T-shirt. He was showing Amparo a wooden carving. Statch waved as she passed into the house, and Amparo waved back distractedly. The young man looked up, smiled, a flash of white against dark skin, and then wrote in a notebook.

Statch went to the kitchen to get a cold drink. There was a large, middle-aged woman, another stranger, stirring a pot, from which entrancing *mole*-ish smells arose. Her name, it turned out, was Evangelista, and she was a cousin of Amparo's, brought in from Apatzingán to help with the housekeeping, since Amparo was now too busy with setting up the *comuna de los artesanos* to keep up with it all. Statch commented favorably on the sauce, grabbed a beer from the refrigerator, went to her room, took a fast shower, and donned a tank suit.

She swam. She had to do twice as many laps, because this pool was shorter than standard Olympic size, something of a pain but at least she got to practice more turns. She recalled the last time she swam so, back at MIT, and how she was thinking about her father and what he'd been up to; now she knew, but she was more concerned about him than she had been in her ignorance. Coming here was strange enough, but what he was doing here, the engineering specs behind it all, were still obscure, as were, she now realized, her own reasons for staying on. She'd seen him; he was healthy and no crazier than he was before. He was shooting people and getting shot at—not the usual plan for a midlife crisis—but it was his life. She was not ever going to be the kind of daughter who infantilized her parent out of some misbegotten guilt.

She did a hundred laps, not bothering much about her time, focusing on perfecting the turns. After the final lap, with her limbs burning and her breath coming in gasps, she slid in her usual dolphinesque way up on the edge of the pool. As she sat there, recovering her breath, someone handed her a towel.

It was the young man who had been standing with Amparo at the gate. She took the towel and wiped the water from her face and looked at him again. He had, she now observed, a young man's look and carriage, but there were fine lines on his brown face that indicated he was not quite as young as he appeared. He was wearing worn jeans and a white short-sleeved shirt, and he had sunglasses pushed up over his crow-black coarse *indio* hair. He smiled delightedly at her and said, "That was quite a performance. I've never seen anyone swim like that."

"Well, I practice a lot," she replied. "Do I know you?"

He held out his hand. She took it. It was warm and rough. "You do now. I'm Miguel Santana."

"Carmel Marder," she responded.

She noticed he was looking intently at her, but she didn't pick up what she normally felt when an attractive man stared at her, as, for example, Major Naca had. Santana was looking at her face and not her nipples, which the cooling of evaporation had caused to berry out through the thin nylon of her Speedo suit. She stood and wrapped the towel around her and sat on the side of one of the lounge chairs. He followed and perched on the edge of another.

A moment later Pepa Espinoza walked onto the pool deck, wearing a short terry robe and a bikini that was remarkable for both the brightness of its colors and its exiguous dimensions. Statch thought that women of Señora Espinoza's age should not wear such outfits, but she had to admit that she carried it off well. The reporter nodded briefly and went off to the other end of the pool. She took a cell phone out of her straw bag and tried to make a call. Statch noticed that Santana's eyes had not followed the reporter's progress across the deck. Gay, perhaps? Or only polite?

"Was that you I saw with Amparo a while ago?" she asked. "Out by the gate?"

"Yes. With all the people coming in here from the countryside and La Cielo, she's a little swamped."

"So you're like the administrative assistant?"

"Something like that. I've got some experience managing things, and she asked me to help with assigning homesites and registering names and figuring out who can do what. I mean the crafts. There's actually a strong craft tradition in the area. The Tarascos were fairly isolated until recently, and their traditions are more or less intact. And we have a number of migrants from Oaxaca."

"The Tarascos are the Indians?"

"Yes, including me, as a matter of fact."

"No kidding? You know, I'm embarrassed to say this, but you're the first Indian I've ever met. I mean aside from the ones from India, who're all over the place where I come from. But you got an education."

"I did," he said, but in a tone that did not encourage inquiry.

Pepa Espinoza let out a vile curse and tossed her cell back in the straw bag. She had discovered the unreliability of cell service at Casa Feliz. She pulled a laptop out of the bag and began to type.

"And what do you do when you're not organizing a craft commune?" Statch asked.

"I work at San Ignacio."

"Where's that?"

"It's the church. Here in Playa Diamante?" He grinned at her. "You're not a Catholic, I'm assuming."

"Oh, but I am. Baptized, confirmed, and everything. My father's a pillar of the Church."

"But you're not."

"No, I ditched it when I was thirteen. I decided to believe in facts."

"Yes, that too is a very ancient religion. What do *you* do when you're not in our beautiful town?"

"I'm in grad school at MIT. I'm an engineer."

In Statch's experience, this admission tended to stop conversation, except if the other person was similarly engaged in engineering. But

Santana's faced flashed an interested look and he said, "That's wonderful! It must be a terrific thing to be able to do, build and design things. What kind of engineering are you studying?"

She began to talk and, amazing herself, she kept on talking: about her work at MIT and Schue and her team, and her problems with the Escher machines and her gigantic breakthrough and what it meant and how she had apparently thrown it away to come here, and why she stayed and watched manufacturing by hand and how it made her feel. And she talked beyond that, about her life, and the swimming, and why she didn't have the champion's edge, and what that meant, and about her emotional life and why that didn't seem to be working out so well either. And about her family, her dead crazy mother and her father, and how she felt that there was something she had to *do* so that her father didn't go down the crazy tube too. She hadn't had an intimate conversation in Spanish for a long time, but she used to all the time with her mother, and she found herself telling him things she could not have readily articulated in English.

The sun crossed the terrace as she talked. Pepa Espinoza swam briefly and left. The children came home from school. Amparo brought out a tray of taco chips and salsa and a tin bucket filled with ice and local beer, and still Statch talked, now beyond embarrassment, pouring it all out into the remarkable, depthless black eyes of Miguel Santana. Throughout he had asked few questions and had not (remarkably, him being a man) offered a word of advice, yet she found herself wishing for his approval and feeling, as she recounted some of her life's more outrageous incidents, an unfamiliar sense of shame.

When the sun began to dip behind the roof of the house, Santana looked at his wristwatch and said, "Unfortunately, there is something I have to do."

"Throw up from boredom?"

He didn't smile. She felt a brief embarrassment at the remark and reflected upon how often she did this, made a silly joke to dispel the burden of sincerity. "Not at all," he said. "I enjoyed hearing about your life. It's so different from my own experience. I have four sisters, and all are married and living within a few kilometers of where they were born. You're a remarkable young woman." He held out his hand and she shook it. "Well, I expect I'll be seeing you again." He smiled. "In church perhaps." He left.

She went back inside the house, changed into shorts and a Hawaiian shirt, and followed the sound of voices to the kitchen. The voices were loud and angry and belonged to Lourdes and her aunt. When Statch walked in, she saw that Epifania and Ariel were sitting at one end of the long table, apparently doing homework, in the extreme quiet mode that children adopt when their elders are behaving like children. Amparo and Lourdes were standing by the kitchen doorway, clearly in the midst of some confrontation, flashing eyes and flushed faces much in evidence. They fell silent when Statch entered.

"What's going on?" she asked.

Lourdes said, "She says I can't go on Monday. She's stupid!"

"I'm stupid? I'm not the one who's failing in school." Amparo turned to Statch. "The school called me today. She hasn't even been going half the time." She made a helpless gesture with her hands, and Statch saw that she was close to breaking down. "I can't do all these things, all these *new* things, and keep up with her."

"Who asked you to?" shouted Lourdes. "You're not my mother. And when I'm on television no one will care if I can do geometry."

Some more shouting back and forth ensued, until Marder walked into the room.

He took in the scene and asked Amparo what was going on. She told him, and when Lourdes tried to butt in, Marder stopped her with a look.

"Lourdes, I suggest you go back to your room until dinner. We'll talk about this later."

Statch watched as Lourdes transformed into a little girl under Marder's gaze and left the kitchen without another word.

In the silence that followed, Evangelista, who had been working invisibly throughout, said, "Señor Marder, when would you like supper and how many will there be, please?"

Statch stared at her father, surprised and a bit dismayed. The familiar, gentle, humorously casual New York liberal dad she'd known all her life seemed to have vanished and been replaced with a Mexican patriarch. She was not at all sure that she liked it.

* * *

On Sunday they all went to church; Skelly joined them, and drove too. Amparo and her family rode in the back of the camper, and the red truck led a convoy of rattletrap vehicles, all of them jammed with people in their best clothes. Front and rear, the convoy was guarded by Templo gangsters in pickup trucks bristling with automatic weapons. Of the inhabitants of Casa Feliz, only Pepa Espinoza declined worship. Statch almost did the same but forbore in memory of her mother, who, though scarcely a believer, had brought her two children to church on every required occasion, out of love for Marder. Statch expected only the usual and predictable tedium, but in the event discovered three surprising things.

The first was the church itself. On the outside, San Ignacio was an ordinary, somewhat clumsy whitewashed adobe shell, but inside it was unlike any church that Statch had ever seen. Instead of the lugubrious nineteenth-century statues and paintings she had expected, the interior walls shone vivid with color. Murals in the local folk-art style depicted Biblical scenes peopled with Indians in the white cotton clothes, straw sombreros, and striped serapes of a former age, and the statues were hand-carved, brightly painted suffering saints and prophets made by people who understood suffering: a pietà, a San Sebastián stuck with arrows, and—huge, behind the altar—an enormous crucifix with the body of Christ hideously twisted, nailed to a heavy, raw-wood cross with great cast-iron nails, spouting pints of gore from the Five Wounds.

The second surprise was Skelly, placed on the other side of her father, going through the usual motions, making the required responses with every indication of sincerity, although she knew for a fact that Skelly was as pagan as a Viking and an aggressive mocker. She couldn't quite understand it: again, perhaps something in the water, or was he, like herself, just deferring to her father?

The church was about two-thirds full with women and children, but there were men too, hard-faced guys with tattooed teardrops on their faces. That was interesting, she thought, and wondered briefly about what the spiritual life of killers might be like.

As was her habit on the few recent occasions when she'd found herself in church, Statch let her mind drift away from the ritual to the contemplation of herself and her affairs. She thought she might be having some kind of breakdown, the sort of collapse that sometimes affected driving, hyperambitious people. She knew former classmates, people who'd propelled themselves through high school into top-flight colleges, then into the best grad school programs, and then, in what should have been the epitome of their careers, simply vanished. One girl had hanged herself; others had taken off for communes in the country, or for India, or gone sailing around the world. And here she was, living with her father, who had gone nuts in some way she couldn't quite figure out yet (but she would, it having become a point of pride), in the middle of a kind of civil war, in her mother's hometown. How weird was that?

The priest was talking about the prodigal son. He said most people identify with the bad son, the runaway, because it's easy. You do bad, you get forgiven. But most people aren't like the bad son—they're like the good son. They want to know how come the wicked prosper, how come *they* get to eat the fatted calf. They're full of resentment against the father and full of envy, and their danger is much subtler, because the bad son knows he's bad and seeks forgiveness, but the good son thinks he's good and doesn't, and so the devil gets him.

Statch was attentive to the homily, although its message went in one ear and out the other, because she did not believe in any morality beyond you-can-do-what-you-want-as-long-as-you-don't-hurt-anyone. The priest looked rather different in his green robes and his sacerdotal face, but it was clearly Miguel Santana: the third surprise.

"You didn't tell me you were a priest," she said to him in mock accusation as he stood at the door of the church after the service.

"You didn't ask," he said, "but you must have known, or else you wouldn't have made such a good confession."

"I wasn't *confessing*. Aren't you supposed to be sorry for your sinful behavior and promise to refrain from it?"

"And weren't you?" he asked, giving her a peculiar look that made her drop her eyes and change the subject.

"That's quite a church you have there. Whatever happened to the weepy old statues?"

"Burned in the revolution. The priest back then, Father Jimenez, was something of a genius, I'm told. He let the revolutionaries have all the bad-taste stuff, then turned the church into a museum of folk art and organized the people to decorate it with traditional designs and sculpture. He opened a sort of craft school too, and when the agriculture collapsed and people were starving, he got local people who retained the traditional crafts to teach kids. That's why you've got so many people in your *colonia* who produce excellent work. By the time the secularists caught on, the place was a national treasure, and after the revolutionary zeal died down, Father Jimenez quietly started to hold services, and here we all are."

He seemed about to say something else, but Statch drew his attention to a ragged man standing in the doorway of the church, clearly waiting for the priest to finish. The man wanted to have a rosary blessed. Father Santana solemnly performed the small rite; the thin brown peasant thanked him briefly and then vanished.

"It must be nice to have supernatural power," Statch observed.

"One would think so," said Father Santana, smiling again, "but one would be mistaken. I'm sure you know enough theology not to make an error like that."

Marder walked up and shook the priest's hand. He complimented him on his homily and added, "It must be hard to be a priest in a region where murder, torture, and kidnapping are the order of the day. How do you handle it?"

"I don't, usually. I perform services for the dead."

"You don't speak out against the violence?"

"No, I don't."

"Are you afraid?" asked Statch.

"Not personally, no. But if I did speak out, I would be assassinated instantly, and then for a long while there would be no one to perform services for the dead. I see you're disappointed. Well, the fact is that the Church spent most of its history working in communities where murder and rapine were far more common than in Michoacán today. Any of the Angevins or the Sforzas, not to mention the average conquistador, could have eaten La Familia for breakfast. You may have noticed that the church was full of Templos and their families, whereas La Familia's religious orientation is somewhat different."

"Some kind of muscular Christian cult, I understand," said Marder.

"Christian only in that they still murder people in the name of God," said the priest, snuffing out his smile. "And may God forgive us all."

11

The ride to the airport was uneventful, probably because Marder's camper truck was accompanied by two SUVs and a pickup full of heavily armed men. El Gordo was delivering protection, which made Marder feel a little less like a fool. Lourdes was chattering away without letup to Statch, who was being more tolerant of this babble than Marder would've credited. Pepa was also chattering nonstop but on her cell phone, clearly delighted to be at long last back among the airwaves of civilization. The plane Skelly had chartered, from one of the apparently limitless legion of "guys he knew," was a King Air 350, a twin-engined turboprop that would make it from Cárdenas to Mexico City's Juarez International Airport in a little under an hour, and was apparently innocent of any association with La Familia. The plane was configured for twelve; they were five—Marder, his daughter, Skelly, Pepa Espinoza, and Lourdes Almones—and so they were able to sit where they pleased. Marder pleased to sit in the wonderfully luxurious seat next to Pepa Espinoza.

"What are you writing?" asked Marder. It was twenty minutes into the flight, and while he had attempted the usual conversational gambits, he had received nothing but short, impatient answers.

"A book," she replied, tapping skillfully at the keys of her laptop. He sighed and looked past her face at the terrain below, the green-clothed mountains of the Sierra Madre del Sur. They were at twelve thousand feet or so, far too high to make out any detail, but the country seemed devoid of any human mark. It was similar in that respect to the mountains of Vietnam. It looked like an uninhabited, unbroken green cover but was deceptive, for below the undulating emerald duvet lay a whole civilization and armies at war.

"What's it about?" he ventured.

"It's about the nastiness and perfidy of your country, Mr. Marder. It's what every book written by a Mexican must necessarily be about. It is our one miserable, inescapable subject."

"Which aspect of the perfidy? There are so many."

"The drug wars. Are you aware of how this monstrous business began? No? Of course you aren't; you are bathed in righteous innocence, like all your nation."

"Why not tell me? It would pass the time and abash me."

Again that almost smile. Charming! She said, "Fine. Well, when the Second World War broke out, the Japanese cut off your supplies of opium from the Far East. The American government prevailed on Mexico to establish vast plantations of poppies to supply the morphine needed in the war. After the war there was no need for the Mexican opium, and all the farmers in Sinaloa and Michoacán would have been ruined had they not begun to grow for the illegal trade. And, naturally, as in all of Mexico, what is illegal is a source of profit and political deals. The eternally ruling party, the PRI, came to an understanding with the drug lords. The *caciques* of the party each had his relationship with the local mafias. Things barreled along very well until your government became *shocked* by the flow of heroin to the United States and put pressure on the Mexican government to suppress the opium farmers, so all the fields were sprayed, using equipment generously supplied by the gringos. The peasants were ruined, but the gangs went on to other things, importing and transshipping cocaine and meth and, of course, tons and tons of marijuana. Now, at around this time, *El Norte* became displeased with the state of Mexican democracy. A one-party system? It assaulted the fine sensibilities of Washington. Other parties were encouraged, secretly or not, and so the PRI state collapsed and now we have in half the country a regime, or series of regimes, based on murder, extortion, and kidnap, funded by money from the United States and armed with automatic weapons courtesy of your constitutional right to bear arms. That's what my book is about, Mr. Marder."

The color had risen to her cheeks as she spoke, and her hazel eyes were sparking. He had heard all this before, from his one beloved, and so it was more like a love song to him than the diatribe she intended.

"I have nothing to do with the drug policies of the United States. I deplore them, in fact. And, as I think I've mentioned before, I consider myself just as much of a Mexican as I am an American."

"No, you are a gringo of the purest type. Who asked you to come down here and interfere with the lives of our people? I see you organizing, directing, bullying, spreading dollars around so you can feel good about yourself: Oh, look at me, I'm *helping*!"

"Are you sorry I helped *you*?" he asked mildly.

She opened her mouth to reply, snapped it closed, and her face darkened again, but not in anger this time.

She took a breath and said, avoiding his eyes, "Yes, I'm being a bitch. I beg your pardon. I *am* grateful, but . . ."

"It irks you to be beholden to an American?"

"Yes. It irks me very much."

"If I may say so, that seems uncharacteristically illiberal for someone of your cast of mind. You surely don't approve of Americans generalizing about all Mexicans. And as I told you, I consider myself as much a Mexican as I am an American."

"That's ridiculous. You've never really lived here."

"On the contrary. I spent the last thirty years living in a Mexican home. It was in Manhattan, but as soon as the door shut it was Mexico. We spoke nothing but Spanish. We ate mainly Mexican food. We watched Mexican media and went to church in Spanish. I have a very substantial familiarity with Mexican culture, including literature and poetry, almost all of which I've read in the original. My children are perfectly bilingual and bicultural. It's true that I'm not *profoundly* Mexican; I'm not a tortilla and *pulque* peon, I'm not a *pelado* in a barrio, but neither are you. In fact, I'd venture to say that if we sat down and had a *ranchera*-singing contest, you might not win."

"Fine, you've convinced me. You're a Mexican. Just as a matter of curiosity, did you beat up on your wife and run around with younger women?"

"I was unfaithful, yes. Once. But no beating. We were insanely in love for nearly the entire time we were together."

"*Maricón!*"

Marder laughed. "So you don't care for Mexican men either. A bad experience?"

She shook her head, shuddering like a horse, and now she looked him in the eye. "Look, Marder, what do you want from me? I said I was grateful for what you did, and I am. But we don't have a *relationship*. That thing about if you save someone's life you're tied together forever is only in the movies, okay?"

"Why don't we have a relationship? Do I disgust you physically?"

"Oh, Jesus fuck! I don't know who you are or what you're doing. For all I know you're some kind of gangster yourself. You certainly don't handle a gun like a book editor, and I've known a few. Or, worse, you're a rich guy with a guilty conscience and some crackpot ideas about how to save the poor of Mexico. And, as long as I'm being frank, I think it's appalling what you're doing with that little girl."

"Lourdes? What do you think I'm doing with her?"

"You're feeding her fantasies of becoming a television star. It's terribly cruel and I have no idea why you're doing it."

"You don't think she's beautiful enough?"

"She's exquisite, for an *indio* peasant. She doesn't know how to move or talk or dress, and even if she could be taught, her skin is three shades too dark. I'll tell you what her film career will be like, Señor Expert on Mexican Culture. If she spreads her legs for the producer and the director and the assistant director and the assistant director's best friend, she will get a walk-on part as a maid or a nanny, and the only lines she'll say are 'Yes, Señora,' and 'Right away, Señor.' If she's extremely clever, which by the way I don't see any evidence of so far, she'll be the girlfriend of a star or semi-star, kept in a tiny apartment in Polanco until she gets boring or ages out. After that, high-class call girl, then a low-class call girl, and then, if she's really lucky and hasn't died from drugs or abuse, she'll be back in Playa Diamante as a fifty-year-old waitress."

"I don't believe it," said Marder. "That's just *no importa madre* and unworthy of you. Why in hell are you risking your skin to tell the truth about what's happening here? Because you believe things can change even in timeless Mexico. Things *are* changing. And even if you're right and she's doomed, it's still a good thing if once in her life a completely disinterested person does something nice for her. She thinks expensive junk will make her happy. I intend to buy her all the expensive junk she can handle, and maybe she'll find that expensive junk isn't what life's about. Who knows? Maybe she'll learn to act. As I'm sure you know, Mexico City has more theaters than practically any other city in the world. Maybe she won't fuck the producer, or turn whore; maybe in ten years she'll be with a nice guy and doing Lope de Vega or Felipe Santander in a side-street playhouse in Coyoacán and very happy. And, yes, it's Mexico, the land that consists entirely of the fucker and the one who is fucked, but it's not actually a requirement. I mean, it's not written on the passport, *chingón* or *chingada*, and in fact there are millions of Mexicans who don't believe that either. My wife was one. And I'm sorry you have that view of life. You must be unhappy a lot of the time."

"I'm *not* unhappy," she snapped. "What the hell gave you the idea I was unhappy? I'm at the top of my profession. I'm a reporter for Televisa, for God's sake!"

"The camera certainly loves you."

"What's that supposed to mean? That I'm a bimbo?"

"Of course not, but clearly you're sensitive to the accusation, and that's why you're writing what you hope will be a serious book." He pointed to her laptop screen. "Which it may well be, but judging from what I can see here, you're going to need a good editor."

"Oh, go fuck yourself, Marder!" she cried. "Why don't you go sit somewhere else? The fucking plane's half empty."

True, but it was also a small, quiet aircraft and she had not toned down the volume of her last remarks. Marder saw Skelly's eyes appear over the back of his seat and then Statch's face poking out into the aisle. Skelly's look was antic; Statch's, worried.

Marder said, "I will, if you want. I'm sorry to have disturbed you so much."

He sat next to Skelly, who said, "Shot down in flames. I'm going to have to give you some tips, chief, or you're never going to get into those pants."

"I wasn't trying to get into her pants."

"Really."

"Yes. To be honest, I was lonely. I miss Chole and I thought I could have a little intelligent conversation, possibly of a literary nature, with an attractive and intelligent and *literary* Mexican woman. And I embarrassed myself. I forgot that a certain class of Mexican looks on Americans very much like Americans look on . . . I don't know, who's the lowest, most vulgar, most violent scum on earth?"

"Mexican drug gangs?"

"Like that. Russian oligarchs, African kleptocrats. Hedge fund criminals. Anyway, beneath contempt, and white American middle-class people aren't used to that, especially from a people they've been taught to think of as producing nannies and fruit pickers."

"But Chole—"

"Yes, Chole was different. She communicated at the level of pure spirit, lucky for me. Her father was a different story, an old-school Mexican aristocrat, and extra-spiky because he wasn't a *hacendado* anymore; he was running a second-class hotel in a second-class beach town, and he thought I was taking advantage of his—well, you know all that. But she *reminds* me of Chole in a lot of ways. The intelligence, the fire, even her face and the way she carries herself. It got under my guard and I made a fool of myself."

"I don't know, Marder. She was traipsing around the pool in a bikini that could've fit into a cigarette pack. I think she's hot and she wants people to know it. Maybe I should take a crack myself."

"I think you should. She mentioned she was in the market for a short, violent, *gaucho* American who can barely speak kitchen Spanish."

"But with an enormous penis."

"That too. You could go down the aisle right now and wave it in her face. Be my guest."

"You know, you're right—she does remind me of Chole a little," said Skelly. "Maybe she's what Chole would have been if her life had played out the way it was supposed to, if you hadn't yanked her out of her native soil."

He knew that Skelly had not meant this remark to be cruel, but its cruel truth pierced Marder and stunned him out of any casual rejoinder. He rose and sat down in the aisle seat next to his daughter, who was wearing earbuds while plying her laptop. He noticed that the computer screen was covered with complex engineering diagrams. When he sat, she snapped the screen down and popped the earbuds out.

"What was that yelling all about? I could hear it through the music."

"La Espinoza objected to my presence."

"Oh, yeah? Well, fuck her! It's your plane. And didn't you save her from a bunch of thugs?"

"I'm tired of talking about her, if you don't mind. You were conversing with Lourdes earlier. What did she have to say?"

"Well, she's a happy camper, all right. But I've never met anyone quite so immersed in popular culture. It's all celebrities and personal adornment and the opinions of her friends. She has no doubt that she's going to be famous and rich and that this is her due. But basically she's a decent kid. She's going to bring her mother home and put her in a big house. She was surprised that I worked, since you're so rich."

She stopped and regarded him curiously. "But you're not really rich, are you? I mean American rich. I admit I was wondering where you got the money to buy Casa Feliz and toss it around like you're doing. Chartered planes?"

"I got lucky with some investments is all," said Marder, and hoped it would not lead to one of those star-chamber interviews he'd occasionally had with his daughter.

It did not. She shrugged and continued, "Anyway, when it was clear that I wasn't up on the latest telenovela plots, she stuck her earbuds in and went to sit next to a window."

"It seems like a simple life. I almost envy her. And how is your complex life, daughter mine? How are you doing?"

"I'm a little freaked, to be honest. I didn't expect this."

"What did you expect?"

"I don't know. A depressed father lying in a hotel room drinking himself to death. Instead, Skelly's here and all this . . . I don't know, *stuff* is going on. And somehow I'm in the middle of it, I've totally blown my whole grad school thing—"

"Surely not. They can give you a couple of weeks off, can't they?"

"It doesn't work that way, Dad. Not in a program like the one I'm in, and not with the competition I have. I made a serious breakthrough in the project design. Schue jumped at it, backed it to the max, and instead of working twice as hard, I took off. He was not pleased."

"We're going to an airport. You could be back in Boston tonight."

"I know. I was thinking about it. But . . . did you ever, like, get totally dissatisfied with your life? I don't mean being miserable or anything. I mean your life is going along a track, you have good work, shelter, enough money, friends, sex, but there's something *wrong*?"

"Yes, I know exactly what you mean. I was like that when I was about your age: settled, decent job, wife, and then one day I got on my bike and rode off to Mexico."

"Yeah, I know. And the same thing now. I mean you bailing out of New York and coming here."

"In a way," said Marder, bending the truth. "But there were some things I had to do. And I've been an editor for a long time. I just got up one morning and it was over. And I love Mexico. Being here reminds me of your mother, you know, the voices and the smells and the colors."

"Yeah, it's like our loft expanded to the whole world."

"Exactly. But it sounds as if you really have your life up in Cambridge."

"I do, but . . . look, I don't want this to sound weird, but are you on some kind of suicide trip?"

Marder felt a brief chill. This was the trouble with an intelligent daughter, and moreover one with her mother's remarkable penetration. "I don't know what you mean."

"I mean the guns, and Skelly being here, and what happened the other day, the attack. You're not trying to, like, *defeat* these guys, are you?"

Marder managed a laugh. "That would be somewhat grandiose as well as suicidal, don't you think? No, but it's the case that I want to live here and also that I don't want to drive off the squatters, and to do that I have to show the gangsters that I'm not someone they can push around without getting their fingers burned. I've allied myself with one faction, and I think that'll suffice. Unfortunately, it's a cost of doing business in Michoacán just now. But this isn't your life. I didn't expect you to come down here, and I think you should go right back to Boston when we get to the airport."

"Yeah, I get that you're trying to get rid of me. But, somehow, you seem to be responsible for constructing a small town. Skelly's a pretty good field engineer, but he's no me. You're going to need some type of sewage treatment and a solar generation-and-distribution system, and you need to be wired to the Net, and there's all the logistics and phasing— someone has got to be the honcho. You could hire someone, I guess . . . but I think it's something I could do. Everyone in America expects their kids to go off on their careers and get together once a year, but that's not the way people are supposed to live. It's not the way they live here, or at least not the way they want to live. It kills them that their people have to go north to earn a buck. It's funny—I'm always bullshitting about poor areas leapfrogging technology, jumping to the next level, like they did with cell phones, and here's the opportunity, dropped in my lap. We could go solar, wireless, state of the art, adapted to a rural craft economy. Autonomous three-D manufacturing—what I was working on—is the obvious next thing in the industrial world, but I've been thinking that when everyone has practically free automatically produced stuff, they're going to want some one-of-a-kind items, lovingly produced by human hands. It's happening now, and it's going to get bigger. And then there's the whole Web marketing thing. We need a webpage and an Etsy account and a fulfillment system and an accounting system—"

"Do you know anything about that? I thought you were a mechanical engineer."

"Dad, it's the kind of stuff fourteen-year-olds can do now. Engineering is all about solving problems, and this is a really interesting set of problems. It'd be years before I got this kind of responsibility, and I bet if I wrote it up I could use it as a thesis project. I bet I could get Schue interested in it. I mean, aside from anything else, if I applied for the job, wouldn't you hire me?"

"Are you sure about this?" asked Marder. His heart was doing peculiar things in his chest.

"No, but it seems like the right thing to do now. I think Mom would've wanted me to do it."

"Okay, you're hired," he said, now barely able to get out the words. He hugged Carmel and kissed her on the temple.

Where did this desperate caring come from, he now wondered; what was its source? Something latent in him, was it, or something expressed out of the land of Mexico, out of the situation in which he found himself? He had come down here thinking that it was a shucking off, a preparation for the nakedness of death, but from almost the first minute of his supposed escape, entanglements had reached out like jungle vines and clung to him. And yet he felt no desire to disentangle himself again, to tell the pilot of this plane to take off from Mexico City and go far away, leaving him among strangers. He had tried and failed to escape, and now he was being drawn ever deeper into something strange and dangerous, and he was dragging his daughter into it too. Or not him, really; the ghost of his wife was the strength behind all this.

He looked out the window. The plane had descended to around ten thousand feet. Beneath them the land had turned sere, the desert eastern slopes of the Sierra, and beyond this landscape he could now make out what appeared to be an immense brownish smear extending to the northern horizon.

"That's the Valley of Mexico," he said, pointing. "Chilangolandia."

"Why do they call Mexico City people *Chilangos*?"

"I have no idea. And I believe the more common term nowadays is

Defeños, those from the *distrito federal*, Defe, as they say. God, it's certainly huge."

"It looks like L.A."

"Oh, it's a lot bigger than L.A. L.A. is a hick provincial town compared to Defe. And this huge thing occupies practically no cultural space in the minds of most Americans, even though it's the largest city on the planet and the real capital of Latin America, of half a billion people. Cultural imperialism in action. It has more museums than any other city in the world, more concert halls, the works. If you were a European intellectual in the eighteenth or early nineteenth century and you came to the New World, this would be the place you'd visit to see peers, not New York or Boston, which were a tenth its size back then."

"Yeah, I got all that from Mom. Are you going to show me the sights?"

"I don't know the sights. I passed through here only once. I married your mother here and then we left Mexico."

The plane dropped through the smog, the blue sky vanished, and the plane lighted gently on the runway and taxied to the general aviation terminal. They trooped down the lowered stairway into thin, throat-biting air smelling of fuel and exhaust. Behind a low fence were a man in uniform, holding a SR. MARDER sign, and a waving young man in a tan photographer's vest, obviously waiting for Pepa. She strode out ahead without a word to anyone and then, to Marder's surprise, halted, spun on her heel, and walked back to look him in the face.

"I'm sorry," she said. "Truly. I think I'm having post-traumatic shock or something. I had no right to speak to you that way. Please forgive me."

"There's nothing to forgive," said Marder. "I was out of line with that comment on your writing."

She smiled. "With respect to manners, perhaps, but not substantively. I know what I want to say, but I have trouble with the actual words."

"Many quite famous writers say the same," he replied, returning the smile.

"And . . . well, I was on the phone with my producer just now and I mentioned you and what you were doing—not in a complimentary way, I confess—but he suggested that you might be a story, I mean, who you are, the background, and it ties in with what we've been running recently about the violence. I have video of what went on on the causeway the other day, and we're going to run it. Would you be open to, say, interviews, camera crews on your property . . . ?"

"As long as they include you," he said.

"I think I can guarantee that." She held out her hand. "Thank you. I think I have your number at the house. I'll be in touch."

"Not so fast. I'd like a favor in return."

"Oh?" Suspiciously.

"I have an appointment with Marcial Jura, to introduce Lourdes."

"Marcial? Really? I'm impressed. You're full of surprises, Señor Marder."

"It's Rick, please. Yes, we have some mutual connections in New York. I called in a bunch of chips and he kindly agreed to spare us a few minutes. But I'd consider it a great favor if you'd spend some time with Lourdes beforehand—help her shop for clothes, you know, an impressive outfit so she won't look like she just walked in from the *rancho*, and show her how to use makeup. And talk to her, all the things you mentioned, how to walk and hold her hands and so on. I think she'll listen to you. She thinks you walk on water."

"You're the water-walker if you arranged for Marcial Jura to look at an unknown child."

Spontaneously, they both looked over at the unknown child. She was standing near the door to the general aviation terminal, swaying to the music coursing through her earbuds, smiling, her long black hair flipping about in the light breeze, radiating gorgeousness to every eye. A baggage handler, they observed, had been so transfixed in his dutiful passage that he clipped a cart and sent a cascade of suitcases crashing to the tarmac.

"I rest my case," Marder remarked, and Pepa laughed freely, an appealing sound he had not heard before but wished to hear again.

"Well, I'll do it," she said. "When's the interview?"

"Tomorrow at four. We're at the Marquis Reforma."

"Of course you are. Where do you get your money, Rick, if I may ask an American question to a distinguished Mexican gentleman?"

"Investments," he replied.

"The safest possible answer. I'll be there at ten." She stuck out her hand. He declined to kiss it, an entirely proper gesture, but instead shook it firmly, like a gringo.

* * *

The last time Marder was in a bed in Mexico City, the bed had been in a tiny upstairs room in a *pensión* in Tepito. The room had smelled of grease from the *taquería* downstairs, and enormous roaches scuttled noisily along the baseboards, but the bed had contained one who made it an enchanted bower. They had just been married. The smell and the scuttling distracted not a bit from that well-remembered carnal paradise. The Reforma's lonely bed was vast and comfortable, however, and Marder spent the first hypnagogic moments sunk in a pleasant fantasy involving various potential partners and in regretful memory.

From this he was roused by a pounding on the door. He rose, groaned when the full force of gravity pulled at his head, threw on a hotel bathrobe, and opened the door to Skelly.

"What time is it?"

"Around eight."

"Scram. I'm going back to bed."

"Uh-uh, chief. We have a big day. I need to see some people and you need to come with me. I brought you a present."

Skelly handed him a large paper bag. From this Marder removed a contraption of leather straps; he held it up, shook it out, and finally identified it.

"A shoulder holster?"

"Yeah. You're going to shoot your ass off if you keep carrying that cannon stuck in the back of your pants."

"That's very considerate of you. I assume it's to be used when we see these people? I mean, they're the kind of people one visits armed."

"Not at all. They're respectable merchants of death, but they do a cash business, and they're located in one of the underprivileged regions of the city. You know Itzapalapa?"

"I've heard of it. How much cash?"

"A hundred large, more or less."

"Pesos?"

Skelly rolled his eyes. "I assume you can get the cash, no problem."

"Sure, I'll just call Bernie and have it transferred to an HSBC branch here. I assume this is why we're going strapped."

"Exactly. I thought of hiring a *sicario* or two, but you never can tell with guys you don't know; they might decide to go into business for themselves. And being you're Deadeye Dick . . ."

"Right. Let me make that call now."

He used the hotel phone and caught the accountant at home.

"I hope you know what you're doing, Rick," Bernie Nathan said when Marder told him what he wanted. His voice over the wires sounded strange to Marder, the tone of someone who did not shoot and get shot at, an echo of a former life.

"Yeah, Bernie, it's a property deal. I can get a real bargain if I show some cash up front." He finished the conversation and turned to Skelly. "So, what are we buying for all this money?"

"Just enough basic machinery to make the *casa* not such a pushover if anyone decides to get serious, just whatever they have immediately available. It'll all be ex-Soviet stuff, but I don't want to be handed off any condemned crap, so we have to pay top dollar. Put some clothes on, chief, I don't want to keep my guy waiting."

"So early?" said Marder, dropping the robe and pulling on chinos, T-shirt, and his old leather huaraches. "I thought this kind of stuff got done by dead of night."

"Only in the movies. You look like shit, by the way. What did you do last night?"

"Nothing much—while you were out with your international criminals, we had a nice dinner at Aura downstairs, and then Carmel and Lourdes went clubbing."

"You let that girl out on the street at night in the big town? I'm surprised she didn't get snatched out of her high heels."

"Oh, you know, she was with Carmel. And Carmel can take care of herself." He fumbled into the shoulder holster, stuck the Kimber in it, and Skelly helped him adjust the straps. Marder sighed. Another aspect of a trip he had definitely not signed on for was learning that his little girl was packing. The previous night he'd raised the same issue about Lourdes that Skelly had just mentioned, and Statch had flashed his father's Colt Woodsman at him and promised she wouldn't let the dazzling charmer out of her sight. He'd watched them go and then walked around the ritzy neighborhood for a while, found a bar, and watched Los Tigres beat Morelia 3–0 on the TV while downing an unaccustomed quantity of old brown tequila, much of which he could still taste on the back of his tongue. He brushed his teeth, however, which helped, and drenched his face with cold water; then he slipped into his jacket and they left.

Skelly had rented a battered white Jetta. They drove to an HSBC on

Paseo de la Reforma a few blocks from the hotel. Marder discovered that the seat belts were reluctant to stop providing safety, and he cursed and clicked while Skelly (who never used them) chuckled cruelly. Once free, he went into the bank carrying a nylon duffel bag like a bandito, spoke with a manager, and related his business. He showed his passport and his credit card, and there were a number of phone calls made and doubtful looks exchanged. Marder overheard the phrase "eccentric American millionaire" several times. He had to accept part of the cash in pesos, unless the señor wished to wait. The señor did not wish, but then they had to go to a guy Skelly knew and turn the paper pesos into fifty-peso gold coins. Apparently the international illegal-arms market recognized only dollars, euros, and gold.

After that, Skelly took them around the south end of Chapultepec Park, onto the La Piedad expressway east. He drove with his usual brio, weaving, speeding, hunched over the wheel, checking the mirrors with quick jerks of his head.

"Something wrong?" Marder asked.

"Two cars behind us in the right lane, a dark-blue Dodge van."

Marder looked. The van was there, but the reflected sun on the windshield made it impossible to see the occupants.

"What about it?"

"It's been there since we left the bank on Reforma."

"A tail?"

"Possibly. Let's find out." Skelly floored it, shot around a semi, raced ahead on the left for half a mile, cut right again to the center lane, and checked his mirrors. Marder twisted in his seat and looked behind. He could make out the top of the blue van two cars behind in the center lane: certainly a tail.

Skelly said, "Okay, let's lose them and hope they weren't smart enough to use more than one chase car."

Marder sat back in his seat and braced himself. Skelly swung the car into the passing lane again and slowed down. A Mercedes moved up into tailgate position, flashing its lights. Marder studied his friend's face. He saw the jaw tighten, the skin of the forehead take on a dull shine from tiny beads of sweat. Skelly was frightened, but Skelly was always frightened. Marder remembered realizing that in the bamboo forest and recalled how it surprised him then, that Skelly was terrified of dying and he himself was not.

* * *

What frightened Marder was imprisonment, being confined and tormented. He remembered crouching there, with the striped shadows of the bamboo giving a tigerish appearance to the faces of the men crouching around him. They were trapped on a little knoll in a tiny perimeter, less than a quarter mile below its blunt summit, with nowhere to go and no chance of being airlifted out, not with the dense growth of bamboo and thick forestation on the top of the knoll. The firing had slackened because they had very little ammunition left. Marder had kept his M79, even though he had no ammunition for it, only a couple of smoke grenades. And he had his .45. The NVA company that had chased them here was probably running out of ammo too, but obviously they could send for reinforcements; they had thousands of men in the immediate area, and they still had quite enough ammunition to keep the SOG detachment pinned down. He could see Skelly with his radio operator through the green poles of the bamboo; he was talking into the plastic handset, his voice calm, his eyes wild and staring.

But Skelly stood up with bullets snapping around him and came over to Marder and asked him for the grenade launcher and a red smoke grenade and he had shot the grenade a hundred or so meters upslope. And then he'd come back and told Marder that there would be a C-130 flying over fairly soon and that when he heard the sound of its engine he should lie flat and cover his ears with his hands. Then Skelly had walked through the bullets and told all his surviving troops the same thing. Marder could not, however, resist looking up as the sound of heavy engines passed overhead. He saw a scant few lines of green tracer, seeking for the Hercules, and then it was over and gone, leaving a tiny black dot in the air behind it.

Skelly tromped on the gas again, the engine screamed, and the Jetta shot forward and cut right across the traffic, passing in front of a big diesel truck with less than a yard of clearance. Marder heard air horns, the roar of air brakes, screeches of tires, the blaring of offended vehicles. The Jetta gunned across two lanes of traffic, crossed the hatch lines of an exit ramp, bounced against the near shoulder, and careered up the ramp on two wheels. The blue van, neatly boxed in, could only speed on down the freeway.

Marder considered his friend, whose demeanor had now relaxed into one appropriate for a Sunday drive through the park, and he wondered yet again about the peculiar nature of Skelly's bravery. Terror did not paralyze him, far less cause him to cower or retreat. Rather, it prompted a cool consideration of the probabilities and an instant commitment to whatever desperate action was most likely to bring about an agreeable solution. Thus this latest death-defying driving stunt, and thus also that long-ago decision to lie to his control about where his detachment was pinned down, so that they would deliver a fifteen-thousand-pound Daisy Cutter bomb to the top of the knoll while a couple of dozen men crouched on the very edge of the thing's kill radius. The black dot had dropped to earth and the earth had moved, popping Marder five inches into the air, and the sound had entered his bones, turning them to liquid, and he had wet his pants. Then the gunship had come over and sprayed their pursuers with cannon and minigun fire, and the helicopters had landed on the mountaintop buzz-cut by the bomb and taken them for the short ride back to Bronco One.

"What are you smiling about?" Skelly asked. "Did you piss yourself *again*?"

"No, and speaking about pissing myself, I was just thinking about how you dropped that Daisy Cutter on top of us."

"Jesus! What the hell brought that to mind?"

"This last little escapade, I guess. That ride back to the base, the way the bird stank. I think half the people had messed their pants. It must've brought up my album of insane things Patrick Skelly has done to get out of situations he got himself into. A substantial volume, I might say."

"It worked."

"It always does," said Marder. "And when it stops working, we'll never know about it. This looks a little like south-central L.A."

The exit had led onto Calzada Ermita Itzapalapa, the main drag of the eponymous district. The broad thoroughfare was jammed with traffic, consisting largely of the small jitney buses that poor Defeños depended upon to get around their sprawling city. Itzapalapa had been a colonial town and before that a space sacred to the Aztecs, but now it was just another swallowed area, with almost no water and more crime than any other part of the DF. Dwellings of various classes, from quite respectable homes to miserable tenements, were strung and scattered among shops and industrial sites, zoning having not been heard of in those parts, and as a result it was livelier and more democratic and filthier than an equivalent section of an American city.

Skelly pulled the car onto a narrow side street, bordered on one side by a factory yard protected by a high barbed-wire-topped cyclone fence and on the other by a row of miscellaneous dwellings, all with heavy barred gratings on their lower windows and doorways. At the end of the short street stood an incongruous clump of manzanita trees, in the shade of which a group of old people sat around on decrepit couches and lawn chairs. Skelly parked, opened the trunk, took out the nylon duffel bag with the money and gold in it, and said, "If I'm not out in three days, take the emeralds to Mombasa and sell them to Farouk."

"Seriously."

"Seriously, I know these guys. No problems with them at all. I've done good business with them before."

"These are Mexicans?"

"Chinese. No, what you need to watch out for is that blue van. Move the car down to the corner—I don't want us to get blocked in by some goddamn garbage truck or a delivery. I shouldn't be more than half an hour."

Skelly hoisted the bag and marched off across the street to a steel door on which painted letters announced HERMANOS SING LLC. He took a throwaway cell phone from his pocket, made a call. A minute later, the door swung open and Skelly disappeared.

Marder stared at the door for a moment, then moved to the driver's seat and drove down to the avenue end of the block. He got out of the car to stretch and to study the little street. A food shop stood directly to his left, filling the air with the scent of spiced meat frying, and there was a small bodega in the middle of the block, to which the lounging *viejos* went often, returning with beers and snacks. A gang of thuggy-looking kids roared around the corner on motorbikes. They wore the outfits they'd seen in Chicano gangster films from *El Norte*: baggy pants hung absurdly low on their narrow hips, expensive athletic footwear, plaid shirts worn loose over wifebeater undershirts, hairnets on a few. They bought beers in the bodega and stood around pushing one another and trading clever remarks. Some of these were directed at the gringo *maricón,* and Marder supposed that after a while a bunch of them would come over and try to hustle him, take his money, steal his car. He took out his Kimber and jacked the action, casually, as if he were flipping a coin or lighting a cigarette, and replaced it in his shoulder holster. After that the thugs stopped looking at him.

A dusty maroon van with the logo of a roofing company pulled into the street and parked across from the steel door to Hermanos Sing LLC.

Two men in coveralls got out, removed a ladder from the roof rack, and began to set out tools, buckets, and tarpaulins on the sidewalk. They both wore sunglasses, and both of them were good-sized fleshy men. Marder thought they did not look very much like typical wiry sun-tanned dusty Mexican working stiffs. But perhaps these were the supervisory roofers; perhaps the actual crew was coming in another van or on another day, or maybe these guys were the estimators. Marder thought you could go crazy thinking in this way; every single person on the street would be a threat, life would become intolerable.

He got back in the car and turned on the radio, punching the seek button until he had a station that played old-fashioned *ranchera* music. He sat there, foregetting the roofers and the gangsters and soaking up remembered *Mexicanismo* and his former life, sitting in the living room with Chole reading while Lola Beltrán or Rocío Dúrcal played softly in the background.

A motion in the corner of his eye; in the rearview he could see the steel door open, he could see Skelly step out and start to walk toward the car. Marder shifted over to the passenger seat and snapped in the safety belt.

One of the roofers picked up a tarp. The other roofer pulled some kind of tool from his pocket. It took Marder a moment to realize it was a pistol.

Marder pulled out his own pistol, threw open the door, and got hung up on the seat belt. As he struggled with the faulty release, the roofer with the pistol stood in front of Skelly with his back to Marder; the other guy was coming up behind Skelly, ready to throw his tarp over Skelly's head and hustle him into the van's conveniently wide-open sliding side door.

Marder had barely made it out of the car when he heard a bang and saw the head of the man with the pistol burst outward in a geyser of red. Skelly had spun around to face the other man and Marder saw a flash, heard another bang, and the man with the tarpaulin fell over. Skelly trotted down the street, got into the car, and drove off.

"How in hell did you manage that?" asked Marder, as they wove through the traffic on the *calzada*.

"I had this in my hand all the time," Skelly replied, flipping a tiny pistol into Marder's lap. It was still warm when he handled it.

"It fires a .410 shotgun shell. I raised my hands like I was surrendering and begged for my life, and then I shot the bastard in the face. And the other one too. It looks like they were pros and had a following car, or two."

"But they saw you weren't carrying the bag. Why did they want to snatch you?"

"I don't think it had anything to do with the money. I think it was our friend Cuello."

"You think? In the DF?"

"It's a matter of a phone call. And it's Itzapalapa—kidnapping's a cottage industry around here. No, I don't think it was a spontaneous thing. It was planned. They probably tailed us from the airport."

"But why you? Why not me?"

"Oh, they probably figured I was the brains behind the operation. Or the muscle." He gave Marder a grin. "Don't feel bad, Marder. They'll come after you next."

12

Marder was waiting by the plane the next morning, nervous, constantly looking at his watch, imagining the worst, when Skelly drove up in the Jetta with Statch in the front seat, followed by a truck inscribed with the name of a meatpacking firm.

"I had to pick up a few items, chief," said Skelly. "Statch put them on her card."

"What items? Not the stuff you bought yesterday?" Marder looked at the truck, from which four men were unloading large cartons and wheeling them over to the yawning cargo bay of the King Air.

"No, no, all that has to come via shipping container. This is just some useful electronics."

"He bought a cell-phone tower," said Statch.

"And cell phones, lots of cell phones," Skelly added. "Our little community is going to be wired to the nipples."

"I don't understand," said Marder. "Is it legal to have your own cell-phone tower?"

"It's legal-ish in a Mexican kind of way. Statch will explain the technical details. My God, is that our Lourdes?"

"Yes," said Marder, looking over at the terminal building, from which the girl had emerged. "Or Lo, as we're now supposed to call her. She's had the whole works, courtesy of Señora Espinoza and my credit card."

Via a little pink Bottega Veneta suit, Blahnik heeled sandals at a hundred dollars an ounce, plus a four-hundred-dollar haircut and a long evening of training in poise and makeup and other aspects of stardom, Lourdes Almones had transformed herself from a sulky provincial teenager into a reasonable simulacrum of a telenovela star. The effect was perfectly artificial to Marder's eyes, and he was sensible of a certain Frankensteinian horror in his breast, but the girl was glowing with happiness and, starlike, she communicated this to nearly everyone in her immediate orbit.

"I'm in love," said Skelly.

"She's seventeen," said Marder.

"We'll grow old together," said Skelly, approaching the girl with his arms thrown wide.

In the air again, Marder sat next to his daughter, whom he had seen but briefly since the previous evening. Neither she nor Skelly had been at the dinner to celebrate Lourdes's triumphant interview with Marcial Jura.

"We missed you last night," he said. "You ran off with Skelly."

"Yeah, he wanted to pump my brain about cellular systems, and then we went to this guy he knew—"

"Yet another guy of Skelly's innumerable guys. Did this one have a name?"

"Mr. Lopez. He was in the back room of a warehouse in Tepito with a lot of what looked like shady inventory."

"Why did you go with Skelly anyway? I thought you were coming to Televisa with us."

"I thought my expertise would be more useful with Skelly than in getting Lourdes ready. I figured Pepa had that down—I mean the makeup and the haircut and the clothes and all. It was a little rich for me—as you know, I'm a T and shorts kind of girl. How did she do, by the way?"

"Unexpectedly great. You know, you figure a Mexican telenovela guy, a big-shot producer, he's got to be a fat lecher with a cigar and a mustache, Zero Mostel, but no. He looks like a ballet master, like Balanchine: black shirt, short hair, slight build, heavy round glasses. We walk in there—a regular office, big video monitors, small messy desk, with couches and a coffee table, nothing fancy—me and Pepa and the girl, and after the usual greeting and small talk he ignores us. He's totally focused on Lourdes. They talked about telenovelas. He drew her out, what she liked, what she didn't, the actors, the plots . . . I was amazed at how articulate the kid became when she was talking about something she loved. Ordinarily you can't get a word out of her."

"I know guys who're like that with video games. It's sort of pathetic."

"Is it? I don't know. Popular culture is hard to figure. Billions of people watch these things religiously—maybe literally religiously. I don't think that it's an accident that almost all telenovelas are produced by Catholic countries. Anyway, we had a screen test, we went to a studio, and he had Lourdes improvise in front of a camera—he would set up a situation and give her some lead-in lines. It was amazing. She just sort of occupied a classic character—the spurned lover, the defiant daughter. I'd never seen anything like it. Pepa was blown away."

"Why was that?"

"Because she'd given me this line about how an *indio* like Lourdes would be abused, the whole casting-couch business and how she would never get real roles, only maids and servants, but apparently Jura's moving in a new direction; he wants to develop some *indio* actors to become real stars. He thinks the market is ready for it. Girls first, of course."

"Of course. Well, it's not my thing, but I'm happy for her. Is she going to get a contract?"

"Apparently he wants her in some kind of training school for young actors they have in Defe. But there didn't seem to be any doubt in his mind that she'd get a part when she graduated. I think she'll do well. You saw her—blooming like a rose. I'm very pleased."

His daughter made no response, and Marder had the thought that, though a T-shirt-and-shorts person, his daughter perhaps resented the attention he'd given to the lovely little stranger. "I'm sorry you weren't there," he added.

"Yes, well, as I said, it's not my kind of thing. Anyway, I like hanging out with Skelly. He's a laugh a minute."

"Is he? The last time I was out with him it was only mildly amusing. He shot two men in the head."

"You're kidding."

"I wish I was." He briefly related what had gone down in Itzapalapa.

"Well," she said, "it sounds like he didn't have much of a choice."

"Right, but, still, terminating two human lives should make a difference—I mean outside the heat of combat, when you really don't know what you're doing. And he was completely unaffected by it, smiling, joking, like it was crushing out a cigarette or an insect. I still can't believe I shot a bunch of men the other day, and whenever I think about it I get a little nauseous. It's not normal."

"Maybe he's used to it. Maybe he's a famous international hit man."

"There's no such thing. As far as I'm aware, no heavily protected person has ever been killed by a professional assassin. There's no money in it. If you want someone dead, you hire a couple of teenagers who don't give a shit. No, I think he's in the security business just like he says. I think he protects some fairly bad people, though, and hires mercenaries and like that. What I can't quite figure out is why he hangs out with me. I mean, what's in it for him?"

Girlish giggling and Skelly's booming laugh sounded from the front of the plane.

"I'm going to kill him if he hits on that girl," said Marder.

"I don't see why you should care," she said. "You're not responsible for her, and from what I've seen she's perfectly capable of looking out for herself, nor is she a blushing innocent. Really, Dad—it's not like you're her father. In fact, if he's bonking her, everyone will stop thinking you're bonking her."

Marder looked at her, amazed. "Why would they think that?"

"Oh, maybe because you took her to Mexico City in a chartered plane to buy her lots of fancy stuff and set her up with the most famous telenovela director in the country. Why would you do that unless you were pulling down her new La Perlas?"

"Wait . . . people in Colonia Feliz are talking about this?"

"Of course. You're the sun around which their lives revolve. You're the *patrón*. Your moods are consulted like the weather. When you frown, the clouds darken—"

"Oh, cut it out, Carmel!"

"It's true. I thought that was the point of you coming down here, to be a big shot in Mom's hometown."

"Did you really think that? What possible word or deed of mine in all the time you've known me would give you to believe that I was that kind of man?"

"None. But I thought you'd gone crazy, remember?"

"And now?"

"I don't know. The jury is still out. I mean, one day I'm, like, oh, my dad's an editor in New York, and the next it's, oh, my dad's a feudal lord in Michoacán. It takes some getting used to."

Another gust of laughter and high spirits from forward.

"And I agree about your boy up there. That's the other thing I can't figure out: What's in it for him? Why is he hanging around and doing all this stuff?"

"Did you ask him?"

"Yeah, I did. He said he just wanted to help out a pal."

"And . . ."

"Moving an apartment, lending a car, letting him sleep on your couch, is what you do to help out a pal. Not dropping your whole life and setting up a state-of-the-art security system for him and shooting people. You have no idea the kind of surveillance and commo equipment he bought last night, tens of thousands of dollars' worth, besides that whole damn private cell-phone system. And I bet you went shopping with him when you took off yesterday morning."

"He did. I waited in the car."

"What did he get?"

It passed briefly through Marder's mind to dissimulate, to get Carmel into the zone of deniability, to protect her from whatever consequences Skelly's purchases might have, but then he dismissed the idea. Marder had never been the kind of father who treated his adult daughter like a perpetual daddy's little girl. Sometimes he thought it was a little unnatural, but there it was.

He said, "He bought heavy weapons, military grade. It was part of the deal with the Templos, in exchange for protection." Marder felt it was fair to leave out the China White, since he didn't officially know about that yet.

"Do you think that's wise? These guys seem to do enough damage with American gun-shop stuff and machetes."

"I don't know. Skelly's in charge of security. And I think that in this particular situation, there's nobody better."

"What do you mean, situation?"

"A people occupied by an oppressive force, or forces, and wanting to resist. That's what he trained for; it's what he knows how to do."

"Well, I hope it works out better than Vietnam," she said.

When she said that, something clicked in Marder's mind, and he understood why Skelly stuck around and why he was expending so much effort to make Colonia Feliz secure from the forces of evil. He's making up for the failures, for the way his army and his country abandoned the Hmong forty years ago. And for the destruction of Moon River.

It came back to Marder clearly now, like the fight in the bamboo forest, the names and faces still obscured but the visceral memories arriving in waves, like the onset of a drug.

It was a day or so after the firefight. They were back in the village, the wounded had been evacuated, the dead in their dripping poncho liners had been taken away. Hayden and Lascaglia were dead; Pogo too—he'd died in the helicopter, with the medic working against the wound shock and Skelly gripping the man's shoulder, his mouth an inch from the dying man's ear, shouting against the chopper's roar, demanding that he not die, that he stay with the living, stay with me, stay with me . . .

He'd seen Skelly's tears clearing bright runnels in his grimy face and had wondered then (and still did) why he himself was tearless at the death of comrades. Maybe what Skelly had said was true, that his body might be here but the essential Marder was not, was a tourist, a visitor. Or perhaps, being diffident by nature, he lacked the basis for the intense comradeship he observed among the SOGs and among the Hmong soldiers. Or perhaps it was simple denial—his mind had closed off the war, shut down all feelings; I am not really here, so I can't die. But these considerations did not occur to him until much later. At the time he simply experienced a terrible isolating chill and felt badly about himself because of it.

Despite this, Skelly persisted in cultivating him. At the time, Marder imagined that it was because he was the sole surviving airman, the last helpless kitten in the litter, and that the SOGs regretted losing Sweathog and Pinto, but then Marder decided it was more personal than that. Skelly was *interested* in him.

After the firefight, Marder had little to do. The sensor system was complete and apparently operational. Occasionally they could hear and see, far off over the jungle ridges, the flash and rumble of the Arc Light strikes that the vast machinery of Igloo White had vectored in on the sounds of transit on the trail, invisible B-52s dropping hundreds of tons of explosives on truckloads of rice and ammunition. There was no radio traffic for him from Naked Fanny; the air force seemed to have forgotten him, at least temporarily, and he thought that was fine. He had no real desire to go back to Task Force Alpha. He volunteered to monitor the radio nets and made himself useful maintaining various electronic devices. The SOGs were famously unconcerned with military occupation specialties; people did whatever was necessary, and Marder learned how to call in air support from the forward air controllers during operations. The SOGs went out on missions and returned—most of them. New people arrived and were absorbed and were wounded or killed or served out their tours and variously departed, but Marder didn't really go to the war anymore.

He spent a lot of his time in the village. He talked to the children, enticing them with PX potato chips. That was one nice thing about the SOG: it had its own air force and supply lines, and the Ponies—their private helicopter pilots—would bring in almost anything you wanted from Long Binh or Saigon. All of the SOGs were comfortable dealing with the Hmong—they had been trained to be nice to freedom-fighting natives—but none more so than Skelly. He was forever bending Marder's ear with descriptions of the beauty of their culture, its integrity, its spirit. He thought it was how human beings were meant to live. Skelly spent whatever free time he had in Moon River, surrendering his turn to fly to Saigon and its delights in order to submerge himself ever deeper in the culture of the Hmong. He very much wanted Marder to be inducted into his tribe and clan, even volunteering to buy the buffalo required for the ceremony.

Marder put him off for a long time and then gave in. He did so because he did not wish to offend Skelly or to be the only American without a bracelet, but in fact he did not take the induction seriously. Unlike Skelly, who was essentially an outcast, Marder had been a member of an intact tribal society for his whole life, having been brought up in a Brooklyn Irish parish under the old ecclesial regime. He thought there was something unpleasantly desperate in the way Skelly had plunged into Hmong culture, and he felt it even more when he discovered that Skelly had taken a Hmong wife, had married with all ceremony a girl name Joong, who could not have been more than seventeen. The other SOGs seemed to accept this Hmongness in Skelly as another of the eccentricities they all exhibited as members of an unconventional army, along with their exotic weapons and uniforms, the quasi-legal supply system, and their relative freedom from the MACV chickenshit that characterized the rest of the war.

What Marder saw, and he thought that perhaps they did not, was that Skelly took it very seriously indeed, that for him the entire war was about the preservation of the Hmong in this village, that this was, in fact, the only honorable facet of the immense waste of life and treasure that was tearing his native land to pieces. Like everyone else who'd been in-country for more than a week and had half a brain, Skelly understood that the Republic of South Vietnam was worthless and unsalvageable. The ARVN was corrupt at every level and completely penetrated by the enemy. MACV was a house of lies, devoid of honor, whose only strategy was throwing hapless draftees out in the bush until they got blasted by the NVA and the remnants of the VC and then sending bombers and artillery to blow holes in the forest in hopes of adding to the (largely fictitious) body counts. Skelly dismissed all that—he knew the NVA, he knew they would never give up, they would sacrifice their entire population before they'd tolerate any foreign soldiers on their soil.

The montagnards were different, though. They were their own nation, and they would fight. They'd been fighting the Vietnamese for centuries—they were like the Indians in America—and with just a little help they could build an independent nation in their mountains that would be proof against any attack and that would inspire the sympathy of the world. The United States would at last be fighting a good fight—even the fucking hippies, even fucking Jane Fonda, would see it was a good fight—and the Americans would support it.

Marder allowed himself to agree with this vision, but he had a lot less faith in the wisdom of America than Skelly did. Although he was a product of an intensely patriotic working-class community and had no connection with the college-kid antiwar movement, Marder had been raised by a couple of Catholic lefties, that rare breed. His father knew what a rich man's war and a poor man's fight was, and his mother, whose weekly letters kept him apprised of what was going on back in the world, was a Catholic Worker, who'd known and loved Dorothy Day for decades. Marder thought Skelly was a little nuts, but he was also eighteen and not entirely a cynic, and he was willing to dip a toe into Skelly's deep reservoir of faith.

And he liked seeing Skelly with the Hmong, with Joong and her siblings and cousins; he liked the sweetness of their natures, how gentle they were with their kids, how gentle horrible old Sergeant Skelly was with the wand-like creature he loved. Marder liked how they honored their old people and how those old people tried to keep intact the rituals, the spiritual tendons, so badly frayed now, that kept the Hmong from a dissolution worse than death.

So Marder relented, said he would buy the buffalo and be inducted, and one morning he squatted in the public room of the *root*, or longhouse, of Baap Can, the headman of the village, and listened uncomprehendingly to Skelly bargain (if that was the word) about the buffalo necessary to the cere- mony. It seemed that much had to be done to prepare the spirits for the event. Baap Can had apparently grown ever more conservative with respect to ritual, since it was obvious that the failure of the people to observe every detail of ritual was what had brought about their present calamities. In the past, Marder learned, a single act of violence would have paralyzed the village with cleansing ceremonies for weeks, but now they lived in the midst of continuous violence and the spirits were silent.

It went on for hours, giving Marder plenty of time to think about religion in all its varieties. Did Skelly really believe all this? That the universe was packed with malignant spirits that had to be propitiated with animal sacrifices? That all illness and catastrophe was the action of some sorcery or the caprice of ghosts? Perhaps he didn't believe it, perhaps it was part of his training, to immerse himself in the culture of the people he sought as allies, not to give offense. Later on, but not then, Marder would come to understand that what Skelly believed in was Training.

The Catcher in the Rye had wandered into the army, and the army had offered him the salvation of eternal boyhood through suffering. If he would torment his body, if he would ascend step by step through the sweaty heirarchy of boot camp, advanced infantry school, airborne, Special Forces, then he would become part of a boys' gang that couldn't be beat, that aspired to purity amid the chickenshit of this miserable fraudulent war, that supplied all the brotherhood that a man could handle, that wasn't phony. Marder had watched them at their play—the roughhousing, the practical jokes, the arrant, gleeful violation of military regulations. He recalled behaving just that way as a kid. And so, when Marder came to think about it, it must've been no trouble at all for Skelly to slide into simple paganism—all of them were halfway there already, all more or less worshippers of the Lord of the Flies.

And maybe the girl was part of it. Maybe Joong had converted him—it had happened before. He knew his own father had little or no personal religion, but he went regularly to Mass out of love for his wife, and never a remark about the well-known deficiencies of the one, holy, and apostolic Church. He thought about the girl, Joong. She seemed a blankness to Marder, a sweet, lovely, singing creature who was kind to animals and children. He recalled a conversation he'd had with her once. She was playing with a white cat. Marder had arranged a sentence in his head and tried it. "Do you like cats, Joong? My mother likes cats."

She looked at him with a puzzled smile and asked whether in America cats were sacrificed as they were among real people. Marder said they were not. She shrugged—it was known that Americans were infected with spirits. This cat would be sacrificed soon to heal her aunt Jieng-Tang. It would take a cock and a cat and perhaps a dog. The cats and the cock would have their throats cut, but, of course, the dog would be burned alive.

The negotiations ended and then they brought out jars of *rhööm*, sour rice beer, and drank a lot of it through straws. When they came out into the gathering dusk, Skelly said, "You're all set. They have to do a lot of stuff first, cut some big bombax posts and put bamboo finials on them, all carved up in a special way, and there's a whole ceremony. I'll explain it later. It'll probably go down tomorrow evening or the one after." He slapped Marder on the back, grinning. "We'll be tribal brothers. How about that shit?"

But, in the event, Marder never became a member of the tribe, because that very night a reinforced battalion of the 174th Regiment, People's Army of Vietnam, attacked Moon River.

Marder snapped out of the reverie to find his daughter regarding him with a peculiar expression.

"What?" he said. His mouth felt clotted and sour, as if he had just finished a gourd of Hmong beer.

"You were mumbling and making funny noises."

"Was I? I guess I drifted off . . . some dream or other."

"No, your eyes were wide open, but you weren't here."

"Well, I'm here now," said Marder brightly, and then changed the subject. "Look, Carmel, I'd like to inter your mother's ashes in the family tomb at La Huacana as soon as we can catch a break in all the construction work. I assume you'll be coming."

"Of course."

"And I intend to invite your uncle Angel and his family. He's not in a good way, and I'd like to help him out if I can."

Statch said nothing to this but felt something close to irritation, and some shame as well for feeling it. What was so bad about trying to help people, after all? But what her father appeared to be doing seemed a little off, this extraordinary desire to improve the lives of others. It irked her, and she recalled feeling something similar as a child, trying to warm herself on the edges of the great romantic furnace that was her parents' marriage. And even now that death had ended it, her father was still not quite present. He had not rebounded into another romance, as did so many men in similar situations, but had turned instead to this almost hectic philanthropy.

When she was back in her room at Casa Feliz, after the landing and the convoyed journey—El Gordo was certainly providing good service so far—Statch got out her cell to make some necessary calls. The first call was to Karen Liu. Statch asked what was going on in the lab. Liu's responses were flat, tinged with what seemed like embarrassment. At last Statch extracted the information that Schuemacher was preparing to pull her off the grant; he had an Indian boy genius on tap as a replacement. Statch got off the line as soon as she decently could and decided that she could not bear talking to any of the other people she had thought of calling. Instead, she opened her laptop and composed a long email to Erwin Schuemacher. She thanked him for all the help he'd given her and wished him success in his vision. She said she was resigning because she didn't think it was fair for him to hold her assistantship vacant while she was away for an indefinite period. She paused here. Should she try to communicate why she was staying? Did she even know? Dr. Schuemacher was, of course, an expert on every one of the forces known to physics, but she doubted if he would understand the forces now working on her. He would think she had gone crazy.

As she had, in a way, but not like the people who dropped out of MIT engineering because they had *actually* gone nuts, the kind who stayed in their rooms and never bathed and wrote in tiny letters on the walls. She wasn't crazy in that way. If you looked at it from a slightly different angle, you could even say that she had gone sane. In an effort to justify herself, to explain herself to her professor, she kept typing, and as the letter became longer, as it turned into something close to a Unabomber screed, she found that she was talking not to Dr. Schue but to Carmel Marder, whoever she now was. The burden of this was that, all things considered, she no longer thought that the future of manufacturing was the development of self-contained factories that could forage for raw materials and shit appliances. People, she had recently learned, could get by with many fewer appliances, or none at all. She wanted to try to use engineering in service of modesty, of scarcity, of getting by with less.

She read this email over. Sweat started on her forehead and trickled down her flanks. Did she really believe this? She recalled Dr. Schuemacher exploding the whole small-is-beautiful worldview, what he called hippie-dippie whole-earth crapola. The future belonged to automated factories using solar and nuclear power, making everything anyone could conceive of essentially for free, distributed by automated systems. Physical labor would become an anachronism, like slavery and religion, and people would increasingly become one with their machines. No one would die, and humanity would reach out to the stars in virtual form at the speed of light.

Carmel believed this as an intellectual proposition, but somehow she'd lost her *faith* in it, and she couldn't understand why. There appeared in her mind now the concept of "conversion experience." She was having one of these, she thought; it had taken her over and had destroyed the life she had known, even though she didn't really believe in conversion experiences and didn't know what she was converting to. She didn't even know whether she believed in the stuff she just wrote. The one thing she knew for sure was that if she pushed the button with the cursor on the send icon on this particular email, it would end forever any chance of getting back into Schuemacher's kind of engineering.

She read it over, revised it, and paused for a long sweaty moment with her finger over the fatal Chiclet. These irrecoverable acts! She thought about how nice Cambridge was in the autumn, the leaves crunching underfoot, the crisp days, going to the pool and swimming her limbs off, the intellectual stimulation of the labs, the steamy coffee bars, the unforgiving competition, the convenient sex. She sighed, she pressed.

And it was as if the button were also connected to her sympathetic nervous system: chill sweat popped out all over her skin, her belly roiled, her limbs trembled, her heart tripped. Depression descended like a gray mist, and crazy thoughts flitted through her head—write another email, drive to the airport, get on a bus, shoot herself in the head . . .

She ran out of the room, out of the house, and down to the beach. The beauty of the scene, the balmy air, seemed mocking, demonic, void of comfort; the water itself cried failure, all those countless hours of training a cruel joke.

"What's wrong, kid? You look like your cat died."

This was Skelly, encountering her on an aimless ramble down by the boat harbor.

"My career died," she responded. "Is that worse than a cat dying? If a museum was burning down and you could save only a cat, the *Mona Lisa*, or your career, which would you choose?"

"The cat. Seriously, though."

"Oh, I don't know, Skelly. I just resigned my assistantship, and I feel miserable and liberated at the same time. Does that mean I was fooling myself, doing the work I was doing? I mean, why else feel the liberation?"

"Yeah, I know what you mean. I felt like that when I declined re-upping in 1975. The army was my life and then it wasn't. I was supposed to be a command sergeant major, crusty, covered in privilege and perks, and then when I saw myself doing that it was a little puke-making."

She was all attention: a personal confession from *Skelly*?

"Why?" she asked, when he didn't continue. "Why did it stop being your life?"

He gave her a look that was for an instant terribly sad; then it changed and he slipped back into his persona, like a gecko scuttling behind a rock.

"I don't know—the dry-cleaning bills are huge, for one, and, two, I stopped being sure my country needed to be defended in the way I was trained to defend it. We're going to the market in a while. Want to come?"

"No, thanks. I want to stay here by myself and obsess and be miserable. I might even have a cry."

Skelly patted her shoulder and walked off. She watched him go, then stared out at the sea. I could just walk into it and swim out toward Asia until I sink, she thought, and entertained a short stack of similar moronic thoughts. She had her cry, then had a mildly hysterical laugh at her own expense. She waded into the clear water and washed her face in the sea. While she thus engaged, she heard a high voice saying, "Are you coming? It's time to go."

Oh, terrific, I'm hallucinating voices now, she thought, and then she felt a small hand clasp hers. She yelped and jumped half a yard backward.

The boy Ariel was standing there, smiling uncertainly. "Señorita? It's time to go. We're all going to the market. Don Eskelly is driving us in the truck."

Don Eskelly? Oh, right, him. It was Don Ricardo and Don Eskelly now around the *colonia*, and she was La Señorita, or sometimes La Marder, everyone slotted into semi-feudal roles, her new fate. The boy's smile resumed its joyful blaze, he reached out his hand again and she took it and allowed herself to be led. It was curiously comforting, she found, to be led by a child, she felt that the horrendous decisions were behind her now, *no importa madre*—a deplorable take on life, perhaps, but one with hitherto unexpected benefits. So she walked along and climbed onto the bed of the Ford, along with a dozen or so other people—Amparo and Epifania, Bartolomeo and Rosita—with the boy chattering away, explaining to her that this was the market where they would buy necessities for the Day of the Dead, the decorations and masks and toys, and the *candies*! But they were not to eat any of them until the day itself. The last one to board was Lourdes, who did not climb into the back but into the shotgun seat with Skelly. No one commented on this, and Statch, in her new version, did not register it as significant.

Off they went, swaying and laughing as the truck bumped over the rough causeway road. By the time they reached the plaza, Statch was herself again, although it was a different self from the one who had pressed the send key. Now she wandered through the market in this new self, not in a daze but in the opposite of a daze: a heightened awareness in which the anti-engineering portions of her brain seemed to have regained control. She stood transfixed for long minutes before pyramids of papayas, sapotes, cherimoyas, mangoes, and *aguajes*, before fans and stacks of bananas in all their varieties, red, mauve, yellow, and green; she walked through the butchers' aisles and saw the heads of cows and hogs, their violet tongues lolling, their clouded eyes crawling with flies, and felt the absence of gringa disgust; she stopped at a stall and ate a tortilla filled with *jumile* sauce—a delicacy of the season, made with tomatoes, serrano chilies, onions, and the ground bodies of mountain beetles; it tasted of iodine and cinnamon—something she would not have done in her former being, something even her mother had never served.

The hilarious aspects of death seemed to be a theme of this market, as the boy had foretold: skeleton masks in cloth and papier-mâché, sugar skulls, and elaborate dioramas of the dancing dead, all done in sugar and cake; costumes and shirts, flags, and ornaments, all marked with bones and grinning skulls. Statch bought a straw bag and filled it, buying almost at random—toys, garments, confections—and finished with a present for Skelly, an unlabeled long-necked tequila bottle half full of a habanero chili sauce guaranteeed by the old gentleman who made it to be the hottest in Mexico. One drop, Señorita, please, one drop only; she would be interested to see what Skelly made of it. As she strolled, she sampled foods from the various stalls, resonant of her childhood but in a major key, meat of uncertain provenance and unwashed fruits, knowing the consequences of this but not caring much, then having to find a public toilet and finding herself glad of the urgent evacuations, as if some part of her needed to be washed out; and she thought, irrationally, that this was the last bout of *turista* she would ever have, that she wanted to go back and eat and drink the foods of this country until she had re-created her physical body to fit her new Mexican self.

When she emerged from the toilet, she cut through an unfamiliar alley, seeking a shortcut back to the plaza, and came upon Lourdes. The girl was leaning against a green Navigator, talking to two men. The men were both in their late twenties and dressed in dark suits and white shirts with open collars, the uniform of La Familia *sicarios*, and of a superior grade.

Statch stopped, observing the scene. Lourdes seemed happy, joking with the taller of the two men, a good-looking fellow with that ever-attractive bad-boy smirk, and the other one, a squat toadish number with a wide leering mouth and an overhanging brow, an especially unfortunate look when coupled with the shaved-side buzz cut that his kind favored. Statch didn't usually think in such terms, but she now understood that she was looking at an evil face.

This man said something to Lourdes, bending over to say it into her ear, and Lourdes jerked her head away and responded loudly and with passion. She started to walk away, but the toad grabbed her arm.

Statch slung her bag across her chest and strode toward them. "Oh, hi, Lourdes," she called out. "I'm so glad I found you. We're just about to go home."

"Who's this?" asked the handsome one.

"That's the daughter," said Lourdes. "From the gringo who bought the house."

"Come on, Lourdes. We have to go," said Statch.

"From the gringo who bought the house," repeated the toad, looking Statch up and down in an unpleasant way. "You know, *chica*, your daddy shouldn't have done that. I think he should leave that house and go back to *El Norte* where he belongs."

"Lourdes—" said Statch.

"But since you're here, we were just going to have a party. The two of us and Lourdes, but now you'll come along too. It's a better number, don't you think, more interesting combinations. Salvador, put your girl-friend in the car."

The other man looped an arm around the girl's waist from behind and reached back for the rear door handle. The toad grabbed Statch's left arm.

But Lourdes, without warning, screamed and heaved forward. Her captor was off balance and let slip his grip, and Lourdes cannoned into the toad, who cursed, let go of Statch, and turned slightly, raising his hand to slap Lourdes. The other man recovered his balance and moved a step toward Lourdes. He grabbed at the back of her blouse. Lourdes twisted and ducked down and tried to squirm away between the two men.

Thus it was that the two men's heads were close together when Statch pulled out a bottle of the hottest chili sauce in Mexico and smashed it over the head of the toad, sending him to his knees and splashing the bulk of the bottle's fiery contents into the face of his friend.

The two women ran down the alley and out into a street that led back to the plaza. Statch was looking around wildly to see if she could spot Skelly, but to her surprise Lourdes stopped and would go no farther.

"I can't go out there with no blouse."

"Girl, those guys are going to kill us if they catch us. Now, come on!"

"No, I need something to wear. Why did you hit Gabriel with that bottle?"

"Why did I . . . ? For God's sake, Lourdes, they were going to kidnap us and do who knows what. Don't you have any sense at all? Here, put this on and let's go!"

She handed the girl a T-shirt she'd just bought, black with rows of printed red skulls. Lourdes put it on and had to stop to admire herself in a window. When they heard the sound of the SUV's motor, at last some primitive switch in Lourdes's brain closed and they ran back to the market.

When they'd caught their breath and were standing by the red Ford, where Skelly and the others had gathered, Statch asked, "Who were those guys, by the way? It looked like you knew them."

"I do know them. Salvador is my boyfriend."

"Your *boyfriend*?"

"Yes. He wants to marry me, but I don't know anymore, not since I have this opportunity. But it would be a big wedding, you know, he promised me, in the church and at the Hotel Diamante after. He's very rich."

"Lourdes, he's a gangster."

"Yes, but maybe he'll do something else. Only I got mad when El Cochinillo said he wanted to fuck me at, you know, the same time as Salvador. I thought that wasn't very nice. And Salvador didn't say anything, he just stood there grinning. And I got mad. And then you came along."

Lourdes said this with a faintly accusing tone, as if Statch had rudely interrupted a lovely party.

"And who's El Cochinillo?"

"He's Salvador's best friend. They call him the Piglet because he's the son of El Jabalí, the Boar; you know, the *jefe* of the plaza in Cárdenas."

She lowered her voice, as the locals did when they discussed *los malosos*. "You know, La Familia Michoacána. They don't usually hurt women, except El Jabalí lets El Cochinillo do it. I think you should go away from here, Carmel."

"I think you should pick better boyfriends. Anyway, you'll be in Defe soon and you'll have plenty of non-gangster guys at your disposal."

"Yes, I will," said Lourdes. "Look, do you ever wear a padded bra? You know, with push-up?" She demonstrated on her own flawless examples.

"No, I don't. Why do you ask?"

"Because men like it, and you'll never get a boyfriend without a set of *bombas*. My girlfriend Pilar got one and she has a boyfriend now. You know, they're probably going to kill your father. El Jabalí is very mad at him, Salvador said. And now they'll probably kill you too, because you hit the Piglet with a bottle of hot sauce. But, really, it was very funny. Why did you go crazy like that? They weren't going to rape you or anything."

"Oh, you know that for a fact?"

"Yes. El Jabalí doesn't like rapes, and he kills rapists and cuts off their *chiles* first. He's a Christian. He only does what God says."

13

Marder walked out on his terrace and watched his daughter helping Skelly and a crew of *colonia* men bolt the shaft of the cell-phone mast to one of the squat towers that guarded the four corners of Casa Feliz. The towers were actual rooms, unfinished but weather-tight, devised, he imagined, for the storage of terrace furniture. One of them was electrified and piped for a wet bar that had never been installed, and Skelly planned to use it for the base station of the cell. One of his "guys" was in contact with someone from Telmex, who, for the usual consideration, would mate the cell to his company's system. This was not an unusual arrangement, Marder had learned, provided so that the wealthy in isolated haciendas need not give up the benefits of modern technology. Cheap cell phones had been distributed generally around the *colonia*—nice for the people and vital to what Skelly hoped to develop into an efficient little militia and threat-detection network.

With deep pleasure, Marder observed the fierce concentration with which his girl fired bolts into the concrete to hold the brackets for the antenna mast while also joking with Skelly and the crew as they worked. She seemed happy and unaffected by the encounter yesterday with the younger Cuello. Marder felt now that, curiously, he had come out on the other side of worry, because worry was useless and degrading. This was the upside of *no importa madre*—a man did not spend energy on obsessing about what could not be helped. His daughter's breaking a bottle over the Piglet's head would not make Cuello hate Marder more than he already did, and in a way it furthered Marder's cause. He wanted Cuello enraged, in fact.

Marder himself had spent the day setting up a Web marketing system. He had edited a book about it some years back and found it a fairly painless exercise. Young Epifania had been tasked to go around to the small factories and take digital photos of their work, and the thing was coming along nicely. He'd hired an outfit in New York to set up fulfillment software and handle billing and tax matters and a firm in Santa Clara to market the goods to high-end crafts shops in big American and European cities. Thus commerce progressed in the wired global marketplace. He had no great hopes of making a fortune for these people, but he wished at least to secure a better living than they had been used to, as well as a place for them to live.

Life flowed on smoothly for the next week or so, and the house was indeed as happy as its name. The cell phones went on. A prefab steel building was delivered by flatbed truck and assembled on a concrete slab to serve as an office and warehouse. The animals (except poultry) were herded away from the humans and corralled at the northern end of the island. The septic field went in, and plastic pipes were laid to distribute water. Marder was startled and gratified by the way the people organized themselves for communal tasks like this. Skelly or Carmel would lay out the technical requirements, and they would set up the project and carry it forth without altercation or confusion, which was what one might expect from a people with a thousand years' experience in self-directed communal water engineering and agriculture.

In this period, Marder was conscious of a kind of unreal lightness of spirit that was supposed to be typical of long sea voyages before the era of instant communication. Anything might be happening, anything may be waiting when one struck port, but now, in the instant, all was peace and contentment. He loved sitting with a drink in his hand, on his rooftop, looking at the lights of the *colonia* and listening to the music drift up, depending on the breeze, from this or that radio. In the other direction, from the pool, came the sound of Lourdes and her court of maidens. Since her audition, Lourdes had become the happy genius of the house and instantly the most popular figure at her school. Everyone wanted to be a friend of the future star, and this attention, far from making the girl insufferable, had tapped hitherto unsuspected springs of charity. She loaned clothing and baubles, she shared the makeup tips she had learned from Pepa herself, and if there was envy bubbling up from the maidens, somehow Lourdes floated above it on the fluffy cloud of satisfied aspiration.

In the mornings, Marder would often awaken to the sound of churned water—his daughter dutifully doing her hundred laps—and he would peer out through his shutters to watch her long body slice through the pool. It was amazing to him that she had the energy. She worked harder than anyone else; she was at every work site in her shorts and sweat-soaked T-shirt and her tin hard hat with the butterfly decal on it. She was cordial enough to him when they happened to get together, for meals or in passing, but she did not seem at all interested in a deeper relationship with her father; she appeared to be locked in some private quandary, excluding him. What he'd wanted when he left New York was a withdrawal from contact, so now this pain could not in decency be acknowledged. The joke was on him.

For her part, Carmel found herself full of joyful energy during most of her working day. There was something about dealing directly with mud and steel, stone, fire, glass, and clay that made her silly happy, like a little girl puttering around a sand pile, and there was also something about working with people like Rosita Morales that she did not get from sharing a cube with Karen Liu. It was like being with her mother again, learning how to make meals from scratch, from the raw foodstuffs brought home from Mexican markets. Yes, she understood intellectually that all that D. H. Lawrence stuff about primal-life-force energies and the moral superiority of the uncivilized was bullshit, but here it was, undeniable in her body. It annoyed her, this disconnect between what was supposed to be and how she felt, and she took it out on her father, the source.

And another thing: in the days that had passed since the visit to Mexico City, she had taken to avoiding breakfast at the house and having coffee at a little chica-hut place on the beach north of town. Amparo's coffee was first-rate, and Casa Feliz was of course wonderful, but not, she had decided, every fucking minute of the day. She'd bought a motorcycle, a used Suzuki 250, so that she didn't have to take one of the trucks every time she had to go to town or to Cárdenas to order supplies. She would ride it to Miguelito's shack early in the morning and sit there with a *café con leche* and a tamarind *torta* or a *gordita,* the typical brown-sugar cookie of Michoacán, which she had baked innumerable times with her mother.

Now, sitting on her favorite bench, gazing at the ocean, with the sun rising over the sierra and just starting to warm her back, she felt, in that strange way, another kind of prickle in that spot and turned abruptly to see if someone was in fact staring at her or if she had descended another notch into crazy. But it was an actual stare: Major Naca, pretending not to be watching her through his aviator sunglasses.

Caught, he smiled, nodded, asked if he could join her. A slight bob of her head and he came over. A few pleasantries—the weather, the sea— and then, "I hear you're doing wonderful things on the island," he said. "Many busy hands, money flowing, trucks in and out all day. Everyone is impressed."

"Even the army?"

"I can't speak for the army. But the Casa Feliz is well regarded in the district. The army is more concerned with, can I say, the peripheral relationships you've established with the gangs. For example, we find it interesting that people from Casa Feliz, such as yourself, are typically followed around by vehicles full of gun thugs. There's one such car on the road out there."

"It's no crime to hire security. This is a dangerous region, and you yourself observed that we have reason to fear at least one of the many drug gangs."

"Yes, but in this part of the world it's often the case that to protect is to own."

"And if the army were doing its job properly, we would have no need to hire gun thugs."

Naca looked startled for a moment and then laughed. "On the other hand, lie down with dogs, get up with fleas, as my dear grandmother used to say. Of course we should do better, but the country is very large and the army is small and the drug gangs increase without limit. In fact, my unit is pulling out tomorrow."

"Where are you going?"

"That is a state secret, I'm afraid." He drew a thin cigar out of a case, asked her if she minded, got a no, lit it with a silver lighter, and left both case and lighter on the bench. He added, "You will have to rely on the federal drug police for the time being."

"I thought they were corrupt."

"Some are, and some are not. Again, poor Mexico. But I didn't follow you here to discuss poor Mexico. How did you enjoy your trip to Chilangolandia?"

"It was fine."

"It must have been. A shopping spree and an interview with a famous telenovela producer for that pretty girl. Did you buy anything yourself?"

"Not much," she said. "I'm happy to see that the army is keeping track of our movements."

"To an extent, and only for protective purposes. And, also, your father's involvement with that little girl has set tongues wagging. It is very like a telenovela. The rich American comes to town, fights off the bad guys, scoops up the town beauty for himself—what could possibly happen next?"

"My father is not having an affair with Lourdes Almones. I thought the same when I came down here, but it's not so. He decided to help her into a career as a TV star out of pure generosity."

"Really. You amaze me."

"Yes, well, my father is an amazing man in many ways. He believes in helping people obtain their heart's desire. It's part of his religious practice."

"How so? I thought religion was about rejecting the world."

"True. But people fixate on some secular prize they think will make them happy, and in general they don't get it and so spend their lives thinking that they would achieve paradise if they did get it; therefore, they ignore God. Whereas if they did get it, they would realize it was all ashes and turn instead to the true source of happiness."

"He has explained this to you?"

"Of course not. It's just a theory, based on a lifetime of studying Richard Marder."

"So you're telling me he has bought this girl expensive clothing and obtained an opening for her with the biggest telenovela producer in Mexico so that eventually she will become a star and see that stardom is ashes compared to God?"

"Something like that. I see you're astounded. You disbelieve it."

"I would never doubt the word of a lady, Señorita. But it seems an unusually long game to play."

"My father *is* unusual, Major, far more than he seems. He is certainly the most genuinely religious man in my experience, yet he didn't insist that my brother and I participate in the Church, and we don't. When we jumped ship, he barely said a word in defense of his religion, only . . . what you just said reminds me of an exception to that. He often used to say, 'God plays a very long game.' It was often in response to our childish challenges, as, for example, how do you believe in a good God when there's so much misery around? God plays a very long game, and so does my father, I believe. Perhaps he will even provide you with your heart's desire."

Major Naca was silent for a moment, perhaps thinking of what this might be, then he smiled—not the tight official grin he'd been using but a far more boyish and charming expression. "Well, I would like this campaign to succeed and to reap honors and promotion. I am in intelligence, and promotion is very slow in intelligence." He tapped the colored insignia flashes on his uniform that supported his major's star. "They think we are all *maricónes* in intelligence, and the very *macho* guys who run the army don't trust us. But I would like very much to be a colonel. Could he arrange that, do you think?"

She smiled back at him. "*Narcoviolencia* suppressed? Consider it done. But, really, there's something I've been wondering. Why exactly is it so hard to round up these guys? I mean, they're pretty open, and surely it shouldn't be that hard to disrupt their operations, the meth labs and all that, when you have essentially a free hand."

"Oh, we round them up all right, but their soldiers are easily replaceable from our infinite supply of *ni-nis,* and the leaders are in deep hiding. And, of course—"

"Servando Gomez isn't in deep hiding. He spends all day in the back room of Los Tres Hermanos in the middle of Playa Diamante."

"Yes, I know. And if I launched an assault with heavy weapons on that cantina, I might be able to kill him, along with a few dozen civilians. The problem is that shooting a leader is nothing. Another leader arises and is challenged and then there's even more violence. If we could sweep all of them into a football arena at once, that would be wonderful, but we can't, and soldiers are not undercover cops, after all. We can chuck them out of a town or village that they've taken over, but when we leave they come back and suborn or terrify the local police. Also, Mexico is always on the verge of an insurrection of some kind, and we are close to such a tipping point now, with all this violence. More than forty thousand people dead—and it would not take a lot to turn this country into something more like Afghanistan, with drug gangs posing as popular movements controlling big swaths of country. Some might say we're there already." He let out a self-deprecating laugh. "This is why I don't pursue a career in the tourism industry. I have a deep pessimism of my native land."

"*No importa madre*," she said.

"Just so. But one does what one can."

Statch couldn't think of anything to say to this but had a strong sense, almost a déjà vu, that so far every single man she'd liked, sexually or not, had evinced this attitude toward the generally crappy mess mankind had made of the world. She now became aware of a private soldier standing at attention a few feet behind Major Naca, waiting to be noticed, hesitant about moving into his superior's field of view while he was putting the make on the gringa, a situation apparently not covered in whatever passed for the Mexican Soldier's Guide.

She motioned to the man, who trotted forward, saluted, and informed the major that brigade was on the radio and wanted to talk to him immediately. Naca dismissed the private, who saluted again and disappeared.

"I must go now," the major said. "It's been a pleasure, this conversation, and I hope to have another—that is, if you are staying in the area."

"I will be here for a while, I believe. And I would hope so too."

He reached into his tunic pocket and brought out a leather-covered notebook.

"Here is my card. Please call me at any time."

She took the card and smiled. A charming smile from the major in return. She extended her hand; he took it, kissed it, and turned to leave then back to face her again, now no longer smiling.

"There is one thing I should tell you, in the nature of 'lie down with dogs, get up with fleas.' Do you know who Salvador Manuel García is?"

She did not.

"Well, then, you know who Melchor Gabriel Cuello is. El Cochinillo?"

"Yes, I do." She felt a brief chill and a strong desire to tell the major about what had transpired in the street near the market, but she suppressed both.

"Then you must know he's not a pleasant fellow, but he does have friends, of a sort, and the closest of these friends is Salvador García. For the past month or so, Señor García has been trying to seduce Lourdes Amparo, perhaps with success, perhaps not. Our intel goes only so far. But I'm sure he's heard the rumors about Lourdes and your father, and he'll not be overly concerned whether or not they're true. The world must acknowledge that the girl is his to take. Quite to one side is the possibility that, having seen the big world now and having this splendid opportunity before her, she might not be as interested in a provincial villain with a grade school education and a short future. García has not been brought up to deal well with rejection. Perhaps you should be on your guard."

"Thank you. I'll tell my father," she said. For an unknown reason she felt like weeping for an instant, but this passed. She said, "'Mexicans, at the cry of war, make ready the steel and the bridle!'"

The major sang the next lines of the national anthem in a fine baritone: "'And may the earth tremble to its core at the resounding roar of the cannon!'" Then he departed, still singing.

Marder awoke from his siesta that afternoon to what sounded like automatic-weapons fire. He fumbled for his pistol, slipped into huaraches, and was halfway down the stairs before he correctly identified the percussive bangs as coming from nail guns. He recalled Statch asking him about buying a compressor and guns to speed up construction, and he must have agreed. Or maybe Amparo had asked him. He was not sure who was in charge of what anymore, and that was fine with him. He was not running a corporation, precisely, but something older and more Mexican. He imagined that the *latifundistas* of old, including Chole's ancestors, had dealt in this way with the details of the vast estates.

He descended to the kitchen and had a few words with Evangelista, the cook, who pressed on him a glass of cold fresh orange juice. He drank it, smiled, said it was good; she beamed in delight. Everyone was happy when the *patrón* was happy. Marder could see how easily corruption might seep into the soul through this pleasant path, until one became a petulant monster, and resolved yet again that this would not happen to him.

He went toward the small room at the back of the house that Amparo used as her office. When he walked in, she was talking on a landline phone and peering at a laptop screen, looking very much like an executive. But when she caught sight of Marder in her doorway, she immediately became a servant again, terminating her call abruptly and standing up, awaiting orders.

Marder sighed. He had no talent at this, navigating through the fogs of class and status. Chole had done it naturally, but he did not; they

didn't teach that in America, because in that nation class had to be concealed behind a scrim of hypocrisy—the waiter, the domestic, the nanny;
were they not all equal, all pals?

"You don't have to stop what you're doing and stand up when I come
in, Amparo. I'm not the president."

She sat down, obedient; the mask dropped and she waited passively
for his command. He asked her what she was doing, and after a few
moments the intelligence lit up in her face again and she enthusiastically
described how she was working with Statch to set up a website for the
Feliz co-op and establish accounts to sell goods via Etsy. The nail guns
were apparently in use to set up a prefab warehouse and office. When
Amparo finished this account, Marder complimented her work and asked
if she knew where Don Eskelly and Statch were now.

She pointed upward. "They're in the tower, installing the cell-phone
machine with the man from Telmex."

They were indeed. The man from Telmex was a pudgy pale-for-
a-Mexican fellow in a short-sleeved striped shirt, a big-knotted tie, and—
was it possible?—a plastic pocket protector and rack of pens. He was in
the small tower room with Carmel and Skelly and a collection of gray
metal cases wired to one another and to the tower above. They were deep
into techland and not happy with Marder's interruption. He motioned to
Skelly, who came out to the terrace.

"What's going on?"

"We're rolling good. We should have service supremo by dinner-
time."

"Who's the guy?"

"José from Telmex. He's being very helpful. Statch's nerdar lit up the
minute he walked in, and, as for him, he's putty in her hands. He says
no problemo, there's line of sight between us and a Telmex array up on
the nearest ridge of the Sierra. You can just about see it from here. So
we're fine."

"Does Telmex know about this?"

"In a manner of speaking. Elements of the Telmex company are
aware."

"*Elements?* What does that mean?"

Skelly made an impatient gesture. "Stop *worrying*, Marder! Everything's been smoothed out. I mean, it's Mexico, you know? Speaking of
which, Statch ran into Major Naca out on the beach. He said Lo's ex-

boyfriend is a big gun with La Fam. He said this gentlemen has a beef with you now that you're enjoying her luscious young body."

"Do you think there's any way we can suppress that rumor?"

"I don't know. Leaflets, maybe, from a light plane. A TV ad? Or you and I could start kissing and feeling each other up in public. That, by the way, is an entirely independent rumor that's going around."

"Wonderful. 'The idiocy of village life'—Marx. What's this *guapo*'s name?"

"Salvador Manuel García."

"We know what he looks like, I presume."

"I'll check, but he's probably on Facebook."

"I'm sure. My interests: long walks on the beach, travel, dismembering enemies. But you'll tell your boys to keep an eye out, yes?"

"Right. And you might want to have a conversation with young Lourdes about the 'ex' status of Salvador. Statch thinks she might be using her new career ops to stick the knife in a little. Before that, he was the big shot offering her a boost, and now it's she who's going to go off and be a star. Not a good position for Lourdes to be in, given we can presume Salvador is a vengeful decapitator type of person. I'm concerned about her face, specifically."

"We're in a telenovela, Skelly."

"To an extent, yes. I have to keep reminding you it's Mexico."

"Speaking of which, how's the security thing going? I haven't been keeping track."

"Pretty well, considering it's early days and we don't have most of our weapons. My guys are in fair physical shape—a little underweight maybe, but that's better than starting with fatties. They can shoot pistols, and I'm working on basic hand-to-hand. They don't know how to move worth a shit, but that's hard to teach. As you know. On the other hand, we'll be on defense for a while, until . . ."

Marder saw that Skelly had been about to say something and then thought better of it. "Until what?"

"Oh, you know—until I can work them up a little more," he replied smoothly. "I should get back and see if I can help Statch and José," he added, and headed toward the tower, forestalling the inquisition that Marder clearly had in mind.

Am I the last to know anything around here? Marder thought. Are they protecting me from the burden of command or manipulating me?

Is there a difference? He had a good deal of paper and computer work to accomplish, but he didn't feel like going to his office just yet and, being the lord, he could do as he pleased. He walked down through the house and out through the grounds of the *casa* and through the gate that led to the *colonia*.

School had obviously let out and the bus must have deposited the children some minutes ago, because the street was full of kids in uniforms. Among them was Lourdes, surrounded by her court of devotees. Since the triumph of Mexico City, Lourdes had been punctilious about attending school, good as gold was our Lourdes, a girl who could keep a bargain. Marder paused and watched the girls run past, their slim brown legs flashing under hems hoisted by rolled waistbands far higher than their mothers had sewn. It was like having a flock of birds of paradise on the place, and Marder enjoyed the aesthetic pleasures of watching them, without—so far as he was aware—the lecherousness attributed by his community. One of the girls caught sight of him, and there passed a flurry of whispers and loud giggles. Lourdes, however, kept her head, did not join in the giggling, but met his eye and delivered a courtly inclination of her head, which he returned. Then they ran down the gravel path to the servants' house.

Marder continued past that to the main street of the *colonia*. This had been graded and graveled, and a crew of men was ditching on the side of the road and laying fat white plastic piping. Marder didn't recall authorizing any of this, but he imagined he was paying for it. No one seemed to be in charge, but the work was being done anyway. The houses along the road looked neater, less like favela shacks and more like little homes. They had put up poles for running current from the diesel generator.

As he strolled along, he noticed that the people paused in their work when they saw him and took the time to nod or wave or call out a greeting, nothing embarrassingly deferential, but they were happy and knew that it was his doing and they wanted him to know that they knew it. He recalled how similarly the villagers in Laos had responded to Skelly and the other soldiers and felt a pang. Here, too, a simple and reasonably happy life was surrounded by demons who wanted to destroy it—there politics, here greed and the need to dominate and control. Somehow he had acquired the responsibilty for preventing that from happening in this domain. In that instant he felt the true weight and a blast of pathetic self-pity: he wanted to be back in his comfortable loft, in his nice leather chair, with a thick galley his only task, a thousand pages about North Korea, so easy to grasp compared with the current tangle, and no lives at stake.

He shook himself out of this—physically shaking, like a horse, drawing looks. Moving on, he observed the start of local commerce. There was a tiny bodega selling canned goods, beer, candy, sweet drinks, and flour and a place that washed clothing and a woman with a sewing machine and a man with piles of used clothing, tires, and batteries. And a cantina consisting of a scatter of miscellaneous plastic chairs and tables, a sunshade of corrugated green fiberglass on posts, and a flush door set across oil drums, the bar.

At one of the tables, in the back, in deep shade, sat the priest, Father Santana, his head bent in conversation with a woman. Marder sat at another table and the proprietor came out immediately, smiling, asking what he could offer Don Ricardo. A beer, which arrived in a flash, icy, and a glass, the same, and a plate of tortilla chips with a small pot of *mole* to dip them in. The proprietor was a squat man everyone called Juan Pequeño. After he served the beer, Juan Pequeño lingered, and Marder could see he wanted to say something and so asked him if there was anything he could do for him. After several mumbling starts and apologies, it being such a small matter, far too small to interest Don Ricardo, and so on, the proprietor told his tale: *los malosos* had been ripping off his beer and *pulque* deliveries, and he was a poor man and could do nothing himself, but since Señor, as was well known, had no fear of *los malosos*, had driven them out like dogs, could he perhaps . . .

Marder said he'd look into it; effusions of gratitude, and the man withdrew. Marder drank his beer and noticed that a small crowd, of perhaps seven or eight people, had gathered in the street, forming what was not quite a waiting line. He noticed, too, that the priest's woman had left and another woman had moved into the chair opposite him; he had a line as well. Marder looked across and met Santana's eye for a moment. The eye rolled up slightly, humorously, and teeth shone in a smile. Then the man's face grew serious again and he turned to his supplicant.

After the final petitioner, Marder pulled out the little notebook he always carried and made notes. When he looked up from this task, Father Santana was sliding into the chair opposite and gesturing for a beer.

When this had been delivered and half of it drunk in one long set of swallows, Marder said, "Come here often?"

A weak joke, but Santana took it literally. "A couple of times a week. It's hard for the older people to get to the church in town, so I make house calls, so to speak. How often do you come?"

"Never. Or I should say this is the first time. But I'm glad I ran into you. I'm planning to inter the ashes of my late wife in her family's crypt in La Huacana. I was wondering if you would consent to come along and say the proper words."

"I would be happy to. Have you considered that the Day of the Dead is almost upon us? Perhaps that would be the appropriate time. I have Masses to say in the morning and other duties, but I would be available later. We could drive up there in the afternoon."

Marder thanked him and they both drank their beers for a while. No one else approached them. Then Marder said, "What just happened—it's a little weird, I have to say. I sit down for a beer and all of a sudden I'm holding court."

"Well, you're the *patrón*. It's part of the job. And, to be honest, I'd much rather see you do it than El Gordo or the Piglet."

"Yes, but I'm not very good at it. I don't know these people at all. I have no sense of who's right or wrong, honest or dishonest."

"You'll learn. The people here are nothing if not patient. And you're a decent man."

"Am I? They think I'm sleeping with a teenager."

The priest laughed. "Well, of course they do, but they don't think badly of you for it. The men admire, the women are envious: it's the way things are. The richest man gets the most beautiful girl, and they have every confidence that you will take care of her and provide for the children. And in any case it's a preferable outcome to the alternative, which is that she would be snatched up by one of *los malosos*. In fact, I believe that this has already occurred."

"Yes, I heard that too, and I have no idea what I'm supposed to do about it. Do you have any advice for me?"

"Oh, it's not a case for advice, my friend. It would be like advising the river how to flow or the tide when to turn."

"Meaning?"

"Meaning this is your fate, obviously, and the people here understand this. Two men arrive in town out of nowhere, bringing a shower of gold and casting out the villains. And we here are of two minds. First we put out our tubs to catch whatever part of the shower we can. Then we sit and watch the show; we cannot take our eyes away, even though we know it will end badly, for this is Mexico, the graveyard of hope."

"But this is real life, not a telenovela," said Marder. "We have free will, or has the Church changed that too?"

"No, but the belief in fate is much older around these parts than the Church and its teachings. In pre-Conquest times, when my ancestors fought their wars, the point of battle was not to kill the enemy but to capture him, so he could have his heart torn out atop a pyramid. And for the sacrifice to be perfect, the victim had to be almost uninjured, save for some ritualized cuts. This is why they were called the striped ones. Therefore, when a warrior was cut in this way, he would surrender and resign himself to that fate. They were outraged when the Spanish murdered them in their thousands and even more outraged when the Spanish fought to the death rather than surrender. The Spaniards were ruled by an entirely different story, the story of chivalry, knights fighting for glory and sacrificing *themselves*, do you see, and not their captives. A more compelling story, perhaps, but, in any case, that narrative was victorious. Though not entirely victorious: the two stories blended and became Mexico, and that is why, although we have had white knight after white knight—Hidalgo, Morelos, Zapata, Madero, Villa, Cárdenas—crusade after crusade, still everything remains the same. No, I tell a lie—things are not quite the same. Now we tear out people's hearts figuratively instead of literally atop a pyramid in Tenochtitlán."

"That's a little cynical and bitter for a priest, don't you think?"

"No, you mistake me, sir. I am neither bitter nor cynical. I remain interested, indeed fascinated, by the story that is playing out. I have hope. Miracles occur, to be sure, and perhaps you are one of them." He looked past Marder and added, "And here is your beautiful daughter coming down the street. Of course the knight must have a beautiful daughter. A beautiful daughter and an ugly sidekick—it is almost a requirement. Not to mention that the beautiful daughter can transform herself into a man and do man's work when needed. This is also in the legends, the magical girl." Then, to the girl, "Good day to you, my dear. What have you in that bag?"

Statch greeted the priest and took from the fat plastic bag she was carrying a cheap prepaid cell phone. "The tower is up. I'm giving out cell phones."

Father Santana studied the thing, turning it over in his brown hands, an expression of delight on his face. "A marvel rather than a miracle, I think, but it will do for the present. I have been meaning to get one of these, but they're so expensive here and the reception is so bad. Now I can please my mother and annoy the bishop. Thank you, Señor Marder and daughter!"

Marder did not know how many cell phones had been distributed in the *casa* and the *colonia*, but through the remainder of the day he observed nearly everyone he encountered walking in the way that characterized modern man, with a hand pressed to the ear and a faraway look. While he understood the benefits, he found it made him a bit sad.

He was therefore somewhat withdrawn at dinner, saying little, while Statch and Skelly were almost antic with their success, trading jokes about their exploits and about the phenomenon of José the Telmex nerd, about how the cultures of nerd and machismo had produced a being who managed remarkably to be both at the same time, like a torero with Asperger's.

Marder went to bed early and checked in with both God and Mr. Thing, praying orthodoxly to the one and superstitiously to the other that if tonight was the night, it should be done completely, not leaving him a husk or impaired, and if not, then that would be preferable for the moment. Marder felt stupid when he did this, but he always did it. He didn't think that feeling stupid was such a bad thing.

Another ritual at bedtime was to stand naked in front of the window and look out past the terraces to the sea. A half-moon hung low in the cloudless night, making a stripe of cold fire on the backs of the waves. He used to do this in his loft and at various places where he spent the night, vacation lodgings and so on, and on many of these occasions his wife would come up soundlessly and embrace him from behind and kiss him at just the height her lips could reach between his shoulder blades. He never heard her coming, it was always a delight and a surprise and a prelude to a particularly wonderful kind of sex.

Chole's ghost tiptoed out of the bathroom, and he felt her lips on that spot and let out a cry and whirled around in terror. An enormous moth. Still trembling, he urged the creature out of the window and closed it, then dived into bed and pulled the coverlet up to his chin, like a frightened child.

Marder awoke in the dark to gunshots and a shrill scream. He rose sluggishly out of a dream in which both he and Skelly and a man whose book he had edited twenty years ago were behaving inappropriately with Lourdes Almones. Shaking himself awake, Marder stumbled into shorts and slippers, grabbed his pistol, and ran out of his bedroom.

The screams continued, and he recognized them as coming from Lourdes and their location as the wooded area below the terraces and above the beach, where palms and *cocolobos* grew. Someone turned on the outside floodlights, and Marder therefore did not break his neck crossing the terraces and descending the stairs that led to the beach. There, in a sandy clearing in a grove of palms lit weirdly by slats of light streaming through the fronds, he found the source of the screaming. Lourdes, her face and hair covered with blood, was shrieking curses and beating at Skelly, with him blocking blows and chanting calming phrases at her to no great effect. Lying on the sand was a young man. He was crying out too but more weakly, declaring his undying love even to the point of actual death. Marder knelt down by the man's side. Marder assumed this was the expected Salvador Manuel García and so addressed him and asked him how he was, promising help was on its way. He'd been shot twice through the torso, one high, one low, and he did not look good, although he had clearly looked quite good previously—a slim, handsome *guapo* with the cropped hair and the tattoos. When he registered who Marder was, García uttered a string of curses. This was all Marder's fault, it turned out, and García pledged fearsome revenge, describing the excruciations that Marder would undergo at the hands of his compadres in La Familia, interrupting the dreadful catalog only to shout out the name of his beloved.

People were arriving now, from the nearer areas of the *colonia* and the house. The indispensable Amparo was one of these, dressed in a robe and slippers. She took in the scene, yanked her niece away from Skelly, delivered two slaps like whip cracks to the girl's face, and dragged her weeping away. Marder organized some of the men to carry Salvador Manuel up to the house and used his new cell phone to dial 060 and request an ambulance.

When this was done, he turned to Skelly. "What the fuck, Skelly?"

"He was going to cut her face. As it was, he gashed her scalp pretty good, as you saw. I yelled for him to get away from her and drop the blade, but he raised it again and was going for another swipe when I shot him. This is García the boyfriend, as you probably gathered."

"Yes. And why did he decide to cut her, do you know?"

"From what I overheard, she was trying to let him down easy, on account of having to go to Defe for her career, and he went nuts and said it was because everyone knew she was fucking you and he was going to kill you and cut her face off, and then he pulled out the knife."

"So you saved her and she attacked *you*?"

"What can I say—it's Mexico. They're living out their parts in a *narcocorrido*. Speaking of which, how are we going to play this?"

"Just a second—how come you were out here?"

"I get up every night to check the perimeter. We don't have enough guns to mount a full guard with our guys, and I don't exactly trust the Templos. I was walking the beach—where we're wide open, by the way—and heard voices, so I walked up the steps to check out what was going on."

A plausible story, and the darkness kept Marder from reading Skelly's face. A little too plausible, he thought, but that was a side issue at this point.

"Give me the gun," Marder said.

"Why?"

"Because it makes a better story if I'm the shooter. I'm a Mexican citizen, and you're here on papers that won't stand up. You can have my Kimber, and it'd be a good idea if you went back to your room for a little while, just until the cops have done their business. And before you do that, I'd like you to get with Statch—I don't want her involved in this. Tie her down if you have to, but keep her away from the cops."

Skelly started to protest but then grasped the wisdom of this solution, exchanged pistols with Marder, and disappeared in the direction of the beach. Marder climbed back to the house.

The men had rolled a chaise longue out from the terrace, laid García on it, and covered him with a blanket. He was unconscious now and looking gray. Marder went up to his room, dressed, splashed some water on his face, cleared the pistol, picked up his wallet and Mexican passport, and went downstairs, just as sirens announced the arrival of the ambulance and the cops.

In the servants' apartment, he found Amparo tending to the now-exhausted girl. Amparo seemed to have stopped the bleeding and had cleaned the blood from Lourdes's face. Marder explained the new story of what had happened and why Lourdes had to confirm it if the police asked. Lourdes nodded her agreement; of course one lied to the police—how else could one live?

That settled, Marder went back to the front of the house and watched García being loaded into the ambulance. When this had departed, two men in good-looking business suits and handsome shoes approached him; both of them were light-skinned with good haircuts. They showed their credentials—*federales*, it appeared. They also announced their membership in the elite drug police: officers Varela and Gil. Varela had a mustache and Gil did not, but besides that they could have been brothers, so similar did they appear. Or perhaps, Marder thought, it was fatigue and the late hour. Marder showed them his Mexican passport and explained who he was.

"We know who you are, Señor," said Gil, glancing without much interest at the passport. "Perhaps you can explain what happened here, how the young man came to be shot."

Then Marder told his convenient lie to a pair of blank faces. They asked no questions, nor did they seem interested in talking to anyone else. Marder thought this was a bad sign. When Marder had finished, Gil said, "This is a serious crime—you'll have to come with us."

"Can't it wait until morning? I own this property. Do you think I'm going to flee because I shot a trespasser who was trying to kill one of my servants?"

"Your girlfriend," said Varela, and the two of them moved closer.

"She's not my girlfriend," said Marder, but they had already grabbed his arms, cuffed his wrists, and forced him into the back of their SUV.

14

For as long as Marder could recall, his singular horror was being tied up, confined, or physically helpless. When he was a small boy, a pair of older cousins—sadists in the usual way of older cousins—liked to play cowboys and Indians with him, the climax of this game being little Rick bound and gagged in a dark closet in the basement of their Brooklyn home. He would become hysterical and wet himself when they did this, which only added to the fun. During his time in Vietnam, Marder's chief fear was not death or maiming but being captured by the enemy, trussed up, stuck in a tiny cage. He'd resolved that he'd never surrender, he'd fight to the death. This resolve had been tested back then: after what happened in Moon River, Marder had not, in fact, surrendered.

Now, handcuffed in the back of a car, in the custody of men who, if not actual sadists, certainly meant him no good, Marder felt the beginnings of that hysteria pluck at his vitals. He took deep breaths and wished he had paid attention to the YouTube clips on how to escape from handcuffs in fifteen seconds.

Quite aside from this particular neurosis, Marder was conscious of something wrong about the current situation. He had never been arrested before, but, like every American, he'd seen fictional representations of thousands of arrests, and he'd edited several true-crime books, and these officers were not acting like any officers he'd ever learned about, fictional or real. Perhaps they weren't officers at all. He braked this morbid speculation with a conscious effort. There was something wrong, but it was more complicated than a simple assassination. What, for example, were the federal drug police doing investigating a crime of passion? And if they were corrupt, why hadn't they suggested a bribe?

The car drove along for what seemed like hours to Marder, but he knew that was an illusion. The windows had been darkened so heavily that he could not see where they were headed, but the sounds that penetrated had changed from rural to urban. They must be somewhere in Cárdenas. The car slowed, turned sharply, and halted.

Gil opened the door and pulled Marder out. They were in what appeared to be a parking space under a building. Marder did not ask where they were or what was happening, because he knew they wouldn't answer and that he would lose dignity by being ignored. The two *federales* (if they were) led him up a few steps onto a landing, through an unmarked steel door, then up two flights of concrete steps and through a glass door marked "213." The light in the office was bright enough to make Marder squint, and it was uninhabited by office workers or policemen so far as he could observe. They frisked him efficiently, removing his cell phone and wallet and popping both into a plastic bag. He was relieved to see them do this, because if they had pulled the cash and dumped the rest, it would have been a different kind of Mexican arrest and not good news. Then they placed him in a small room containing the canonical table and three chairs and left him alone there, sitting in the chair with the wall at his back, still with his hands cuffed behind him.

The room was small, stuffy, and windowless, but it did not look like an official interrogation venue. For one thing, it lacked the expected and useful one-way mirror. Also, neither the chairs nor the table were fixed to the floor. Time passed, and after a while Marder allowed himself to be amused. Mr. Thing had rendered him helpless, and he had thrust himself into a life-changing action to regain control; now here he was helpless again. In any case, he was not particularly fearful, and the experience seemed to have finally scotched his childhood trauma. Rudy and Stan were the cousins, and he recalled the schadenfreude he had felt on learning their adult fate, which in both cases consisted of dull and unremunerative jobs in the nearer suburbs of New York. He still got an annual Christmas card from Stan, picturing him smiling stiffly out of his fat, together with a hefty wife and a number of unusually unattractive children. Marder had run into Rudy on the street in the city about fifteen years ago; Rudy had been effusive, wanted to go for drinks, renew the family connection and so on, but Marder had begged off, hoping he had kept the disgust from his face.

As Marder drifted throught this litter-and-graffiti section of memory lane, a man with the soft, pleasant, and neutral face of a suburban pedophile walked through the door and sat down at the table opposite, followed by Varela, who closed the door behind him and took up a position against the wall just out of Marder's sight. The man opened a folder and read it for a minute, turning pages in silence. Then he looked up at Marder and said, "Well, Richard—or do you prefer Dick? Ricky?" He was speaking English, with a flat midwestern accent.

"I prefer Mr. Marder. Who are you?"

The man shifted his gaze to a point behind Marder, and Varela hit Marder behind the ear with something solid enough to rock his head and make his ear ring but not hard enough to knock him off his chair or, apparently, to wake Mr. Thing up from his slumber.

"That's what happens when you ask questions, Ricky. You need to let me ask the questions. Do we understand each other?"

"Yes."

"All right, then. First question: What are you doing in Mexico?"

"I'm a retiree. I was a book editor in New York, and I used my savings to buy a house and some land in Playa Diamante as a retirement home."

Varela hit him again. It was not a devastating blow but nicely gauged to be painful and humiliating, and Marder understood that the man was prepared to keep it up all night. After a while, as with the boxers and football players you heard about, there might be some brain damage. In his own case, there was probably less "might" involved.

Marder said, "I think you should know that one reason I moved here is that I was recently diagnosed with an inoperable brain aneurysm. If your man keeps slugging me like that, it's going to pop and I'll die. You may not care about that, but there are people who will, including Pepa Espinoza. She might wonder why an offical of—I'm guessing here—the U.S. Drug Enforcement Administration was presiding over the torture of an American citizen that resulted in his death."

The man's glance flipped up past Marder's head and he must have received a signal from Varela, because he smiled again and said, "No one is torturing anyone. You haven't got a mark on you. Let's go on. Maybe you can tell me why a retiree would go into business with Servando Gomez, a known drug trafficker."

THE RETURN | 221

"I'm not in business with Servando Gomez. It's a protection racket. He's shaking me down for five grand a month. I thought it was worth it because the previous owner was murdered."

"Really? Then why haven't you gone to the police?"

"That's an excellent idea," said Marder, and twisting his neck around, added, "Señor Varela, I am being extorted by the criminal Servando Gomez. Please make him stop."

Varela hit him again, but not quite as hard.

"Nobody likes a wiseass, Ricky. So you're a poor extorted retiree. Who just happened to bring a heavily armed gunslinger with him. Why don't you tell me a little about Patrick Skelly."

"He's a friend of mine. He's in the security business, and when he heard I was coming to Michoacán, he insisted on coming with me to provide security."

"A security consultant, eh? That's a job description that covers a multitude of sins. Who're his other clients?"

"I have no idea. We don't discuss his other business. In fact, I believe confidentiality is an important consideration in that field."

"Even extending to entering Mexico under false pretenses?"

Marder said nothing to that, and after a pause, the man continued. "And I'm sure you don't know that Patrick Skelly, under several aliases, has been deeply involved with the Khun Sa cartel in Asia and with gun-running out of China. He deals with terrorists and drug smugglers and human traffickers, the worst of the worst. It surprises me that you should have a friend like that. Book editors don't usually have international criminals as pals."

"We were in the Vietnam War together. He saved my life."

Marder had noticed this before, what happened when he mentioned that he'd been in combat in Vietnam to American men who hadn't been there and were trying to act tough. A small deflation appeared in their faces, certainly involuntary. And, as now, they acted even tougher in compensation.

"Okay, Ricky, let me tell you what's really going on. Your pal is setting up an operation here, maybe for some U.S. outfit, maybe for the Asians. The situation with the cartels is fluid, and this section of the coast is up for grabs. He's using you as cover, you and your retirement and this stupid crafts bullshit you're involved in. Crafts my ass! He's training a private army to defend his drug operation, and I'll bet my next three paychecks he's got some kind of arms delivery on the way. Now, I don't know how you feature in his plans, and I don't care, but let me say this, and you can take it to the bank. From now on we are going to be all *over* your case. We are going to know who you meet and what comes in and out of that place. We're going to be closer to you than that little *chica* you're fucking, and you're not going to get rid of us like you got rid of the bitch's ex tonight. You're dirty, Ricky, and I'm going to bring you down. You're going to spend your retirement in a super-max cell with the other wiseguys." He tore a piece of paper from his notebook, wrote on it, and stuck it in Marder's shirt pocket. "There's my direct number. If you ever want to stop your bullshit and stay out of jail, you'll give me a ring." He picked up his folder, said, "Hasta la vista, asshole," and walked out.

Varela bent over and unlocked the handcuffs. He went over to the door and held it open and Marder walked through. Down the lit hallway again, Varela leading. He stopped at an unmarked door, knocked.

Gil opened it and they exchanged some words, speaking too softly for Marder to understand. Then Gil left the doorway, and for a moment Marder could see that he was not alone in the room. There was a young man in there, wearing a silky pale-tan suit over a white turtleneck with a gold-chain pendant. It was a memorable face, and Marder had seen it before: through the excellent optics of his rifle scope. It was the face of the man who had run out of one of the cars that Skelly had disabled when La Familia had attacked the house, the man who seemed to be in charge.

Gil returned and handed Marder the plastic bag with his wallet and cell phone. When Marder opened it, a burned smell floated free. He looked at the cell phone, sniffed it. He imagined that someone had popped it into a microwave for thirty seconds, turning it into a desk ornament.

Varela said, "You're free to go."

"How am I supposed to get back home?"

The policeman shrugged. "You could call a cab. Use your cell phone."

"It's dead."

"Find a pay phone, then. There's one at the end of the street. Just get out of here." He made a shooing motion with his hand.

Marder left the office and walked down the concrete steps until he reached the small landing that led to the parking area. He switched the landing light off, opened the steel door a crack, crouched down, and peered out. The vehicle he had arrived in was still parked there. He dropped to the floor, shoved the door outward very slowly, just enough to pass his body through, and closed it as silently as he could. The click it made as the latch engaged sounded like a gunshot as he low-crawled down from the little platform in front of the door and squatted in its shadow, sheltered by the bulk of the SUV.

He chanced a look around the curve of its front fender. There were two cars parked at the curb, a dark van and a large sedan of some kind. They should have been illuminated by a nearby streetlamp, but the bulb had conveniently gone out. All he could see from his present location was the red spark of the cigarette being smoked by someone leaning against the side of the van. The plan was obviously to snatch him as he walked unwarily out of the building to look for the supposed pay phone, as he would certainly have done had he not spotted the La Familia hon-cho in the office with Gil.

Marder received something of an illumination at this point. He thought he had come to terms with death, or at least with Mr. Thing, but he now found that he really, really did not want to be dismembered alive by the butchers of La Familia and his torso left in the plaza with an illit-erate scrawl as his epitaph. It offended his editorial taste, for one thing, and he thought it would hurt his daughter and the community that had formed around Casa Feliz. I have a reason to live, he thought, surprising himself, or at least a reason to avoid dying in that particular way, which at present amounted to the same thing.

He heard scuffling sounds and a quick curse, and then the door behind him opened and a man came through. He must have stumbled on the darkened landing; Marder could not see who it was, but it had to be the man who'd been with Gil. He must be coming out all confident that Marder had already been grabbed and packaged by the men lying in wait over by the van. Marder watched him disappear into the dark and then heard someone being yelled at.

Marder made his move, hoping that the current distraction would cover any noise. Bent over low, he slid along the wall of the building until he reached its end. To his left was a blind alley that led to what appeared to be a delivery entrance; to his right was the street, the only way to go. If he was lucky, they wouldn't be looking his way. The cars were pointed in the other direction, and to pursue him with the vehicles they would have to back and fill a couple of times on the narrow street. If he could cross unobserved, he could hide in the shadows of the buildings opposite and cut right down the first side street he came to. Then eventually he might come across a non-imaginary pay phone or a twenty-four-hour business.

He took several deep breaths, dashed out across the street, and was spotted immediately. He heard a shout and the sound of a big engine starting. He was across the street, running, a clumsy run: unhappily, he'd never been much of a runner. He was a swimmer like his daughter. But he tried to control his breathing and smooth out his pace.

He reached the end of a short street and cut right. It was a commercial district, full of machine shops, small factories, and mean little office buildings, all closed at this hour, lit intermittently by a stingy line of streetlamps with fluted metal shades. Marder heard someone running behind him—they must have sent someone on foot to keep him under observation. The person was undoubtedly armed, which meant Marder was doomed.

The steps behind him sounder closer, and he risked a look over his shoulder. His pursuer was maybe ten yards behind him, a man in a white T-shirt and dark trousers, twenty years younger than Marder, and running like a deer. Marder tried to increase his pace, but it was clear that the man could catch up anytime he liked; he had probably been told to keep his distance until the van arrived. They wanted Marder alive.

He kept running, his breath now burning and coming ragged into his chest. He heard the screech of a vehicle turning a sharp corner; its headlamps threw crazy shadows of two running men onto the street before him. An alley appeared on his right and he made for it. Perhaps there'd be an open building or a weapon—an old tool or a chunk of wood or even a bottle—so he could go down fighting and not slaughtered like a pig, screaming.

Marder had just ducked into the alley when he heard something unexpected: a long burst of automatic fire and then a crash, the kind made by a large vehicle driving at speed into an immovable object. Marder paused in the darkness. He heard a car or a truck roar down the street and another brief exchange of gunfire—a pistol and another burst of full auto. Cautiously, he went back to the head of the alley and looked out. The van had crushed itself against a power pole; smoke and steam were coming off it. In the center of the street lay his pursuer, the white shirt now black with blood. Near him sat a pickup truck containing half a dozen men, all armed with automatic rifles. One of the men was Skelly.

Marder walked to the truck on rubbery legs, heaving breath into his lungs, shaking with the aftermath of terror. Skelly leaned over the dropped tailgate and helped him into the truck. One of the men rapped on the cab roof with the butt of his rifle, and the truck drove off.

When Marder had caught his breath, Skelly asked him how he was.

"I'm in one piece. Fuck! I'm too old for this shit anymore, you know that? I can't run worth a damn."

"You can still shoot," said Skelly. "If you can shoot well enough, you hardly ever have to run."

"Oh, let me write that down. I'll add that to the wit and wisdom of Patrick F. Skelly, soon in your local bookstores. How in hell did you find me?"

"Well, obviously, our Templos followed you and those *federales* out of our place and to where you were taken. Then Reyes called me and sent this truck by to pick me up. We saw the crew waiting for you and laid low and waited for developments. We thought we'd have to yank you out of that van, but you made a break for it, and the rest is history. An uncharacteristically smart move on your part. How did you know La Fam was waiting for you?"

Marder explained about the guy and the rifle-scope memory, then described the man.

"That sounds like the junior Cuello, El Cochinillo. You're an important man, boss, to bring Numero Dos into action personally. He usually has his people do that shit."

"I'm flattered. But how did you know that the *federales* would turn me over to La Familia?"

"Oh, Gil and Varela have been in Cuello's pocket since forever. It's well known."

Marder was shaking his head. "No, it wasn't just that. There was a DEA guy there, in the building. He interrogated me, mainly about who you were. He thought we were starting our own little cartel."

"Well, that's not good. Was it an enhanced interrogation?"

"Somewhat enhanced. The main thing he wanted to impress on me is that he had our number and was going to be all over us henceforth, with his gang of tame *federales*. I wanted to tell him he was wasting his time, but I forbore."

"Yes, but it's going to be hard to set up our own little cartel with him breathing down our necks. I guess you would be opposed to direct action?"

"You meaning whacking him?"

"Like that."

"Skelly, quite aside from the fact that we don't whack people who are not actually firing weapons at us, killing a DEA agent would bring a forty-man DEA strike force into the area, with ten helicopters and a light aircraft carrier. We'll have to figure out some other way of getting him off our backs."

"In that case, I'm open to suggestions. What's this asshole's name, by the way?"

"He didn't offer it," said Marder. "It wasn't exactly a social occasion. By the way, what did you mean about setting up our cartel?"

Skelly ignored this and turned to one of the men in the truck. "Crusellas, what's the name of the DEA guy who works with Gil and Varela and them?"

Despite the darkness, Marder recognized one of the men who had paid that extortionate visit to Casa Feliz on the day after their arrival. And the other one, Tomas Gasco, was there too, glaring at him.

Crusellas answered, "Warren Alsop."

"Thank you," said Marder, and to Skelly, "Our cartel?"

"Yeah, I explained this to you already. We need to supply some product to the Templos along with the weapons. It's part of the deal."

"You can't do that. I thought I had made myself clear."

"Don't worry about it, Marder. You'll have full deniability. You won't know a thing."

"I don't want deniability. I want it not to be an actuality."

"Hey, did you just get rescued or not? You'd be losing vital body parts right now if these guys weren't doing their jobs. What we pay them is chump change; it's not even a rounding error on their monthly take. They're in it for dope and weapons. I hope my fucking boat isn't delayed. It should've been steaming into Cárdenas about now. Uh-oh, what's this?"

The truck had been traveling along the coast road north out of Lázaro

Cárdenas, heading for Isla de los Pájaros and home, but now it slowed as it came to the junction with Route 37 and pulled to the side of the road. Crusellas shoved the muzzle of his AR into Skelly's side, and the man sitting across from him lifted Skelly's weapon. The other three men in the back of the truck pointed their rifles at Marder and Skelly. Marder could see the flash of their teeth as they smiled.

They heard the door of the cab open, and in a moment Mateo Reyes appeared and dropped the tailgate.

"What's going on, Reyes?" Skelly asked.

"A change of plans. The *jefe* is concerned about the weapons and product you promised us."

"Jesus, man, I told you, they left Hong Kong twenty-five days ago. They should be here any day."

"Twenty-three days is the normal transit time between China and Lázaro Cárdenas."

"So? It's not like driving a car down a highway. There are winds and currents and shit, or things break. They'll be here."

"I'm sure, but in the meantime you'll be our guests." With that, he put up the tailgate and went back to the cab.

Marder and Skelly had their wrists bound with cable ties, flour sacks were placed on their heads, and the truck drove off north on 37.

Marder leaned his head next to Skelly's and said, "Well, this is a fine kettle of fish."

"It's no big deal," said Skelly. His voice was muffled but clear enough to understand. "It's a normal business practice with these guys. Don't worry. We're not going to be in a cell. We'll hang out by the pool a few days, play cards, and then the boat will get here and we'll be golden. Also, it could've been worse."

"How worse?"

"Oh, you know—they could've snatched your kid."

The unsnatched kid spent the start of the day after the night of her father's arrest swimming laps in the pool, hoping that the endorphins produced by grueling exercise might help to calm her excoriated nerves, but no luck. Of course she was worried about her father's fate, but what made her grind her teeth and curse was the way that Skelly had man-handled her the previous night. When Skelly explained that Marder had decided to get arrested for shooting the boyfriend, Statch had flatly refused to countenance it and had immediately tried to run out of her bedroom to stop the outrage. And Skelly had grabbed her, restrained her as she had not been restrained since the age of six, a degrading, insulting restraint. She had screamed like a cat, had used all her curses in two languages, to no avail. He had held her in one of his famous Special Forces grips with contemptuous ease, until both the ambulance and the police car had gone. Now Skelly himself was gone, God knew where, leaving her alone—no, not in the least alone; alone would have been fine, but she was far from that. All the problems of this ridiculous establishment had fallen on her shoulders.

And this fucking pool was too short for proper laps, an absurd eight meters in length, a pool suitable only for the sport of children with inflated animals. She stopped swimming with a curse and slithered up to sit on the tiled rim of the pool. She could see them now, despite Amparo's efforts, gathering like abandoned pets on the edges of the terrace. They were terrified, the poor bastards. The sun that had illuminated their lives for the past few weeks had departed, who knew where? Off with the police, into a black hole, and what would become of them all? This was what they wanted her—La Señorita, perhaps the new *patrona*—to tell them, and she hadn't any idea.

However, eighteen years of high-quality American education had given her sufficient expertise at impromptu bullshitting, so she dried herself off, slipped into a terry-cloth robe, and addressed the little crowd. She said she had heard from her father and that he was fine, that he would be back soon, and that everything would remain as it was. He had promised them, and he was a man of his word. She saw nods, hesitant smiles. These people wanted to believe, even in the land of *no importa*. The group dispersed, with some of the women coming up to her with little touches, as she were a statue of the Virgin of Guadalupe in a church.

To her surprise and relief, she found that she didn't mind it. Her mother had something to do with this; maybe this was the unlived life of the mother sprouting in her child, like a seed long buried in unsuitable earth, turgid, bearing spines, hungry for the light, irresistible. Or maybe old D. H. Lawrence was right about Mexico; maybe the chthonic powers still ruled at some deep level, because what else would explain what had happened to her father and what, obviously, was now happening to her. Of course, Statch had never exactly been ashamed of being a Mexican, but she hadn't advertised it either. It was like the label on the back of a blouse: no need to tear it out, but you tucked it away when it popped out and tickled your neck, a label like those worn by everyone in America's diversity-obsessed anomic society, ultimately of slight importance compared to talent and looks and money.

Still, she was enough of an American to want to cause an action, to generate some change. She fished through her bag and found Major Naca's card. She called him on her now-functional (five bar!) cell and he answered, with a lightness in his voice that told her the call was not an imposition. She told Major Naca what had happened last night, leaving out the business of who had really fired the shots. The point was that Richard Marder had been picked up by the *federales* and she wanted to know what had happened to him.

Naca listened, asked no irritating questions, promised he would check and get back to her as soon as he knew anything.

Statch waited. She fired up the laptop, played a little solitaire, read her Facebook and LinkedIn pages, declined to update her hundreds of friends ("Guess what? Dad arrested for shooting Mexican gangster—arrested by federal cops!!!! LOL!").

Her phone rang. Major Naca reported that the *federales* had released her father after questioning on the previous night. They had declined to charge him, pending an investigation.

"But they won't charge him," he added, "not for shooting a thug who was trying to stab a girl. I would say they would regard such an act as a public service."

"Fine, but where is he, then?" she asked.

"Our informants report Templos in the area where he was released, and there was a minor gun battle there last night too. A bunch of La Familia gangsters got shot up in a car."

"So the Templos have him?"

"It looks that way. Assuming your father's deal with them is still in place, he should be fine."

"And if not?"

"Then I don't know what to say. I truly wish I could marshal the Mexican Army to help find him, but just now we're in the middle of an operation and I'm not free. I will alert our intel resources to keep an eye out, but I'm afraid that's all I can do at the present moment. I am most dreadfully sorry, Señorita Marder."

She thanked him for the information, said that she understood his problem and that she'd make inquiries of her own. Lourdes didn't mind distracting the sole Templo guard at the roadhead, and Statch was able to roll her motorcycle by the vehicle in which the distracting was taking place. Then she went to visit the only Templo who might be inclined to give her information: her uncle, Angel d'Ariés.

15

They drove into the mountains for what seemed to Marder a long time. Remarkably, Skelly had fallen asleep, his body loose and jouncing against Marder's shoulder as the truck turned on the twisting roads, demonstrating yet again the man's astounding ability to sack out in absolutely any situation that did not require thought or violent activity. Marder was wide awake and suffering: from the bondage, from the bag on his head that muffled his senses, from rising visceral panic. He felt the scream build in his throat as the old nightmare returned but worse, because this was more real. He was not in the grip of sadistic children but of awful men who cared nothing for him, and the grown-ups would never come. He was going to lose control. He would piss and shit himself or fling himself off the truck—anything was better than this constraint in the dark.

Then there floated into his memory a story he'd read as a boy. He recalled in detail the book it came from, a green-colored hardback he'd bought for a dime in a used bookstore on Fourth Avenue in New York. It was a Jack London novel about a man held captive by an evil warden, condemned to lie in a straitjacket in a black room for weeks on end to make him submit. But he would not submit, and the story told how he had passed through madness into a world of fantastic adventure that was more real than the cell and so survived his torment.

Marder recalled the book, its brittle yellowed pages, its old book smell, and the dense dusty smell of the old bookstores and how wonderful it was to travel to Union Square on the subway with his mother. It was a special thing they did together, cruising through the bookstores and coming home with piles of used books in shopping bags. And her smell, the sharp odor of the cologne she used, and also the smell of the army, tent canvas, and gun oil, and burnt gunpowder, and sweat, and latrines. Skelly had a peculiar smell too, when you were close to him. Marder took a deep breath, but all he could get now was the smell of the burlap bag, damp from his breath. They said you couldn't remember smells as you could sounds and sights; the wiring wasn't there, apparently. He'd edited a book about that too, one of many on the mysteries of the brain. But he could recall the fact of experiencing a smell, and he supposed everyone who'd had that experience remembered it, although it didn't often show up in accounts of war: what a human body smelled like when it was eviscerated by high explosives.

And on this olfactory stream Marder was now borne away, out of darkness and confinement, into the past, to the first time he'd had that singular experience.

Marder was awake when it started, and he would've been killed with the rest of the men in the command bunker had he not gone out for a piss at a little after four in the morning of September 18, 1969. The command post was in a longhouse, and below it was a bunker where you could go for shelter during an attack, but there had been no warning at all, because the PAVN had packed in big 107-mm mortars with the range to hit the command post from beyond the wire. And they knew just where it was too; they must've had a perfectly accurate map of the village and the Special Forces base, and also more than their fair share of the fortune of war, because the first salvo of mortar bombs was right on target. That first concussion knocked Marder off his feet and over the buried piss barrel, and when he staggered upright again, bleeding from a dozen shrapnel wounds in his back and buttocks, he found that the command hooch had collapsed into a mass of shattered timbers.

Marder stumbled toward this smoking heap, which was visible only by the glow of its own small fires and by the streaks of tracer incoming and outgoing, green and red, and the ghastly intermittent light of the illumination rounds flying above the perimeter. His foot slipped, and he fell and discovered that what had tripped him up was a mass of entrails. It was vaguely attached to shredded limbs and a head he refused to recognize. The head had its eyes open, and every time an illumination round appeared in the black sky, these dead eyes shone with an obscene parody of life. Marder was puking his guts out, helpless, repeating childhood prayers, when he was grabbed by the arm and hauled to his feet.

"Everyone's dead," he told the grabber, and it was more than a moment before he realized that the man was Skelly. By then Marder had been pushed into action, loaded down with a bag of grenades and two boxes of machine-gun ammunition, with extra belts draped around his neck. Skelly should have been in the command hooch and dead, but here he was, running, screaming orders to the men who drifted out of the dark. The Hmong and the Vietnamese Rangers had been trained for such attacks, but the destruction of the command and the local radio net had unnerved them. Skelly had spontaneously reverted to a preindustrial mode of command, using Hmong kids as messengers and leading by shoving, cursing, and example.

He set up the M60 in a prepared position, commanded two men to operate it, and moved on, dragging Marder and a couple of squads of montagnards with him. It was obvious, even in the dark, where the PAVN sappers had broken through the wire. Claymores were exploding, flares were going up, tracer sparks were flying back and forth all along the northern edge of the village. Marder had picked up an AR and a bandolier of magazines for it and had assigned himself the duty of following Skelly, on the principle that in combat you wanted to stick as close as possible to anyone who knew what the fuck they were doing, which in this case was Skelly. Ordinary command had disappeared in the ruins of the HQ hooch; Skelly was clearly in charge of the battle and was leading from in front.

With some part of his mind, Marder was observing Skelly in action even as he fired his weapon and tried to stay alive. He saw that Skelly was trying to keep the PAVN sappers out of the village and at the same time sweep them into the fields of fire of the machine guns he had just emplaced. Marder assumed naturally the responsibility of watching Skelly's back and flanks and of shooting anyone who was shooting at Skelly while Skelly dealt out efficient slaughter, moving and firing with an almost balletic grace, knocking the PAVNs down like fairground targets as they emerged from the shadows. Despite his terror, Marder could not help but be full of admiration; it was like something out of Homer, he thought later, the brilliant Achilles among the Trojans, divinely protected, unbeatable.

The savage little firefight did not last long. When all the intruders were dead or captive (and, if captive, soon dead as well), Skelly and Marder walked to the perimeter, counting casualties and preparing for what Skelly was sure would be another assault. Aside from that first devastating blow, they had suffered surprisingly few casualties, and none of the civilians had been hurt. But although they repaired their wire and stayed alert all that night, no further attack came. Skelly kept saying that they had to come now, that the whole point of spotting and destroying the base's radio contact with the outside world was so that they could wipe out the SOG encampment without having to worry about assault from the air or reinforcements. In fact, every such encampment was an open invitation for the PAVN to do just that, laying out American meat as bait and waiting for an attack that would garner the body counts on which the high command doted.

In the morning, they cleaned up and placed body parts in poncho liners. Skelly and the three surviving SOGs frankly wept as they did this, and they alone were allowed to do it. Marder understood that when SOG didn't get a morning radio check from their outpost, they'd send out a plane, and with this expectation, Skelly had caused a huge "R" to be constructed by charring the character into the short grass on the field where helicopters and light planes usually landed, to indicate that they had no radio working that could reach the SOG net.

Skelly remained obsessed with the notion that something was wrong, that the attack as it had gone down did not make sense: they cut us off, they destroy our command structure, they penetrate our perimeter, and then give up? He threw out patrols to the north and east, the two obvious routes of attack, and he himself led a patrol to the south, where Yeng Mountain formed an almost impassable barrier. Almost, but there were trails up there: maybe they were moving people up to the heights. Marder was left in Moon River so that he could try to assemble a working radio from the hulks of those caught in the barrage. It was while he was doing this that he discovered what the clever enemy was actually doing, by which time it was too late.

The truck stopped and Marder came out of his waking dream. Someone pulled the hood off his head and clipped his handcuffs off. They were in a shed of some kind that smelled of fodder and horse and nose-prickling dust, obviously a former stable. The men led them wordlessly through a door into a low-ceilinged adobe house and down a narrow hallway to a room. There they were left. The door was not locked. In the room were two old-fashioned steel beds, with bedding, crisp and white; there was a pine bureau and a large wardrobe with cast-iron hinges, a sturdy table, and a couple of heavy chairs of local manufacture. Marder went to the single small-paned window. Through it he could see the edge of an orchard—some kind of citrus, he supposed—and part of a large long windowless building.

"Well, this is very nice," said Skelly, throwing himself on one of the beds and propping his head on the pillow. "It's a lot nicer than the last time I was kidnapped. Have you got any idea where we are?"

"Up in the *tierra caliente*, I think, in one of the old *ranchos*. This area used to be a pretty lush agricultural district fifty years ago—citrus, avocados, all kinds of produce. Then the government fucked it up somehow—I don't recall the details—and everything went bust." He opened the window and sniffed: warm dust and that horsey ranch smell and something else, harsh and phenolic. "The narcos use these little *ranchos* to cook up meth, which is what I think is going on in that building. It probably used to be a packing shed." Marder left the window open and sat on the other bed. He was exhausted but still too wired to collapse. Unlike his friend, he could not sleep at will.

"When were you kidnapped?" Marder asked.

"It's a long story."

"We have nothing but time. Or we could talk about what happened that night at Moon River. I was thinking about that on the ride up here. How they hit the command hooch on the first shot and what happened after. It just came into my mind after decades of not thinking about it. Strange, no? I always wondered how in hell they hit it on the first shot. Sheer bad luck?"

Skelly said, "It wasn't luck," and at that moment the door opened and El Gordo walked in. The big man sat on one of the chairs, which creaked under his weight. A Templo followed, carrying a tray on which sat four bottles of beer and two plates covered with napkins.

El Gordo said, "Gentlemen, I regret the present inconvenience, and I hope you will regard yourselves as my guests."

The man left the tray on the table and went out.

"You have the freedom of the place, which I hope you will find comfortable enough. If Señor Skelly is true to his word, it should not be a matter of more than a day or so. If not . . ." He waved his hands in a small gesture indicating uncertainty. "If not, then we have a problem."

"I take it you intend to keep us here until, so to speak, our ship comes in," said Marder.

"Yes. Then we will all drive down to the port and find your shipping container and we will do our business."

"Yes, but there's another problem," said Marder.

"Oh?"

"Yeah, his name is Warren Alsop. He's got a couple of *federales* in his pocket, and I hear they're working for La Familia."

"So?"

"So Mr. Alsop has expressed a great deal of interest in why I'm down here in Playa Diamante. Everyone seems to be interested in that, of course, but Mr. Alsop's in a position to do something about it. He told me he intends to watch me very closely from now on. He doesn't know the *federales* meant to give me to La Familia and so he's going to want to make sure that I'm back at my place, which I'm not. Then where am I? He's going to wonder what I'm doing, and that's not good for this operation. It's important that I don't lose my character as an innocent American retiree. What you don't want is a lot of *federales* and DEA guys on the roads looking for me while you're trying to transport a shipment of arms and heroin."

"I take your point," said El Gordo after a moment's thought. "What do you suggest?"

"You should immediately transport me back to Isla de los Pájaros. I believe that I can convince Alsop that I'm of no interest to him."

"How will you do that?"

"I have a distraction in mind," said Marder, "one that will neutralize Alsop and probably his *federale* friends."

"May I know its details?"

"You'll have to trust me on that."

"I will. I think you're an honest man. But I'll also keep your friend here. Until your ship comes in." El Gordo smiled, rose ponderously from his chair, and left.

"That was neatly done, chief," said Skelly. "May *I* know the details?"

"I was bluffing. But I'm sure I'll think of something. Alsop had the look of a GS-11 dullard and shouldn't be that hard to scam. What did you mean when you said it wasn't luck at Moon River?"

"Oh, just that Charlie—you remember old Charlie, the LLDB?"

"Yeah, the one we used to rib about being VC."

"He *was* VC, or actually PAVN military intelligence. He engineered the whole thing. He even put the idea in my mind that the next assault was coming from over the mountains."

"Well. And he got away with it."

"Not really. After we figured out it had to be him—this was long after you were out, late '74—they sent me back in and I killed him. We killed a bunch of guys like that. It was like the Phoenix program but not as famous, and nearly unofficial, getting the guys who'd shafted us while posing as friendlies."

"You were an assassin?"

"More or less. Not that it made any difference, but I enjoyed the work. I really dislike betrayal."

Later that afternoon Marder was deposited at the gates of Casa Feliz, leaving Skelly at the secret *rancho* as security. Skelly made no objection, and Marder was not particularly worried about him, because this thing he had in mind was going to work, and if not, he had no doubt that Skelly could handle twenty or so heavily armed *malosos*.

He received a gratifyingly warm greeting at the *casa*. Everyone was happy to see the *patrón* back safely, as yet another indication of Marder's vast protective powers. His daughter was not among the greeters, and when Marder asked where she was, Amparo told him that she had gone off somewhere, without guards. Lourdes was then quizzed, who answered that the señorita had gone off to meet a boyfriend, but she hadn't said who or where.

Marder spent the next hour or so pacing his roof terrace. He'd brought half a dozen bottles of Dos Equis in an ice bucket up there and he drank one after another, spinning the recent events in his mind and trying not to scan the causeway more than every ten minutes. Boyfriend? In Michoacán? Finally he saw the yellow motorcycle turn off the road, pass the guard car, and drive on toward the house, with an intact daughter aboard.

"Where have you been?" he demanded when she walked out onto the roof. "I've been worried sick about you."

"Oh, hello? I've been worried sick about *you*. You totally disappeared, and the *federales* had no information about you—I checked with Major Naca—so I was out cruising the roadsides for artistically arranged limb piles."

"But really."

"Really, I went to see my uncle Angel at the famous hotel."

"Why would you do that?"

"Because he's a Templo, and Skelly went off with the Templos and didn't come back, and he might have known something."

"And did he?"

"Well, at first he didn't want to talk to me. And then he said that you both were with El Gordo and he didn't think anything bad was going to happen to you. I think he's incredibly ashamed about what he's come to. Did you know that place is almost a brothel now?"

"Yeah, I gathered that. Did you eventually find a topic of conversation?"

"You, actually. He wanted to know what you were really doing here."

"Yes, everyone asks me that and then they don't believe me when I tell them."

"Because you're devious in a perfectly sincere way. Anyway, Angel is terrified of you. He thinks the gangsters you've pissed off are going to come after him."

"They might. Maybe I should get him to come here."

"I suggested that," she said, "but that scared him too. People watch him, and, of course, this place is guarded by Templos. Honestly, he was the saddest man, and he looks just like Mom did when we were kids. Could I have a beer too?"

He handed her one from the ice bucket.

"It was freaky, Dad. This guy, this stranger with Mom's face, and I was talking to him, familiarly, like I'd known him as a kid, and the funny thing was, he started talking the same way. He showed me photographs of the family. I noticed there were none of Mom."

"There's one. I'll show it to you."

"Don Esteban must've been a piece of work—I mean, to get that mad that his daughter married without his permission. And in the sixties too."

"The seventies, actually, but to him it could've been the *eighteen* seventies. It was all about shame. *His* grandfather, before the revolution, was the absolute monarch of an area the size of a county. Las Palmas Floridas was their hacienda, hence the name of the hotel, the lost golden place, the legend passed down generation to generation, that family pride; they were *hidalgos, criollos* of the purest blood, that whole pile of shit, and so nothing they ever did would make up for the loss of that status. For a d'Ariés to be reduced to hotelkeeping was shameful enough, but at least he still had absolute rule over his family. Until he didn't and a gringo ran off with his daughter, a girl he'd already promised to someone. He erased her—well, you know the sad story."

"Yes, but talking to Angel, I had this—what do you call it? Not déjà vu but spooky in the same way. For a little while I had the sensation of being in an alternate life, as if I had always been Mexican and lived here and had known Angel and his wife and all my cousins, been part of a huge Mexican family. And while I was feeling that, a bunch of drunk guys came in with girls and wanted booze and rooms, and one of them hit on me. It was pretty gross, and Angel, like, totally *disappeared*—I mean, he became another person in front of my eyes, a really sort of nasty person. So I came back."

She took a long draft. "And I'll be here for a while, I guess. I didn't tell you, but a while ago I emailed Schuemacher and ditched my assistantship. Someone else will have to build the next frontier of engineering."

"That seems a little radical."

"I don't know. No more radical than a book editor setting up as a player in the Mexican drug wars."

"I'm not a player in the drug wars."

"Actually, you are. Uncle Angel told me all about the arms-and-heroin deal. And since I seem to have committed my life to this enterprise, could you just promise me one thing? Could you for once tell me the fucking truth?"

"I'm sorry, Carmelita. I will endeavor to be more forthcoming in the future."

"Why am I not convinced?" she said, but under her breath. Then she asked, "Is Skelly back too?"

"No, he remains as a guest of El Gordo against the arrival of the package we promised him."

"He's a hostage?"

"In a manner of speaking."

"Then how come they let you go?"

"Well, that's something I need to talk with you about." And he told her the Warren Alsop story and what he proposed to do and asked her if it could, in fact, be done.

"Oh, sure. Hacking the backhaul of a cell system is fairly trivial, if you have access to the router and the other hardware, which we do. I can set it up in . . . well, with testing and all, it'll take a couple of hours."

"Wonderful! Could you start now? I haven't slept in almost forty hours, and I need to collapse after I call our guy."

They both stood up and she hugged him, the first spontaneous hug he'd had from his girl in a while, and it made up for a good deal. She left and entered the rooftop storeroom where they had housed the cell tower.

Marder took out one of the house's many prepaid cell phones and called the number Alsop had given him.

"This is Marder. I've decided to come clean," he said when Alsop answered.

"Well, Mr. Marder! I kind of figured you'd be calling."

"Yeah, you were right. I'm not a retiree at all."

"No, you're not. And what have you got to say to me?"

"It's not something I can discuss on an unsecured line. I need to make some calls and then I'll be ready to make a full and frank confession. And when you hear what I've got to say, I believe you'll be in a much better professional situation than you are at present. I'll call you later."

With that, he hung up on the expostulating voice, went to his room, stripped and showered, and collapsed facedown on his bed like a man shot through the heart.

When he awoke, the setting sun was reddening his windows. He shaved and dressed with particular care, in his only suit, a pale-silk-and-linen number, no socks, worn huaraches—a suitable outfit, he thought, for an international man of mystery.

He went downstairs and found his daughter, who raised her eyebrows.

"Impressive," she said. "You should dress like that all the time; you'd get a little more respect around here."

"I get far too much respect around here as it is. So—did you do the thing?"

"The thing is done. Do you have the number the call's going to be routed to?"

"Yeah, your cell phone, and then you'll send it off to this one." He punched a number into his phone and let the call go through.

"Ornstein? Marder. How're you doing?"

"Wonderfully. I am the envy of every starving lefty in New York and enjoying it immensely. So *this* is why people sell their souls to capital! And you're calling to evict me, right?"

"No, not at all. But I do need a small favor."

"A kidney? Not an issue. Let me get a knife from the kitchen and I'll have it out in a jiffy."

Marder laughed and told Ornstein that he wanted him to impersonate a federal official—a serious felony—and Ornstein said it would be his pleasure and who was the bozo, and Marder told him and Ornstein soon found a YouTube of the bozo making a speech, and Ornstein said it would be a piece of cake. Then Marder gave him the scenario and they closed the conversation.

He called Alsop again (the man picked up on the second ring) and in peremptory tones told him to be at Casa Feliz in half an hour, alone, no wires.

Alsop came—somewhat late, to show who was in charge—and he had a couple of heavies in the car with him but entered the house by himself. Marder took him out to the pool deck and sat him at a chair under an umbrella. The sun was just touching its rim to the cobalt line of the sea.

Marder said, "I hope you aren't wired, Alsop, but I'm not going to determine whether you are or not. It'll be on your head if any of this gets out."

"If any of what gets out?"

"Tell me, did you ever hear of an operation called Southern Gadget?"

"No. What's it supposed to be?"

"I'll give you a little background. Approximately five months ago, a convoy of three trucks left a research reactor outside of Perm, Russia, carrying twenty-three hundred canisters of plutonium reactor fuel in the form of metallic buttons, for transport to the Russian Nuclear Center at Sarov in the Nizhny Novgorod region. The trucks arrived safely, but there were only twenty-two hundred and twelve canisters aboard when they arrived. Eighty-eight canisters, each about the size of a coffee can, each containing about 10.25 kilograms of plutonium, were in the wind. The Russians kept this very, very quiet."

"Then how come *you* know?"

"National technical means," Marder replied. "Later it was found that one of the workers at Perm had been suborned by Ilyas Musadov. Do you know who he is?"

"No. Why should I? What does this have to do with you, anyway?"

"Be patient, I'll get to that. Musadov is a Chechen terrorist. He has wide contacts in central Asia and via Afghanistan with the drug trade in the western hemisphere. In any case, we believe the material was transported via Kazakhstan and Afghanistan to Karachi, where it was apparently put aboard a ship, although at the time we had no idea which ship. About six weeks ago, we received reliable intel that the shipment had reached the hemisphere and had been off-loaded at the port of Lázaro Cárdenas and into the possession of Melchor Cuello, of the La Familia cartel. That's when my team and I were mobilized. The operation to locate and secure the plutonium is called Southern Gadget. It is now the single highest priority of the U.S. intelligence community."

Alsop stared at him for a moment and then laughed. "You must think I'm fucking stupid."

"Not at all. You spotted right away that I was not what I said I was. Now I'm telling you the full story, because I can't have you interfering with my operations or movements."

"And you expect me to believe that you're a, what, a CIA agent?"

"I don't expect you to believe anything. I want you to call Carleton Everett. I assume you're familiar with the name." Marder took out his cell phone. "Here, I'll dial his number."

"It's after eight in D.C. There won't be anyone there."

"Yes, there will. No one at the top of U.S. intel is going home until we have the cans. There are eighty-eight of them. Just one of them surrounded by explosives and detonated would render a city center uninhabitable for decades. It might not kill a lot of people, but the economic costs would be devastating. It's a perfect terror weapon. Everett is obviously one of the people involved, because it looks like a drug gang is getting into the contract terrorism business. You know what they say— the best way to smuggle a terror weapon into the United States is to hide it in a shipment of cocaine or heroin. What are you people catching now? Ten, fifteen percent? And these are the boys who know how to ship major weight. Or maybe—best case—they're going to try to make the Mexican Army back off by threatening to use them in Mexico City. It doesn't matter. We have to get control of that material. So? You want me to call him, or would you rather use your phone?"

For the first time, Marder saw the man drop his confident mien.

Alsop pulled out his own cell phone and dialed a familiar number, that of the deputy administrator of the Drug Enforcement Administration.

Up in the little room on the roof, Carmel Marder's cell phone vibrated. She took the call and said, "Drug Enforcement Administration, Deputy Administrator Everett's office."

"I'd like . . . I mean, this is Warren Alsop, the head of the Rabbit Punch operation in Michoacán. In Mexico? I'd like to speak with Deputy Administrator Everett, please."

"Yes, sir. May I ask what this is in reference to?"

"Ah, well, it's in reference to an operation called Southern Gadget. I have this man here who claims he's—"

"Please, sir! This is an unsecured line," said Statch in a shocked tone. "Hold please for the deputy administrator."

She waited for half a minute, then worked her computer keys and heard the sound of ringing.

"Everett," said a voice.

"Sir, this is Warren Alsop. I'm sorry to trouble you this late, but—"

"Shut up, Alsop! What the fuck possessed you to blurt out the name of that operation on an unsecured line?" The voice was deep and rich and had the twangy East Texas drawl familiar to all the minions of the DEA.

"I'm sorry, sir. I have this man named Ma—"

"I told you to shut up! Listen to me carefully now. One, you will forget you ever heard of the operation in question. Erase it from your mind, speak to no one about it, especially to no Mexican national. Two, you will immediately sever all connection with the gentleman in question. I mean the *editorial* gentleman and any of his associates. You will not watch him or interfere with him in any way. Three, if this gentleman or his associates ask you for any help whatever, you will give it to the fullest extent of your power, asking no questions. Four, you will not refer these orders to your chain of command; you will communicate only with me, at my discretion. Five, you are never to call here again for any reason. Now, those are five orders, and while I can't write them down, I expect you to remember every one of them and comply. Can you do that, Alsop?"

"Yes, sir."

"Good. If you don't, my friend, I will drop more shit on your head than you knew existed in the world. And we never had this conversation. Are we clear on this?"

"Yes, sir."

The connection was broken. Alsop stared at his phone as if it would of itself make the world what it once was.

Marder said, "Good conversation?"

Alsop gave him a look in which fear, anger, and hatred were equally blended, stood up, and walked out without another word.

Marder watched him go. When he heard the sound of gravel spraying as the man's car took off, he went to the landline in the kitchen and called El Gordo.

Someone answered. Marder identified himself, and El Gordo came on the line a few moments later.

"Our problem is resolved," said Marder.

"That's good. May I ask how?"

"Through what we call national technical means. But he won't cause us any trouble. Any word on our business?"

"Yes. I'm informed that our business is where it should be. I am very pleased and will be more so when we have delivery." He paused. "I'd like you to be there."

"Not a problem."

"Good. There will be a car at the head of your road at eleven-thirty tonight. Perhaps we can get together when the delivery has been made, to discuss subjects of mutual interest."

Marder agreed that this would be nice, hung up the phone, and was about to leave the kitchen when Evangelista, the cook, asked him whether he wanted something to eat. Marder realized that he had not eaten anything solid since the kidnappers' food the previous night. Thinking thus, he immediately felt weak and ravenous. He sat in a kitchen chair.

"I'll make you *chilaquiles*," she said.

"You don't have to bother. We could just heat something in the microwave."

The woman cast a baleful look at that appliance. "You don't want to eat from that, Señor. It has rays that soften the bones. I'll make you a nice dish in ten minutes, and meanwhile you can have a beer and I'll get you some fresh *plátanos*." She served these out, clanged a large iron fry-

ing pan on the burner, and started to chop garlic. *Chilaquiles* was a fru-
gal dish, a way to use up stale tortillas and any odd bits you had left over.
Marder watched as Evangelista cut up and fried onions, a heel of chorizo,
chipotles, and a stack of yesterday's tortillas; he smelled it too, and he
was back in the first apartment they'd lived in up by Columbia, where
his wife was making this very dish as he came in after work.

A moment of dizziness then, a disorientation, and for a second or
two he wondered whether it was Mr. Thing performing at last. But, no, it
was only the false Mexico Chole had created speaking past the years to
the true Mexico Marder now inhabited. He sensed a presence behind
him and felt a pang of terror, as he had in the degraded hotel, that if he
turned around she'd be there, still young.

But it was only Carmel, who said, "That smells great. I'm starving—is
there enough?"

Of course there was enough. Evangelista loaded two plates and
watched contentedly, her big arms folded, while they ate. "We're glad to
have you back, Don Ricardo," said the cook. "The place does not go well
when you're gone. You know, the foot of the master is the best manure."

Statch laughed, rolled her eyes, and smiled at her father. It was funny
but also true, like most proverbs. If Marder only knew what crop he was
growing.

He spent the next couple of hours wandering through the *colonia*, observing, showing himself, letting people buy him drinks at the tiny cantina,
solving problems for people or declining to solve them. Sort it out for
yourselves, he told them, and sometimes they did. He understood that in
any village there were feuds, resentments, but although this was not a
hacienda where one man's word was law, he felt the tug of former times
built into the character of the Mexicans. They wanted to make him that
sort of man, so they could relax into their traditional helplessness, and
blame him when things went badly, and nourish themselves on hate.

He walked down to the beach and was surprised to find a group of
men filling sandbags and passing them up the bluff via a human chain.
A whole pallet full of the bags, green and made of tough plastic weave,
waited to be filled. He went over to one of the men and said, "Rafael,
what's this about? Why do we need sandbags?" Rafael was a big, dark,
stone-faced man with a cropped head and arms full of tattoos, a former
soldier, Marder recalled, who was one of Skelly's security subalterns.

The man shrugged. "It's Don Eskelly's orders. It's for our bunkers."

"Bunkers? Why do we need bunkers?"

The man seemed a little embarrassed to be telling this to Marder, who should know all. "For when the war comes, Señor," he replied. Marder nodded and walked back up the stairs. Of course there would be a war. How could he have thought otherwise?

At eleven, Marder proceeded down the causeway for his appointment with El Gordo's men. He'd told Carmel where he was going and, somewhat to his surprise, she hadn't tried to talk him out of it. A few days ago she would have, but now she was a little more Mexican. She looked into his face soberly, and gravely, kissed him on the cheek and wished him good fortune.

An SUV waited there with two men he didn't know. He got in the back as directed, and one of the men sat next to him. They drove off down the coast road toward Cárdenas, then east through the city until they reached the container port. There was a gate around the whole place and a gatehouse, but the guard on duty gave them no problem. They drove slowly through aisles of shipping containers stacked six high.

The man sitting next to Marder took out a cell phone, dialed a number, spoke, listened, and told the driver, "Second right and then left. We should see them."

He put the phone away and smiled at Marder. He had a teardrop tattoo at the corner of his eye. Marder said, "I don't see how you can do this. I thought La Familia had the port locked up."

The man shrugged. "It's a big port."

They made their turns and saw a white five-ton Volvo truck with the logo of a beer company—HERNANDEZ Y CIA, CERVEZAS Y MAS—painted on the side, featuring a picture of a frosty Carta Blanca.

Marder pointed to the vehicle and said, "I thought Hernandez was a La Familia outfit."

"Yes, we've borrowed it for this thing," said the man, and laughed. "They won't bother it when we drive through the city."

Marder got out of the SUV and then, in the glare from an overhead lamp, he could see that there was also a small van parked alongside the beer truck and a group of about half a dozen men standing around, among whom were Reyes and Skelly.

Skelly and Reyes were deep in conversation, Marder observed, but when Skelly saw him he waved and walked over.

"I hear you took care of our problem with that guy."

"I did. The man turned out to be open to reason."

"Yeah, El Gordo was impressed. He had the sense that Alsop was using Cuello as a friendly to get the other cartels. Don't you love when they do that?"

"It makes me proud to be an American. What's going on here?"

"We've been reading serial numbers. It's that orange one on the bottom level. We are about to have the grand opening, as soon as Reyes's boy can get a bolt cutter out of his van."

Here Skelly gripped Marder's arm in a manner that focused his attention. Skelly was looking him straight in the eye as he said, "Now, in the most casual way you can, I want you to lean against the hood of the car you came in, and when they open the door of that container, I want you to sort of slide down so that the engine block is between you and the door of the container. Can you do that without asking a single fucking question and keep smiling because we're just a couple of buddies meeting up after a worrisome interval?"

Skelly gave him a little pat on the arm and walked back to the door of the orange container. The Templos all gathered around, like children before the piñata, as Reyes cut the lock and lifted the handle that released the door latch. No one was watching Marder, so he, the good soldier, did as he was told and slid off the hood of the SUV.

He heard the metallic creak of the container door opening and he crouched as ordered. Then came a peculiar clattering sound that reminded him of a Linotype in operation, followed by shouts and agonized cries and a scatter of pistol shots, more clattering, and silence. He waited, then risked a peek over the hood. All the Templos lay on the ground, glistening with blood. Skelly was down too, cursing, and leaning over him were three Asian men, all small and well knit, dressed only in underwear shorts, and carrying MP5 submachine guns equipped with long black suppressors.

Marder stepped out into the pool of light. Instantly the muzzles of the submachine guns came up, until Skelly yelled something that Marder recalled was the Hmong language, and the guns dropped again. He knelt by Skelly.

"Are you okay?"

"Yeah, just shot. One of those fuckers got off a few rounds."

"What's going on, Skelly? Who are these guys?"

"Oh, some associates from our old stomping grounds. Njaang, Kroong, and Baan, this is Marder."

The three men looked at Marder with the blank faces of seals.

Skelly said, "Marder, we've got a lot of stuff to unload. You'd better get busy before someone shows up."

"I don't understand," said Marder.

"I'll explain later, chief. Meanwhile, I'm bleeding here."

Marder examined Skelly's wound, a hole in the center of a platter-sized bloodstain just above the beltline on the extreme left. "You're gutshot, man," he said. "We need to get you to a hospital."

"I'm not gutshot. It's a through-and-through—you can take me later," said Skelly. "Just help the boys load the truck."

A grin split his pale face, and his teeth shone startlingly in the sodium light.

"This is like old times," he said. "But without the fucking air force."

Marder didn't think it was like old times at all. Skelly was still talking, but more weakly, and Marder had to lean closer to his mouth. "The boys will take the truck to the *casa*. Rafael knows to expect them. Did they do the sandbags?"

"Yes. You planned this whole thing?"

"Of course I planned it. You didn't really think I was going to let that fat asshole get his hands on heavy weapons, did you? They'd have you out of there so fast you wouldn't have time to put on shoes. No, they're ours, and we're going to keep them. Oh, and there's a big suitcase you need to keep your eyes on."

"What's in it?"

"You don't want to know," said Skelly, and closed his eyes.

16

"I feel like shit, but you look like shit, Marder," said Skelly from his hospital bed in Cárdenas General. "You're out of shape. I've been telling you that for years."

Marder looked at his hands, which were torn and blistered. "I'll take your word for it, but in fairness, I feel like shit too. I'm at the age where a man of means expects others to do the heavy lifting. Your guys were amazing, I have to say. It was like watching an old-time movie, the way they moved. Little guys, but they could heave crates up on their shoulders that I could barely budge. Who are they, anyway?"

"Just some tough Hmong I work with when I'm back with the Shans. They'll be useful in the coming days."

"You think we're going to be attacked."

"I don't know, you talked to El Gordo—what do you think?"

"Well, it's hard to tell over the phone. He didn't actually accuse me of ripping him off. I think the fact you were shot meant something. He asked how you were."

"Did you tell him I was here?"

"Well, yeah. He asked, and I thought I was on sketchy ground already without making up an easily checked lie."

Skelly was quiet for a moment, a look of concentration on his face. "He'll be a little slowed down because he doesn't have Reyes anymore, but I have to get out of here."

He pushed a button, and in a shorter time than Marder would have expected, a nurse appeared. Skelly asked her to send Dr. Rodriguez along and she departed.

"You seem to have them well trained."

"My winning personality or bribes, you choose. Ah, here's my personal physician."

A youngish man in a white coat walked into the room. He seemed happy to see Skelly but looked doubtfully at Marder, as if he were carrying staph.

Skelly said, "If you'll excuse us, Marder, Dr. Rodriguez is going to practice the healing arts."

Marder walked down the halls, glancing in the rooms he passed. Around nearly every bedside was the Mexican Family, almost always the mother, often spooning food into the patients, since everyone knew the hospitals fed you trash. Marder thought they weren't feeding Skelly trash, and he doubted that these others got the kind of service he received.

He passed Dr. Rodriguez in the hall and paused to address him, but the man rushed by and did not meet his eye. A busy man, it seemed, or perhaps he was still unaccustomed to bribery and was ashamed.

Skelly was getting dressed. As he'd predicted, the slug had torn up the muscles of his flank but had done no intestinal damage. Another noble scar for Skelly.

They drove back to the *casa* in the SUV Marder had left in just a few hours ago. Everyone was glad to see Marder, again, and some were just as glad to see Skelly, including Rafael and his band of militia—and Lourdes. Skelly was conferring with his men in the front driveway; they were telling him how *los chinos* had arrived, how they were already setting up strongpoints with the powerful new weapons, how everyone was doing as they asked although they could speak no Spanish and barely any English. Marder was about to move off and inspect these wonders, when the beauty came racing up from the servants' house and flung herself at Skelly, hanging on his neck and covering his face with kisses.

Skelly clutched the delicious body to him, grinning, and over her head passed Marder a satyric look and a wink. Marder turned away into a chaster embrace: his daughter.

"You're back again," she said, "miraculously preserved. When those guys came in with the guns, we didn't know what to think, and they're not very communicative. What language is that they're speaking?"

"Hmong. They came over from China in the shipping container with the weapons, and when the container was opened, they came out and massacred all the Templos. How long has that been going on?" He gestured to where Skelly was walking away with his minions, Lourdes glued to his side.

"Poor Daddy—the *patrón* is the last to know what his peasants are up to."

"He's sleeping with her?"

"I've always liked that euphemism. My room adjoins Skelly's, and I can assure you, sleep is not involved in their connection."

"That bastard!"

"I don't see what your objection is. If she's Skelly's girl, it'll suppress the other guys' fighting over her. No one will challenge the big kahuna."

"For God's sake, Carmel, she's sixteen."

"She'll be seventeen next month, which I believe was approximately my mother's age when you took her out of here."

"I was twenty-four. He's sixty-something."

"And sexy as hell. I'm sorry, but I don't see what the big deal is. Girls fall for older men all the time. It's a trade-off. They get a leg up in life, financially and career-wise, and the old guys get to feast on young flesh. And Skelly's not going to slash her face or treat her like shit."

Marder didn't know what the big deal was either—not rationally at any rate—but, viscerally, thinking about them together made him want to kill his friend. Insane, insane, but there was burning in his belly, as if he'd eaten a spoonful of habaneros.

"Unless you're envious . . . ," his daughter ventured.

"Oh, don't be stupid! I have no sexual interest in that little girl."

Statch studied her father for a moment, then said, "I believe you. I think your current sexual interest is sitting in your office."

"What?"

"La Espinoza showed up a couple of hours ago. She's going to do a story about us. I told her she could use your office. She was very concerned about your fate, perhaps a little more than journalistic interest would suggest."

"Why are you always fantasizing sexual imbroglios for me? First Lourdes, now Pepa. It's unseemly."

Statch held a finger next to her nose and put on a knowing grin. "I call 'em like I see 'em, Dad. If you'll excuse me, Skelly wanted me to check out the sandbagging on the diesel tank and take a look at the machine-gun nests that *los chinos* are supposed to be setting up."

"Do you actually know anything about that kind of stuff?"

"Oh, I skipped the course on field fortifications, but we MIT engineers are pretty flexible." She waved and tripped off, whistling. The song was "La Adelita," the famous *corrido* of the 1910 revolution. She had learned it at her mother's knee, as had Marder, a ballad of love and death, like every other Mexican *corrido*.

He entered his house and found it transformed. All the furniture in the living room had been pushed to the walls and stacked there, and men from the *colonia* swarmed about, heaving up walls of sandbags to cover the windows, cutting off the light from the sea, and changing the place into something more like a cavern or an immense bunker. The dining room had been lined with rows of pallets, and the dining table had been draped with cloths; the cabinets where the dishes had been kept now showed various sorts of medical apparatuses. A woman in pink scrubs, whom Marder had never seen before, was arranging supplies. She smiled at him but did not introduce herself. Proceeding to Amparo's small office, in search of some explanation for the metamorphosis, he found twelve-year-old Epifania sitting at her mother's desk. This had been cleared of everything but a couple of dozen cell phones, set in small groups and bearing labels neatly printed on masking tape. Epifania had a Bluetooth rig in her ear, and as Marder came in, she was talking, apparently, to thin air: "Copy that, alpha two-five. Feliz one out."

"What are you doing, Epifania?" he asked, and she swung around in the swivel chair, startled. "Oh, hi, Don Ricardo. I'm doing a comm check. Don Eskelly said we had to have a comm check four times a day. This is our comm center, and I'm in charge from after school until my bedtime." She smiled and rummaged through a drawer in the desk, retrieved a cell phone. "This is yours. All the command points and some of the actuals are preprogrammed into it."

Marder took the phone. It was a "Nokla" made in China, and it had his name in marker on the back.

"Actuals," he repeated.

"Yes, people in the chain of command. Don Eskelly explained it to us. Like if you wanted to talk to the alpha platoon leader or if he was on the line—"

"Yes, dear, I know what 'actual' means in this context. I just haven't heard it used that way in a long time. I see we have a nurse."

"Hilda Salinas, yes. She's from the clinic in El Cielo. She's a cousin of Chiquita Ferrar and she volunteered. Lots of people from El Cielo would like to come, but there's not enough room for them. And some of them are afraid of *los otros*."

But you're not, thought Marder as he left, and he recalled the terrified child he had met on his arrival at Casa Feliz. He passed the kitchen with just a glance. It was crammed ridiculously full of large women chopping and chattering among steaming pots of what smelled like rice and beans, obviously a communal kitchen for the whole estate. He waved to the women, received their smiles, and went to his office.

Pepa Espinoza was at his desk, tapping at a laptop computer, and did not look up when he came in and sat on a couch. The room was growing dim as the men built up the sandbag barricades outside the windows. He rose and switched on the overhead lighting and sat down again. She finished what she was doing, closed her laptop, and looked up at him.

"So, Marder," she said, "are you ready for your close-up?" She reached down and brought up a Sony HDR digital camcorder, then switched it on.

"You want to interview me?"

"I am interviewing you. My first question is, what do you hope to accomplish by turning your house and grounds into a fortress?"

"I don't understand, I thought you were bringing a crew. I thought we'd sit on a couch like they do on TV. I always wondered how they got the logo in the corner of the screen to stay up there."

She put the camera down on the desk and frowned. "There's no crew because my producer turned me down. He doesn't think you're newsworthy."

"Gosh, that's a disappointment. I was hoping for the canonical fifteen minutes. And I'm surprised. An inside look at the newest chapter in the narco wars: '*Campesinos* beat back La Familia; American ex-Special Forces trooper trains militia to fight *malosos*.' Probably the biggest story of the year, if not the decade. Did he say why not?"

"Oh, he got the canonical envelope in the mail—a photograph of his wife and children outside their school with black crosses drawn on their faces. I can't say I blame him. On the other hand, I have no children and no one's life I care much about saving. I'm here as a freelancer, recording for YouTube and posterity. And you're right: it's going to be gigantic."

The door flew open and a group of dusty men appeared. The foremost said, "Oh, sorry, Señor, I thought no one was here; we have to make holes." He indicated the walls generally.

"Let's let these men have the room," said Marder. "We'll go up on the roof."

Espinoza shoved her laptop and camera into a large red canvas bag and followed him out. "What are the holes for?" she asked as they climbed the stairs.

"Well, when they defend a building in the movies, they shoot out of the windows, but in real life they barricade the windows and shoot out of loopholes."

"You planned all of this? That the narcos would attack you here?"

"Skelly did. I told you, I just came down here to retire in the sun, but that doesn't seem to be possible at present. Given the situation that we would not be allowed to live in peace, Skelly decided that a showdown was inevitable at some point, and he arranged for us to have heavy weapons to defend ourselves."

"And stealing these weapons from the Templos made it inevitable that your place would be attacked. Very neat."

"You're well informed, I see."

"It's my métier. But what I don't quite get is why you think you can get away with defying the narcos. El Gordo must have four hundred men under arms, trained killers, completely merciless. They're not going to have much trouble with a hundred or so campesinos."

"That's an odd statement coming from a Mexican patriot. Zapata and Villa did pretty well with just that kind of people."

"And they failed."

"Well, yes, but maybe we won't."

"They have tanks. Did you know that? Huge armored trucks with machine guns."

"Mercy me! I guess we should surrender, then. But on the other hand, you're here. You must not be that worried about your own safety. There's a contract out on you. Don't you think that one of your merciless killers will collect on it?"

"Perhaps. This is where I shrug fatalistically like a good Mexican and say, Everyone has to die."

"Or it might not come to that," said Marder. He pointed to where groups of men were constructing positions for the two huge Soviet DShK 12.7-mm machine guns, one commanding the road and the other the shoreline. "They might see that we're well defended and look for easier prey. That's why people keep dogs, you know. The kid who's looking to smash a window and grab the computer would rather not deal with a dog, so he moves on to the quiet house down the street."

"But El Gordo is not a street punk, and if he lets you off, people will see *him* as a punk, and he'll be finished. His own people will take him out."

"Then let them do their worst," said Marder.

"You're not concerned that you're risking the lives of all these people?"

"I *am* concerned. What do you think I should do? Leave and let all these people go back to the barrios and decrepit *ranchos* they came from? Let the narcos fight over who gets to build a casino resort on my land? No one has to stay and fight. Some people have left, as a matter of fact, but others have come. A few people, at least, seem to be happy that someone is fighting the narcos."

"And how long will you be able to survive a siege? How will you feed these people or get goods off the land, this absurd crafts thing you've concocted—"

"Why absurd?"

"Oh, crafts! People have been trying to make a go of Mexican crafts for decades, and as soon as a market is created it's destroyed by mass production. You can buy embroidered *huipiles* in the market here in town that are made in Chinese factories. And hats—every village used to have women who wove straw into sombreros; each village was different, each hat was a creative act. A man would buy a hat and leave it to his son, that's how long they lasted. But they were too expensive—a hat for a hen, they used to say—and so people started to buy hats made of crap in sweatshops, because poor people don't need a work of art to keep the sun off their heads, and so the weavers, the women, all became beggars and starved."

"Well, if you're right, we won't have to worry about the economics of the handmade; we'll all be shot dead way before we can starve. And speaking of shooting . . ."

A crackle of small arms fire was coming from the far side of the *colonia*.

The men working on the gun emplacements looked up. Marder saw that one of them was Njaang, late of the shipping container. Marder saw him listen for a moment and then smile. He drew a circle in the air and jabbed his finger through it several times, then went back to work.

"It's just target practice with the new rifles," said Marder. "Shall we go down and look? I'm sure you'd like to get it recorded."

They descended and walked through the *colonia*.

"It seems unusually bustling," she said.

People were in fact moving more quickly than was common, carrying loads to and fro on wheelbarrows, carts, three-wheelers made from motorcycles, and there was an atmosphere of tension, or anticipation, as if everyone were preparing for a fiesta. Marder got the usual smiles and waves, except from one family who had everything they owned on a pushcart and were clearly going elsewhere. But another family, with a similar cart, was just as clearly waiting to take their little house; their children smiled shyly, and the woman stepped forward and introduced her family and said that the man was down at *el golf*, practicing on the new rifles.

They walked on, and Marder said, "Did you ever read Orwell's description of what it was like in Barcelona when the anarchists took over during the civil war?"

"I may have," she said. "Why?"

"He wrote that the most remarkable thing he saw was that, when you went into a restaurant or walked the streets, all signs of servility had disappeared. The waiters held themselves like grandees and refused tips. The signs of class had vanished overnight."

"But they lost, didn't they, Orwell's people?"

"Yes, but they had something for a while, and we have it here now. I've been trying to stop people from treating me like I'm another rich asshole, and now they have. And what have we here?"

He had stopped in front of a metalworking shop belonging to a man named Enrique Valdes, who usually made candle lanterns and religious images out of tinned sheet metal. In front of his shop/house were now arranged a number of wide curved boxes, the size of small attaché cases, open at the top and with brazed-on legs that enabled them to either stand upright or be fixed vertically in soft earth. A teenaged boy was using an electric grinder to score lines in the concave faces, and his younger brother was cutting short pieces of heavy barbed wire off a spool and dropping them into a pail. Valdes himself was ladling a grayish paste from a fifty-five-gallon drum into one of the metal boxes.

"It's amazing, you know—I live here and I had no idea that all this preparation was going on."

"What are they making?"

"They're claymore mines. That stuff he's putting in there is fuel oil–fertilizer explosive. Well, we have enough of those ingredients, and I'm sure Skelly has arranged for detonators. When they're set off, you get a one-directional blast—that's why the kid is weakening the front face of the mine. The enemy gets a face full of shrapnel, which is barbed wire in this case. You'll notice the kid is inscribing a slightly different pattern in each one. How horribly wonderful and Mexican!"

Marder smiled at her, but she gave him a look that he could not decipher. "You're enjoying being a warlord, aren't you?"

"Not at all. I would much rather live in peace and develop a crafts-export business. But since I'm in this situation, you'll allow me to find any amusement I can. Besides, I'm obliged to show a cheerful face."

"You should be cheerful. When this thing collapses, you can take off to some other beach and leave the *campesinos* in the shit."

Marder said, "You're quite mistaken. I intend to die here." He stamped his foot. "Here, on my land. And also, if I may, I find your cynical nihilism excessive, even by the standards of journalism. I would think that you'd cheer for a bunch of people trying to make a stand against a loathsome social cancer that's killed forty thousand Mexicans, but all I hear is carping and nasty insinuations about my motives. It's not objectivity; it's personal, for some reason. Either your dislike of me is skewing your attitude or you've totally succumbed to *no importa madrismo.* In either case, I don't want to hear that crap anymore. If you can't stop sniping, you can take a hike."

He walked away, not caring whether she followed or not. The sounds of firing grew louder, and soon he came to the edge of the inhabited part of the *colonia* and the area everyone called *el golf.* Skelly had rigged poles and wires from which hung paper silhouette targets, and men were lined up firing at them, in single-shot and three-round bursts. A larger group of men was standing behind the firing line, smoking and calling out to the shooters. Rafael was acting as the range officer, and Skelly was squatting on the ground among a group of men, showing them how to field-strip and clean a Kalashnikov.

It was like watching Nureyev dance, observing someone who could do something better than practically anyone else. Skelly really knew how to defend an area using irregular troops, how to train and inspire them, how to augment their qualities and compensate for their defects.

Marder watched the young men learn until they could all do the simple task, on a weapon, after all, designed specifically to be used by careless, simple soldiers.

"I'm impressed," said Marder, when the lesson was over and he and Skelly had walked a little distance away from the trainees. "You've done a lot in an incredibly short time. Do you think we have a chance?"

Skelly shrugged. "Yeah, if they run out of gun thugs before we run out of bullets." He looked down toward the firing line, where Pepa Espinoza was videoing the shooters and interviewing the men who were waiting. "How's your girlfriend? She seems to be in her element."

The reporter paused and looked at the two men. It was a peculiar look, defiant and a bit hurt at the same time.

"Yes," said Marder. "She has that in common with you. Speaking of girlfriends, where's Lourdes?"

"Watching the little kids. Rosita's got a day-care center set up."

"We need to talk about that."

"The day-care center?"

"No—Lourdes. I want to get her out of here. She should be in acting school in Mexico City. That's what we arranged."

"Maybe you should ask her what she wants."

"Maybe the adults should make decisions for the children. What are you going to do, Skelly? Marry her? Give her a career, a home, and children? You're old enough to be her grandfather, for God's sake."

"Maybe you're taking this paternalism stuff too seriously, chief. Let's drop the subject, okay? And let me say that if you were getting some nookie yourself, you might not be so concerned about the nookie other people are getting."

"It's not about sex," said Marder. "It's about someone's life. I'm sending her to Defe."

They had a staring contest then, which Skelly broke off first, laughing. "Look, Marder, here's the way it is. This is a war and I'm the war lord, so I get any girl I want, for as long as I want, and Lourdes is the girl I want. It's real simple. After the war, assuming we win, then we can talk about *arrangements*. Meanwhile, I got to go check the perimeter."

He walked off, leaving Marder struggling to control his rage, which was made worse because he did not understand its source. He hadn't been this furious in years at anyone but himself.

"What was *that* about?"

He spun around and there was Pepa. "Nothing," he replied. "A small glitch."

"It wasn't nothing," she said. "You should've seen your face; you looked like you wanted to shoot him."

He gave her a sour look. "You never stop being a reporter for one second, do you?"

"Not with you I don't. You're a big bag full of secrets and lies, and I hope that if I keep poking you, some of them will leak out."

"I've been nothing but frank with you."

"Really. So tell me frankly what was that argument about."

"Off the record?"

"If you like."

He told her what the argument was about.

"What are you going to do?"

He looked at her avid face and the solution popped into his mind. "I'm going to get her out of here, and you're going to help."

"Oh, no, Señor. I was happy to help once, but I am not going to involve myself in any—"

"Yes, you will. I can tell you're one of those new journalists who want to be involved in the story. No mere objectivity for Josefina Espinoza, oh, no—"

"—abductions from the seraglio. And, besides, why do you need me? Just pop the kid into a car and—"

"No, it has to be you. If I try to get her to go, she'll run to Skelly and the two of them will be singing a *corrido* duet, with me as the villain. This is a Mexican romance, and the boyfriend can't know that the girl-friend is leaving town. No, she'll listen to you; she worships the ground beneath your Jimmy Choos. You tell her she has to go to Chilangolandia like I arranged and she'll go. Now, we'll need a car that can pass safely through the streets—"

"You're not listening. I'm not going to do it."

"Fine. Then you can leave my property. I'll have to call around and see if there are any other reporters who want the biggest story of the decade. In fact, now that I think about it, I would rather have a man do it. It's going to get pretty rough here over the next couple of days, and I'm not entirely sure you'd be up to it. So . . . it was nice knowing you, Señora Espinoza. I'll look for you on the decapitation beat."

He turned and walked away from her, back down the village street toward his house. He heard a shrieking, as from tropical birds or small children, and a mass of the latter ran past him toward a patch of beaten earth the community used for a playground. All of them wore skeleton masks on their faces, and their grubby fists clutched stick-mounted sugar skulls. At the back of the mob was an adult, also in a skull mask but with a body that was anything but skeletal and was instantly identifiable as that of the troublesome Lourdes.

He hailed her, and she tilted her skull back and gave him the Smile.

"Lourdes," he said, extending his hand to her. "I'm so glad I ran into you. I was just talking about you with Pepa. She has some exciting news for you."

Marder turned and called, "Pepa!" and made a fetching gesture with his hand. Espinoza was standing in the middle of the road, her head forward, her mouth unattractively agape, looking much like the bull after the matador has finished his bamboozling capework.

After a moment, Pepa arranged a TV smile on her face, came forward, and embraced the girl, but not before snarling *"Chingaquedito!"* in his ear as she passed.

Marder walked away from them both with a last friendly wave. Indeed he was a *chingaquedito*, Mexican slang for a sneaky, manipulative, sandbagging son of a bitch. His wife had introduced him to that word early in their relationship when he departed even a bit from the openhearted honesty she practiced herself and demanded of him. "If I wanted a macho, two-faced, lying dog," she often told him, "I would've married a Mexican."

The children had recalled him to the calendar. It was nearly the end of October, and the Day of the Dead was upon them. Of course that was what the cooking was for, not a tactical kitchen for a war but preparation for the fiesta. They would eat and drink and have music and dancing, and all the grave Mexican faces would split, revealing the antic trickster spirit they all kept carefully hidden. There would be fights and love affairs and drunken insults. Marder would be particularly insulted then, being the *patrón*, and he would not mind, because he would be dead drunk too. And after that, they all would string wreaths of marigolds and make altars to their dead, with sugar skulls and *pan de muerto* iced white as bones and molded in the shapes of bones. The first day of the fiesta would be for the little angels, the dead children, and the next day would be for the other dead; the families would travel to the cemeteries and have picnics at the gravesides of their defunct kin and prepare *ofrendas*, so the dead could eat too when they returned to earth, according to the will of Mictecacihuatl, the Queen of Death and of the land beyond death.

The preparation had passed without Marder paying it much attention, although he was more than familiar with preparations for Día de los Muertos and with the difficulty of getting just the right kinds of marigolds in New York, not that such was the chief difficulty at chez Marder in those years. No, it was that the señora could not, in fact, visit the graves of her ancestors along with her family and so had to content herself with drinking and insulting Marder. El Día was not Marder's favorite festival as a result, and he must have suppressed the many signs that it was upon them—the stink of marigolds in piles, for example, coming from the doorways he passed, the scent of baking. Of course, one could buy *pan de muerto* in the shops now, but many believed the dead were not fooled.

Marder's dead was in a jar in his bedroom. As he thought about this and about why he had banished this particular season from his mind, he experienced one of those little miracles of coincidence that occur in all lives. He was thinking that he had to talk to the priest, and there the man was, walking down the street, chatting, hand in hand with two kids in skeleton gear. Marder wanted a long talk with the priest but not here in the middle of the street. He explained his problem, though, and Father Santana was helpful as always.

"You're worried about being stopped and abducted," the priest said. "But I don't think there's much of a chance of that. In the first place, we'll be traveling in my car. Everyone knows my old VW and it passes pretty freely, even when things are as bad as they are now. Though they live lives of depravity and murder, they all want the sacraments when they're dying. Besides that, it's the Day of the Dead. Banks and businesses close down, and so does the narco war. You know, even *los otros* have their dead to visit, and no one wants to get on the wrong side of Mictecacihuatl."

"That's good, then. I assume I'll see you at the fiesta here."

"Well, no, actually, which is why I'm here now. I'll be at my own church and the celebration in the town. Señor Cuello always throws a big party, and I'm expected to sit with the notables and give countenance."

"That's not very good company for a priest, is it?"

"Yes, everyone says that, but sitting down with thieves, murderers, and torturers is exactly the sort of company a priest should keep, if he wants to imitate Christ. Which I try to do. Our Lord, you know, never turned down a nice meal."

"Your imitation doesn't go as far as seeking crucifixion, I suppose."

The priest laughed. "Oh, that too, if necessary, but let this cup pass and so on. Cuello is curious about you, by the way. He was pumping me for information the last time we met."

"What did you tell him?"

"That you were an American retiree with philanthropic ambitions."

"And did he believe you?"

"Of course not. At first he thought you were an agent of some other cartel. Now he thinks you're an agent of *El Norte*."

"And who do *you* say I am, Father?"

Father Santana laughed again. "Very good. I say you are a soul in trouble, like most of those I meet." He held out his hand. "Let us say ten o'clock, the day after tomorrow, in front of the house here. I'll probably be late, but you won't mind that, given the Day."

17

"You look like death warmed over," said Marder to his daughter.

"Thank you. It was a communal effort."

"I bet. Where did you get that dress?"

"This old thing?" She flounced and twirled it. It was yellow, made of satin, ankle length, with a low ruffled top that bared her shoulders and elevated her small breasts. "I don't know—Rosita and the ladies had a trove of them. They did my makeup too."

"I like it. You seem happy to be deceased."

All of Statch's exposed skin had been painted matte black, upon which had been skillfully drawn the shapes of the underlying bones, in white. Her face had been painted to look like a skull; her short red hair had been center-parted and slicked down with gel, and she wore a kind of tiara made of colored ribbons from which depended a long yellow wig. She was impersonating La Calavera Catrina, the upper-class lady who is a feature of every Día de los Muertos.

"I *am* happy. This is the first Halloween party I've been to since I was eleven that I didn't go as the you-know-what. I used to get so tired of carrying around that book and flashlight. The walking dead is much more restful. How're you doing? I notice you're not dancing."

Marder indicated the bottle of old brown tequila in front of him. "No, I'm working on my drunk. I fear it would impair my dignity were I to fall on my face, even though this is an occasion for the *hidalgos* to make asses of themselves and for the people to have a good laugh at my expense."

"You should dance with La Espinoza, though."

"Oh?"

"Yes, she's been looking at you with hot eyes all evening."

Marder spontaneously cast his gaze around the terrace but found no hot eyes. He did see Lourdes, also dressed as La Caterina but in red satin, filling out the dress more lusciously than his own girl, and dancing with Skelly, who was wearing a silk-screened skeleton shirt and a skull mask. Skelly was a good dancer; they were both good dancers. It was a pleasure for all the people to watch them—the most fearsome man and the most beautiful girl. It was like a *corrido* being written before their eyes; all that remained was the tragic ending they knew had to come. Marder, who had arranged the tragic ending himself, wondered whether Pepa Espinoza had made her move and whether it had worked, and whether, having made the decision to leave, the girl Lourdes had enough brass and self-command to keep it from her aging desperado.

"That's your romantic imagination," said Marder.

Statch, who was sipping at a margarita, sputtered at this, causing a plume of fine spray that glittered in the light of the dozens of luminaria placed around the terrace.

"Says the most romantic person in the world to the absolute least."

"Maybe you're changing. Maybe we're switching personalities: maybe it's your turn to be romantic and mine to be the coldly calculating one."

A certain bitterness in this remark struck her, and she said, "Excuse me, but is anything wrong?"

"Not really. I'm just fine, if you ignore that I've turned my house into a fortress bristling with military hardware, controlled by mercenary killers under the command of a gentleman who, to my certain knowledge, has been a few bricks shy of a load since 1969. I'm looking at a party full of nice people dressed as corpses and wondering which of them is going to be actually dead in the next few days, the deaths being my fault, my fault, my grievous fault. And all because I . . . ."

"All because what, Dad?"

He could feel her interest focusing on him, the primary urge to comprehend that she'd had since age five, the thing that kept her here, where she too was probably going to get shot.

"Because I liked the view from this terrace."

She waited, but nothing more than this evasion came. He drank another couple of swallows of the *añejo*.

"I think you're exaggerating, Dad. The army will be back through here in a couple of days and the bad guys will return to skulking and a little light dismemberment. They're not going to launch a mass attack againt this house with Major Naca and his tanks in the district."

"You've been apprised of Major Naca's motions?"

"In a way. He called me and I wormed it out of him. He'd just come back from the cemetery and he wanted to talk."

"He lost a child?" asked Marder, for today had been the first Day of the Dead. In the old days there had, of course, been many, many little angels, and although there were fewer now, there were still plenty among the poor of Mexico.

"Wife and two little kids, in the earthquake."

"Not the big one in Defe, surely. He'd be way too young."

"No, the Manzanillo one in '95. They were on vacation and they were strolling down the street after lunch and a façade fell on them. Missed him, killed them."

"Good Christ! He told you this on the phone?"

"He did. I was surprised too."

"Do you have a . . . relationship with this man?"

"I had coffee with him once. But on the other hand, it's El Día de los Muertos. Normal rules don't apply. He seemed like a lonely person who wanted to talk to a sympathetic stranger about his loss. It happens on trains and airplanes all the time. Sometimes it's the beginning of a relationship and sometimes it's just what it is, a reaching out to an anonymous human, like a secular confessional."

"Which is it in this case, do you think?"

"Oh, I don't know—he's an attractive guy, a little old maybe, but isn't that what they say about daddy's girls? I certainly haven't been overly successful in establishing lasting relationships with my contemporaries, and when I think about the kind of dating I was doing in Cambridge, it's like it was happening to a different person. He's up in Apatzingán, and when he passes through here again we'll see how it goes. Don't hire the hall yet."

Now a figure approached, dressed like many others in a skeleton-printed long-sleeved T-shirt. To this had been added a stylish wraparound calf-length skirt and a skull mask with a pre-Columbian look: bright red, studded with glass jewels, and sporting a long red plume above.

Statch said, "Speaking of inamorata . . . I'm going to find someone to dance with. See you on the battlements, Daddy."

She bounced away, waving gaily at the red mask as she left.

Who sat at Marder's table and tilted up her horrid visage.

"If your wars are as good as your parties, Marder, the narcos haven't a hope."

"It *is* a good party," said Marder. She had a hectic look quite different from her usual severe professional visage—a mask, he thought, just as artificial as the scarlet thing perched on her head. "Have you been dancing and drinking your fill?"

"Drinking, not dancing, I'm afraid. It was drummed into me as a little girl that our kind does not whirl around the floor to the strains of the mariachi. They rendered me a perfect little tight-ass. God forbid someone should mistake me for a *naca*."

At this moment, the band—four guys from Playa Diamante, from the El Cielo end of town, the cousins of someone, with a guitar, a *guitarrón*, a fiddle, and a trumpet—started a bolero after a spate of bouncing *canciones rancheras*. Almost without thought, Marder rose and took Pepa's hand. "No one would ever suspect you of being a *naca*, Señora," he said. "You are as *fresa* as it is possible to be, nor could the most abandoned dancing detract an iota from your *fresismo*. Which we will now demonstrate," he added, and led her onto the dance floor.

Marder knew a good deal about Mexican dancing, and it was clear after a few minutes that his partner did not. He therefore took her in hand; at least she knew how to follow his lead as they cruised through the evolutions of the bolero. He did some fancy work, not discreditably, and she registered an amused appreciation.

"I'm starting to believe you *are* a Mexican, Marder," she said. "Where did you learn to do those moves?"

"In Sunset Park. That's a Mexican neighborhood near where we used to live. My wife liked to dance. She was very good at it too."

"She sounds wonderful."

Marder picked up the tone of this remark. "She *was* wonderful. She was graceful, intelligent, creative—Maria Soledad Beatriz de Haro d'Ariés. Perhaps you've read her poetry?"

"I'm afraid not, but that's certainly an interesting name. My parents come from high *criollos* but not quite as high as that. My, my, you are a surprising man. So she was a poet too. I am myself prosy, and clumsy, as you are no doubt observing this minute."

"I'm observing nothing of the kind. And she was wonderfully beautiful, a superb mother, and a terrific cook."

"I'm shriveling: say her bad points, please."

"There are only two I can think of. One was that she was a little crazy. Every so often she would have a screaming fit. I mean she practically had to be physically restrained to keep from hurting me, or herself. And she would direct this insane rage only at me, never at the kids, thank God, or at anyone else, because I was responsible for uprooting her from her native soil and leading her into loathsome exile."

"If you don't mind me saying so, that's ridiculous. Why couldn't she hop on a plane? Or, for that matter, you could have settled here if it was so important to her."

"No, I *said* she was a little *crazy*. The point of the madness was that her father had to forgive her or she couldn't return. And he wouldn't. He was that kind of man. He had fallen to zero in the eyes of the world, maybe, but to his family he was still the *hidalgo*, the *hacendado*."

"Yes. I know men like that. What happened to him?"

"He was assassinated. He resisted extortion from *los malosos* and they sent a couple of *sicarios* after him. Her mother was killed in the same attack. No one in the family bothered to tell her. When the lawyers made the distribution after the will was read, it turned out that her mother hadn't forgotten her. There was some old family jewelry she wanted Chole to have. That's how she found out. A FedEx package with a pearl-and-garnet necklace, some silver, a couple of brooches, and a letter from a lawyer. And she came apart."

The bolero ended and the band took up a sprightly *corrido* in the *tierra caliente* style.

"Could we sit this one out?" said La Espinoza. "I could use another drink."

They sat, and in a moment or two Epifania came by with a cold pitcher and filled Pepa's glass with margarita.

"I don't know why I'm telling you this," said Marder. He poured and drank another shot. Around him the fiesta had become blurry, like an arty photograph of a fiesta, and the shrill trumpet seemed unnaturally loud. He heard a woman scream and the sound of men shouting at one another. Well, that was all right—there were inevitably fights at fiestas. He wondered if Skelly had posted guards. No, it was still the truce of Santa Muerte, the white goddess whom the murderers all worshipped. In another day the killing would begin again.

"I know why," she said confidently. "So then what happened? She came apart and . . ."

"She was sort of gone. The kids were away at college by then, and somehow the woman I'd loved for over twenty years just wasn't there anymore. She'd been replaced by someone who screamed curses at me when she wasn't in a drugged-out sleep. It was very strange, like being in a dream. I said to her, let's go to Mexico, find out what happened, get back with your family. No, she didn't want that, it was too late, I'd ruined her life, and so on and so on. I figured I could set something up, get a place down where she used to live, a nice house, and surprise her, somehow get her on a plane and when she got there everything would work out. Somehow. I was not thinking too clearly, obviously, but I pushed ahead. I found a woman who specialized in rentals in the right area, and I started looking at properties with her, and . . . what can I say? I was miserable, she was attractive, and we started a thing. I mean right there in her office, on the desks, on the floor."

She listened as the rest of the awful story came out. Her face was hard to read: encouraging, impassive, sympathetic? Marder suspected that, given her profession it was a professional face, developed to maximize the flow of tragic tales in a country unusually rich in them.

When he was done, she did not comment or offer condolences or, worse, tell him he shouldn't blame himself. She only took his hand and said, "Let's dance some more." Out on the floor she clutched him, pressing her body against his, ignoring the tempo of the current song; they circled slowly in a corner, like a toy spun by a soft wind. As he circled, Marder caught a periodic glimpse of Skelly and Lourdes, who were really dancing to the tune; he could see sparks of sweat lit by the glowing pepper lights as they whirled. He felt of stab of irritated pain—not quite envy, because he would not have traded his own life for Skelly's, but rather a wish that he had more of the man's talent for life in the moment. Skelly looked young in the colored lights, far younger than Marder. Was it the life he'd chosen or the human growth hormones? Pepa was now pushing her breasts into his chest and resting her head against his collarbone. What was this? Marder decided not to think about it, to live like Skelly for the space of a dance.

But not quite. "Have you been able to talk to Lourdes?" he asked.

He felt her stiffen. "As a matter of fact, I have."

"And?"

She pulled away from him and looked into his face. "You're really interested in this, aren't you?"

"Yes. Are you going to interview me about why?"

"No. I owe you any number of favors, and I'm as completely indifferent to the fate of beautiful young girls as it is possible to be. I spoke with her. I reminded her of the delights of fame and wealth. The girl has the attention span of a seagull, although she seems to like conspiracies and so should do well in Mexican television. I haven't spoken to the priest about his car."

"I'll arrange that. I'm going up to La Huacana tomorrow morning to inter my wife's ashes. The two of you can come along."

"The two—"

"Yes, you have to come too. To keep the seagull focused on getting on her plane."

She paused for a moment, her hand resting on his shoulder. They both regarded the dancing Lourdes. The perfect face was alive with pleasure and the promise of undying love. Skelly was soaking it up; they could see the delight on his face, the hard planes, the hard eyes all made soft by her presence, by her delight in him.

"That's one of the most amazing pieces of acting I've ever seen," said Pepa, "and I speak as a professional." She leaned again into Marder and they continued their own, more ambiguous dance.

Somewhere past three in the morning, the band closed down, collected its fee plus a substantial tip from Marder, and drove off to their barrio. The women cleared the foodstuffs away and the lights went out. Marder walked his dancing partner up to the second floor, both of them very drunk and giggling with it, stumbling down the darkened hallway. They stopped at the door to her bedroom and he clasped her hand.

"Well, this has been very pleasant," he said, "really the most pleasant evening I've had in a long time. Everyone had a good time, didn't you think? Maybe it was the situation—maybe they all thought it was going to be the *last* good time."

"Mexicans always party like it's going to be the last good time. It's a national trait. And for so many of us it *is*. I mean, it's a good bet, especially in Michoacán."

"Yes, there's that. But we also believe that the dead are always with us, and maybe the dead enjoyed the party too, maybe life and death don't matter quite so much as we've been taught. Or do the dead like to see the living having a good time? Are they jealous? I wouldn't be, I don't think. When I'm dead I plan to be a happy spirit."

"What was the second thing about your wife?" she asked.

"Excuse me?" Marder was having trouble standing up. He threw an arm around the woman and leaned into her.

"Before, you were telling me about your wife and I admitted that she sounded superior to me in every way, and you said, no, she was deficient in two things and one of them was that she was crazy. What was the other?"

"Oh. I meant she was dead and you're not. Assuming alive is better, which is sometimes difficult to believe. I'm starting to talk nonsense. Maybe it's time to sleep."

He hugged her, the two of them swayed, he kissed on her cheek and breathed deeply of the air above her skin: a little perfume, a little meat smoke, a little chili, a little tequila, and beneath these the mysterious, the pheromones from the Pleistocene, the girl-stuff itself. He sighed out that breath and said, "Good night, sleep well," and was turning away when he discovered she had hold of his belt, with her warm fingers inside his waistband.

"Oh, don't be an idiot," said the woman. "Take me to bed."

Lying naked with him, she said, "There's no moon tonight. There should be shafts of pale moonlight illuminating my perfect body."

It's true, he thought. The only light through the window came from distant stars shining over the sea, and there was a profound absence of vision, but this made the other senses, touch and smell and hearing, more keen. They touched therefore, and listened, and smelled.

"What's that heavenly odor?" she asked, shifting slightly to better enable his current touch.

"It's night-blooming cereus. The late Guzmán planted a patch of it under his bedroom window. Listen: What's that sound?"

They listened. A rhythmic high-pitched cry, like the sound a mechanical bird might make, floated in through the open window, along with the rush of the surf.

"I think it must be Lourdes getting laid," she said after a moment.

They listened for a full minute, stifling hilarity. "Well, they're certainly putting us to shame," he said. "Can you forgive me?"

"Oh, she's faking that. Seventeen years old? She has no idea what an orgasm with a man is."

"How can you tell?"

"My dear man, was I not once a hot seventeen-year-old Mexican girl, and not so long ago that I've forgotten how it was? One learns to masturbate, of course, and perhaps there is fooling around with one's girl-friends, and one is puzzled and dismayed when the same thing doesn't happen with the first man. There are other rewards, but not that. If she's lucky, an older man will teach her about her body."

"Skelly is certainly that," said Marder.

"Yes, but he doesn't really care about her, which is why I agreed to help get her out of here."

"He seems to. I almost had a fight with him about it."

"No, the fight was the *point*. You didn't want him to have her, so naturally he had to have her. It's all about you. Yes, he enjoys her youth and perfection, but at bottom everything he does with respect to her is about you."

"I don't understand."

"I know you don't. It's one of the charming things about you, Marder, a kind of negative narcissism. You are blissfully unaware of affection or interest on the part of others, as if you were a leper. That's why I had to drag you in here by your *chile* or nothing would have happened, and it's why Skelly is in Playa Diamante risking his neck. He's in love with you."

"That's ridiculous!"

"It's the case, whether you believe it or not. And you pay him no real attention and it drives him crazy, and so he does feats of heroism or prodigies of annoyance so that you *will* pay attention to him. And if you stop that stroking every time I say something that astonishes you, we will not get along. Thank you, that's better."

She writhed a little, and sighed, and said, "*Everyone* loves you,

Marder. Amparo is your absolute slave; I see her watching you like old *campesinos* watch the monstrance with the blessed sacrament in a procession. Your daughter has sacrificed her whole life to be here with you. And I am here. Yes, I'm a journalist and this is, as you say, the story of the decade, but it's mainly you. I don't think I've ever met anyone quite like Richard Marder. It's embarrassing to admit to fascination, but there it is. And I like the way you smell."

"So fascination and smell were able to overcome your dislike of Americans. In my case, at least."

"Oh, I fuck Americans all the time. Germans. Australians. It's the Mexicans I avoid in that department. No, when I feel like getting off, I usually fly up to L.A. or New Orleans. I have a number of colleagues I frequent, nice men, occasionally married ones, no attachments, no job-related *caca*."

"That seems unpatriotic, if you don't mind me saying so. As an honorary Mexican, I am inclined to be offended. What's wrong with Mexicans?"

"Nothing. A noble race. Perhaps I just had a run of bad luck. No, keep doing what you were doing. No, further in. Yes. Well, my Mexican horror stories. They court you, you're the moon and the stars, and then after they fuck you you're just a *chingada*, a kind of human garbage that they don't have to consider. I have been with Mexican men who have called their wives on their cell phones, sitting naked on the side of my bed while their semen was still dripping out of me. The very last one I had was doing me from behind, and I recall thinking that my feet were feeling a little rough and that it was time for a pedicure—and, by the way, foreplay to these guys is a couple of drinks at the bar—when his cell warbled. It was *La Paloma*, if you can believe it, and he actually picked it up. While he was fucking me. And had a conversation with his wife. Why was he out of breath, she asked. Oh, the elevator was broken, he had to walk up six flights. This is the kind of romantic interaction I have had innumerable times with my countrymen, God bless them!"

Her speech was now interpersed with heavier breathing and sounds indicative of the catlike pleasure she was apparently capable of and desired, and which, Marder believed, had not been part of her liaisons all that often.

"So which is it?" he asked. "Marder is unique or just another in a line of non-Mexican rigid objects?"

"Oh, closer to unique. I can usually figure out what makes a man tick before the coffee cools, but not you. And I tried. I used every likely contact I have in New York to find out who you were, and I drew a blank. You're no one special, it seems. But now you're in the middle of a drug war with a lot of money that doesn't seem to come from anywhere. You take the part of a bunch of *pelados* that no one has ever given a shit about, and you defy the two major drug gangs in the neighborhood— not one but *two*—and turn your house into a fort and stock it with heavy weaponry—and where did *that* come from, she wonders—and get the whole thing organized by a fairly serious mercenary and drug-lord bodyguard—and, let me tell you, *he's* something special anyway— and . . . *and* you proceed to shaft not only El Gordo, your chief ally, but also shoot the best pal of the meanest *narco* in the area, this totally dangerous felon, because of a teenage girl you barely know, out of what appears to be sheer decency. Such things don't happen, *querido*, not in Mexico."

"They happen everywhere. As you point out, I'm no one special, yet here I am. Skelly is special, but he's here too, which I find only a little short of miraculous. I'm surprised, by the way, that you were able to uncover much about him in your researches. He tends to keep a low profile."

"Not low enough. His war record is fairly public, and as for his career afterward—well, let's say I'm part of the reportorial fraternity that spends a lot of time looking into the doings of the big drug cartels. I specialize in Mexico, obviously, but I know the people who know the narcos of Asia and Russia and so on. Did you know he worked for Khun Sa?"

"I had no idea. He's mentioned the name."

"The lord of the Golden Triangle. He could eat El Gordo dipped in salsa. In any case, your Skelly's a mercenary. He sets up security operations for the worst people in the world. You would imagine him to be on a moral plane with someone like Servando Gomez, and yet here he is, the best friend of a man I would call . . . I suppose 'saintly' would be the wrong word considering what you're doing at the moment. But don't stop! And kiss me a little here."

"Mother of God, that was wonderful," she said after an extended nonverbal interval. "I haven't had anything like this in ages."

"I'm surprised you stopped talking."

She laughed. "Oh, the talking is what *makes* it wonderful. And you'll have noted the difference in the audio effects from what came in through the window from little Lourdes."

"More full-throated, I'd judge," he said, "more sincere, less influenced by hard-core porn. Speaking of which, what do you think of Fuentes's notion in *The Old Gringo* that the old *hacendados* had their peasants whipped if they made any sounds of pleasure during lovemaking? Did that really happen?"

"Assuredly. Their ladies insisted on it. It was intolerable for peasants to have something that was denied to them by their status and their Church, and the masters complied, because they, of course, had all the sex they wanted from those very peasant women. And when the *patrón* had such a woman, it went without saying that she could not share any pleasure with that farm animal, her husband, ever again. However, thanks to our glorious revolution, I have no hesitation about making any sounds that . . . yes, keep doing that, press harder . . . yes, oh, that's excellent. Viva Zapata!"

Somewhat later, she shifted position, drew a line of small kisses down his belly; he felt the fall of her hair following this damp line. Then some moist noises and again her voice from the darkness, "So, about Skelly: How do you come to be such buddies? You were in the war together, yes?"

"Yes. It's a long story, and how will you continue the interview if your mouth is full?"

"I will take small breaks. I find it enhances the lubricity."

He was drunk, so he told her the whole story, starting with Naked Fanny, and the voodoos, and Moon River, the montagnards, Joong, and what Skelly was, and the firefights on the trail, and the assault on the SOG outpost, and about all the dead. Then he stopped, and after a moment there came a sound amusingly similar to the withdrawing of a cork from a bottle.

"And what happened then? Did the communists attack again?"

"No, not exactly. What happened was, I got up in the morning after the assault. I was sleeping in one of the longhouses because all my stuff had been burned up in the attack. It was Joong's father's longhouse, as a matter of fact. I went out to piss and when I came back through the village I noticed that some kids were playing with a ball, throwing it back and forth, and some other kids were knocking another ball around with sticks, and a couple of real little kids had balls attached to strings that they were whirling around their heads. Everyone was having a great time, and it was strange that it took so long for it to occur to me that I'd never seen so many balls in the village before. Skelly was gone with the surviving Vietnamese rangers up the mountainside to the south to see if he could make contact with any bad guys, and I was poking through the ruins of the command hooch to see if there was any radio stuff that I could salvage, when a kid flung his ball and it bounced by me and I saw that it was a voodoo. Long story short: it turned out that the PAVN had been gathering these things for weeks. I mean, we put out thousands, and they'd picked up hundreds and left them in the village after the attack. That had been the real reason for the attack in the first place and also why they hadn't pressed it harder. They didn't have to: yet another way in which we'd underestimated our enemies. Also, the kids had been playing with them all morning, and therefore to the pinball wizards back in Naked Fanny, all those voodoos moving around must have looked like the central marshaling yard of the northern Ho Chi Minh Trail. If you keep that up I will lose interest in my story."

"Really?"

"Yes, I suddenly find that telling this is more important than getting blown, because, while I've had a blow job before, I've never told this whole thing to anyone. Slide up here, would you?" After a moment, she did.

"That's better," he said.

"Never? Not even to your wife, during that long marriage?"

"No. Chole wasn't interested in war stories, and besides . . . maybe I wanted to start fresh with her; we were both escapees from our lives. But now it's not like real life; it's the Day of the Dead, when everything is permitted, and I want to vomit out this lump of shit and you're a woman who can take it, you're the great chronicler of artistically dismembered corpses."

"Can I do *this*?"

"Yes. Conservatively, if you please. Okay, so when I saw the voodoos there, I ran for the hills. I mean, I was nineteen, an air force electronics guy, and so I ran to find Skelly. He was the *man*, he had the voice of command, he had the training. I found him coming down a mountain track. He was alone, because the LLDBs had run off. They figured they could exfiltrate back to Vietnam by themselves, and they had no partic- ular interest in defending a yard village or hanging out with a couple of

Americans who had no radio contact anymore and hence no money and
no resupply. They hadn't found any sign of the PAVN. And then I told
him about the voodoos and what I thought it meant. It took him a little
while to get it, and as I looked at him . . . you know the expression 'hollow eyes'? Yeah, we know what it means, the metaphor, but Skelly really
had hollow eyes. His eyes are deep-sunk eyes anyway, but these didn't
look like any eyes I ever saw on a person before, a living human being.
You saw a look like that occasionally on the wounded, the ones who
knew they were goners. He'd lost all his friends at once, all these beautifully trained tough guys, invincible warriors, and some enemy mortars
had caught a break and they were all dead. Oh, and I just found out why:
one of our Vietnamese was a spy, and the whole mission was a setup, a
joke. Ha-ha. I had to pull him, to yell at him that we needed to get back
to the village and evacuate it, that they'd send the bombers in.

"So then he got it and we ran like madmen down the mountain. By
that time the B-52s had probably already taken off from U Tapao in
Thailand, maybe a forty-five-minute flight for an Arc Light mission, six
planes, thirty tons of bombs per plane. They fly so high you can't see or
hear them, and you only know it's happening when the bombs start to
explode. We heard the first blasts when we were still in the forest, and
when we came out into the open the whole area was full of smoke and
dust and this overwhelming, colossal noise. Skelly kept going, just dived
into the dust, and I figured later he must've got knocked down by the
edge of the blast from a five-hundred-pound bomb. But I thought he'd
been killed for sure, that I was alone on a mountain in Laos."

"What did you do?"

"I lay flat on the ground and cried and pissed in my pants. After it
was over, I got up and found Skelly. He was bleeding from lots of little
wounds and he was concussed, completely out of it. The village was
gone, not even ruins, a field of craters, and . . . well, four, five hundred
people—it's hard to actually dispose of that much human flesh, so there
were pieces, gobbets, I guess you could call them, all over where the village had been and on the outskirts where we were. Mostly unidentifi-
able, like in a butcher's shop, but also the occasional piece where you
could tell what it was despite the dust—a shoulder and part of an arm or
a torso with breasts on it or a little kid's head. Some of it was stuck on
Skelly and I picked it off him, bits of people he'd known and loved, courtesy of the USAF. Well, mistakes happen, what can you do? *There it is*, as

we all used to say in the war. I kept saying it like a mantra all that first day when I had Skelly on my back and was walking to Vietnam."

"How far was it?" asked the good reporter. She made no sympathetic comment, for which he was grateful, although he wished he could see her face. Should he light a candle? No, he had to have the dark to tell this.

"A little over twenty-five klicks," he said after a longish pause. "I was heading for a Special Forces camp I knew they had at Quang Loc. I had a compass but no maps, no radio, of course, no weapons but my sidearm and Skelly's K submachine gun, a couple of C-rats, and four canteens of water. Also I had to actually walk across the Ho Chi Minh Trail and find my way through thousands of active PAVN and Vietcong."

"And you survived, obviously. The two of you survived."

"Our bodies survived," he corrected. "Even that was ridiculous, when you think about it. I was in pretty good shape and I'm big enough, but I certainly wasn't a SOG elite soldier, and Skelly was in and out of consciousness. The route led straight through a dozen miles of thick rain forest. I couldn't use the trails and I had to pick the steepest routes, because those were where I had the best chance of avoiding patrols." He stopped.

"Go on," she said.

"I can't," he replied. "I'm starting to sweat and I'm getting nauseous. I think this was a mistake. The only thing I can think about now is getting away from here and finding a small white room and spending the rest of my life in it, never talking to anyone."

"Yes, but you're here now and you can't leave."

"Why not?"

"Because I have a firm grip on your sexual organ."

He laughed, and his tension faded a little. "Yes, the classic barrier to male flight. Okay, think of the hardest thing you ever did—physically, I mean—and up it by a factor of ten. After the first day, I was wiped and we'd made it maybe two klicks. It was like walking through sheets of drywall; every foot of vines and bushes and bamboo had to be hacked through with Skelly's Ka-Bar knife. I'd dump him on the ground and make a five-meter tunnel and then go back and pick him up and lay him down and take a drink of water and start hacking again. And it wasn't even hacking, really, because I couldn't make any noise; I was terrified of being found and shut up in a little cage. I had to slowly slice through every fucking branch. At the end of the second day I sat down to die. It is simply a technically impossible feat to cut your way through twenty-five kilometers of triple-canopy highland Asian forest with a knife, while carrying an unconscious man, on essentially no food or water."

"But you did it."

He swallowed several times and willed calm upon his heaving belly. "No, that's just the point. I didn't do it. I had supernatural help."

"What! You're saying *God* made a miraculous tunnel through the forest?"

"More or less. I was lying there waiting to die, with my nose and mouth covered in insects, bitten all to hell, and I heard a voice in my head that wasn't me. If this has never happened to you, it's impossible to convey the reality of it, but there it was, as real as your voice coming to me in this dark room."

"So you're saying that God, after letting however many millions of people die in that miserable war, just decided that Richard Marder and Patrick Skelly were indispensable in his great scheme of things?"

"Yeah, I am. I'm sorry if it doesn't make journalistic sense, but that's how it was. Anyway, I got up and started to cut again, and somehow it was easier. It was like I was out of my exhausted body; I could see the patterns of the vines and shit blocking our way, and I found myself passing through them with the bare minimum of effort. I felt like I wasn't alone there in my tunnel—there were *beings* in there with me. And when we got to the bottoms, I just knew when and where to cross the streams. And the roads. I actually crossed branches of the Ho Chi Minh Trail. Patrols and convoys went by us and no one ever saw us. The voice told me when to move and when to stay still. After that we only moved at night, and I was guided through the night too. I didn't step on a mine, or fall off a dike, and again no one saw us. It must have taken us a week. And then I was sleeping, or not really sleeping but in a deeper trance. I have a sense of what I was seeing in the trance, but I don't have words to describe it, only this being supported by *powers*.

"And then I felt that they were leaving me and I cried out, like don't leave, don't leave me! It turned out I was actually yelling, because I woke to find a hand across my mouth. It was Skelly. He'd come to sometime in the night, and he was the old Skelly again. He asked me where we were and I said I thought we were about two klicks southeast of route 14 and if we hit the road where I thought we would, we'd be less than five klicks south of Quang Loc. He just nodded like this was a routine report. He told me I looked like shit and that he'd get me back alive, and not to worry. And it was like he'd been in charge and he'd been carrying *me* all that way. I was so glad not to be responsible anymore that I just fell into it and that was the story we told when we ran into a patrol out of the Special Forces base later that day. He got a Silver Star for that, by that way."

"And you never told him the truth."

"What, that angels had guided me through the jungle? No, as a matter of fact I didn't mention that part, because everyone in the army knew for a fact that if a SOG operative and an air force puke had to get out of a situation, it'd be the SOG guy who led the way, eating snakes and being the total warrior that he was. And so I left it at that and later . . . it's hard to explain, I sort of sank into passivity. My dad got me a job with his sister in the restaurant she owned up by Columbia, and I fell into a marriage with a girl I liked well enough but didn't really love, and so life went on, until one day I woke up and there was a voice telling me, go to Mexico. Which I did, and I met Chole and had that life. It was Chole who made me go back to school. I got a degree from General Studies at Columbia and went to work in a big publishing house and worked my way up through the editorial ranks."

"Until she killed herself, and what then? Another voice telling you to come to Mexico?"

"Something like that. Now you know all."

"Not quite all, I think."

"No, not quite," he agreed.

"Well, maybe you'll tell me another time. If there's another time. Do you think they'll come? I mean in force."

"I expect so, as early as the day after tomorrow, in fact. You really should get out while you can."

"No, I'll stay, if you don't mind. I'm tired of being a pretty face reading the news. I had to fuck a Mexican to get this pissy little assignment doing commentary on gang murders. After this story breaks, as you keep telling me, I'll be a made woman, an actual reporter, like Christiane Amanpour or Alex Crawford. War impresses people—risking life, hearing the bullets fly."

"And won't have to fuck any more Mexicans ever."

A giggle in the dark. "No, I just said that to annoy you. I didn't really have to, but I had to crawl, which was even worse, if you want to know.

But we could die. I mean if Cuello gets his hands on me, it's over, and not in a pleasant way."

"Because you shoot video and talk about his murders?"

"No, because of El Cochinillo, his kid. You don't know this story? Okay, El Cochinillo, it turns out, once demanded a bride, a girl who'd won a local beauty contest. Nothing like our Lourdes, but young, pretty, and sweet, and El Cochinillo went to the father and said the wedding would take place on such and such a day, and what could the guy do? And so it took place, a huge affair, gangsters and politicians from all over. Unfortunately, the girl hanged herself on her wedding night, still a virgin. One has to wonder about the foreplay."

"That was the story?"

"No. The story was that when El Cochinillo found her hanging there, he was so enraged that he fucked the corpse. And he got a taste for it. Girls have disappeared off the streets. We think he—"

"Yes, I get it," said Marder. "But if I jump on you now, will you stop talking about murder, evil, and depravity?"

"Yes, I will," she said.

18

Hungover and afflicted by uncertainty about what had occurred on the previous night, Marder lolled miserably in the shotgun seat of Father Santana's venerable VW Kombi, as the van rolled from the causeway out onto the beach road, its destination the private cemetery at the former d'Ariés estate, Las Palmas Floridas, at La Huacana, up north in the *tierra caliente*. Marder was going to inter the ashes of his wife, which now rested in a ceramic urn on his lap. The car carried an uncomfortable company, all unresponsive to the priest's cheerful morning chatter. In the back, Carmel Marder and Pepa Espinoza sat at opposite ends of the seat, both of them frowsy, glum, and silent.

They were probably hungover too, Marder thought, as he tried to make sense of the memories of the previous night. How much had been fantasy and how much real? His body told him that he had engaged in a sexual extravaganza, but he had awakened in his own bed, and La Espinoza had not with either word or look this morning given him the impression that there was any change in their relationship beyond that of reporter and subject. Statch had been a little cool this morning too, and Amparo had been all formality as she dished out breakfast, calling him El Señor, as in, Would El Señor like some more coffee?

Perhaps it was the occasion; perhaps there was a social taboo in Mexico against screwing one's brains out on the eve of burying one's wife, even though one's wife was three years dead and one hadn't had any sex at all in the period. Marder wished that he had garnered more of his late wife's confrontational style. Had her ashes retained the power of speech, there would had been a barrage of *"Qué pasas?"* rattling around the bus, the reasons for the glumness would have been wormed out of each unwilling heart, advice would have been dispensed, tears shed, guts wrenched, shoulders dampened, and hearts eased.

At the occasion during which that woman had actually become the present ashes, Marder had impressed or dismayed his loved ones by his stoicism—not a sob from Marder at the crowded funeral service, not even when the casket had rolled through the curtain to the flames. The kids had been howling and clutching each other, but not Marder. Now he felt something collapsing inside him; his hands trembled around the urn, he found it hard to speak. He wondered if this was it: he would fall into fragments and Mr. Thing would pop and perhaps they could just leave him there at the cemetery with her, perhaps this was yet another of God's happy jests.

He looked over his shoulder. Pepa had her eyes closed, her head jammed in the corner between the top of the bench seat and the van body. She had put together a funeral outfit—black skirt and a matching jacket over a bloodred shirt. Carmel was wearing loose dark trousers and one of her many safari shirts, this one charcoal, untucked, and on top of that was a garment that for Marder had no name but resembled a kind of duster. It came down to her knees and had a very large number of buttons. He thought she looked good in it, but Marder thought she looked good in everything, so his opinion did not count. He caught her eye, and she smiled wanly at him before also closing her eyes and assuming the position that Pepa was in, on the opposite side of the seat.

The car stopped in front of the Cangrejo Rojo cantina. This was part of the escape plan, for Lourdes could not be seen leaving the *casa* with the funeral party. Instead, Amparo had taken her in the back of her old pickup truck, concealed under a tarp, and dropped her at the cantina on the way to Mass. Now the girl came bubbling from the door of the cantina and into the car, carrying a huge wreath of Mexican marigolds. Instantly the mood of the passengers lifted. Lourdes was happy, and therefore the world had to be happy, and her talent was such that the world could not but comply. Nearly against his will, Marder found himself smiling; one would have had to be a corpse not to bask in the radiance of her delight. Marder thanked her for the flowers, feeling irritated at himself for forgetting to buy any. Her smile flashed out as she gave him the *de nada*.

The noise of the old VW prevented Marder from following the conversation among the three in the rear seat. The priest was saying that he hoped there was not going to be much traffic on 37 north or in the city of Lázaro Cárdenas, because he had to get back for a special Mass at five-thirty. Roads were often crowded on the second Day of the Dead, as families visited their deceased members in various cemeteries and went to the favorite shrines. Besides that, El Día was a prime time for religious visions and there would be a line of people at the rectory this evening, all claiming to have seen wonders and miracles.

Marder had been letting the priest's chatter wash over him, like the noise of the tires and the wind, but this remark caught his attention. "That's interesting," he said. "How do you tell if they're real?"

"You mean visions?"

"Yes, like a sense of God or angels directing you, telling you things. I mean, lots of people hear voices, and generally we lock them up and medicate their heads for them. But obviously the Church believes that kind of thing is not all craziness, no?"

"No. With the greatest reluctance, the Church has agreed that the Holy Spirit is allowed to talk to people directly, without having first cleared it with the appropriate ecclesiastical authorities. It falls to us, its servants, to distinguish between the three possibilities—madness, the divine, or the demonic."

"That's what I meant," said Marder. "How do you do that?"

"Well, it's fairly easy to distinguish the mad. We do it all the time. Madmen are withdrawn or manic, they don't think clearly, they're unnaturally fearful or unnaturally bold. Most of all, they develop a kind of flawless logic that doesn't admit to any challenge from another mind. You could say the mad are sealed off from the human community by their affliction. That's why we say they're in a world of their own."

"And saints aren't?"

"Oh, no. The great thing about saints is not so much that they get messages from God but how they behave toward others. People recognize saints because of their actions. In contrast, you have people who imagine messages from God and then go out and violate every one of God's laws. They're puffed up with pride—God has chosen *me* to accomplish this great deed. Which is how we know they've been contacted by the devil. The devil most often presents as God, which is one reason for the perpetual demonic behavior of the Church. It's not surprising when you think about it. What else has the devil to do but wreck the Church and thereby keep people from God? In contrast, the person touched by God is characterized by great humility, even perfect humility in some cases. Are you familiar with *The Cloud of Unknowing*, by any chance?"

"The name rings a bell. I haven't read it."

"Well, it's mainly a guide to the contemplative life. At one point I was about to join the Cistercians, and I read it and discovered I was not meant for a life of quiet contemplation. In any case, the author distinguishes between imperfect and perfect humility, which he considers the predicate for any real sustaining contact with God. By imperfect humility, he means our consciousness of our sinful nature and our utter inability to escape from it by our own efforts. It's what modern people would call self-knowledge. It's a necessary first step, he says, but inferior to what he calls perfect humility, which is the direct experience of the superabundant love of God. They have the sense of what grace really is, that they have been chosen not because of anything personal to them but as a pure act of loving. I know people who are in that state, and I am hard pressed to avoid the sin of envy when I consider them. I'm doomed to be Martha, I'm afraid, repairing the roofs of churches and carrying soup and putting up with suffering humanity. As are you, I think."

"But I had a vision," said Marder. "I heard the voices of angels."

"Did you?"

And now, for the second time in as many days, Marder poured out the story of the destruction of Moon River and his own mystically guided hegira to Quang Loc, a story he had kept from everyone, often including himself, for more than forty years. A thought flew around in his head as he did so that this was not him, that something was impelling him to purge the secrets, and he wondered whether Mr. Thing had something to do with this, whether it was a tiny leakage in the zones of the brain that involved inhibition. Perhaps he would start stripping in public and sputtering false angelic messages to the world. In any case, it was all of a piece with this grand dismantling of the old Marder that had begun in a doctor's office in New York some eight weeks ago.

The priest listened silently, and Marder was uncomfortably aware that this particular confession was by no means the weirdest account that Father Santana had heard in his career or even the weirdest of the past week.

"That's a wonderful story," he said when Marder had done. "What do you make of it?"

"I was hoping you'd tell me."

"Well, you don't seem crazy to me now, and I suppose one could make up a story about the stress of combat. Yet you did something that competent judges would have considered impossible, which is one definition of a miracle. And afterward—did you ever have the sense of being guided by still, small voices?"

"Not in the same way, no. The idea of coming down here exploded fully formed into my mind, with no prior warning. Maybe that's a similar phenomenon."

"You think God wants you to live in Playa Diamante and do what you're doing here?"

Marder choked out a laugh. "Well, when you put it that way . . ."

"Yes, it sounds insane, obeying the voice of God, like American politicians, or Hitler. Still, we have this thing called discernment."

"Meaning?"

"Well, we start with this outrageous idea that the ground of being, existence itself, is a person, and that this person is intimately concerned with each of our lives and desires us to turn our hearts toward him. Once you accept that level of insanity—or faith, as we prefer to call it— then it makes perfect sense to try to discern what God's purpose is for your life through a disciplined process of prayer and self-examination, discernment, as we say."

"You think I should do that?"

"I think you're doing it. I think that's all you've been doing since you got here. And we are all extremely interested in what you ultimately decide. Here is the oven."

"What?" said Marder, startled, but the priest was not making a theological point but only gesturing at the view, which had come to include a flat sheet of water surrounded by low hills. This, Marder now recalled, was the vast impoundment known as Oven Dam, *Presa el Infiernillo*. After this they spoke about the countryside, the development thereof, the decision to drown villages and their churches under water for the sake of irrigation and hydropower, and other nonreligious topics, as the VW strained noisily to mount the Sierra Madre.

In the backseat of this vehicle, Carmel was experiencing yet another life-changing illumination. Lourdes had jumped in, flushed and excited from her escape, shining with the romance of it and the promise of her future, and Carmel had responded, grinning and giggling along with the other two women. Then, gradually, as the conversation went on, she began to feel odd. Of course, she spoke the language fluently—a cradle tongue, after all—but she soon became conscious that she was not getting it, that she was not inside the conversation but outside, looking in. Partly this was because of the subject under discussion—life in Mexico City, a place she'd never lived. Pepa had apparently arranged for Lourdes to stay with a friend of hers, a well-known television producer, and her talk was all about the telenovela game and what life would be like for a beautiful young actress in the capital. But now Statch thought that even had the discussion been about Boston, she'd still be a little out of it, a little slow on the uptake, incapable of easy repartee. She thought back to the talk in Cambridge, in the labs, the hallways, the bars; she thought about the foreign students, the glazed expressions on their faces when the Americans got going on some riff or climbed the staircase of an idea, and she felt that the same expression was congealing on her own face now. And it struck her like a physical blow: this is what her mother's whole life in America had been like, this was the life of the exile.

And she recoiled from this feeling, calling herself a fool. It was not the same. She could go back to America, to Cambridge, at any time; she still had her friends from college, her peers at grad school, her various lovers. Yes, but unless she left now and talked her way back into her former life, unless she abandoned Casa Feliz and all it represented and climbed aboard a plane with Lourdes, she would in short order become a stranger in Cambridge too. Like an ancient trilobite falling to the bed of a shallow Paleozoic sea, she'd be covered in sediment, fossilized; she would never again be current in the life of a lab, or a field, would be, perhaps, "interesting" to those people, a novelty, but never again at home.

She felt a dreadful tug, as if her heart were being wrenched from her breast, and then a release. She would have her mother's life, or at least a version of it, she would be a *gringita* henceforth and forever. This realization seemed to suck all the energy out of her, and she slumped against the window. The sounds of the chatter from the two true Mexicanas faded in her ears, and she focused her attention on what her father was saying to the priest.

They passed through orchards and fields of maize and tiny dusty villages barely named—a bodega, a gas pump, a cantina, and gone. At the town of La Huacana they slowed for a church procession: the local saint carried high, the crucifix, the monstrance, the altar boys, dark skins against white surplices, and crowds of kids in bright clothing, sucking on skull lollipops and wearing the white bone masks of the day. Then they came up over a ridge, the tiny engine roaring, wheezing, and there on its hill was the hacienda of Las Palmas Floridas, just a glimpse, white walls and the red roof, and then it vanished again in foliage. Father Santana turned his Kombi off the main road and they traveled in dust for a while, then turned into a drive past orderly orchards of mango, avocado, grapefruit, and at last stopped in a graveled parking lot before the great house. A fairly new dusty Dodge pickup truck was the only other inhabitant of the parking lot, and Marder thought he knew whose it was.

Marder studied the house. Although he was seeing it for the first time, he'd heard about it for longer than he'd been married to the woman whose family had once owned it. It was a great hollow square of whitewashed adobe brick, with a tile roof and a courtyard with a bronze fountain in it, a Flora with flowing horn, imported from France. The fountain had hosted golden carp, but these had not survived the revolution, nor had the ballroom mirrors, smashed by the rebels. It held more than twenty bedrooms. Such tales had been handed down from the grandfather, to the father, to Soledad, to Marder, becoming ironic in the final telling, for in the New York of the seventies in the circles frequented by literary types, one could not (unless one was Nabokov) boast of ancestral palaces built on the sweat of the oppressed. The Zapatistas had seized it in 1910 and turned it into a field hospital, which was why it hadn't been burned like so many other haciendas in Mexico, those symbols of unbearable grief and oppression. Now it was an agricultural institute, as the sign outside it announced. It was closed for the Day of the Dead.

They all left the VW and stood in the warm sun and the silence; wind and the cheeping of small birds was all they heard, and then the crunch of gravel as Statch strode away.

"Where are you going?" Marder called out, but got no answer.

"I believe the cemetery is in the rear of the property," said the priest, and they all walked down a path, past test plots of infant plants with fluttering plastic labels. Marder strode over the neat gravel, carrying the urn. He had imagined he'd be arm in arm with his daughter, mutually grieving, but this was apparently not part of the actuality, nor was it the sort of dim rainy day he'd always associated with funereal occasions. He'd buried both his parents on rainy days, but here in coastal Mexico there was bright sun; the pathetic fallacy was not in play here, and Marder felt oddly disappointed. And what was wrong with Statch? She'd practically trotted ahead, and now he could see that she was at the gate of the little cemetery, looking up at something enclosed by a round lunette in the arch above it.

When he reached the gate, he saw that it was a patinaed bronze of some saint, green as the sea, but which saint could not be told, because it had been defaced by dozens of bullet holes. The stone of the gate was similarly pocked.

"It must have been an unusually anticlerical battalion of the Zapatistas who came through here," Marder remarked. Statch did not respond but pushed open the creaky, rusted iron gate and went through. Marder followed, as did the rest of the party. The place was about the size of a backyard in an American subdivision. In the center, on a small rise of ground, was a large stone crypt with a leaded roof and marble columns supporting a classical pediment, on the base of which was inscribed the name DE HARO D'ARIÉS, this heavily defaced as well. The other graves were more modest by far, crumbling stones for the overseers and upper servants, and for the peons only mounds, marked here and there by rotting wooden crosses or, where the descendants had come into some money, a scatter of small memorial stones.

On a rusted iron bench next to the crypt they found the last of the d'Ariéses, Angel, with a bottle of *aguardiente* and a store-bought packaged *ofrenda*, a plastic tray laden with sweetmeats and wrapped in orange cellophane. The man was red-eyed and drunk, but Marder embraced him formally and asked him whether the crypt plate had been prepared according to Marder's instructions. Angel said yes, it was inside the mausoleum, and he had arranged for a local man to come by on another day and mortar it in place.

They all stood in front of the mausoleum door. The priest put on his stole and recited the few words prescribed by the Church for such occasions.

The priest said, "Grant this mercy, O Lord, we beseech thee, to thy servant departed, that she may not receive in punishment the requital of her deeds, who in desire did keep thy will, and as the true faith here united her to the company of the faithful, so may thy mercy unite her above to the choirs of angels. Through Jesus Christ our Lord. Amen."

The priest sprinkled holy water on the urn and on the mausoleum, and Marder carried the urn into the cool, dim space. The walls were lined with marble plaques naming a couple of centuries' worth of dead d'Ariéses. He found the parents, the slain Don Esteban, his unforgiving pride turned literally now to dust, and the mother, resting eternally as she had lived her life, under her husband's stony weight. There was a square hole large enough for a coffin to slide into, and Marder placed the urn in its cool depths and then lifted up the heavy marble plaque and slid it into place and hid Maria Soledad Beatriz de Haro d'Ariés Marder, as the plaque announced, until the Last Day.

He stood there for a moment, thinking about the last day and judgment and resurrection, a confused welter of thought skirting madness, for who could really believe all that stuff? And who could really believe the opposite?

"My heart, loyal, atones in the darkness," said Marder, a line of Velarde from a poem she'd loved, and he thought of the billion contingencies of life. Had Velarde never written, had Marder not found that dusty book and wooed her with half-understood poems, would he be standing here with her ashes? Another route to madness. Or faith: he walked out into the glare of the sun.

He took a few steps, and it seemed to him that he was looking down a tunnel, like the one he'd cut through the Laotian forest. He was alone; perhaps the people had vanished or had left him, perhaps they saw him as he really was and were appalled and had fled him as from a leper. There was a great Montezuma cypress there, the *ahuehuete*, sacred to the rulers of ancient Mexico. He walked toward it, stumbling a little on the gravel, and its branches reached out, dark and terrible like the fingers of the old gods. There was a sound now; the gravel was surprisingly comfortable as he listened, some kind of animal in pain—perhaps they were slaughtering hogs. But it was also vaguely familiar. There was something tugging at him; perhaps the cypress wanted to take him into its boughs. This was one thought in Marder's disintegrating brain, and the other was that Mr. Thing had made himself known at last, and Marder could not help agreeing that the guy had a terrific sense of timing. Marder waited for them to switch the white light on in the tunnel; he waited to hear the choirs of angels, the beckoning figure.

But in the event, no angels, only that voice. He'd heard it before, a quiet one in his head, but clearly not of his own production, like a remark heard in a dark theater from a stranger: ordinary, terrifying because of its simple banality, its inarguable existence. It said, *It's all right. You'll be fine.*

Marder was aware first of pain as he came up from wherever he'd been, the pain in his throat, and it also came to him that the sound he'd been hearing was his own voice, howling. He listened to the howl for a few more seconds and then there didn't seem to be a need to howl anymore. He opened his eyes. The tunnel was gone and his field of vision was full of his daughter's face, haloed like an angel's by the shafts of sun coming down through the dark foliage of the *ahuehuete*. Her dusty cheeks had bright runnels cut by tears. She wiped her nose with the back of her hand.

"Are you okay now?"

"She's dead," said Marder.

"I know, Dad. It's been three years."

"Three minutes," said Marder. "Are you furious with me now, like Peter?"

"No. I was a *little* furious when I heard you tell Father Santana about being guided by angels in Vietnam. That was a story I could've used when I was growing up. You didn't say you were this hero."

"It wasn't like that. Skelly's the Special Forces hero."

"But *you* saved *him*. And he got the credit and the medal."

"I didn't want the medal and he did. What does it matter now, anyway?"

"I hate secrets. I despise not knowing what's going on. Don't you get that at long last?"

"I do, and I'm sorry. Speaking of secrets, are you ready to tell me how you found out where I was?"

"Obviously I hacked into Nina Ibanez's email. I thought you were hiding down here in a love nest with her."

"I thought you didn't care who I boffed."

"I don't, with that exception. I'm sorry, it's totally irrational. But as I stand here, I can tell you that if you were here with her, after what happened to Mom, I couldn't be friends with you. I would have to agree with Peter."

"Yes, I would too."

Marder got to his feet, feeling terribly old and not only in his back. He walked slowly to the car, arm in arm with his daughter. He stopped and placed his hand on her shoulder. Looking into her eyes, he said, "Carmelita. You remember we used to call you that, before Statch?"

"Yeah. When I was a kid I hated the name, for obvious reasons. They used to call me 'Caramel,' you know? A brown sticky substance that gets in your teeth. Statch is the right name for an oversized, gawky jock with peculiar Germano-Mexican features. Look, I'm sorry I blew up just now. It seems kind of silly given our current situation."

"Yes, that situation. Part of me desperately wants you to get on that plane with Lourdes and fly out of here. I'm your father, and I'm supposed to protect you, but I can't protect you. Maybe that's an illusion we have to maintain, that we can protect our kids, otherwise no one could bear the pain of loving children. But, on the other hand, I'm incredibly proud of you, for what you're doing here, for the sacrifice you've made, for what you're doing for me and for our people."

"I appreciate that, Dad, but, you know, I'm an adult; it's my choice."

"Yes, another illusion, maybe. The interaction of fate and choice, something I've been contemplating a great deal lately. And it's something you might want to think about as you walk through the graveyard of your ancestors. It wasn't only your mother I was howling about a minute ago, by the way. I was also thinking about what it would feel like to slide you into one of those square holes, and I thought that my very deepest prayer was that I would be too dead to do it."

"Dad, come on, that's just morbid."

"For God's sake, we're *supposed* to be morbid. It's the Day of the Dead."

In this conversation they had switched without thought from English to Spanish, for in their family that tongue had always been the one in which grave things had their voice. He saw that his words had stung her and saw also, with relief, that she was abashed, that she was not going to withdraw in the way that American girls did when checked. He saw her turning more Mexican before his eyes.

"Anyway, there it is: I surrender you to your fate, the last gesture of fatherhood. Christ! First she learns how to walk, then how to read, then she goes out of the house alone, then she has sex . . . Everyone talks about the great transitions of the kid—they're big deals—but nobody says what it does to the dad. There are no *quinceañeras* for the dad."

"We could start a tradition," she said and they both laughed, and thus relieved the unbearable pressure and they walked, joking about that, back to the car. In which no one mentioned the recent operatic performance, but resumed speaking on other topics as if nothing gigantic had just occurred. Marder was still in something of a daze, staring out the window, but he did see Angel d'Ariés getting into his pickup and he seemed to be talking into a cell phone.

Marder remembered that when they hit the roadblock. He had, of course, understood that it was a risk to invite Angel to the interment—the man had, after all, confessed that the Templos were his family—but strategy had not been uppermost in his mind. He'd thought it worthwhile to give Angel a chance to connect with a real family, he felt he owed that much to Chole. That no good deed goes unpunished was a cynical banality he'd heard often in New York, and it always made him want to snarl, So what? He'd been told all would be well as he lay in his agony on the gravel, and so he waited calmly for what God would send.

At a nameless hamlet, the bad guys had parked a big SUV athwart the road. Half a dozen or so pickups had been stationed in clumps along the roadside, and dozens of armed men stood there too, watching the VW roll to a stop. One of the men came forward and told everyone to get out of the van, and they did.

"This is very unusual," the priest said to Marder. "My bus is considered neutral territory ordinarily. I take them to the hospital when they're hurt and drive their families to their hideouts. But I don't think we should worry. Besides, it's the Day of the Dead."

"I think they're making an exception for me," said Marder, and it was so. A man Marder recognized from his visit to the meth-lab *rancho* now led Marder away from the others to a tiny cantina, one room with a plank-and-barrel bar and three tables, at one of which sat El Gordo.

"Don Servando," said Marder, nodding politely. "I'm happy to see you well."

El Gordo gestured to a chair. "Sit, Don Ricardo. A beer for you?"

Marder said that would be nice, and a beer was brought. Marder drank from it deeply. His throat was still raw.

"We have a problem, my friend," said El Gordo.

"I'm sure we can work it out. But this is a day when such problems are usually forgotten. We don't indulge in violence on the Day of the Dead, or so I imagined."

"No violence is being offered. We are merely two associates having a drink. We will use the holiday to clear up issues that may lead to violence in the future. No one could object to that."

"No one could," Marder agreed. "I would be honored to be of assistance. So what is your problem?"

"I want my guns and my product. This was our agreement, was it not, in exchange for my protection? And I have neither guns nor product, although I have kept you under my protection and even saved you from the hands of the Family."

"I thought I had explained that, Don Servando. The Family raided the cargo container and stole the goods."

"Yes, so you said. But my informants tell me that there was no such raid. And you must credit me with having informants in Don Melchor's organization, as I'm sure he has his in mine. We used to be one body, as you know, and loyalties are mixed. My understanding is that the very weapons you promised me are at this moment emplaced on Isla de los Pájaros. And that you have Chinese mercenaries as well."

"There are no Chinese mercenaries, sir. I can assure you of that. I have taken defensive measures, of course."

"Against me?"

"Against everyone. Every man must protect what's his, don't you agree?"

"Absolutely. These are perilous times and Mexico is not all it should be." He leaned back in his chair and folded his hands across his keglike belly. His eyes showed amusement.

"You know, I like you, Señor Marder, I truly do. You are an interesting man and you are not afraid of me. Most of the people I come in contact with are either one or the other. Those who are not afraid of me, like those boys out there, are too stupid to be afraid of anything, and the interesting people are all frightened out of their wits, just because of who I am. I sincerely hope I don't have to kill you."

"I feel very much the same."

The man smiled, showing remarkably white teeth. "Then we must always stay in close contact. My father used to say, hold your friends close but your enemies closer."

"Yes, I've heard that too."

"Still, I hope we can be friends, once this little matter is cleared up.

There are depths to you that I wish to explore. For example, there are rumors flying about that you are with the authorities, that you have some sort of secret mission—the CIA, perhaps."

Marder shrugged and said, "I'm a newcomer here. Newcomers always generate rumors."

"But you deny this one."

"Categorically. As I keep telling everyone, I am a retired editor from New York."

"Then how is a retired editor going to arrange my murder? If necessary, of course."

"I may have skills and resources not immediately apparent, as you've already learned. *My* father used to say everybody in a Santa Claus suit isn't Santa Claus."

El Gordo had a look of confusion—a familiar intercultural phenomenon—and then he laughed aloud and heartily.

"Very good! I will remember that one. Now, as to our current problem. You will drive back to your house and you will obtain for me what you have promised, for I do not for a moment believe that these are in the hands of La Familia. In the meantime, your daughter and your little girlfriend will remain with me, as my guests. The reporter and the priest do not interest me at present. I would expect to hear from you by, let us say, midnight tonight, telling me that my goods are ready to be transported. Failing that, I will come there and bring the girl, in a manner you will not like."

"Well, I'm obliged to tell you that this would be a terrible mistake on your part. The child, by the way, is not my girlfriend—"

"Oh, nonsense! Do you think I'm a fool? All the world knows she's your *chingada.*"

"—and all the world is mistaken. As for my daughter, I was under the impression that the Templos did not kidnap, and especially not women."

"We do not. Therefore, if I don't get what belongs to me, I will sell her to someone who does. I will sell her to El Cochinillo. See if you like dealing with him."

Marder stood up and said, "I don't understand why you're doing this, Don Servando. I would be happy to arrange another shipment of the same items, at my own expense, and convey them to you as a gift."

The big man rose slowly to his feet, took Marder by the shoulder, and brought his face close.

"That's a generous offer, Señor, but to accept it would require that I trust you, do you see? And I don't. There is nothing personal in this, you understand. In this part of the world, someone in my business must live without trust. It saddens me, but there it is."

"Then you should find some other business, Don Servando. You could leave all this. God knows, you must have enough money salted away. You could go to a place where you could trust people and need not kidnap girls."

"That is an excellent suggestion, but we can discuss my future career some other time. Now we are where we are, and I've told you what must happen and what will happen if not. It's time for you to go."

"I would like to say goodbye to my daughter first."

"Of course. But you should say *hasta la vista*. I'm sure you will arrange it so that you see her again quite soon."

19

As soon as she saw the roadblock and realized what was happening, Statch Marder took her grandfather's Colt Woodsman out of her bag and shoved it in her waistband, in the small of her back, pulling her safari shirt out to cover it. When she got out of the van with the others, a *sicario* stepped up, demanded the handbags of the three women, and dumped their contents on the ground. There came a shout. A huge man strode across the street and berated the bag-spiller in colorful language, the burden of which was that the Templos did not abuse women, the Templos protected women, and he made the man pick up everything and give the bag back to Statch. He apologized to the señorita, nodding politely to her, smiled at Pepa and Lourdes, shook hands with the priest, and walked away.

Statch turned to her father, who had approached in the trail of the big man, and said, "Dad, what the hell is going on? Who are these people?"

"They're Templos. You just met El Gordo, the *jefe* thereof. As for what's going on, I'm afraid that you and Lourdes are being kidnapped."

"What!"

"Yeah, El Gordo wants his guns. Don't worry, I don't think he means to hurt either of you."

"What if he doesn't get his guns?"

"I'll pay a ransom. That usually works."

Statch felt her knees start to tremble, so she sat down on the edge of the VW's floor, in the open doorway. The priest was on the other side of the street. He seemed to be arguing with El Gordo.

"Well, this is a kick in the pants. No sooner have I made a noble speech than I get the snap quiz: Does the girl really have serious guts or is she a bullshitter? It doesn't usually work that way; usually you get to keep your wonderful illusions for a while."

"It's Mexico," said Marder. "It doesn't work that way here." He pulled out his wallet and handed a wad of currency to his daughter. "Here's all the money I have. I don't know what good it'll do, but . . ."

She took it, a thick wad of violet five-hundred peso notes. "It's okay, Dad. It'll be fine," she told him, although she didn't think it would be fine at all, but rather to make him feel better, so that her panic did not add to his. She'd always thought her father was the acme of cool, but with his crack-up at the tomb and now, this pale and sweating, this trembling figure before her, she felt the axis of her life starting to go eccentric.

"It's okay," she repeated. "I have a gun."

"Oh, no, you don't want a gun! Give it to me!"

He looked around frantically to see if they were being observed, and they were—more than observed. There were two men coming toward the truck, and Marder had to stand by helplessly while they took his daughter and Lourdes away. He heard Lourdes ask, "What's going on? Are these guys taking us to the airport?" before the sound of revving engines from all the Templo vehicles drowned out any response that might have been made.

In the VW, both priest and reporter demanded explanations too.

"Drive," said Marder. "Drive fast."

So they flew down the sierra, the priest's foot to the floorboards over long stretches, scattering chickens in the tiny settlements, and Marder told them the situation. Pepa was leaning forward in the backseat, clutching Marder's seat, her face close to his so she could hear above the sound of the poorly muffled engine and the wind.

"But you're going to give him his stuff, aren't you?"

"I don't think I will," said Marder. "Skelly told me once that any group with those weapons could just grab Casa Feliz and toss everyone out, which is why he arranged for us to take them. As long as we hold them, we hold the land. And, of course, there's no guarantee that Gomez will return the hostages even if he has the weapons. We're not going to take him to court. And he'd be worried that a couple of guys who've shown the ability to import heavy weapons and heroin into Michoacán would go over to La Familia or even one of the other cartels. He'd shoot us both out of hand and probably kill anyone he thought might be a popular leader in the *colonia*."

"But your daughter," she said, "she's your *daughter*. You're risking her life for a *house* and for people you don't even know?"

"I'm terrified," he said, turning toward her, and she could see it in his face, pale beneath its tan, white around the lips, the pain in his eyes. "But the point of this whole thing is *not* to surrender to the terror. I'm not going to act like a typical kidnap victim's parent, giving up everything to buy back the child, frantic, totally controlled by the kidnappers. I'm not doing that, even though I *feel* that way. I get you don't understand this, but I've learned to accept whatever God sends. If it's a disaster, I'll mourn the loss. If not, I'll rejoice. It's not in my hands. I didn't ask for this fate, but it's the one I've been given, and so I intend to hold the land and protect the people in my care as long as I have life and let come whatever. I had a thought also, speaking about fate, back at the cemetery; the thought was that years ago I stole a girl out of Mexico and now Mexico wanted one in return. It's an absurd thought if you think life is just one thing after another, with no meaning, but not if you think there's a deep plan going on in every life. Which I do."

Pepa had nothing to say to this, and they drove on, not speaking, wrapped in the roar of the engine and the scream of the tires on the mountain curves.

Statch and Lourdes were shut up in the back of a windowless truck furnished with a pile of blankets, padded shipping mats, a bucket, and a two-liter plastic container of water. A faint gleam of light penetrated the interior from small holes in the roof. The truck jounced into motion and Lourdes said, "We're going to the airport, right?"

"Actually, no. The Templos are kidnapping us."

A small frown marred the matte perfection of the girl's brow. "You're joking."

"I wish I were. The thing of it is, El Gordo wants something from my father and Skelly, and they're holding us until they get it."

"Well, they'll give it and then I'll be able to go to Defe. How long will it take, do you think?"

"I don't know, Lourdes. It could be a while, because I don't think Skelly wants to give up the stuff."

"It's drugs, right? I knew Skelly was a *narcotraficante*. He said no, but I could tell. But, you know, he'll give it because he loves me, even if they kill him."

"Well, perhaps—"

"No question," said the girl. "And Don Ricardo, your father, will pay for you too. It's a common thing; everyone understands how it goes, although usually they take the boys. People will pay more for a boy, they say."

She stretched luxuriously and tossed the shipping mats and blankets into a simple pallet. "I'm going to take a nap," said Lourdes, arranging herself on the floor. "I was up all night—who would think that an old man like that would want to do it all night long? It's the Viagra or something, I don't know." She looked up at Statch. "So, do you have a boyfriend?" "Boyfren," not *novio*; Lourdes was a modern girl.

"Not at the moment."

"What, you don't like it with boys?"

"I like it fine," said Statch. "I just have a lot of other stuff to do, and a boyfriend takes up time and energy."

"Yes, that's what Pepa says too. She says don't let the boyfriends mess up your career. Pick someone who can help you out and stick with him until you can stand on your own. That's good advice, don't you think?"

Statch thought briefly of Dr. Schuemacher and the lab at MIT. "Yes, good advice," she agreed, and thought, Would I trade places with this kid? Quite apart from the dazzling looks, could I ever achieve that unthinking physical *being*, without all the thoughts and plans, the continual self-appraisal, the measuring of every action? She hadn't been anything like Lourdes since the age of six, and now here she was, all plans and control having been taken from her. And, to her surprise, she was riding on top of the whole thing; being kidnapped was apparently a natural extension of having kidnapped herself from the life she'd thought she wanted. Again she decided that, whatever happened, she would not have changed the path that had led to this strange and more intense life.

The truck drove on, and from the angle of the bed Statch could tell that they were climbing. They'd taken her bag but hadn't searched her, nor had they taken her watch, so she knew, when the truck slowed, made some intricate turns, and then reversed and stopped, that they had been traveling for about two and a half hours; somewhere in the *tierra caliente*, then, up in the hill country.

The doors swung open and a man called for them to come out. It was dark and warm, and the air smelled of dust and, faintly, of horses. They were in a stable. Two men led them across a concrete floor to a side door, across an alley, and into another building. Lourdes wanted to know where her bags were—she had all her stuff for Mexico City in those bags, her clothes, her makeup—but the men didn't answer her. They moved through a large kitchen smelling of lye and frying grease and down a hallway. A ranch house, thought Statch, and wondered if it was the same one in which her father and Skelly had been confined. The men put her in a room by herself. It had a hasp and padlock on the door, and she heard it being fastened. Throughout this brief walk she'd heard the sounds of roaring engines and of a crowd of people, and she assumed that there was someone in the house watching television, perhaps an auto race. For some reason this made her feel better. No one had yet said a word to her.

The room contained a pipe bed with a bare mattress, a covered bucket, and a washstand with a white enamel basin. The single window was barred with a wooden shutter, which, on inspection, proved to be wired shut. But one of the slats was cracked, and by prying at it with her pen, Statch was able to snap it in two, so that she could peek through and see what was going on outside. Like many such mountain *ranchos,* this one was built around a walled courtyard, and Statch's window provided an oblique view of that area. The sounds she had heard were not from a television broadcast at all, she now found. The courtyard was full of vehicles, pickups and SUVs and sedans, revving engines, moving around, arranging themselves into columns, and around them were scores, perhaps hundreds, of men, all wearing black baseball hats and dark shirts, many of them carrying assault weapons. It looked, and Statch thought it probably was, an army about to go to war.

At the extreme corner of her field of view was a big ten-wheeled truck, curiously modified. Steel plates had been welded to its side—overlapping plates, like the scales of a pangolin—and a kind of cupola had been built on the top of the cargo hold, protected with sandbags held in place by cyclone fencing, leaving dark slits that could only be meant for gun ports. The front of this vehicle bore a steel plate that covered the windshield and the hood, with a narrow opening cut into it to allow the driver to see. The bumper had been extended by another thick steel plate, and an I-beam was welded to that, to make a heavy ram. Above this shelf, sandbags had been piled, secured by more cyclone fencing. The sides of the cab had been similarly armored and there was a hinged hatch where the window had been, to give access to the cab's interior. As an engineer, Statch could not help admiring the design—it was the first narco-tank she'd seen in real life—although her heart quailed at the thought of its obvious target. The thing would go through the gate of Casa Feliz like a bullet through a Barbie doll, and the front wall of the house wouldn't slow it down much either. In one charge, it would deposit fifty armed men in her father's command post.

As she watched, engines roared, the men mounted their vehicles, and the convoy rolled out of the yard, leaving behind a cloud of yellow dust that hung in the air for a long time. Panic touched her with little electric jabs in the belly; chill sweat bloomed on her face. She had to escape from here. She had to find a phone and get through to her father and warn him, and she had to call Major Naca and get the army involved. They'd taken her bag, so the cell phone and the money were gone, but she still had a number of interesting things in her pockets. And, of course, the pistol, pressing against her spine. Maybe she should have handed it over to her father, but there hadn't been time. She had never shot anyone, and although she was an excellent target shot, both her father and Skelly had impressed upon her the difference between target shooting and shooting people. She recalled Skelly's advice about pointing guns: never point a gun at someone you don't intend to shoot, and if you do point it, shoot them. It's not like the movies, where the two guys have a conversation at gunpoint. In her mind's eye, she saw herself shooting a man and also saw herself freezing and having the man take the gun away from her. She moved her thinking away from that dire topic and looked at the stuff she'd taken from her pockets: a small leatherbound notebook, a black Rotring rollerball pen, a tiny flashlight attached to the keys to her motorcycle, a thumb drive, twenty-seven pesos in coins, a red Bic lighter, and a miniature Swiss Army knife containing a tiny scissors, a nail file/screwdriver, a toothpick, and a thirty-two-millimeter blade.

The question of escape: in the movies, the hero always tries to escape, but Statch was not sure if this was the correct solution. Getting out of the room would be trivial. A quick inspection told her she could unscrew the bed frame and that the steel levers provided by its parts would be more than sufficient to break out the shutters. But what then? She had no idea if there was a guard looking out into the courtyard. She could shoot the guard (could she, *really*?) and then skip lightly over the wall and use her transparent airplane to fly a couple of hundred kilometers to Apatzingán, where Major Naca would immediately put his forces at her disposal, assuming he was not someplace else by now.

No, it was too stupid to move without more data, and, besides, she had some responsibility for the idiot child, Lourdes. She couldn't leave without learning where she was and what they planned to do with her. On the other hand, there was the night. Depending on what she learned during the next few hours, she might try to slip away in the darkness. She could hot-wire a car—an older model, without all the security crap in it—disable any other vehicles, and drive away. Interesting fantasy, anyway—did anyone actually ever escape from kidnappers? She didn't know, and although it was now unfashionable, Statch never liked committing to anything in the absence of evidence.

So she waited. In all this consideration, it never occurred to her that she might be in danger of death. Her whole life was a record of success and obstacles conquered, and so she thought she had an advantage over anyone who might wish to harm her and was able to scotch most negative thoughts. And as one who despised the wasted minute, she now lay down on the bed, propped her back against the wall, and picked up her notebook and pen. Turning to a fresh page, she began to design a twenty-first century leapfrog energy and manufacturing economy for Colonia Feliz.

They heard honking behind them. Father Santana checked his mirrors and then pulled to the side of the road to allow a convoy of pickup trucks to pass. Each one carried a posse of hard-faced young men, standing and swaying, the barrels of their assault rifles making a picket around their close-cropped skulls.

"I wonder what that's about," said the reporter.

"The clans are gathering, it seems," said Marder.

"Let me check the Net." Pepa twiddled her smartphone for a few minutes and then exclaimed, "Jesus Maria!"

"What?" The two men in unison.

"The Templos bombed one of Cuello's boats in the marina at Playa Diamante and machine-gunned one of their cantinas."

"Did they get the *jefe*?" Marder asked.

"It's not being reported. I rather doubt it; he's careful and he has a lot of boats, both in the Playa and in Cárdenas, and any number of properties he controls. In any case, it looks like the war is heating up, and it's apparently going to happen here, on the coast."

This idea was confirmed when two more such convoys, with dozens of vehicles and hundreds of men, passed before they hit the coastal road. As they made their northward turn, Marder said, "Look, I'd appreciate it if you kept quiet about Carmel and Lourdes for a while. I want to tell Skelly about it myself."

In the event, Skelly got only a partial truth. Marder found him in the command center, formerly the living room of the mansion, now packed with the adult population of the island, and many of the children. Skelly stood soldier-straight in front of a whitewashed half sheet of plywood, upon which had been drawn a large-scale map of Isla de los Pájaros. Marder waited by the door at the back and watched; Skelly saw him but did not acknowledge his presence.

Skelly was, of course, an excellent military briefer, and Marder could see he was getting his points across despite his halting Spanish. He even had a sheet of clear plastic that he dropped over his map and drew on with china markers to show the locations of his troops. The tactical situation was not complex. The island was a hog-backed, egg-shaped territory oriented north–south, connected to the mainland slightly below its equator by the causeway, a distance of perhaps one hundred meters. There were a hundred or so meters of beach on the seaward side, with the remainder of the northern coast occupied by cliffs plunging directly into the sea. The house, now the final redoubt, was located on the peak of the ridge in the center of the southern hemisphere, directly in line with the causeway.

Skelly's shining pointer—a recycled car aerial—flitted over the chart, indicating the only possible routes of attack: the causeway itself, the beach, and the south side of the island, where the former owner had constructed a tiny marina, with a semicircular basin and two wooden docks. The defending forces owned three DShK heavy machine guns and six PKM light machine guns, all ex–Soviet Army, and, from the same source, seventy-two AK-47 rifles. Skelly had eighty-four men at his disposal, including the three Hmong—*los chinos*, as the people called them—who now sat together in one corner of the room, squatting against the walls and whispering together in their chirring tongue. *Los chinos* would each command one of the DShKs—huge 12.7-mm machine guns on wheeled carriages—and these would constitute the heart of the three strong points on which the defense was based and which were directed against the three supposed routes of attack.

Flick flick flick went the pointer. The other men had been arranged in four platoons. Three would support the strong points: Alpha on the roof terrace and house approaches, commanding the causeway; Bravo to the south, above the marina; and Charlie, deployed below the terraces of the house and directed at the beach. Delta would be based in the house proper and be used as a reserve or the core of a last-ditch defense.

A simple plan, Marder thought, but they could have only simple plans with the kind of half-trained soldiers they had. He looked at their faces as Skelly concluded his talk. "Any questions?" Skelly asked. There were none. The peasants and artisans of the Colonia Feliz defense force clutched their unfamiliar rifles and moved uneasily within their web-gear, and most of them wore on their mild brown faces the look of boys standing along the wall at their first dance. Some of the younger ones, of course, had tied on red headbands and looked fierce, and now Marder found that almost everyone was looking at him. After a moment's hesitation, he went to the front of the room.

Marder had not given many speeches in his life, and certainly none like this, but he relied on the generic type of such speeches, many of which had been given to people such as these in the history of their unhappy land. He told them that they were about to make history, that they fought against wicked people who were trying to steal their land and destroy everything they had worked for and steal the future of their children. He said that he had come here as a stranger but that his late wife was from around here and that he had resolved to build a monument to her memory by doing something she would have done, had she been able. He told them that his wife's parents had been murdered, as so many others had been, by the evil ones, the same ones who would shortly come here with their weapons, thinking that they could simply take anything they wanted by violence. He said he swore to them on his wife's memory and by the Blessed Virgin that he would never give in, that he would resist to his last drop of blood. He said that if anyone wanted to leave, they could go now, without shame, but once the battle started he expected everyone to give what he himself would be happy to give, his life for peace and justice and a better future for them and their children. Long live the Colonia Feliz!

Marder raised his fist as he said this last, feeling like a fool and a fraud, but in fact the people cheered; they cheered, Viva Don Ricardo, Viva Don Eskelly, Viva la Colonia Feliz. *Arriba los Felizistas!* Marder caught Pepa Espinoza staring at him with a look he had not seen on her face before, a kind of stunned surprise.

The people started to leave for their posts and other duties. Marder took Skelly's arm and suggested they take a walk. They went out through the front door, through the gardens of the house, and onto the road that led to the village. They passed the beer truck that Skelly had used to transport the weapons from Asia. Marder noticed that a crew of men was loading it with bags of fertilizer.

"I see you're making good use of La Familia's beer truck," said Marder.

"Yeah, we have to spread the fertilizer around, up where they have crops started."

"If they're still planting stuff, I guess they think we can defend the island."

"And you must think so too. That was quite a speech, boss, I got to say. I didn't know you had it in you."

"But, seriously, what are our chances at this point?"

"Seriously? Like in any combat situation, it depends. I mean, it's not *suicide*, or I wouldn't be here. These boys aren't real soldiers, but they're fighting for their homes, and that counts, as we all learned in Vietnam. I can't try anything fancy, and I'll be satisfied if they just stay in their positions and fire their weapons in a disciplined fashion. On the plus side, we have better weapons, real military pieces, made by people who expected them to be used by peasants. They're reasonably accurate and totally indestructible. The other guys have American fake ARs designed to feed the fantasies of right-wing assholes. If it comes to slaughter, that stuff won't hold up. Also, our enemies aren't soldiers either, and they're fighting for an easy life where they get to push everyone around. Is that as important or as inspiring as fighting for hearth and home? Well, the

Wehrmacht did pretty well for a while on that basis, but, again, *los malo-sos* are not the Wehrmacht. I don't think they'll advance against the kind of automatic fire we can bring on them for a while. 'For a while' is the key point there. We have no resupply, obviously, and not that much ammo, maybe three hundred rounds for each rifle and a couple of thousand for each machine gun. Twenty-six of our homemade claymores, five dozen or so homemade grenades. We were supposed to get RPGs, but they weren't in the shipment. Baan said they're coming on the—get this!—*next* shipment. Everyone's all Amazon dot com nowadays. So, the bottom line is, I think we can hold out for a while, long enough for the story to get out and the army to move in. Absent that—well, we run out of ammo, we use sharp sticks and harsh words."

"What makes you think the army will come?"

Both men turned, surprised, toward the source of this comment. Pepa was there with her Sony, having clearly followed them out and discreetly trailed them.

"Why *wouldn't* they come?" asked Marder.

"First, because the action is up north, in the big cities, and down in Acapulco. There's mass murder in Veracruz, Guadalajara, Monterrey, not to mention the killing zone along the border. And they've started up in the Defe itself and that's intolerable; it's an affront to national sovereignty. The point is, your small war may not be a priority for the army just now. Second, they might see it as a minor skirmish among gang factions. They didn't hear your noble speech about defending hearth and home, besides which, peasants resisting with military arms is not something the rulers of Mexico ever want to encourage. All I'm saying is that if you're counting on the military to bail you out, you may be disappointed."

"I'm counting on you, though," said Marder, "as much as on the soldiers."

"On me."

"Yes. On your talent and on the Internet. You'll record what we're doing and send it out: interviews, action, rockets' red glare, bombs bursting in air, the dead and dying, the whole story of a popular resistance to the rule of the narcos. If you're not killed, you'll be famous."

She looked stunned.

Skelly roared out a laugh. "That's very sweet, Marder. Yet another invitation to join your death trip. Of course, it could be a problem getting the news out, because the first thing they'll do is cut the Internet cable. The box is right there at the foot of the causeway."

"It can go out through the cell tower," said Marder.

"And that's going to be their main target when they get here," said Skelly. "Pepa might have to swim for it with a thumb drive in her mouth."

"If I have to, I will," said Pepa, surprising herself. It was not the sort of thing she usually said; it was like something in a bad film. That's remarkable too, she thought; whenever we make a noble statement it sounds false in our ears. An interesting question, and she considered it for a few moments in silence.

Just then a group of children ran by, carrying ammunition boxes and containers holding food and water for the men on the lines. They were chattering and laughing and having a good time. One of them was the boy Ariel, who turned and waved gaily to Marder and shouted out something Marder didn't quite catch.

"Did he say, 'Victory or death'?"

"I believe he did," said Pepa. "My God!"

Marder turned to Skelly and said, "Well, Patrick, once more we find ourselves in an enterprise likely to lead to the death of numerous children. I wonder why that is."

"I guess we're just lucky," said Skelly, not smiling now. "By the way, do you know where Lourdes is? I haven't seen her around since early this morning."

"She should be in Mexico City," said Marder. "Father Santana left for the airport with her and Statch early today." Misleading, but not exactly lies.

Skelly gave Marder his shark look—something Marder hadn't seen since Vietnam, and it took all his self-control not to quail before it.

"Oh? How did that get arranged?"

"She wanted to go. She's not a prisoner. Didn't she tell you she was going?"

"No. And neither did you. Or your girlfriend." Skelly started to say something, then thought better of it and assumed a grin, although Marder could see by the way his nose pinched and went white around the nostrils that he was very angry.

"Okay, I'm a big boy. I get that she's scared, she's got some opportunities to pursue—I wish her the best. Maybe I'll go up there and see her after this is over." He clapped his hands, once. "Well, this has been pleasant, but right now I have to get to *el golf* and check out the troops."

Skelly started to leave, but Marder touched him on the shoulder. "Wait—when the thing goes down, where do you want me?"

A more genuine smile returned. "Well, not in the command center anyway. Every time I gave an order they'd be looking at the *patrón*. How about up on the roof with the big rifle and your Steyr? You can snipe. I know you enjoy sniping."

They watched him walk away.

"He's as bad as they are," said Pepa.

"Perhaps not quite as bad," replied Marder. "And he's on our side."

"Is he? You're very trusting where he's concerned, Marder, and I have to say it's unusual for such a devious person as yourself to be trusting that way, especially with respect to a *chingaquedito* like him."

"Well, we go back a long way. Can you handle a kayak?"

She giggled, an unusual sound, and gave him a grin that dropped ten years from her face. "Well, change the subject! Can I handle a kayak? I spent three summers on the Sea of Cortez attending a very exclusive camp for rich young ladies, so, yes, I can handle a kayak, although it's been . . . I'm embarrassed to say how many years. Why do you ask?"

"Because, if worse comes to worst and you have to get out of here with, as Skelly said, a thumb drive in your mouth, there's a plastic kayak in an azalea thicket just to the west of the boathouse down by the marina. You'd want to wait for dark."

"You cooked up an escape route for your daughter?"

"For you, actually. Carmel could swim off this island about as fast as you could paddle. And the kayak was here already. From the fun-loving Guzmán. I just stashed it there when they turned the boathouse into a strong point. Of course, there's Skelly's cabin cruiser, but he's got the key to it, and also it's kind of a big target. You'd do better with the kayak."

A peculiar expression appeared on her face. Marder thought it was embarrassment. She looked down and her mouth twisted. Then a nervous laugh. "You're always saving my life, Marder. I'm wondering if this is a good basis for a relationship."

"We'll have to see how that works with our extreme sexual attraction," said Marder lightly, but the remark seemed not to please her.

"Yes, we will, although I hope you're not turning all Mexican on me. First come little flirty comments like that one, and next you're squeezing my ass in public and telling all your boyfriends about what I'm like in bed. I'm nobody's *chingada*, Don Ricardo."

"Point taken. Although the terror I feel when I think about you would militate against your presumptive *chingadismo*. I'm sure you feel the same."

"What, you think I'm afraid of you?"

"Yes. A certain underlying fear of the beloved is part of every real romance. Terrible as an army with banners, as the Bible has it. Obviously, women have every right to be frightened of men, but that's not what I mean. I mean we allow the other to get inside the shell, inside the armor, the—what's another word?"

"The penetralia."

"Yes, and a word we don't hear enough at present. We're not flirting now, Espinoza, we're sharing hearts."

"Yes, and I think you should slow down. I don't know how much this has to do with the situation; the presence of death makes people do crazy things, and . . . quite apart from last night, my penetralia are somewhat occluded at present."

"And tonight? May I expect a visit?"

"Let's leave that open, shall we? If I'm to do a shake-and-bake documentary of this *locura* you've arranged, I have a lot of work to do. But perhaps I will surprise you. *Hasta luego*, Marder."

She turned and took three steps in the direction of the *colonia*, spun on her heel, walked back, kissed him soundly, and, without another word, went on her way.

Speaking of insanity, thought Marder as he watched her walk away.

It was not all that much of a surprise. It was late, just after two; he'd had to accomplish a thousand small tasks that apparently only *el patrón* could do, settling arguments, allotting resources, chiding, calming, pumping up flagging spirits. He was just letting the sound of the surf lull him to sleep when the door opened without a knock and she came in, wearing only a light silk robe and carrying a laptop case, both of which she dropped at the side of the bed. Without a word, she slipped in beside him and gave him the indescribable, familiar, but evergreen shock of a naked body against his own.

She wanted to be on top, to be in control, and he thought that was fine. She was ungentle, nearly violent, as she ground down and pounded against him, making the bed rattle, and there was a good deal of biting and scratching and bad language.

"Yes, I'm your *chingada*," he said after.

"Good. See that you don't forget it."

He laughed, and she did too and punched him in the ribs as she rose from the bed and went to the bathroom. When she came back, she opened the laptop case, slipped on a pair of reading glasses, and worked on the video she'd shot that day.

He watched her as she worked. He recalled sneaking looks at Chole as she worked in the big studio they'd shared in their loft and he felt the same curious semi-erotic thrill, a voyeurism of the spirit.

She felt his eyes on her and said, "Don't peek. I can't stand it when people watch me edit."

"I was actually enjoying the sight of your nipples jiggling as you pounded the keys. You talk to yourself too, little imprecations and queries. Charming. How is it going?"

"Good. Some nice interviews and a lot of background stuff. Of course, the killer part, so to speak, will be the actual fighting."

"You seem to know what you're doing. Not that I looked."

"Yes, I had to learn video editing on my own. When I bailed out of telenovelas, they made me start as the weather girl in Veracruz. I often wore a bikini, if you can believe it, and for a couple of years I shot stories with friends as crew and sent the videos in to my management and got totally ignored, until I did a political exposé of one of the enemies of the guy who owned the station. That got me the reporter's job, and then Televisa picked me up for a magazine show out of Defe. And here I am."

She punched keys for a while, then slammed her finger down on the save button and copied to a thumb drive.

Holding the tiny thing up, she said, "I suppose this will be gripped in my teeth as I paddle away. Or in a more intimate cavity." She snapped the laptop shut and slid it to the floor.

"Speaking of intimate cavities." She rolled on top of him.

"Eek. Not again."

"No. I have to get some sleep, and so do you, my Zapata. I just like to lie on top of you. I like a big guy for that purpose."

In a while they took a break from nuzzling and she said, "You poor doomed man."

"Perhaps not. Change is always possible."

"Yes, this is why you'll never understand Mexico. In my country, politics is tragic, and all our great politicians have been tragic figures, either saints or demons. You, clearly, are one of the saints. But no one expects real change, because the nation reflects the human condition, original sin, call it what you like. There will always be a *chingón* and a *chingada*, and the only question is which men fall into which group. In your country, on the other hand, you believe that change is possible, and so your politics is comic. All your politicians are therefore clowns."

"It's a point of view," said Marder, "although I believe *I'm* enough of a Mexican to have a tragic sense of life. I fell into this situation, you know; I didn't write a manifesto and come down here to carry it out. I'm obliged to hope for the best, but I'm not a fool. I think death will find me very soon, and, *querida*, my dear heart, I can't imagine anyone I'd rather spend my last few hours with."

"You know, you're always saying things like that. I was struck by it earlier when that kid yelled 'victory or death,' and then that crack about swimming off the island, and I said, 'If I have to, I will.' Somehow the irony has left the building. I've been wondering why."

Marder's cell phone rang, the stupid default tone sounding particularly stupid in the circumstances. He left the bed and picked it up, observing that it was just past three a.m.

The caller was El Gordo.

"Well, Don Ricardo, here is your last chance to give me my property back."

"I'm devastated to have to tell you that my colleague and I have decided that it's not presently in our interest to do so. My colleague used an American expression: If you want my gun, you'll have to pry it out of my cold dead hands. How about half a million instead? Dollars."

"I'm happy to hear that you dispose of such resources. When I have you, and your house, and my property, such knowledge will ease negotiations for your personal release. I earnestly hope that I don't have to pry anything out of your cold dead hands, although that's really up to you. *Hasta la vista*, Don Ricardo."

"That was the Templos, no?"

Marder slipped back into bed. "That was Don Servando himself. He as much as told me he's coming to get what he thinks we owe him. I don't see why he shouldn't attack us tomorrow. I expect he's been preparing it for a while."

"I'm trying to think up a witty and insouciant rejoinder, but I'm drawing a blank. We seem to be in an irony-free zone now."

He wrapped his arms around her smooth, warm back. "Yes, well, irony is no protection when you can feel the breeze from his scythe on your skin and hear the rustle of his wings."

She turned in his arms so that she was staring into his face, her eyes wide, the pupils black and huge in the dim light. "Holy Mother! My God, you know you're right too about what you said out on the road before." She was speaking softly, trying not to let her voice break. "You really do frighten me. I can't believe I'm here. I can't believe I'm voluntarily in the path of an entire cartel. *Puerco Dios,* Marder! It's just now hitting me: we are all going to die, aren't we?"

"But not you," he said.

20

"Are you still sleeping?"

There was enough light coming through the windows now to show him her face. He touched her cheek. "Not really. In and out, with unpleasant dreams."

"Me too. Are you worrying about your daughter?"

"Every second it takes all I have not to jump up and start running around in circles, screaming. But the truth is, I'm actually helpless. Either she'll be fine or the opposite, and I resign the outcome to God's hands. It's one of the advantages of the religious imagination, without which ninety percent of the population of this country would have curled up and died a long time ago."

"That's an interesting point of view. Maybe I should interview you right now."

"You got my famous speech on tape. Let that suffice. I'm not the star of the show. Besides, I'm naked."

They laughed, and while they were laughing came the frantic knocking on the door and Ariel's shrill cry. That was the last laugh, thought Marder, as he jumped from the bed and into his pants.

"What, *muchacho*?"

"There are boats coming—a lot of them; a whole army of boats."

"And Don Esquelly, where is he now?"

"Up on the roof, Señor."

"Thank you, Ariel. Now go to your post."

The reporter was up and throwing on her clothing as fast as she could.

Marder grabbed a khaki shirt and his shoulder holster, his binoculars, a ball cap, his Steyr rifle, and his huaraches.

"Good luck, *querida*," he said as he left. "I'll see you when I see you."

The air on the roof still held the damp of the night. Peach tones streaked the sky above the eastern mountains; the sea lay in shadows, iron-colored and calm. Skelly was standing by the 12.7-mm emplacement, staring out to sea through his Zeiss glasses.

Marder raised his own binoculars. There was a large fishing trawler lying to about a thousand meters from the beach, accompanied by a substantial yacht, a forty-footer. The trawler was bringing forth smaller craft, a dozen or so by Marder's count, sliding them efficiently off the rear platform normally used for hauling in loaded nets. They were large Zodiacs, each presumably full of armed men and powered by an outboard engine, but Marder could make out only vague shapes, a duller blackness in the darkness of the sea.

"That's a pretty professional-looking operation," Marder observed.

"Yes. El Gordo owns a marina and guide shop, or extorts one. That's where the boats come from. And his guys tend to be fairly disciplined. Whoops, one boat went over. Well, it happens in the Special Forces too."

Now came the sound of automatic firing from the shore. Lines of the phosphorescent green tracer favored by the Warsaw Pact flew out toward the trawler.

Skelly cursed and got on his cell phone and chewed out Dionisio Portera, the leader of Charlie platoon. The boats were out of effective range, he said, and told them to wait until he fired a flare before shooting, and, for the love of God, short bursts. When he was off the phone, he had some words with Njaang, the 12.7-mm gunner, who immediately yanked the bolt of his weapon back, sighted the weapon, and pressed the triggers.

The sound was so enormous that Marder instinctively stepped away. At the same time he could hear the other 12.7, the one in the bunker on the golf course, sending enfilading fire into the lines of rubber boats. He saw one boat dissolve in a foamy tangle of rubber strips and red mash and looked away. Skelly grabbed his arm and pointed at the 20-mm rifle, standing on its bipod nearby.

He said, "Shoot some HEI rounds downrange. See if you can annoy the bridge of that trawler," and returned to studying the invasion through his glasses.

Marder looked through the scope of the 20-mm, shifting slightly to get the bobbing trawler in his sights. Then the whole scene lit up like a movie set. Skelly had shot off his flare, and the machine guns nested above the beach opened up.

Marder fired three rounds of high-explosive incendiary into the trawler's bridgehouse, starting fires. The boat fell off its station, showing its stern, allowing the 12.7 more play. Through Marder's rifle scope, everyone on the platform looked dead. The deflated remains of two Zodiacs slopped with the small waves against the trawler's low stern.

Marder stepped back from his rifle to find himself a scant foot from the lens of Pepa Espinoza's Sony.

"Is it time for my interview now?"

"No, but I wanted to catch you sinking the invasion armada. Very impressive."

"I don't think it's sinking. It's a very tiny cannon."

"But they're not going to send any more boats in. I need to get down to where the action is."

She trotted off down the inside stairway. He hoped that she'd stop and turn and come back and kiss him, as she had before, but she did not. He looked out through a gap in the sandbag parapet. The beach was strung with black boats, most of them collapsed, many with dead men inside them, and windrows of corpses lay on the sloping beach, a miniature of the grim photographs of D-day.

The 12.7 mm was silent now; Marder saw that the ammunition box was empty, and the area around it was carpeted with brass and links. But the machine guns below were still firing, and so were the AKs of Charlie platoon—firing far too rapidly, it seemed, for Skelly was once again shouting into his cell phone.

He stuck the thing in his pocket and looked at Marder. "These *pendejos* are going to use up every round on the island in the first five minutes. I was afraid this was going to happen. Look, keep an eye on things up here—I'm going to go down and dance on their heads."

He vanished. The Hmong loaded another belt into his gun. Around the terrace, the other men clutched their weapons and peered over the parapet, although there was nothing to see. Marder had another look at the trawler through his scope. The wooden bridge was burning merrily and the craft had developed a list. The large yacht had moved out of range. The men on the beach were isolated and couldn't be resupplied. They'd have to surrender eventually. Could it have been so easy?

And then someone shouted, and in a moment all of the men on the causeway side of the roof were yelling and pointing. Marder crossed to the other side of the roof and saw a large black object moving slowly down the coast road. He ran back to get the 20 mm and set it up on the eastern parapet. Through the scope he could see that it was an example of what Mexicans called a narco-tank. The cartels built them to over-awe rivals, he'd heard, but rarely used them. This was apparently one of the rare times when they rolled one out.

The thing made its turn slowly and began to move up the causeway toward the house, speeding up as it did so. There was something light-colored tied to the front of the rig. Telescopic sights are not optimized for tracking moving objects, and Marder had a hard time keeping it in focus. When it got closer, he could see what they'd done, which was to build a cage of cyclone fencing around the steel plate protecting the front of the vehicle. Within this they had imprisoned Lourdes Almones. Her wrists and ankles had been tied to the fencing, so that she couldn't shift her position, and her head was situated just rightward of the center of the narrow slit that let the driver see where he was going.

A difficult shot, Marder thought; not impossible. He would have only the one shot, because the truck was approaching too fast for a second. All he had to do was place his round into a slit about the size of the opening on an old-fashioned post-mounted letterbox, without hitting Lourdes's head or the armor plate around it—all this made harder by his guilt, by his own terror, by the terror he could see on the girl's tearstained face, by the thought of what would happen when the tank hit the gate. The girl was as good as dead already, and it was his fault. These were his thoughts in the three seconds that elapsed between the time he saw it was Lourdes and the time he would have to either squeeze the trigger or lose the house, unless he could get the crosshairs of his scope just on the—

He barely heard the shot, or so it seemed. He saw the bright flash in the blackness of the slit and saw that Lourdes still had a head, and then dirty yellow smoke gushed out of the slit and the tank veered left—lazily, like a hippo going for a wallow in the sea—off the road, down among the boulders, slamming into them with a mighty grinding crash, and turning over onto its side.

Before the monster had completed this evolution, Marder was down the stairs, and since everyone on the roof had seen what happened, he was followed by a dozen men. He dashed through the house, shouting for people to follow him; he had his pistol out; he was running out the front door, past the men in sandbagged bunkers guarding the gate, out the small side gate, and onto the causeway.

He heard heavy steps close behind him and snapped a look over his shoulder. It was a kid named . . . he couldn't remember now, a former *ni-ni*, worked in the glass factory; he was wearing a Lakers basketball shirt and a red headband and was carrying a PKM machine gun.

Marder heard the roar of engines, distant pops, and the snap of bullets overhead. He looked down the causeway. A long column of vehicles, mainly large pickup trucks, was careening down the road; the men standing in the bed of the foremost were firing at him. He crouched and ran, stumbling off the roadway and down onto the boulders, jumping like a goat from one to another, heading for the careened tank.

She was lying still in a fold of fencing, her skin blackened with soot and dappled with splashes of blood. He forced his hand through a space in the fence, reached her wrist. A pulse. A scatter of bullets pinged and whined off the side of the tank and the rocks.

Marder turned to the kid. "What's your name, *muchacho*?"

"Juan Benevista, Don Ricardo, from Delta platoon."

"Okay, Juan Benevista, I want you to give me your weapon, and then I want you to run as fast as you can to the toolshed behind the house and come back here with a bolt cutter and stretcher bearers. Is your ammo box full?"

"I haven't fired it yet, Señor," he said, looking a little sad.

"Good. Now, you go wait behind those rocks until I start firing, and then run like the wind!"

Marder set up his machine gun in the shadow under the overhang of the capsized tank. He started firing when the lead pickup was barely a hundred feet from him, letting the green tracers walk up from the front grille to the windshield and onto the the men clustered in the back. He saw the windshield fall apart and the truck swerve violently to the left. Its wheel went off the roadway, struck a rock, and the truck overturned and continued down the road on its back for thirty yards, leaving a smear of blood and shattered men. The next truck in the convoy braked, skidding on the mire of blood and leaked fuel and oil. Marder sent a short burst into it, which was hardly necessary. It crashed into the wreck, scattering its passengers like discarded dolls. Marder shot down the few staggering survivors.

The remaining attack force stopped some thirty meters away, swung a truck and an SUV across the road, and began a lively fusillade. At that point the spilled fuel from the wrecks ignited, sending dense clouds of black smoke across the scene, masking Marder's position.

Men had arrived from the house, twenty or so, under the command of Luis Araiza, the Delta platoon leader. The man squatted down next to Marder and peered out at the enemy position. A bullet spanged off the steel above them. Araiza tried not to flinch, Marder observed, but flinched nonetheless.

"How's it going, Luis? Are you having fun yet?"

"We haven't done anything. We were in the house as the reserve. Is this a reserve situation, *jefe*?"

"It is. Here's what I want you to do. Split your guys into two teams and send them to either side of the causeway. Make sure the narcos don't send anyone up the sides—it's dead ground from the front of the house and the roof. We need to keep them as far away from the house as we can. Do you have grenades?"

"Yes, *jefe*."

"You hear that banging sound? That's the guys in the tank trying to get out—there might be forty men in there. I want you to send someone to climb up on top and drop some grenades into that turret thing. Do it now, while it's still smoky."

Araiza looked doubtfully up at the black hulk. More bullets snapped by and ricocheted off the steel plates. He said, "I'll do it myself."

Marder laid down a base of fire with his PKM and the man scrambled up the side of the narco-tank. Three dull booms sounded, after which there was no more banging. Then, during one of those odd lulls that often occur in even the most violent firefights, Marder heard a thin shrill voice crying.

Juan Benevista appeared, sweaty but grinning, and handed Marder a bolt cutter. Marder gave him back his machine gun and ran down to the front of the tank. He snipped away at Lourdes's bonds and the fencing until the girl was free of the cage. As he lifted her out, her hands fluttered at her face. She saw the blood, she plucked at her hair, she saw the black char, she howled in despair. He felt someone tugging at his arm. "Let us through, Don Ricardo, we'll take her."

It was Rosita Morales and another woman. He recalled that the women had decided that they would act as the medics of the defense force, and here they were, with a homemade stretcher on which they tenderly placed the girl, then covered her with a blanket and ran off with her, back to the house.

The smoke from the fire thinned out and the Templos launched several attacks along the boulders. These were ragged, uncoordinated, and easily stopped, which Marder found strange because, from what he could see, they must have had several hundred men on hand, all milling around behind the barrier of the vehicles across the road. It seemed that Skelly had been right: the *sicarios* of Playa Diamante had not signed on for assaulting a position defended by machine guns.

He pulled out his cell phone and pushed the speed dial for Bartolomeo Ortiz, the blacksmith and commander of Alpha platoon on the roof terrace.

"Ortiz, how are you doing? What's happening on the beach?"

"I think they are defeated, Don Ricardo. Don Eskelly says they are just a few hiding in the bushes down there. Our men are shooting them like rabbits."

"That's good, then. Look, Ortiz, I need some heavy fire directed at that roadblock. Let's get the 12.7 on it, and get Rubén on the twenty millimeter. Tell him to start some fires in those cars; tell him to light up the fuel tanks."

"We have only one more box of rounds for the 12.7, Señor."

"Yes, I know, but this could make them leave us alone. I think they might break if we push them now."

Ortiz hesitated, and Marder could tell he was uneasy taking orders from anyone but Don Eskelly, but he didn't like to argue with the *patrón* either. In a few minutes the big machine gun started sending fat green tracer into the SUV barrier, and then came the car-door sound of the 20 mm. Pieces flew off the vehicles of the enemy, a man ran away and was decapitated by one of the 12.7 rounds, and then the gas tanks went up and all of the men sheltering there ran down the road. The Felizistas cheered.

Marder walked back to the house. He felt like shit, the tension of combat having overridden the innumerable bruises and strains that accumulate when one is engaged in shooting and being shot at, which all gave notice now that Marder was no longer nineteen.

Within the house, it felt like a locker room after the victory in the big game—a women's team perhaps, because most of those who greeted Marder with cheers and hugs were women. Marder smiled his way through these and went to the dressing station. According to Hilda Salinas, the nurse, casualties were fairly light: six wounded, only one dead—a kid named Jesús, an ironworker. Marder could not recall the fellow's face. He asked about Lourdes.

The nurse's lips tightened into a wrong smile and she looked away, in the way that people around here used when they were embarrassed before someone in authority.

"He took her."

"Who took her?"

"Don Eskelly. He came up from the beach with one of his wounded men and saw her, and they spoke and then he picked her up and went out."

"I see. And how are you doing, Señora? Do you have everything you need?"

She laughed harshly. "I have nothing I need. I would like a doctor, and some people who had more than a first-aid course, and morphine and an x-ray machine and more plasma. Some of these people are going to die if this doesn't stop before we can get them to a proper hospital."

She took a deep breath and arranged her face into a more professional mask. "I'm sorry, Don Ricardo, I shouldn't complain, but we are not set up for a war here. In the clinic, the *sicarios* walk right in and finish what they have started and no one stops them. They take people right out of the beds, witnesses and rivals and whoever, and they end up on the road, chopped to pieces. That's why I came to you."

"I understand," said Marder. "We'll try to make sure that it doesn't happen here. What about Lourdes—was she badly hurt?"

"Not physically, no. Some cuts, scrapes, and burns, but she was concussed in the crash. She should go to a proper hospital for head shots. He said he was going to take her to one." She looked over Marder's shoulder. "Oh, there he is now."

Marder turned, and Skelly walked up to him and, without a word, socked him in the jaw.

* * *

A woman brought Carmel dinner at seven-ten. She'd been a captive for more than six hours and was feeling odd, not because of the captivity so much but because this period was the first time in a long while that she had been disconnected from the Internet for more than a few minutes. She was designing, she had to look things up, she had to make calculations, and she couldn't; she kept reaching for a smartphone that wasn't there, like a quitting smoker patting pockets. Not having the data was like not having oxygen, she thought; it dulled her thinking, and she had to draw everything up from memory, and who used memory anymore?

She was running out of paper too. The little notebook (itself an anachronism) was filling with calculations about Colonia Feliz—wattage per square meter, flow rates through pipes of different sizes driven by pumps of different designs—that she would've done on a screen if she had one. She had tried using the walls as a scratch pad, but the rough stucco was hard to write on and she didn't want to screw up her pen. And did it really matter? That was a thought that kept coming up. Maybe this was the first symptom of a breakdown, like the guys in the movies *Pi* or *A Beautiful Mind*—obsessive calculation.

Or maybe it was a talisman against death. If she had all these plans, if she was going to do something really good for a lot of people, maybe she wouldn't be killed. But this thought was very deeply buried indeed and barely registered in her consciousness, except as a tone of sadness that made her issue long sighs from time to time.

The meal was fresh hot tortillas and spicy shredded meat, the famous *carnitas* of the region, and green rice and beans, served with a big tin cup of black coffee. Statch tried to engage the woman in comversation, but she pointed to her mouth and ear and shook her head: a deaf mute. There was a man waiting out in the corridor when the woman came in, a big man with a dull, hostile expression and a head that got narrower at the top, a feature exaggerated by the faded buzz-cut hairdo that seemed to be the official Templo look.

She ate the food, which was excellent Michoacán country cooking, the food on which she had been raised, and thought about her mother and tried not to completely break down, but still she wept a little. She used the bucket and washed her face and sat on the bed. They were treating her pretty well, she thought, which was good news. If they were feeding her and leaving her alone and hadn't searched her thoroughly or taken her watch and other items, it meant they were planning to release her. With this thought, she spent her evening comfortably enough. The room had no lamp, and when it become too dark to write, she took her boots off and lay on the bed.

Sleep came to her quickly and she slept soundly until, at about four the next morning, two men burst into the room, dragged her from her bed, tied her hands behind her, taped her mouth, yanked her pants off, found the pistol, laughed, slapped her across the mouth, dropped a sack over her head, frog-marched her shoeless out into the cool of the night, and threw her into the trunk of a car. Okay, she thought, *now* I'm in trouble.

* * *

Marder saw the punch coming and took it, not bothering to duck or slip the blow. It knocked him down and he struck his head, a violent blow against the tiles. Would this be the event that awakened Mr. Thing? Part of him hoped so; how tedious this waiting around had become! He thought of the line from *Ulysses*: she lived as if every moment were her next. Something his mother used to quote, and there she was in that Persian lamb coat she wore in the winter time, always with a little hat. She was playing gin rummy on Newkirk Avenue with Mr. Thing, at a folding card table in front of St. Jerome's church. Marder was happy to observe that this experience was living up to what everyone said: you would see all those who had gone before, and the white light, and there would be the welcoming figure, Jesus or whomever, and that would be it, the beginning of the next great adventure, and here Mr. Thing looked up at him from his cards and threw them down, and his mother said, There was the king I needed, and, looking up at Marder, said, Look at the time! You'll be late again, Ricky.

Marder opened his eyes and murmured, "Late again," and looked into the face of Pepa Espinoza, and at other faces looking down at him, a circle of brown faces, all with worried looks. So—apparently not just yet.

Somewhat later, up on the roof terrace, Marder held a plastic bag of melting ice to his jaw and surveyed the situation on the causeway. The Templos had begun to stoke their troops with crank now and had launched one furious assault with crude Tovex grenades and a charge of massed automatic weapons. The Felizistas had managed to beat it back, but one PKM was destroyed, and four more men had been killed. Marder doubted they would come down the causeway again, at least not without another heavy vehicle to lead the way. He had six HEI rounds left and half a belt of 12.7 ammunition. He had men filling oil drums with fertilizer and fuel oil. He thought the Russian grenades they had would act as detonating charges, and he had an idea that they could place the drums on either side of the gate and blow them when the next narco-tank, or whatever, came through. And then what? They could keep building narco-tanks and he could not make the means to stop them, not indefinitely.

Except for the ache in his jaw, Marder felt numb, stunned, wrapped in invisible batting. Skelly was gone, it seemed; he'd taken Lourdes in the boat and disappeared, along with the three Hmong. The sky pressed down on him like the slats of a tiger cage; he couldn't do this, not without Skelly, and he kept scanning the horizon, half expecting his friend to return with a wicked grin on his face, saying it was one of his jokes. He couldn't get his mind around the occurrence: he felt the way he had when they told him his wife had died.

"Why?" he asked. "I don't get it."

Pepa Espinoza replied, "He's an unstable homicidal lunatic. I know you cared about him, but his relationship to you was not a regular sane human relationship. I think you projected a lot of your good qualities onto him—kindness, responsibility . . . all that."

"Pepa, forgive me, but you don't know what you're talking about. He was my friend, from when I was not much older than Lourdes. I can't believe he just walked off in a fucking huff because I sort of lied to him about a girl."

"Yes, and I wish I had a hundred pesos for every time I've had this conversation with a girlfriend. How *could* he have? I told you before—it wasn't pals between you, old army buddies hanging out. It was a romance. You paid attention to a pretty girl. He took that girl. Because he loved her? Of course not—because he thought you might, and to show who was in control. You wanted to defend this land and the people on it, and he helped you. Because he gave a shit? Of course not—it was because it made you depend on him, need him. Now you break the rules, you lie to him to help the girl escape, and what happens? He acts like a hysterical betrayed *chingada*; he punches you out and takes off. See how well you do without him, that's the message. It's an old story, Marder, maybe the oldest story. It's in the *Iliad*, for God's sake."

"The *Iliad*, huh? Maybe you're the one who's jealous."

"*¡Ay chingate!* What am I doing here, talking to a man who won't listen? Again, it's exactly like talking to an abandoned woman, but the difference is that your *pendejo* friend really *is* essential to your survival."

"You think so?"

"I know it. You didn't see him down there when they attacked on the beach, but I did. My God, I have the most incredible video on the battle. They must have sent a hundred and fifty men against our thirty, and they would've blasted right through them if Skelly hadn't been there. He was everywhere—exposing himself to fire, running back and forth, encouraging the men, stopping those poor kids from throwing their guns down and running away, directing the machine guns . . . He's a one-man army. Are you?"

"No. Skelly is unique as a warrior in my experience. I have a different skill set. In any case, did you collect adequate footage?"

"Yes, but we don't say 'footage' anymore, Marder. What is your skill set?"

"Patience, endurance, guile, and a cavalier disregard for my own survival. Wars have been won with those by people who never fired a shot. This is going to be another spectacular sunset."

Marder looked out at the sea, and as he did he put his arm around Pepa Espinoza. She stiffened and then, after an uncomfortable moment, relaxed. It was lovely standing with her on the roof of his home and watching the sequential conniptions of the light: the scarlet, the magenta, cloud strips lighted with fire in sequence, the wonderful touches of egg-shell blue still surviving amid the furnace colors, intensifying their violence, the perfect glowing ball sinking with increasing speed, throwing a red track on the metallic surface of the sea. And then the last spark gone and the whole sky suffused with a fleshy ridiculous pink, like the penultimate moment of a cosmic striptease act, after which the chaste curtain of the blue hour, twilight.

They were silent while this proceeded, and after it was over, Marder said, "I think they'll try to come at us in the dark tonight, and if that happens I'm going to pull everyone back into the house, kill as many as I can with the claymores, and hold out for as long as I can. How long that will be depends on how the world sees what we're doing, which means you have to get away with your story."

"I can send it out via cellular."

"No, you can't. They've been shooting at our dish for hours. We can get local service, but I'm afraid sending a huge video file with the present equipment is out of the question. Besides, you have to be there, you have to do the talk shows, you have to collect your fame. 'I only am escaped alone to tell thee.' It's a key part of the story. Also, I'd keep the khaki shirt and your hair the way it is, dusty and tangly and tied up with a bandanna. Your slightly battered beauty. You've even got a wound."

She glanced at the filthy bandage on her forearm. "It's from a rock chip. It's nothing."

"It'll help sell the story and bring you international fame—lovely, spirited, brave, filthy, and suffering, just like our poor country. No, you have to leave. But before you go, there's one favor I'll ask of you, and it's sort of in your line of work."

"Ask."

"I want you to record a meeting I'm going to have with a group of our people, late tonight, let's say . . . eleven. I should be finished with what I have to do by then. And it'll give you time to assemble your material and get it on a thumb drive for your escape."

He hugged her and walked away without answering her string of questions.

It was not difficult for Marder to find, in the library of the late *abogado* Guzmán, the forms and the relevant chapters of Mexican law, which, while so often ignored in practice, retained the accessible rationality of French philosophy and the thirst for justice born of violent centuries. He worked in his office; the two men guarding their loopholes enforced silence upon themselves in deference to the *patrón*. At eight, Amparo knocked on the door and asked him if he was coming to supper. He asked for a tray, then told her to wait and wrote out a short list. He wanted those people assembled in the kitchen at eleven tonight. She looked at the list, nodded, and slipped out of the room.

The tray arrived, carried by a silent Epifania. He ate an enchilada and drank most of a pot of strong coffee. He typed, he printed, he revised and printed again. It was comfortable work with words, a memento of the life he'd abandoned, and it had a bittersweet resonance, like perusing a stack of ancient love letters. He finished just after ten-thirty, printed out copies, used some of the former owner's creamy stationery to write out a document by hand, and descended to the kitchen.

They were all waiting for him, the big table had been cleared and scrubbed. He sat down at the head of it and bade the others sit. He'd invited the four military commanders Skelly had appointed, plus Amparo and Rosita Morales, the potter. Pepa Espinoza was there too, leaning against the big refrigerator, her camera in her hands. He regarded the faces around the table, all various shades of brown, all carrying a look of expectancy, perhaps trepidation too, but also a resistant dignity, a deep Mexican seriousness. They owed the señor a good deal, this look said, but they were not his creatures; they had fought for themselves against the *sicarios* and won, and they were wondering if they were now to lose, as their ancestors had won victories and still lost the fruits thereof. They glanced suspiciously at the paperwork he'd brought. In their experience, no good came from papers.

There was none of the joshing that always introduced an important meeting in America. Marder nodded to Pepa, who started her videocam, and began without preamble.

"In the event of my death, an event that is more likely than not given the current situation, I've made provisions for the survival of this community. This," here he held up a thin sheaf, "is a document conveying the ownership of this property—house, lands, and structures—to a trust under Mexican law, this trust to be administered by seven trustees. You are those trustees. Why you? I chose the four commanders because they are men with good heads and are respected by the community, and also because I think they won't be easily frightened. Señora Morales is here because she too is courageous and widely respected and because her pottery business brings in more income than any other. She will speak for the business interests of the community. I strongly recommend that you elect Bartolomeo Ortiz to be your chairman and Amparo Montez to be your executive secretary. Bartolomeo has been the natural leader of this community ever since I've been here. From what I've seen, he's singularly free of corruption. Amparo, as you know, is educated; she has full knowledge of our accounting systems and is skilled with the computers and the Internet, which is going to be the basis of your prosperity. In a few days this place is going to be world famous and many people will want the things that are made here, and not only because they're beautiful."

He now distributed packets of papers to the others at the table. No one read what they were given. Their eyes were fixed on Marder.

"These are copies of trust documents for you to read," he continued, "and here is a legal instrument setting up the trust itself. When it is signed and notarized, you will own this island and everything on it in trust for your families and their descendants, forever. Another document I've prepared is a handwritten instruction to my lawyer, ordering a transfer of certain funds to be used as an endowment for the trust, to tide you over until you become self-supporting through the work of your hands. Yet another document establishes a conservation easement, so that no big development can ever be built here. This is all I can do to ensure that this place can't be taken from you by lawful means. You can still lose it in the old-fashioned Mexican ways, stolen by violence or wrecked by internal squabbling and envy. But at least you have a chance. Are there any questions?"

"This is an *ejido*, isn't it?" asked Amparo.

At this well-known word, murmurs passed around the table. All of them knew the meaning of the ancient cooperative land-tenure system of Mexico, much raped and traduced but still dear to the hearts of the *campesinos*.

"Yes, that's just what it is," said Marder, "and in case you are wondering, in the unlikely event that I live, the trust goes through as written. I hope you will allow me to live out my days here as your guest, or you can throw me out on my ear. It's up to you. Oh, one other thing—we will have to rely on Pepa Espinoza to carry these documents to safety, have them notarized, and tell the world what we're doing here. My hope is that the publicity and the images she's recorded will pressure the government to do its duty and protect us from these gangsters."

Marder looked into the eye of Pepa's camera as he said this.

Later, they were nervous with each other; neither wanted a passionate, tearful goodbye. She hugged him and gave him a formal kiss on both cheeks, as if he were a *Chilango* colleague and not a lover. "Don't die, Marder," she said. "I will never forgive you if you get yourself killed."

"The same goes for you," he said. "Do you think you can find your way?"

"Of course. Around the headland, across the mouth of the river, and I should see the lights of Playa Diamante. It's not exactly a wilderness."

"I was thinking about the human predators."

"Oh, they won't stop a woman in a kayak. I'll just smile and talk kitchen Spanish with a gringa accent. I'll be fine."

"Yes, you will. You'll be a famous television journalist. You'll have your heart's desire."

She slid into the kayak, pushed away from the dock, and spun the craft on its long axis, so Marder could see that she knew what she was doing.

"And is there a place in all this devious planning for Marder's heart's desire? Are we to be allowed to know what it is?"

"Well, I'd like to get my daughter back. That'll do for the moment. Beyond that, I'll be happy with whatever comes." He waved. *"Vaya con Dios, corazón mío,"* he said, and walked away down the dock.

21

In the rattling black of the car trunk, Carmel Marder struggled to control her hysteria. This failed and she screamed, or, rather, made animal noises behind her tape gag. Tears and snot flowed freely out of her, soaking the rough cloth of the bag over her head. She cursed in horrified mumbles, cursed her mother for dying so stupidly, her father for going crazy and coming down to this dreadful place, she cursed Mexico, she cursed herself for her own arrogance, for the bottomless stupidity of her sacrifice.

After some time, this ended and she entered a zone of despair so deep that it passed for calm. I am indeed helpless, she thought, but after all I have been helpless before. Perhaps this passion for control that's been my life is not all it's cracked up to be. Maybe that was an illusion and this is the reality: we are helpless and dependent; it's the human condition; fate takes us when and where it will. Here, her father appeared in the depth of her mind, a memory as fresh as if it had happened yesterday. Her grandmother had just died; it was a funeral Mass with an open coffin. She was ten and viewing the body with her father beside her. People were crying, but her father was not crying and she wanted to know why. She also wanted to know where her grandmother *went*, but she didn't mention that. Even at ten, the logistics of heaven seemed absurd to her. Her little mind skidded away from these mysteries; she was already an engineer. Her father had said—she heard these words now in the roaring darkness, as if he were saying them into her ear—I'm sad because I won't see her again, and I loved her, but I also believe that she still exists and she believed that too, and she's still with me, just like you're with me, but invisible. I can feel her. That's why love is greater than death.

That was one thing: her father was not afraid of death the way everyone else was. Another thing: she remembered driving in the car with him out on Long Island—they were coming back from sailing—and the radio had played one of those civil defense announcements they used to have, and the announcer's voice told them that this is a test, this is only a test, if this had been a real emergency you would have been given instructions, and so on. Her father had said, Thus, the meaning of life, and he'd explained it, as he explained everything to her. It had become a joke in the family, a tagline, when any gnarly difficulty arose: This is a test, this is only a test.

And, of course, he meant death too, although she didn't understand that then. Now she did, and with that came from out of nowhere a feeling of deep peace.

They'd taken Statch to a place that stank of onions, where she'd lain on concrete for a very long time. They'd allowed her to piss in a bucket and then tossed her back in the trunk. The sack had stayed on her head. She was stiff when they dragged her out and sick from the tailpipe fumes. As she stumbled along between the two men, she heard a familiar sound and became aware of a familiar odor. The sound was the jangling of rigging slapping aluminum masts; the smell was the sea. They were taking her aboard a boat. Her heart lifted a little. Water was good.

They stopped. Someone said, "Let's see the little bitch," and the hood was yanked off her head. They were at the end of a dock in the Playa Diamante marina. It was early in the evening, and the lampposts that lined the dock's edge were already lit, illuminating the men standing there as if on a stage. There were three men beside the two thugs who had hold of her, but only one of them was important. She looked at his face and then quickly looked away, as we do when there is a monstrous occurrence on the street, a jumper landing on the sidewalk. She understood that she had never met anyone like that before.

He was a small man, not much taller than she was, and about the same age as her father. She thought, inanely, of the movies, in which actors contrive to express evil, and she thought it was like the difference between a movie explosion, all orange fireballs, and an actual detonation of high explosives in real life: an enormously more bone-chilling event, with the shock wave of invisible death and the predatory hum of flying debris. The photos she and everyone saw of captured drug lords also had nothing to do with this man's face. It was the difference between a tiger in the zoo and a tiger in the wild making its leap at you. This guy was free-ranging, a lord of life and death. He was a fossil from deep Mexico, the land of ripping living hearts out on pyramids, of conquistadores roasting Indians alive. She stared at him and he stared back with his inhuman stare, mildly curious perhaps, with a crude, suspicious intelligence; it was like looking into the black reflective eyes of a mantis.

One of her captors handed Melchor Cuello her .22 pistol and told him where they'd found it. He hefted it, worked the action, and then in a quick movement stuck his arm straight out and pointed the muzzle at her forehead. She made herself hold his gaze, and the tableau lasted for what seemed like a long time. Then Cuello snorted, gave the pistol back to the other man, and said, "Give it to Gabriel. Maybe he'll stick it up her pussy and fire a couple of rounds. He likes that kind of shit, right?"

All the men laughed at this boyish pranksterism, and after a brief conversation that Statch could not hear, the men dragged Statch to the end of the dock and dropped her into a fiberglass skiff with a big outboard on it. They dropped in too and did not bother to replace her hood. It didn't matter what she saw now, nor was there anyone around to recognize her. She was glad to be able to breathe and see, but she thought that no hood was not a good sign with respect to her possibility of survival. They were delivering her into the hands of El Cochinillo himself.

The boat took off with a roar, and soon its hull was planing over the light chop in the harbor, each jolt causing Statch's head to bounce painfully against the deck. She used her legs to shift her position, and now she could see above the gunwale and could watch Playa Diamante recede until it was just a whitish line against the green backdrop of the sierra. They were going quite far out to sea, enough so that she could feel the motion of the craft change, from riding chop to breasting actual Pacific rollers. Her two guards stood by the wheel, talking and smoking, and paid her no attention at all until they cut the throttle and came slowly up under the stern of an enormous white yacht.

Statch had spent a good deal of her life around boats but had never been on a private vessel as large as this one, a great white fiberglass monument at least 140 feet long. As they led her up the ladder, she passed a youth in a white uniform of shorts and tunic, mopping the deck. He met her eyes and then looked quickly away. He hadn't seen anyone.

They led her forward across a broad deck with small round tables and chairs on it, under an awning, then down a set of stairs and through a corridor lined with narrow doors. They went through a hatchway and down another set of stairs and now they were below the waterline, in the working areas of the great yacht. It was hot down here and airless, and she could hear the thud of the diesels.

They opened a door. One of the men grinned at her and pulled the tape off her mouth.

"Scream as much as you want, *chica*. No one to hear you out here."

The man grabbed one of her buttocks, shoved her into the room, and closed the door. She heard the click as it locked.

The room was some kind of storeroom, she imagined, but void of any stores, and its fiberglass surfaces were perfectly clean and smelled faintly of Clorox. Light came from an overhead bulb protected by a steel grille. The thought came that if you wanted to torture someone, and could afford it, an offshore yacht would be a great choice. No one would hear the screams, and disposal of the remains would not be a problem. Fighting the panic—for what would this room be but a torture chamber—she dropped to her knees and lowered her head to the floor and shook her upper body violently. Her notebook, her Rotring 600 pen, and her tiny Swiss Army knife dropped to the deck. She shifted position so she was on her back and wiggled around until she grasped the knife. In a minute she'd used the little razor-sharp blade to slice through the plastic cable ties that bound her hands. She stuck the knife and the notebook into her breast pocket again and took the cap off the pen. It was not much of a weapon, but it was made of solid brass and it had a steel tip. She sat herself in a corner with her hands behind her back and waited.

The horror of the blank room, no watch to mark the passing minutes—time itself dissolved, the present moment, which the sages teach us to live in perpetually, was now the essence of horror. But after some moments of hellish desperation, Statch reached back to the memory of the peace she'd experienced while locked in the trunk. She reflected that she was a trained mind in a trained body, she had resources that her captors did not begin to understand, and so she controlled her breathing as she'd learned to do to still the tension of a swim meet, and from there she moved to contemplating the thrill of competition. While not willing, quite, to work to Olympic standards, she was nevertheless a champion; she liked winning, and it now occurred to her that this was a competition too, with the medal being her life, and a fierce joy bloomed in her heart.

Then without preamble her mental theater lit up with an unnaturally vivid scene. She must have been fourteen or so, she was on a lake in the Berkshires with her father, at a cottage they'd rented for the summer, and they were exhausted and laughing, having just swum to the other side and back. She'd been able to beat him over long distances for several years and had just then done it again, and he was complaining about being an old man; she recalled exactly the moment when she focused on the scars on his back, seeing them as if for the first time, the livid mark above his left hip and the other, like an inverted question mark, over his right shoulder blade. She asked him how he got the scars and he answered that they were old war wounds, as he always did; he said a typewriter had fallen on him, the usual joke; but she was at the age when children acquire a passionate interest in the truth and the evasions that adults have used previously can no longer stand. No, really.

He always said he'd had an office job in air force intelligence, but now she pressed him. Intelligence? Was he a spy, did he go on secret missions, was that how he got the scars? And, after some fencing, which she furiously rejected, he told her the story, in bold strokes. You killed people? Yes, he'd killed people; he'd killed a boy not much older than she was. How did you feel, she asked, and she could see him considering the facile, comfortable lie, and then he said, I felt elated. There's a joy in combat, partly because he's dead and you're not, and partly because we're ferocious creatures, we humans. She had not known then about his escape with Skelly, or about the angelic voices.

Would it have changed her life? It didn't matter, but she now recalled what they *had* talked about, about the war and about Skelly, how he was an extreme example, how he was terrified and exultant at the same time, a born soldier. She wondered why this passage had popped so vividly into her mind, and she decided that it was related to her situation now and what she planned to do with her pathetic weapon. It was chemicals, she guessed, flooding her system—competition, combat, the desire to live and prevail, sports and war, really the same thing. And she recalled another thing her father had said that afternoon, when she'd asked if women could feel like that. He said, Oh, yeah, but in spades. Your mother, for example, is much, much fiercer than I am. You are too. That's the real reason why they don't let women into combat. They'd take over the world.

She heard the key turn in the lock. The door opened and Gabriel Cuello walked in, dressed in a maroon velour bathrobe and canvas slippers. He had her pistol in his hand. He nudged the door shut with his foot and walked into the center of the room.

"Little gringa bitch, I knew I would see you again," he said.

She pushed herself into a corner of the room, as if retreating, holding her hands behind her back. He came closer. She got up into a squat, with her back against the angle where two bulkheads joined.

He waggled the pistol. "Were you going to shoot me with this little thing?"

"If I had the opportunity," she said.

He didn't like her tone; frowning, he came a step closer, until he stood over her. She could smell his cologne.

"You know, *chiquita*, I can tell you have no fucking idea what is going to happen to you. I can tell you think that because you're a gringa, your daddy or the marines are going to save you. You are going to show me some respect now, understand? You are going to do everything I tell you and you are going to smile, because—"

"I thought you only liked to fuck dead girls," she said, "which is fine with me, because, frankly, I'd rather be dead than do anything with an ugly little pervert like you."

He smiled and nodded. "Uh huh. Keep it up, *chiquita*. We'll see how smart you talk when I'm shittin' in your mouth. You'll be begging me to shit in your mouth, you'll see. You can start by sucking on this."

He dropped the pistol into his bathrobe pocket, opened the robe, and leaned forward, his right hand reaching for her hair.

She exploded out of her crouch with all the force of her powerful leg muscles, ramming the crown of her head into his nose. He staggered back, but she followed him, her left hand grasping the collar of his robe. Her right hand drove the steel pen tip into his throat. She felt it penetrate deep into his trachea.

He tore himself away now, his eyes bulging, hands clutching at his throat. He grasped the pen, tore it out. Blood gushed from the wound in a spray. He was coughing; she could hear the blood gurgling in his trachea as he struggled to breathe against the blood that dripped down from the wound into his bronchial tubes. She took careful aim, set herself, and kicked him as hard as she could, driving her foot into his naked genitals. His knees sagged, he doubled over, his face was going purple. She backed up and took a short run, hitting him low, and knocking him off his feet. The pistol flew from the pocket of his robe and skittered, spinning, across the floor. She picked it up. It was still cocked. She shot once into his head. He collapsed and lay still.

She waited, gun in hand, facing the door. Silence. Perhaps the crew thought he had killed her and was now enjoying a session of necrophilia. She opened the door and looked both ways down the corridor, which proved to be deserted. She ran, reversing the direction she had come, up the two flights of stairs and then to the door that led to the deck. She looked through the glass set into the door and saw two men sitting at one of the tables with drinks, smoking, their backs to her, looking out to sea. She opened the door as quietly as she could, took a careful two-handed firing position, and shot one of the men in the back of the head. The other one spun around, leaped to his feet. He was reaching to his beltline when she put three hollow-point bullets into the middle of his chest. The man looked surprised, pulled his own gun, sat down, and died. Then, still holding her grandfather's Colt .22, she went over the rail into the sea.

Diving below the surface, she swam under the stern of the boat, where she bobbed up under the overhang of the dive platform, grasping one of its supports, invisible from the deck. The yacht was moving slowly in a southerly direction. The tender that had brought her here still towed along on its line. For a moment she considered stealing it but instantly dismissed the thought. The yacht could travel much faster than the tender, and they would have the weapons on board to kill her from a distance. Instead, she floated silently, taking deep slow breaths. She heard shouts, commotion, the tread of many feet. Perhaps they had already discovered the dead piglet; perhaps they were arguing about what to do and who was in charge. No one would be in a hurry to tell El Jabalí that his son and heir had been killed by a girl. They would *really* like to have her head in a box when they brought that news.

Someone turned on a spotlight and swept it over the sea. After a while, that person might think to look under the dive platform. She had to leave. She placed the pistol butt-down in the capacious breast pocket of her shirt and secured the button around the jutting barrel. Taking one deep breath, she dived and started to swim underwater, east toward the land. She had swum more than a hundred meters underwater before this, and now she was going for a personal best. The water was blood-warm; she swam easily, breaststroking and frog-kicking, streamlining her body after every kick to maximize the glide. When she finally surfaced and looked back, the yacht was at a gratifying distance, and the traverse of the searchlight's bright disk stopped twenty meters short of where she floated. She waited, dog-paddling until a roller could lift her up so she could spot the lights of the shore.

But there were no lights. She was in the middle of a dark bowl, lit by a crescent moon and speckled with stars, the sea interrupted only by her head and the increasingly distant yacht. The yacht had been moving during the hours she'd been confined and she had no idea of how far it had traveled. If it had been heading directly out to sea, she might be thirty miles from land. But why would it head out to sea? So that the pieces of a chopped-up woman would not wash up onshore? At least she knew in which direction to swim, for an imaginary line dropped from the points of the moon's crescent would touch the southern horizon. She floated on her back and strained her eyes. Was that a faint glow in the east? She convinced herself that it was and started swimming toward it. The pistol dragged at her with every stroke, but she was not about to let it fall to the bottom of the sea.

* * *

Before he went to bed that night, Marder had a brief conversation with Bartolomeo Ortiz. They were at the long table under Skelly's big map, alone; the other men had been sent away. Marder looked at the soiled piece of notebook paper on which Ortiz had written, in a schoolboy scrawl, the ammunition inventory of his little army. It was pathetically meager but not as meager as it had been, for in the hours of darkness a crew of picked men had opened up the wrecked narco-tank and extracted thirty-two AR-15 assault rifles and thousands of rounds of ammunition from among the shattered corpses of their enemies.

"What do you think? Can we hold the existing perimeter with the weapons at our disposal?"

Ortiz looked uncomfortable. His eyes wandered and his huge scarred hands twisted around each other, as if trying to wring a solution from the space between them.

"Well? You're the commander, Ortiz. This is a command decision."

"Don Ricardo, I know how to shape iron I can tell men what to do and usually they do it or, you know, I use this." He held up a massive fist. "And I was in the army, and this is why Don Eskelly chose me to lead a platoon. But I was only a motor-pool corporal. I welded, I cut and fitted and pounded metal. I did not dispose of troops, you understand?"

"Yes, I do, because I was a book editor. And Hidalgo was a priest, Zapata was a peon, and Villa was a bandit, but they all led armies much larger than ours. We do what we can and what's given to us to do. Now, can we hold the perimeter?"

The big man lowered his head for a moment and then raised it and looked Marder in the eye. "No, Señor, we cannot. Even with the new weapons and ammunition, we have only seventy-one effectives, not counting women. I mean with rifles. None of our machine guns has much more than two hundred rounds. We have a total of three hundred rounds for all of the big machine guns together."

"All right. Pull them back to the secondary positions on Skelly's map. If I may make one small suggestion . . . ?"

"Of course, Señor."

"Put a couple of good men on the north cliff. And pull the 12.7 out from the bunker overlooking the beach and re-emplace it—here, outside the village, facing the track through the golf course." Marder made a cross on the map.

Ortiz knotted his brow and his mouth twisted in a doubtful grimace. "But why? No one can come up those cliffs, and there's no beach to land on."

"There *is* a small beach and there *is* a path up the cliffside. If a force should appear there, they would take us by surprise; there are no defenses at all on the northern flank."

"But who would know about that? And before they came by the big beach and the causeway."

"Yes, and we stopped them there. I'm sure they'll try the causeway again, but they won't come through the beach or the marina. As to how they might find out—it would take only one strong swimmer to swim to the mainland and tell them. Mexican revolutions are always betrayed, as you well know. So let's be careful. And how are the mines?"

"We have ten filled and enough diesel for two more. They are being buried where you said."

"Good. Have one brought into the house."

"The house?"

"Yes. We may lose, but they won't get the house. I will bring it down on their heads if I have to."

"Like Samson in the Bible?" asked Ortiz, with an awestruck look on his face.

"Just so," said Marder.

He was awakened by the firing. He jumped from his bed, dressed, and armed himself. He took his Kimber and his Steyr rifle and a box of bullets for the rifle and two extra magazines. Then he ran down to the living room headquarters to see what was going on. Amparo greeted him with a glowing smile.

"It's the army. They've come, and they're attacking the Templos. That place on the beach road where they have all their trucks—they're all exploding. And Father Santana is here. We are saved!"

Besides the torrent of small-arms fire, Marder could hear intermittent loud bangs. But they were the wrong kind of bangs. He said, "Get Ortiz! I'm going up to the roof to take a look."

He ran up the stairs and onto the roof. To the west the sea was buried in a blanket of mist; to the east the sky showed the faintest blush of the rising sun. It was the hour when a white thread could just be told from a black one, the traditional time for military assaults. The men of Alpha platoon were all gathered at the parapet to watch the fireworks. Red tracers flew back and forth, and it was easy to tell that the Templos' base was being overwhelmed by a much larger force, an enormous force. This force had probably moved into the surrounding hillside by stealth in the hours before dawn and now was directing torrential fire down into the closely packed vehicles. Other forces had blocked the road on either side, and from these arose an occasional bright flash and then a blazing line, whose terminus was a violent explosion. Marder had not heard the characteristic *bang-whoosh-BANG* of an RPG-7 in a long time, but it was not something one easily forgot.

Ortiz arrived, out of breath, and Marder clasped his thick arm and drew him away from the others.

"You have to pull back to the secondary positions. We might not be able to hold even those for very long. Also, it would be—"

"But, Don Ricardo, we are saved. The army has arrived."

"It's not the army, my friend. It's La Familia. They mean to wipe out their rivals and then take the *colonia*."

"I don't understand. How do you—"

"They're using RPGs. And, look: you can see there are no military vehicles, no armored cars. No, it's La Familia—they must have pulled troops in from the whole region. There must be a thousand rifles. I think—"

A little tune sounded.

"Answer your phone, Ortiz."

The man pulled a cell phone out of his pocket. "Alpha actual," he said, even though he was now Casa actual. He listened, asked a few questions, gave a brief order, and switched off.

Marder could barely see his features in the dim light, only the flash of eyes and teeth, but Ortiz's voice was shaky.

"It's what you said, Señor. They've beached a trawler under the cliffs and men are pouring out. Dionisio says many men, as many as fifty. I told them to go back to where the big machine gun is."

"Good. As to that, there's only one place where they can come over the lip of the cliffs, and you can shoot them down like bowling pins, one at a time. When the 12.7 is out of ammo, tell them to pull the bolt and smash the receiver with a hammer. Do they have a hammer?"

"I will get one to them." Ortiz looked around the roof and saw a small figure standing on a pile of sandbags, enjoying the fireworks. He called out and Ariel came trotting over. Ortiz told the boy to go to his shop and get his big hammer—not the sledgehammer but the smaller one with the chisel end—and take it to Hector Sosa at the big machine gun on the golf course. And hurry.

Marder saw the flash of the child's grin before he dashed off, and he thought it was wise of Ortiz to use the kid for an errand like that and not deplete his defenses by detailing an armed man.

The sun now crested the top of the mountain, sending picturesque shafts through the smoke at the foot of the causeway, but it hardly required sunlight to see what was happening. Dozens of vehicles smoldered and blazed there. The Templos had literally circled their wagons, but almost all of them were ablaze, and very little return fire issued from them in response to the continuing fusillade from the Familia positions. Soon the return fire ceased entirely, and Marder could see through his binoculars hordes of men, many wearing camouflage outfits, pouring down out of the brush and along the roads to overwhelm the Templos.

He heard the 12.7's characteristic roar from the north and he trotted across the roof terrace in that direction, reaching the sandbag palisade only to find that the scrubby growth of Jalisco firs blocked his view of the northern end of the golf course. He used a ladder to climb up onto the roof of the northwest square tower and lay prone at the roof peak, looking through his scope.

He was focused on the place where the trail through the woods joined the main road of the *colonia*. The 12.7 fell silent, and in another minute a Felizista appeared, then another. They took up a position behind tree trunks and began to fire back along the trail. A group of their comrades ran past them down the road, clumped up in a group running for their lives. Some of them were burdened by wounded, although Marder couldn't see who they were. The rear guards fired until they were out of ammunition, then they ran too.

A Familia *sicario* appeared at the head of the trail and Marder knocked him down with a single shot, then another and another. No more appeared, and Marder imagined that they would take another route out of the woods—it was no impenetrable jungle, but . . . no they were trying it again, a group of men in a rush. Marder shot two of them, but the others were able to reach shelter in the alleys between the houses of the *colonia*. He simply could not fire fast enough, proving yet again that the fellow who invented the machine gun was no fool. He was about to drop down from his perch when he saw a movement in the field of his scope and paused.

Skelly was standing there at the head of the path, walking slowly onto the road, as if taking a constitutional. He was wearing his pistol but was otherwise unarmed. He looked up, as if he knew he was being watched through the crosshairs of a rifle scope and didn't much care, and then he walked after the *sicarios* and disappeared among the houses.

Well, yes, of course Skelly would go to La Familia. Where else could he go? And he'd reserved the RPGs that had come in the shipment as a bargaining chip. Marder found that he couldn't hate him for the betrayal.

Pepa had been correct. Skelly was not like a regular person; he was more like weather, as amoral and deadly as a hurricane.

Motion caught Marder's eye. A man had climbed onto the flat roof of one of the *colonia* structures, in a place where he could not be seen from the roof parapet. He had a rocket launcher. Marder yelled for everyone to take cover and then heard the rocket go off, and the next moment the roof tower that held the cell-phone equipment blew to pieces.

Marder shot the man down and then scrambled off the roof. Someone else must have brought up another rocket, because the tower Marder had just occupied now erupted in dust and flying shards of stone and tiles. Wounded men lay all around, groaning or crying, some for their mothers, and some others lay still. Marder abandoned his rifle and spent the next minutes helping to carry the wounded men down to the sick bay. Every few minutes the house shook with the explosion of a rocket or the blast of one of the defenders' homemade mines.

On his last trip down to the sick bay, he heard the air torn by an unearthly banshee shriek, and there was Amparo, her fine intelligent face destroyed by inconsolable grief, kneeling by the black and bloody corpse of her little boy. She kept shaking it, slapping at the lolling face, issuing howl after howl, until the other women led her away.

Marder went to find Father Santana. He waited while the priest annointed the head of a dying man, one Henriques, a man who made small glittering glass animals. When the priest looked up, Marder said, "Come with me. I want you to do something."

They moved to a corner of the sick bay. Marder looked Father Santana in the face. His skin and the crow-black hair above it was frosted with plaster dust, like everything else in the room. His Roman collar had flecks of blood on it. His expression was that of a terrified man being brave. Marder thought he looked a little like Patrick Skelly did in battle, and it made him more confident in the man.

"I'm happy to see you here, Father. How did you get through?"

"I arrived before this new attack. The Templos were happy to see me. They have a number of dying men, and they made no objection to me coming here and doing the same for you."

"Well, good. I'm glad you're here. Look, Father, this can't go on. The secondary positions are being pushed in one by one as the men run out of bullets. We haven't the ammunition to keep them away from the house for more than a few hours. I want you to go out there and negotiate a truce."

"What kind of truce? If they've won, what do you have to negotiate with?"

"Me. Cuello will want me alive. He'll want to torture me, display my body with a sign on it, as an example to anyone who thinks of defying him. If not, tell them we'll hold out to the end. He'll have to clear the house room by room. We have plenty of ANFO explosives left. He'll lose hundreds of men, and he'll be so weakened that he'll worry about another gang or another *jefe* taking over his operation. Also, you can tell him I'm prepared to sign over the property to him."

"Really? I heard you'd set up an *ejido*."

"I did, but he doesn't know about the *ejido*. Anything I sign will have no validity under Mexican law. We're buying time, Father. As soon as Pepa's video gets released, there'll be an enormous public pressure to send in the army. Every man Cuello has is on the island right now. It could be a clean sweep."

"But they'll kill you. They'll torture you."

"They might. But as we Felizistas like to say, victory or death. And, also, they might just shoot *you*. So will you do it?"

Marder saw the priest's throat move as he swallowed heavily. Then he grinned. "We'll be fellow martyrs, perhaps. San Miguel and San Ricardo of Michoacán, joined for eternity like Saints Perpetua and Felicity. Tell me, I've always wondered—does a name like Marder predispose you toward martyrdom? Some tiny subconscious message?"

"But my name has nothing to do with martyrdom. Marder is the German for 'marten,' a kind of large weasel. Which you may think is much more appropriate."

Father Santana laughed a laugh that was a little too shrill. Then he let out a long breath, as if expelling some toxic gas. "My Lord! This is interesting in itself. I've been terrified of them for so long, so long, and now I'm not. It seems so awfully stupid to be afraid of death, especially in my profession, and now that I'm not, it's hard to recall the fear. I suppose it's like learning to swim—or, no, like acquiring speech—and not recalling a time when you couldn't. Well, Don Ricardo, my only real regret is not having the long conversations about such elevated subjects that I would've liked us to have had."

"We're not dead yet, Father," said Marder. "You should see about getting yourself a big white flag."

22

Statch kept time by counting her strokes, and this gave her some idea of distance too, since she'd swum eight hundred meters so often that she had a good sense of how many strokes would move her approximately that far. After five of these intervals—four kilometers—she seemed to be fine, at least physically. She'd never swum long distances in the sea before, but she'd thought it wouldn't matter, water was water, and salt water actually buoyed her up more than fresh, a slight advantage. As she swam, she thought of the classic long-distance swims—the English Channel was just about forty of those eight-hundred-meter laps—that had been done hundreds of times, by swimmers of no particular competitive talent. She could do it, twenty-one miles, not a problem. Or twenty-eight and a half, which was the distance around Manhattan, and plenty of duffers did that too.

One the other hand, those people were not entirely alone, in the dark, and at an unknown distance from the shore. How far could it be? As much as thirty miles? Could she swim thirty miles, without months of training, dragged down by a bulky shirt with a pistol in its breast pocket, throwing her balance off at every stroke? Probably not. But the distance was surely less than that, far less. She'd boarded the yacht while it was still in sight of land, she'd been on the tender for less than an hour, surely, and how far could the yacht have traveled afterward? She recalled her time in the blank room. If the vessel had been hurrying along, she would have heard the vibration caused by faster revolutions, and she had not. Or had she? She couldn't recall.

But at least she was swimming in the right direction. She rolled onto her back, resting in an easy float, moving up and down on the regular swells. The stars were all out, burning in their ordered patterns. The Dipper was in the right place and Polaris on her right, and the moon was in the right place too, with a line dropped through its horns touching the southern horizon. She was definitely swimming east; all she had to do was keep swimming and she would strike North America before long.

But her stomach hurt. She hadn't eaten since yesterday, and she was ravenously hungry. She could burn three thousand calories in a day of hard practice, and even though she was taking it easier now, the drain on her glucose reserves would be enormous. She could burn fat, but she didn't have much fat to begin with. Long-distance ocean swimmers tended to be a little heftier, their fat also providing insulation from the cold. Which was going to be a problem if she didn't see some town lights pretty soon. The water was more than eighty degrees, she estimated, but that was still a lot cooler than the human body. Every minute she spent in the water drained heat from her, which had to be cooked up from food or fat, but she was using too much energy for this to work properly, and in the middle of the tenth eight hundred meters, she felt the first stab of a cramp in her thigh.

She rolled over on her back and floated, trying to will the muscle to relax, the fibers to stop their futile, agonized contraction. She should get out of the pool and massage the cramp away. She actually had this thought, and this increased her panic. The chill was starting to steal her mind, her body was resigning the struggle to regulate temperature, the cooling brain was beginning to generate fantasy. She stared at the sky. Polaris was in the wrong place, on her right, not her left. Had she been swimming out to sea? For how long? And did it matter?

She reoriented herself and swam for some minutes, until the cramp hit again and she had to stop and roll onto her back and stare up at the stars. One of her first memories floated into mind. She was sitting on a dock at night—it must have been at that place they rented on the south shore of Long Island for a few summers—and her mother had told her that the stars were little holes in heaven through which the light of God shone. Even at four, this was an unsatisfying explanation, and when she discovered the truth somewhat later, it had instructed her that her mother was not to be trusted in matters concerning the real world. The stars were gigantic balls of flaming gas, their numbers, their distances, stupefying, and God had nothing to do with it, with anything at all; the universe spread in spangled glory above her remained utterly indifferent to her fate.

So she declined to pray, as she knew many people, even atheists, did in the last extremity. Or not for herself: she did stare up at the universe and say out loud a prayer for her father, the true believer, that if there was a Something that cared, it would care for her father, that it would help him through her death, that he not blame himself for it, that he be comforted in whatever way religious people found comfort.

That concluded, she had a spate of shameful self-pity, and salt tears leaked from her eyes and mixed with the salt sea. She'd fucked up her life; no one loved her, nor she anyone; she had not made the slightest real contribution to human happiness or advancement; she would shortly sink and fall down the miles of black water and be consumed by scavengers, and she would dissolve and be nothing again.

After that, she bobbed like flotsam on the rollers, waiting for the cold to rob her of consciousness, for a period of time she could not have measured, minutes, hours—time itself had become meaningless, she had always been here, floating on a sea treacherously warm, waiting helpless for the life in her to depart. The cramps eased, but she had no strength in her limbs anymore; she barely had the energy to hold the float position. She let the pistol slip away, its value now less than a marginal increase in buoyancy; her determination to hold on to it seemed the absurd extravagance of a person she no longer was. Getting sleepy, images from her past, lines of poetry she'd memorized, classroom scenes, the usual embarrassments, bubbling up. She looked up at the star directly overhead. It got blurry, became a looping line, went out; she was underwater, sinking.

Something touched her leg.

As if it were an electrical contact, the touch sent a shot of galvanic energy through her body. Her limbs made the practiced and automatic motions that drove her to the surface. A single light shone above the sea, casting a dim cone of yellowish illumination on the working deck of a shrimp boat and the water around it. They were pulling in their nets— that's what had touched her. Three feeble strokes brought her over to the bight of the net, thick with shining shrimps. She hooked her fingers into it, and in a few minutes she was lying on the plywood deck, staring up at the wondering faces of the fishermen.

"Can I borrow your cell phone?"

Pepa Espinoza turned from her computer screen and there was Carmel Marder. For a moment she did not recognize her, so gaunt was her face, so red and crazy were her eyes.

"Jesus Maria, Carmel! What the devil happened to you? Where have you been?"

"Please, I just want to call my father."

"You can't. The cell service is out at the *casa*. My God, sit down! You look like you're about to collapse."

Pepa had been working at a small table at El Cangrejo Rojo, a table off to the side, an area not clearly visible from the central square of Playa Diamante. She pulled out a wire chair and Statch collapsed into it.

Pepa waved the barmaid over. "You looked starved, *niña*. You should eat something. What did they do to you?"

"I've been in the water," she said. "And, yeah, I could eat."

Pepa watched her eat: stacks of buttered tortillas, chicken soup with rice, half a dozen beef enchiladas, a plate of tacos stuffed with fresh *huachinango*, washed down with glass after glass of iced tea. While she ate, Statch told her tale.

"Wait, you *killed* Gabriel Cuello with a *pen*?"

"Yes. A hundred-forty-nine-dollar Rotring 600. I regret losing the pen."

"Mightier than the sword, to coin a phrase."

"Yes, strange when these old metaphors come literally to life. Although I actually killed him with a .22 hollow point through his skull. But if I'd been carrying a Bic, I'd be dead now, and he'd be cutting pieces off me and throwing them to the crabs."

Statch stopped then and lifted her glass to her lips, with the ice cubes going like castanets, until she could no longer hold on to the plastic cup. It fell clattering to the floor, and Carmel Marder had to endure fifteen minutes of hysterics.

"Post-traumatic stress," said Pepa, when it was all over.

"I guess. Or brain damage. Anyway, after I killed him, I went over the side and swam around for a while in the dark, until these guys on a shrimp boat picked me up. I had two hundred American rolled up in a little steel pill case attached to my knife, and I gave them that and I told them I would pay triple whatever they expected to clear from catching bait shrimp if they'd run me back to the marina at Playa Diamante, and here I am."

"I'm going to interview you as soon as my crew gets here. This is an incredible story. Girl escapes from El Cochinillo, kills him with a pen? I'm pissing in my pants!"

Statch decided in the moment that there would never be an interview. She would never tell anyone about the two other men she'd shot in cold blood, or what happened on the water, or that she'd figured out that she swam more than twenty miles. Or that, as hard as she tried, she could not remove from her mind the fact that the conjunction of her course with that of the fishermen Serafin Montoya and his son Ascensio was nothing but brute chance. It was necessary for her to discount Señor Montoya's excited explanation, delivered as he swathed her in blankets and fed her hot fish soup, that they were far to the south of their usual fishing grounds, that this unusual course derived from a message that had popped into Serafin's mind while praying for a good catch to the Virgin of Guadalupe, as he did every night, and that this rescue was beyond all question a miracle of God and the Virgin. Nor could she believe that the reason Serafin had been willing to take her fifty miles out of his way on the mere promise of a reward from a stranger was that, in the hour preceding the rescue, he had caught more shrimp than he ever had in a lifetime of fishing.

Statch also grasped for the first time the actuality of her father's pain, and Skelly's more cryptic agony, what it was *really* like to kill another human being. She wanted to be with her father, to hug him for a long time, to make him understand that she knew, and to convey her hope that they could forgive each other for these crimes on behalf of the human race.

She said, "Sure, fine. So—what's going on at the *casa*? Why no cell service?"

Pepa explained about Marder's actions the previous night and what she'd surmised since she'd left the island: the massive attack of La Familia on their rivals and the continuation of the attack on Casa Feliz. She'd been up all night, using her cell phone to wake up people, promising them the story of the decade. She'd deposited the land-transfer papers with the one *notario* in town not entirely a creature of the cartels and then gone to an arcade with a Wi-Fi hot spot and uploaded all her video to her producer's computer. It was being prepared for airing as they spoke. Pepa and her producer were positive that when it hit the air and the Internet, the pressure to send in the army would be irresistible.

"But what about now, Pepa? That could take days. You say La Familia has hundreds of *sicarios* on Isla de los Pájaros—they could have killed my father and everyone else on the island by the time the army gets moving. We have to get the army there today, right now, this minute."

"Yes, but I don't see what we can do—"

"Give me your cell!"

Major Naca's card had not survived soaking in the sea, but of course Pepa Espinoza had his number. Statch punched it in.

"Third battalion, Sergeant Sanchez, sir!" said the voice.

Statch cranked her accent as high as it would go in the *fresa* direction and told the sergeant that she was a personal friend of Major Naca, that she had vital and urgent information of a national security nature and had to speak to the major immediately.

The major was out of the office; he was on a field operation and could not be reached.

"Sergeant Sanchez, listen to me carefully! My name is Carmel Beatriz Marder. I must speak with Major Naca this minute. I know you have your orders, but there must be some way to patch this call through to his field HQ. Sergeant Sanchez, I would not want to be the soldier responsible for not forwarding this call."

The use of the man's name (she would remember him!) and the accent seemed to work. "One moment, Señora," the man said, and then there was static and a brief exchange with another intermediary.

"Señorita Marder. This is a pleasant surprise, but I am doubly surprised that they patched you through."

"It's regrettably not a social call, Major. La Familia has attacked my father's house in force. They have killed all the Templos that were previously attacking it, and now they are on the point of capturing the house itself. I don't have to tell you what kind of massacre will ensue. You must move your forces immediately to Isla de los Pájaros and attack them. You have the opportunity to destroy La Familia in southern Michoacán in one blow. But you must move *now*!"

"I can't do that, Señorita. I'd have to go through channels to authorize an operation like that. It might take days to get the plans approved, and I'm afraid—"

"No, Major, you haven't understood. This is your moment. The *sicarios* of La Familia are all on an island connected by a narrow causeway. You can trap them all, like rats in a basket. No breaking into buildings and frightening old ladies, only to find that the *malosos* have all run away. It will be war at last and a great victory for the forces of order. And aside from that, if you come now, I will be here."

A small suppressed chuckle. "You will, will you? I suppose you will do anything I want."

"No. I will do things you haven't even imagined, not even in feverish teenaged dreams. Tijuana itself will cringe in shame."

He laughed, more openly this time.

"Seriously, Cristóbal," she said, "I realize I don't know you very well, but from what I do know, I thought you were an *empeño* kind of guy, that you were tired of this whole *no importa* thing. My father is going to die horribly, along with hundreds of other Mexicans, unless you get here. You can stop it. Only you."

"It's a lot to ask, Señorita. My whole career—"

"Your career will not be harmed. Quite the contrary, in fact. I have Pepa Espinoza sitting here. She's made a video of the Templos attacking the property and being beaten back by the armed citizens. This video will be all over Televisa and the Internet within the hour. And Pepa guarantees that she will use the full resources of Televisa to ensure you're the hero of Mexico. Not only will you not be harmed, but the whole country will demand that you be rewarded."

A silence ensued on the line. Statch heard cracklings and ghost voices of other conversations. At last, Major Naca spoke, and his voice sounded deeper than it had before. "Ah, well. I suppose I'm tired of being a major. I'll do it. We should be there in less than an hour."

"I have to go to the bank," said Statch, after saying goodbye to the major and giving back the phone. "I need ten thousand pesos for Serafin—no, better make that twenty. I'm hiring his boat for the day."

"Wait—why do you need to rent a boat?"

"To watch the battle, of course, and to get onto the island after the army takes over. Come on!"

Statch stood and started to walk away. Pepa noticed she was still wearing her safari shirt, stained with sea salt, and a pair of filthy khaki cutoffs six sizes too big for her and tied with a hank of orange poly line.

"I have to wait for my crew," said Pepa.

"Oh, please! This is the finale of your documentary, the total defeat of the evil ones. And we can land on the island dock after the army takes over and get in on the kill. They'll hold the official press back a mile and you'll get another scoop."

After a tiny, hopeless delay, Pepa picked up her bag, dropped cash on the table, and said, "Do we have time to shop? You really need a new outfit, *chica*."

*　*　*

"Why?"

Marder couldn't see the face very well, because it was dark in the concrete room where he was being held, but enough light shone in from the doorway to produce a silhouette, and the shape was unmistakably Skelly's.

"Because I swore that I would never back a loser again. I learned that in Laos. You obviously learned a different lesson."

"Then why did you even come? Why did you help us in the first place?"

"You keep forgetting I'm a dope lord, Marder. You don't want to believe it, but it's true. My guys over in Asia see what the Mexicans are doing with crank and they want in on it. They've got plenty of smack and they see a big market for crank among all those millions of Chinese working double shifts. Think they could go for a little edge? Of course they could, and what could be more profitable? Heroin goes west, meth goes east. They needed a partner to set it up and they figured Cuello was a good bet. So I figured I'd do him a solid, get rid of the Templos for him and make him a present of your little island. He's real pleased. Speaking of the Templos, they've got El Gordo, and I believe they're planning to peel the fat off him with the kind of hot knife they use for cutting industrial plastics. I'm looking forward to seeing that."

Marder said, "How's Lourdes?"

"She's fine. She's in Defe, just like you planned."

"Well, that's good."

"Yes, now she can fuck her way to the stars. That's a nice little monster you created, by the way, all in the cause of doing good. Moving on, I understand you made no trouble over signing the transfer of title."

"No."

"Very wise. Although they're still going to chop you up, I believe they'll shoot you first, which would not have been the case if you'd given them any trouble on the land deal."

"You know, Skelly, I really don't care at this point. Have you heard anything about Carmel?"

"Oh, Carmel is having a boat trip, is what I hear. She's out there with the Piglet. I expect he's introducing her to his version of dating."

"Can't you do anything?"

"Not me. It's never good policy to get between the *jefe* and his baby boy. You know, La Familia reminds me of another institution that's all holy and Christer on the outside and full of depravity and rapists on the inside. You shouldn't be surprised that old Statch got sucked up into it."

"You used to hold her on your knee. She used to kiss you good night. She loved you."

"Well, that was her fucking mistake, wasn't it. People who love me invariably come to a bad end. And my advice to you is, in your next life, stick with the winners."

"Then go with God, Patrick," said Marder.

Skelly spun and walked out, slamming the door behind him.

Marder lay in the dark, trying not to think, trying to communicate with Mr. Thing. He said that if Mr. Thing didn't mind, now would be a good time to pop his cork. Marder had been reconciled to death for some time, but if he had a choice he did not want it to come under torture, surrounded by the laughing faces of evil men. He'd seen people tortured and he knew that some people would do anything, say anything, for a little surcease, and he didn't trust himself not to be one of these. Skelly had said they'd shoot him, but could he trust Skelly, even on this? In fact, there was something wrong with Skelly; that last gloating speech was not the man he'd known for forty years. Skelly was a very bad man indeed, but he was not a sadist, and that had been a sadistic speech. Or maybe Skelly had a brain problem of his own—anything was possible.

Marder was also sure that Carmel was not dead, not being subjected to horrendous acts. He had a quasi-mystical belief that he remained in spiritual contact with his children; he'd often called them spontaneously when he sensed there was something wrong, and there almost always was, whether they admitted it at the time or not.

That they were going to kill him he had not a doubt. After he surrendered, after he signed the papers, they had brought him to this place without a blindfold, sitting between two silent *sicarios* in the backseat of a car. So he knew they were in the old Hernandez y Cia brewery, which he surmised had been turned into La Familia central for the region. They still made beer here—he could smell the yeasty stench—and they also made meth and transported it using the same trucks. There had been a fleet of them parked neatly behind the main building, and he recalled wondering if, as a minor part of the deal, they'd retrieved the one that Skelly had stolen.

A light came on, issuing from high up on the wall, from a louvered rectangle clearly designed to allow the circulation of air through the various rooms of the warehouse. He could now see that the room he occupied was stacked with steel drums on rolling steel trolleys—drums that obviously did not contain beer. He heard voices through the louver, and laughter, and one voice that he recognized as belonging to El Gordo. He couldn't quite make out the words, but the tone was hysterical, the words delivered rapidly, without pause, until they devolved into a shrill scream. There was the stink of burning hair and of frying fat; the screams went on and on for what seemed like hours. Marder wished he could stop his ears, but his hands were bound and so he had to listen, which was, of course, the point.

At last the screams stopped. Marder heard laughter, joking, and a single shot, and then the *slish* of a wet object being dragged over concrete, another nasty sound. Some minutes passed and then the door to Marder's room opened, the overhead light snapped on, and four men stepped in. Two were *sicarios* with the usual neat attire and blank, merciless faces; one was a man in a fresh white hooded Tyvek suit and a plastic apron, who carried a chain saw; and one was Don Melchor Cuello.

The two *sicarios* rolled an empty drum trolley to a position under the light and then picked up Marder, untied his wrists and ankles, and then retied him to the steel trolley. Marder looked at Cuello and said, "We really need to have a talk about your business model."

The Tyvek man glanced at his *jefe,* his hand on the starter cord of the chain saw. Cuello made an arresting gesture.

"Really. What about my business model?"

"Well, in general, any model that relies on torture and murder is unsustainable in the long run. Clearly you know this; you're an intelligent man. All of the original leaders of La Familia have been killed, and the average life span of a cartel leader once he's reached the top can't be much more than, what? Five years? And during that time you have to live like an animal, hunted from place to place, no security, and, really, no way to enjoy your money. Can you take a girlfriend to Paris on a private jet and stay at the George V? Of course you can't. Can you enjoy the prestige and honors accorded to other wealthy men—a nice house in Chapultepec, invitations to high-society functions, your daughters and granddaughters married to respectable men, a place of honor in the community? You can't. It must be very frustrating for you, and it's all because of your business model."

Cuello wore a patronizing smile now. "And what would you suggest I do instead?"

"Divest the dope business. You've got your capital from it and you don't need it anymore. Educate any of your *sicarios* with the brains for it and pension off the rest. It can be done—it *has* been done. Half a dozen big American fortunes were based on illegal booze during Prohibition, and the smart guys got out when they'd made their pile. The stupid ones died in prison or on the street. Sell the labs and the distribution systems. Use the money to get into politics. Enough bribes and you can probably arrange for amnesty. Invest in securities. Pay your taxes. Contribute to charities. In five years no one will want to know you were a drug lord."

"And I suppose I should start by letting you go?"

"It would be a good symbolic gesture."

Cuello's face took on a thoughtful cast and he gazed for a moment up at one of the room's dark corners. Then he said, "Well, these are interesting ideas, and I confess I've had thoughts along those lines myself. On the other hand, if things go on the way they've been going, the cartels will be as powerful as the state itself here in Mexico. Eventually they will reach an accommodation with the government, as they did in the days of the PRI. We will be able to ship our dope and buy the politicians, and I will then have all of the benefits of respectability that you've just described. And—*and*—I will still be able to watch my enemies being chopped into pieces, which, I have to confess, I do enjoy. But that was a good try. Very original."

He patted Marder on the cheek, stepped away from the trolley, and nodded to the Tyvek man, who yanked his chain saw into a stuttering roar—a sound instantly overwhelmed by the noise of a colossal explosion outside. The ground shook and dust flew from the walls and ceiling. The overhead light flickered.

"Shut that thing off," ordered Cuello. The chain saw went silent. They all listened, straining to hear against the ringing the blast had left in their ears. Then came another, even larger blast, and this time the light stayed out. A battery-operated emergency light over the doorway came on. Cuello ordered the two *sicarios* to find out what had happened. To Marder, he said, "The labs blow up. It's a cost of doing business. But I have a lot of labs. It's a piece of luck for you, though." Without change of tone, he said to the Tyvek man, "We have to get out of here. Just cut off his head."

There was a short coughing noise, and Marder thought that it had something to do with the chain saw. But the Tyvek man dropped the chain saw and fell down. Skelly was standing in the doorway, holding a submachine gun with a long suppressor on it.

He pointed it at Cuello and grinned at Marder. He said, "I had you going there for a while, didn't I?"

Skelly's knife sliced through Marder's bonds and he sat up on the trolley naked and looked at Cuello, who seemed paralyzed by what had happened.

"Keep your hands up, *jefe*," said Skelly, frisking him efficiently. "What have you got there? Oh, a Glock 17? Why am I not surprised?"

Skelly pulled a pistol out of a shoulder holster and handed it to Marder. It was Marder's father's army .45.

"Where the hell did you find this?" Marder asked.

"Oh, you left your pieces lying everywhere—very bad gun-safety practice, Marder. I'm surprised at you. Now, if you would just point it at the *jefe* there while I pull the mag from this."

He slung his submachine gun over his shoulder, turned away briefly with the Glock, dropped the magazine, and tossed it against the far wall of the room. Marder heard it clang as it fell behind the stacked drums. Skelly dropped the Glock on the floor and kicked it away.

"I assume that was your explosion," said Marder.

"Yeah, I returned the beer truck the Templos lifted, as a gesture of goodwill. Three tons of ammonium nitrate fertilizer went off. I don't think there'll be anyone walking around out there."

"No. Tell me, Skelly, was there no other way? Our people died. Kids died."

"What can I say, chief? One man against two big gangs? The *Yojimbo* play is the only play. And it worked, as you see." Skelly unslung his sub-machine gun and said, "I spotted a box of Tyvek outfits outside the room next door. You might want to put one on. Unless you're thinking of cutting this guy up with the chain saw. You might as well stay naked if you're going to do that, you know what I mean?"

A cheery little tune sounded, as jarring in the dreadful room as a fun fair in a gulag.

"What the fuck?" said Skelly, and patted at his clothes. He pulled one of the cheap cell phones from one of his many pockets and took the call, never for an instant taking his eyes or the point of his weapon from Cuello.

He said "Yeah? Oh, man! Well, shit, honey, that's terrific. How did you . . . What? No kidding? But you're okay, right?"

"Is that Statch?" Marder demanded, and reached for the phone.

"Hold on, your dad wants to talk with you."

Marder said, "Carmel—are you okay?"

"I'm fine, Dad. Are you okay?"

"I'm okay," said Marder. "Where are you?"

"At the house. It's all over here. The army came and cleaned out the bad guys." And then she told him the story.

After they were done talking, Marder gave the phone back to Skelly and looked at Cuello, who was standing with a look of stony dignity on his evil face. He's not afraid to die, at any rate, thought Marder; he doesn't know yet about worse things. Then he went out to the hallway, past the bodies of the two *sicarios* Skelly had shot, and found the box of Tyvek suits. He put one on and walked down the hallway to where the door to the outside swung, shattered, from one hinge. Outside was black oily smoke, an infernal stench, and complete devastation. Not a living thing moved among the black and burning shapes that had once been buildings and vehicles. It was a suitable Götterdämmerung for a foul empire.

When Marder returned to the concrete room, he found Cuello collapsed against the back wall, weeping, making huge gasping sobs, *a-hahn-a-hahn, a-hahn, a-hahn,* over and over.

"I told him what happened. He seems to be taking it pretty hard."

Marder said, "My condolences on your loss, Don Melchor. What I predicted has come to pass, but a lot faster than I thought it would. Now I have to explain the reason for this catastrophe."

Cuello stopped sobbing and got to his feet. "Just shoot me, you fucker! *Chingada cabrón!* You want to chop me up, go ahead!"

"No, I want to explain. This concerns the murders of Don Esteban de Haro d'Ariés and his wife, Carmela Asunción Casals."

"Who?"

"Yes, there have been so many murders, it's easy to see that you could have forgotten one or two. Maybe you didn't even order it directly. Let me remind you. You wanted a piece of a small hotel owned by Don Esteban. He refused, having had enough of expropriation, and your organization had him killed, along with his wife. But as it happens they were my wife's parents. Her name was Maria Soledad Beatriz de Haro d'Ariés Marder, and the murders of her parents led directly to her death. That's why we're all here. When I came down to Michoacán, I thought it would be difficult to get to you. I really had no idea how to do it. So I waited. I bought a property sold to me by someone who wished me trouble, and what greater sources of trouble could there be in Playa Diamante than you? I knew that sooner or later, if I kept doing the right thing, doing as much good as I could manage, you would not be able to tolerate it. Even though there's enough loot for everyone, and even though you have more money than you'll ever be able to spend, you couldn't stand the idea of someone else getting Isla de los Pájaros. You *had* to get involved, and I had every confidence that, when you did, my friend here would find some way of destroying you. And so it has proved. I told you it was a bad business model. So, the question is, what will you do now?"

The man stared at him, surprised at the question.

"No," said Marder, "I'm not going to kill you, although if anyone in Mexico deserves death it's you. We're going to walk away from here and let you do the same. I've killed my last human being, or at least I hope so. You might die at the hands of a rival gang, or the army could get you, or you could find your way out of the country to a different life and use your money to do some good. You could seek redemption."

He turned his back on Cuello and walked toward the door.

"Let's go, Patrick," he said. "I want to see my daughter."

The two men walked down the corridor, the only sound the roar and crackle of the burning outside and the swish of Marder's Tyvek. The hazy air stank of chemicals.

"You're making a mistake there, chief," said Skelly. "That guy's not going to make nice."

"I'm not responsible for what he does. I'm responsible for what I do, which in this case is forgiveness."

"Marder, you're such a jerk. I don't know why I hang out with you."

Marder stopped and looked Skelly full in the face.

"You hang out with me *because* you want forgiveness. You should ask God, but you don't believe in God, so you ask me. I'm talking to a man who, once a year, lets a bunch of bums beat and rob him, to punish himself for his unbearable guilt. And you do all these shitty things just to check it out—will Marder forgive me for this one, or will he finally confirm what I believe about Patrick Skelly, that he's utterly without any redeeming value, a complete turd. That's why you kept hitting on my wife, even though she did you the courtesy of not taking it seriously, making it into the family joke. What, you thought I didn't know? And crawling into bed with Nina Ibanez the day after I dumped her? Classy. Yeah, I knew about that too. She told me, needless to say. And of course she would have told you that I bought Isla de los Pájaros and what it meant. Tell me, did you ever wonder why, of all the real estate agents in the world, I should have picked the one I least wanted to deal with, the one who had the most reason to want to do me harm? The minute I sent the check she must've been on the phone with you, gloating. And you know what? I forgive you. I understand you can't help yourself, and it doesn't matter. I came down here to do something good and I needed you and I figured you'd come along only if you thought it was something nasty."

He saw Skelly's eyes shift away, which he thought odd because Skelly was a classic bold-faced liar. "It wasn't like that," Skelly said.

"No? Then what was it like? I'm interested to know."

Now there were sirens approaching. Someone had seen the vast column of smoke and called the fire department.

Skelly opened his mouth, but before he could say a word, Melchor Cuello stepped out of the haze, pointing his Glock at Marder. Skelly moved between Marder and the gun just as it went off. He cried out and fell to the ground, and Marder, without thought or hesitation, raised his Colt and shot Cuello three times, chest, neck, and head.

Skelly lay on his back, staring at his hand, which was covered in blood, as was his shirt, a spreading dark stain above the beltline.

"I can't believe it. I forgot to clear the fucking chamber. How could I forget? I always clear the chamber. And why did I leave the gun?"

"Don't worry about that now. Just lie still. Let me take a look at the wound."

"No!" said Skelly clutching his hands protectively over his belly. "It's not going to do any good. He fucked me up, Marder. I'm finished. He got my spine—I can't feel anything below my waist."

"You'll be fine. Listen, you can hear the sirens. They'll be here soon."

"No, I'm dead. But, Marder, you've got to tell me, level with me now, my dying wish, all right? How the fuck did you do it?"

"Do what?"

"Get me out of Moon River to the Special Forces base. You couldn't have done it. You didn't have the training. You didn't know shit about how to survive in triple-canopy rain forest with the whole PAVN looking for you."

"I thought we agreed that you got me out."

A sleepy grin morphed into a grimace. "Yeah, that bullshit. I knew. I was delirious but not crazy. I always knew. So how . . . how?"

"I had supernatural help. You asked me that when you were waking up out there and I told you and then you forgot it."

"Yes, but, seriously, I'm dying here, Marder, and I want to know."

Now the sirens reached a new peak of volume, and there came the sound of heavy tires and engines, and the sirens growled down into silence.

"Stay cool, Skelly. I'll get help." Marder ran out of the building. His throat was raw and his chest tight. The fumes had become even more oppressive, and when he reached the outside, he saw that the firemen were all wearing breathing apparatuses. Meth-lab explosions, planned or accidental, were not rarities in Michoacán these days. An ambulance pulled up and Marder hailed it in a croaking voice. A doctor and two paramedics leaped out, and Marder was surprised to see that the doctor was Rodriguez, the same man who had treated Skelly at Cárdenas General. He led them into the building and they lifted Skelly up onto a gurney.

Marder grasped Skelly's blood-slick hand as they rolled him down the corridor.

"Tell me!" Skelly said, his voice a faint rasp.

"Okay, on the day of the bombing, I ran into a bunch of Yards working for another Special Forces operation, and they carried you and guided us almost all the way to Quang Loc."

Skelly's face relaxed into a smile. "I knew it," he said, and closed his eyes and said nothing more.

23

Marder had to go to the hospital too, after finding he couldn't breathe anymore, or not enough to stay upright. They took him to the same hospital in Lázaro Cárdenas and flushed him out with oxygen and stuck him in a nice room, because he was an important person and his daughter insisted on it and distributed wads of money to show sincerity.

She came into his room with a big bunch of marigolds and tears streaming from her eyes. Marder knew what the tears were about. He spread his arms and she fell against his chest. He hugged her and made meaningless, calming noises.

"When did you—?"

"Dr. Rodriguez told me. Skelly left a note. A will, I guess. He left everything to me—his place in New York, his car. There are numbers for bank accounts in foreign countries. Why would he do that?"

"He loved you. He loved all of us in his horrible way. We were his family."

"But he kept picking at it. He kept picking at you. And that awful thing at the end, pretending he was betraying us—"

"That was Skelly. He thought everything was false, everything was phony, except us. And then I turned out to be phony—"

"Oh, stop! I can't stand when you beat yourself up over that. You made a mistake, and Mom took too many pills and had an accident. Yeah, it's devastating, but it's not some fucking Greek tragedy. Speaking of which, Peter's on his way here."

"Really?"

"Yes, I told him I would come to Cal Tech and beat the living shit out of him and follow him around campus with a sign and embarrass him in front of all his friends. The self-righteous little twerp! You could've died."

She started crying again, then blew her nose mightily, shook herself, grinned sheepishly at him, and was back in prime engineering mode.

"So, what are you going to do with your new riches?" Marder asked.

"Oh, there's a condition in the will. He wants me to take his ashes and scatter them in Moon River. It sounds nuts, but he said you'd know where that was."

"It's in Laos," said Marder, after a stunned moment. "I believe I can give you the precise coordinates. But you're not going to leave immediately, are you?"

"No. I've got a lot of work to do at the *casa*. Reconstruction, improvements . . . like that. Now that we're internationally famous, I don't think we'll have much trouble making a go of it. I thought after the New Year."

"Okay. Have you seen Pepa around? I kind of thought she'd come by."

"Oh, our Pepa is being the toast of Defe. She's on all the interview shows, and Televisa is apparently going to give her her own investigative program. It doesn't look like she'll be spending a lot of time in Playa Diamante. Uh-oh, does that make you sad?"

"No, not really. I'd like to see her again, of course, but I think we have different destinies. Basically, we did each other a solid and there are no hard feelings. It'd be nice if every relationship turned out like that. How's Major Naca? Is that a *blush*, Carmel?"

"Oh, well, he's definitely *interested*."

"And you back?"

She wriggled, laughed, and her face opened like a flower, in a gum-flashing grin. "Mmm. I might, you know, give it a *whirl*."

"Good. He seems like a nice fellow. Not to mention that you're less likely to be bothered by certain people if you're with a man who commands a battalion." He smiled at her, and she felt a pang because the smile was so sad. "Well," he said, "it looks like my work here is done."

"Why? Are you planning to ride off into the sunset? Again?"

"You never can tell," said Marder, and sank back on the pillows. Statch thought she'd never seen her father's face so peaceful and happy since her mother had died.

* * *

At the end of January, some three weeks after her father's funeral, Carmel Marder boarded an Air Singapore jet and flew first-class from Mexico City to Singapore, paying somewhat more for her ticket than she'd received as an annual stipend as a graduate student. It was not a characteristic expenditure, for she had inherited her father's attitude toward ostentation along with half of his many, many millions of dollars. But she had worked extremely hard over the past few months and was on a mission fraught with tension; she thought that her father would have approved.

From Singapore, she took a flight to Saigon on a blue Vietnam Airlines Airbus, then switched to a smaller plane for the trip to Huê. At the airport there, she met a young man by arrangement, who took her bags, slid her through the customs and immigration bureaucracy, and placed her in a clean white Toyota Land Cruiser. He said to call him "Lucky"; he was connected in some way with the family of her old lab mate, Karen Liu. Karen had been horrified when told that her friend intended to travel to Laos by herself and had insisted on mobilizing her kin's considerable *guanxi* in that part of the world, and here Statch was, riding comfortably through the narrow streets of the old capital, on the way to her room at the Imperial Hotel, wrapped in a duvet of Confucian obligation.

The next day Lucky picked her up early. Without thinking, she jumped into the shotgun seat. He gave her a cloudy look, then shrugged and started the car. They drove through cool, damp streets smelling not unpleasantly of flowers, diesel, and decaying fruits.

When they reached the countryside, she asked Lucky how far it was. "Not far. Fifty, fifty-five kilometers."

"Gosh, that's nothing."

"Yes, but the first forty-five to the border are easy, on highway like this, but the last ten, very tough." He laughed and made a sinuous motion with his hand. "Up and down. But don't worry, this a strong car." He flexed a skinny bicep to illustrate strength.

Then they were on 49, the highway that belted Vietnam at its narrowest point. Like most Americans her age, when she thought of Vietnam at all she thought of steaming jungle, but this country looked more like Virginia, with rolling hills and orchards and small dusty villages, distinguished from time to time by ornate decaying tombs, showing crusty white against the green background of the foliage.

The only sign of the war she observed was a piece of obvious aircraft aluminum, with metal showing through the khaki paint, used as a bit of fencing around a buffalo paddock.

"Lucky, do you ever think about the war?" she asked after this remnant whipped by.

"Why, you want to see battlefields? We are close to Khe San."

"No, just wondering if people thought about it, if they still, you know, resented Americans or felt it was or wasn't worth it."

"It was a long time ago," he said unenthusiastically. "Things are getting better."

"And you don't think it's strange that the grandchildren of the Vietcong are lining up for jobs as bellboys and chambermaids in French- and American-owned hotels?"

"They're good jobs. Better than work on farm, or work for Vietnamese person."

She changed the subject and talked instead about his life. He was studying pharmacy.

The land rose. Now it was more like a warmer West Virginia, and they arrived at a built-up area. Lucky turned the car south on what was clearly an important highway.

"This is the Ho Chi Minh Trail," he said.

She looked through the window at the varied life on the edges of the road—repair shops, places selling tires and batteries, food stalls, and shops selling things she couldn't know because she couldn't read the colorful signage. The road that won their war, and it was not paved with gold.

"My dad's job, in the war," she observed, "was to destroy this road. I mean, he was one of thousands of people trying to do it."

"It was a long time ago," said Lucky in a tone that did not encourage the subject.

They crossed the border at A Yen. A couple of tiny, unkempt Laotian border guards glanced incuriously at her visas and passed them through. Now they traveled on single-lane dirt roads, climbing in low gear around the bends, and now she saw the peculiar humpy green mountains of the region, like illustrations from a children's book, making the horizon amusingly jagged, flashing different hues of green at them as the clouds cast shadows or the sun struck them full on.

They crossed a wide river on a crumbly concrete bridge and drove for a kilometer or so on increasingly narrow tracks. Statch gave Lucky the coordinates her father had given her, and Lucky punched these into his GPS.

"We are close," he said. "We take this first track and head north, and when we cross a . . . what is this word? A little river that comes into the Lun, the one back there?"

"A tributary?"

He flashed a smile. "Just right. This Moon River is a tributary to the Lun. When this track meets the river, we will be there."

The track was rough, and several times Lucky had to get out and clear fallen branches away with a machete. He drove the Land Cruiser until the track ended at what appeared to be a copse of young trees. When the motor was switched off, they could hear the burbling of a small river. Statch took a cylindrical tin can from her bag.

"I think I'd like to be alone when I do this," she said.

A nod from Lucky. "Yes. I will wait here."

She walked toward the river's sound. The ground was hard to traverse; it seemed to consist of steep little ridges and unnatural deep hollows, and then, with a shock, she understood that she was crossing a crater field. Every green thing within her field of vision was younger than the day that Moon River village died under the B-52s.

She reached the river, a café-au-lait stream ten meters across. Kneeling on the mossy bank, she opened the can. The ashes were white and gritty, and as she looked at them, a chill went through her. She felt too alone and at the same time surrounded by the presence of the dead. She shuddered and, with a wide motion of her arm, flung a stream of ash out to the river.

"Goodbye, Skelly," she called into the forest, and cast the rest of the ashes out onto the puckered tan stream.

"Oh, that felt good," said a voice behind her. "It was getting crampy in that can."

She shrieked and spun around.

He had a full beard and was tanned red-brown, but it was clearly the late Patrick Francis Skelly standing there, grinning down at her. She screamed a curse and threw the empty urn at his head, then charged up the bank at him, fists and feet flying. It took him several minutes to get her immobilized and not before she'd landed a few good ones. He had taught her how to fight and had done a good job.

"Are you going to listen now, or do I have to tie you up?"

"What a terrible thing to do, you horrible man! How could you do that to him? He loved you. I cried for a week."

The feel of his arms around her, his familiar smell, flung the years away, and she was back with the man who'd indulged every tomboy fantasy, the naughty uncle of every feisty young girl's dreams. She began to cry.

"Why? Why did you—"

"Because there was a contract out on me. A couple of gun thugs tried to whack me that time we went to Mexico City, and I took the opportunity to arrange my own death."

"You could have told *us*," she wailed.

"No, you were watched, and while the Marders have many talents, acting is not one of them. You had to believe I was gone. Can I let you up now?"

He got off her and went down to the riverside, and after a moment she followed him.

"How did you do it? No, wait, it was Dr. Rodriguez, wasn't it? I noticed he was nervous as a cat and I figured it was because he'd lost an important patient, but you'd bribed him to call the death and arrange for you to get smuggled out of the hospital. But how did you convince my father you'd been shot in the first place? Obviously, Cuello wasn't part of the scam."

"No. I had a blank nine-millimeter round made up. I was carrying it around for days, waiting. I slipped it into his pistol and depended on him to come after your dad. A little knife wound to make some blood and that was it."

"He thought you were a hero. He thought you died saving his life."

"I'm not a hero. I'm a killer. I never claimed to be a hero." He looked out at the river and lit a cigarette.

"I used to come to this very spot with a girl I loved. She used to tell my fortune by the patterns of the leaves floating down the river. We were supposed to be happy forever and have many children. Yet another thing that didn't work out. And . . . I'm sorry I couldn't get to the funeral."

"You could've come. No one would have noticed you. We had over five thousand people at the church. There were delegations from the army and the government, the media. Even the Sinaloa cartel sent a wreath. The coffin was on display for a whole day, with a military honor guard, and *campesinos* were rubbing their scapulars and rosaries against the coffin."

"Well, he always wanted to be a saint."

"No, he wanted other people to be saints. There's a difference. He thought he was a cesspool of vice himself. Or maybe that's a necessary aspect of sainthood."

"Did you take him to La Huacana?"

"Yes, he's next to Mom. But we have our own cemetery now, on the headland beyond the golf course. He commissioned a monument for the people of the *colonia* who died in the fighting; it's a big marble thing with a bronze statue of the Virgin weeping and the names of the people who died on a bronze plaque. The inscription reads, 'In memory of those who died resisting the assaults of the *narcoviolencia* in defense of their homes and for the good of Mexico.'"

"That sounds like something Marder would do."

"Yes, we all have typical behaviors. Why did you bring me here on a fool's errand, Skelly? Throwing ashes into a stupid river, probably from somebody's barbecue or a dog incinerator."

"I wanted to see you."

"What for? To talk about old times?"

"The truth?"

"Oh, don't start now!" she said.

"No, this is the truth. I have a shitty life. Plenty of money, a nice place, all the pleasures, and I feel like shit all the time, scared and looking for oblivion, but I can't look for oblivion, because that would make me less than sharp and that would kill me. And then I think, Oh, fuck, why not just die? But that doesn't feel right either. Marder would say it was because I don't have God, but I can't get my mind around that shit."

"I have the same problem."

"Yes! See, that's what I mean. I can't talk to anyone else about stuff like this. What am I supposed to do now that he's gone?"

She thought about this for a while as the leaves in their different colors and patterns bobbed past on the current, predicting different futures for everyone, one of which would come true.

About the Author

MICHAEL GRUBER, *New York Times*–bestselling author of *The Good Son*, *The Book of Air and Shadows*, *The Forgery of Venus*, *Night of the Jaguar*, *Tropic of Night*, and *Valley of Bones*, has a PhD in marine sciences and began freelance writing while working in Washington, D.C., as a policy analyst and speech-writer. Since 1990, he has been a full-time writer. He lives in Seattle, Washington.